Praise for

laura a gilm

PARANORMAL SCENE INVESTIGATIONS

Hard Magic
"Readers will love the *Mythbusters*-style fun
of smart, sassy people solving mysteries through experimentation,
failure and blowing stuff up."
—*Publishers Weekly,* starred review

"The mystery is solid, the characterization strong,
the plot fast-paced and the final product solid.
This is a great start to a new series."
—*Green Man Review*

Pack of Lies
"Bonnie's intelligence and perceptiveness
really make this book go, and readers will root for her
and the team to solve their investigation."
—*RT Book Reviews,* Top Pick

"*Pack of Lies* is not to be missed by urban fantasy fans
looking for a great mystery."
—*Reading with Tequila*

Tricks of the Trade
"Innovative world building coupled with rich characterization
continues to improve as we enter the third book of this series."
—*Smexy Books Romance Reviews*

"I want the next book now! I was not ready to leave this world
when I finished *Tricks of the Trade.*"
—*Reading Reality*

**Also available from
Laura Anne Gilman
and Harlequin LUNA**

Paranormal Scene Investigations

Retrievers

laura anne gilman

DRAGON JUSTICE

H HARLEQUIN®
entertain, enrich, inspire™

Recycling programs
for this product may
not exist in your area.

DRAGON JUSTICE

ISBN-13: 978-0-373-80348-4

www.Harlequin.com

Printed in U.S.A.

To all the readers who have, over the years,
joined the Cosa Nostradamus.
None of this would have happened without you.

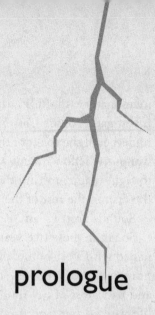

prologue

Yesterday was, unofficially, the second anniversary of PUPI. Two years ago, we were hired, me and Nick, Nifty, Pietr, and Sharon.

Nobody brought cupcakes. Nobody said a word. But we all knew.

You can spend your entire life wondering if you've made a difference. We know. Two years. A lot accomplished. A long way to go.

There's no sign on our building; it's just another mixed-use brickwork like hundreds of others in Manhattan. Too far uptown to be fashionable, too well kept to be fashionably seedy, seven stories and a clean but boring lobby with a row of nameplates and buzzers. Ours simply read P.U.P.I.

The plaque outside our door, on the seventh—top—floor repeated the terseness etched in bronze. If you came this far, you knew who we were and what we did.

My name is Bonnie Torres. A long time ago not so long ago, I was a newly minted college grad with a degree and enthusiasm—and not a clue where to go with it. Now I'm lead investigator with PUPI, the Private, Unaffiliated Paranormal Investigators of the *Cosa Nostradamus*. I spend my days looking underneath the rocks of the magical community, finding the things my fellow Talent want to keep hidden. We use magic to fight magic, to find the evidence the cops can't, to prove the crimes the rest of the world can't see.

Sounds pretty glam, right?

So far, in those two years, I've been shot at, verbally abused, nailed with a psi-bomb, physically threatened, seen people—human and otherwise—die and been unable to prevent it, and had most of my illusions about the inherent fairness of life yanked out from under me. Some days, it's hard to get out of bed in the morning.

And then I think about what we've done, and I haul myself out and get my ass to the office. Because this, PUPI, what we do? It matters.

The boss likes to give a lecture about how we're not crusaders or superheroes. The world's too big a place for us to save all of it. He lectures us, and he knows that we're listening, but we don't believe him. Hell, he doesn't even believe himself, not really, otherwise he wouldn't be here with the rest of us, training us, teaching us enough to stay alive and get our job done.

If he—and Ian Stosser, our founder—didn't believe that we could save someone, maybe not the world, but someone who might otherwise fall, there wouldn't be a PUPI at all.

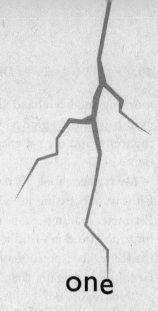

one

We hit the scene, and I started delegating. "All right, I want you to get a perimeter reading—"

"Oh, god. Again?"

I stopped and looked at my companion, puzzled. "What do you mean, again?"

"Again. This." Farshad made a helpless little gesture, indicating the room we'd just walked into.

I put my kit down on the floor and tried to see whatever it was he was reacting to. It was a nice room. It was a nice house, from what I'd seen on the walk through it. The room in front of us had just the right amount of furniture, less than fifty years old but well crafted, not Ikea specials or en suite acquisitions from a "fine furnishings" catalog. Paintings on the wall were original, if not spectacular, the rugs underfoot quality but not hand-woven. It seemed pretty straightforward and ordinary. For a crime scene, anyway.

"What?" I asked again, aware, even if Farshad wasn't, that the client was waiting in the hallway outside the room, impatient for us to get on with it. I'd gotten to the office that morning and been handed a job ticket and a trainee. I hadn't even had time to grab a cup of coffee before we were off to the scene, and my patience might not have been all that patient.

My trainee shook his head, clearly resigned to the fact that I just wasn't getting it. "Don't you ever get tired of all this? Perimeter readings, scan-and-pan, collect evidence, sort and discard? You don't find it boring?" Far swept his hand over the scene, an expression of almost comical resignation on his face. I looked again, then looked back at him.

"Not really, no."

Farshad was one of our new hires; he'd only been on the job for three months. If he was bored with the routine already, he wouldn't last to his half-year evaluation.

He opened his mouth to say something, and I held up a hand to stop him. "Just go into fugue and see what you can find, okay?"

Far nodded, sinking onto his haunches and resting his hands on his knees. I counted silently with him as he slipped into the fugue state that made concentrating current easier, and then followed down after him. Once, when I'd been a new-made pup, I'd had to count back, too. Now it was a matter of breathing deep, once, and sliding into my core.

This was Far's third site. I'd lost count around twenty-five. We'd gotten busy over the past year. That was why we'd hired new staff—and why I was stuck training them.

All right, not entirely fair; everyone was doing newbie-training. But I seemed to be the only one who hated it. Griping, though, did not close the case, and the client was waiting.

An exhale, and I opened my eyes to examine the site again. Seen in mage-sight, the rug and sofa were splattered with a dark stain. Not blood or ichor; that would have shown up with normal eyesight. It didn't carry any of the neon-sharp trace of current, either, so it wasn't magical. Something new? Part of me groaned—an open-and-shut investigation would have been nice, considering the paperwork waiting for me back at the office. On the other hand…something new?

Every sense I had perked up at the thought.

We made it back to the office before lunch, despite the usual Monday transit snafus. At least it hadn't been raining; it had rained every day for the past week. Summer would be starting soon—maybe the sun would show up eventually.

Venec had set up shop today in the smallest conference room, spreading his gear over the table. When we came in, he leaned back in the single chair at the table, an interesting contrast to his usual hold-up-the-wall stance.

"Report."

I'd written my own evaluation of the site while we were there, taking samples both magical and physical, but I let Farshad make his initial report unassisted. Far quavered a little under Venec's sharp bark, but then stood tall and delivered. Good pup.

The job was open-and-shut after all—the client's son had tried to exorcise a family ghost who was annoying him and ended up attracting a succubus. The ghost escaped; the boy did not. We had the succubus's trace now, though, so the client could negotiate for her idiot offspring's return—or not, as she still had two other kids who looked to be smarter than their brother. Whatever happened, it wasn't our concern any longer. PUPI investigated and handed over our findings; we were not judge, jury, or negotiator.

In slightly longer words, Far was telling Venec exactly that. Minus the comment about possibly not ransoming the teenager: it was a common office opinion that three-year-olds had more tact than I did.

he's doing well

The thought came to me, not in the push of emotions or sensations the way pinging—current-to-current communication—usually did, but a soft voice in my ear, clear and defined. It was unnatural as hell, but after a year of it, I didn't even flinch.

he's not going to make it I sent back, with the added implication of a money bet.

There was a sense of snorting amusement and acceptance of my bet. You took your amusement where you could some days.

The source of that mental snort was now leaning forward in his chair, listening to Far's report, not a twitch indicating that he wasn't giving the boy one hundred percent attention. Benjamin Venec. One of the two founding partners of PUPI—Private, Unaffiliated Paranormal Investigations. Tall, dark, and cranky. Sexy as hell, if you liked the type. My boss. And, much to our combined and considerable dismay, my "destined merge," according to every magical source and Talent we could consult.

That had been, putting it mildly, an unpleasant, unwanted surprise. To both of us.

The Merge was—according to legend, because there were no modern references—what happened when two matched Talent encountered each other, when our cores blended or swirled or something equally annoying and sparkly.

The best hypothesis we could put together was that the Merge was some kind of coded breeding program to make sure there were little baby magic users for the next generation. Talent wasn't purely genetic, but it did seem to bud in family trees more often than not.

The idea of magic having an ulterior goal was bad enough;

being its means was worse. I was twenty-four and in no mood to become a broodmare, even if Venec had been so inclined. More to the point, neither of us took very well to anyone telling us what—or who—our destiny was, especially since it would totally screw with the dynamics of a job we both put first, second, and occasionally third in our lives.

In true rational, adult fashion, we'd therefore both spent the first few months ignoring it. That had been pretty much a failure; when you literally spark around someone, you notice. And so does everyone else. So then we tried managing it, maintaining our distance and shutting down everything except essential contact. That hadn't worked so well either, especially after Ben was attacked by a hellhound about seven-eight months ago, and I caught the pain-rebound through our connection.

The cat had been out of the bag then; we'd had to tell the others. *Awkward* didn't even begin to cover it. But the team dealt with it, mostly. Truthfully, being able to communicate so easily, share information along the thinnest line of current other Talent wouldn't even sense, made the job much easier. Only problem was, using it bound us together even more, until it became impossible to shut the other out entirely. The Merge was as stubborn as we were, it seemed.

I kept my walls all the way up off-hours, though, and Venec did the same. We stayed out of each other's personal lives.

Mostly.

Right now, it was all work. Venec now had his gaze fixed on Far in a way that generally made even us old-timers nervous, wondering what we'd missed that the Big Dog was about to point out.

Venec finally relented on the stare and asked, "If you were to approach the scene again, fresh, what would you do differently?"

The right answer to that was "nothing." You approached every scene the same way: with no expectations or assumptions. Far fumbled it the way all the newbies did, trying to determine what he'd missed that the Big Dog was going to slap him down for. I tuned it out and let a tendril of current skim out into the office. My coworkers' individual current brushed against me in absent greeting, the magical equivalent of a raised hand or nod, giving me a sense of the office moving: people coming in and out, talking, working out evidence, or just refilling their brains with caffeine and protein.

Lunchtime was serious business in this office. Current burned calories, and a PUP used more current on a daily basis than most Talent did in a month.

The sense of movement was comforting, like mental white noise. All was right with the world, or at least our small corner of it, and I'd learned enough to cherish the moment.

Far stumbled to a halt in his report and risked looking at me. I kept my face still, not sure if I should be frowning or giving an approving nod.

"All right. Good job, you two." Venec nodded his own approval, making Far sag a little in relief. "Farshad, write up the report and file it. Lou will invoice and close the file. And then go get some lunch. You look paler than normal."

Far grinned at that, accepting the usual joke—he was about as pale as a thundercloud—and beat a hasty retreat.

"You're wrong," Venec said out loud. "He'll make it."

Big Dog was still a better judge of people than I could ever hope to be, so I didn't argue. But the truth was, we'd gone through seven new-hired PUPs in the past nine months, hire-to-fire. One of them, rather spectacularly, had only made it a week before giving notice. Venec had hired all of them; occasionally, even he was wrong.

★ ★ ★

I was amazed, sometimes, when I came into the office in the morning and there were so many people here. We'd started out with five PUPs. We had nine in the field right now, plus our office manager, Lou, and her cousin's daughter Nisa, who helped out in the back office part-time while she went to school. And Venec and Stosser, of course. Thirteen people. Crazy, right?

"If he's doing so well, you'll take me off babysitting duty?" I asked, hopeful but not really expecting a positive response. "Seriously, Venec, I'm better in the lab than I am riding herd. Pietr is way better, and so is Sharon."

"Objection noted," he said calmly. "Again."

"Ben…" I wasn't whining. I wasn't begging, either. The fact that I was using his first name, though, was a warning sign to both of us. Usually I didn't slip in the office. I tested my walls: half-up, so anyone could reach me, but enough that I shouldn't be leaking anything through the Merge. Just like the rest of the magic we worked with, we'd gotten it down to a science. Everything was totally under control—except the sparks that flared through both our cores when we touched, that is. We just made damn sure not to touch anymore.

Which, by the way, sucked. He was nice to touch, toned and muscular, with just enough flesh under the skin to feel good. Months after my hand last touched him, the feel remained.

From the flicker in his gaze, he remembered, too. "You go where you're needed, and right now we need you riding herd as well as being brilliant. Now put some food in your stomach, too. I can hear it growling from here."

Benjamin Venec could be a right proper and deeply irritating bastard when he wanted to be. He was also the boss. And he was right, damn it.

I saluted sloppily and turned on my three-inch boot heel, a flounce of which I was justifiably proud. I did not slam the door shut behind me. That would have been rude.

By the time I'd stalked down the hallway to the break room, the soothing green-and-cream decor had done its job, and my brain had stopped fizzing at me. Calmer now, I was able to see his point: it wasn't about teaching the newbies but working with them. The things we did on a regular basis required everyone to be comfortable with each other, on a level most people aren't ready for—lonejack or Council, we're trained one-on-one, not classroom-style, and group-work takes some getting used to.

So, by putting me in the training rotation, the newbies got used to me being in their personal space, both physical and magical. And vice versa—I might be used to working in a group, but I still needed to learn each individual's signature.

The fact that I hated teaching, would much rather have been in the office working up a new cantrip or spell, didn't matter. Venec was pushing me, making me get out of my comfort zone, and making sure I stayed a viable member of the team.

Making sure I did the best job possible by challenging me in the area of my least competence.

Knowing that you're being manipulated isn't always a bad thing: you can either fight it or let it do its job. Since its job was to ensure that I could do my job, I let it go.

The smell of something warm and meat-filled came through the doorway, drawing me into the break room, my stomach even louder now. The need for more coffee was officially secondary to the need for food.

I noted there was someone else in the break room even as that person greeted me with a wave and "heya, dandelion." I returned the wave, going straight for the fridge.

"Hey, yourself," I said, grabbing a packet of chocolate pudding and an anonymous wrapped sandwich, then turning to face my coworker. "You close your ticket?"

Nicky shook his head mournfully. "Held over by popular demand. Seems our client wasn't quite forthcoming on all that was stolen."

I snorted in a way that would have made my mentor shake his head in genteel dismay. "Surprise. Not."

After the ki-rin disaster we'd somehow gotten a few more jobs, but then came the Tricks case, that damned prankster, and the horse-trading Venec had indulged in to satisfy his sense of fair play. In the aftermath, there had been a month of utter silence when we'd figured it was all over, nobody would trust us to find a missing gerbil. I'd even started browsing the want ads, not that there was anything there I was qualified for, much less interested in.

Then, all of a sudden, it was like the floodgates opened. Okay, a steady trickle through the gates. The Eastern Council hadn't given us their gold seal of approval yet, but the rank-and-file Council were bringing us their troubles.

The problem was, most of them held the "above the rules" attitude that had made Ian Stosser decide there was a need for us in the *Cosa Nostradamus* to begin with. It's tough to solve a supernatural crime. It's almost impossible when the client doesn't give over all the gory details at the start.

Nicky had gotten one of those.

I'd gotten pretty good at holding back exasperated sighs. "At some point, they're going to have to realize that we're not going to judge them. Right?"

Nick snorted in response, and I flopped down on the sofa next to him, swinging my feet up into his lap and unwrapping the sandwich. "Okay, maybe not."

Nick shoved my feet back onto the ground and went back

to marking something in his notebook. Since current messed with electronics something fierce, most Talent couldn't use recorders or cameras, so we all carried notebooks around like twentieth-century beat cops. I'd added a sketchbook to my kit, but Nick couldn't draw a straight line if you gave him a ruler. I know, I'd tried.

"Just be glad you weren't here when the smoke detector went off again," he said.

I groaned. "What's that, the third time this month?"

"Yeah. Scared the crap out of Nisa."

"Poor kid. She so doesn't deserve to be stuck here with us." Nicky just snickered.

"I didn't see anything on the board—I wonder if I could get tomorrow off," I said, biting into my lunch. Ham and cheese. Not bad. Time off would be nice. I'd gotten an invite to go sailing from a woman I'd met the week before, and I wanted to take her up on it before she decided I wasn't interested. Despite the Merge, I was trying to keep some semblance of a normal social life, even if very few of my hookups ended up with an actual hookup these days.

"Doubtful," Nick said, not looking up. "Stosser took a new client into the back office about ten minutes ago. Got your name all over it."

"Oh, gods above and below." I took another bite, that news suggesting that lunch might be abbreviated. "Can't someone else handle it?"

"Fatae."

That one short word made me put down my sandwich, thoughts of my new acquaintance and a lazy afternoon on the water not quite forgotten but shoved aside. "Seriously?"

Nick finally looked up from his notebook. "Serious as a heart attack. No idea the breed. They were cloaked like it was midwinter. Human-tall, human-wide, no visible tails or fur."

That didn't rule much out—most of the fatae in New York City were human-shaped, enough to get by on a casual glance, anyway. There were a few horned and hooved types, and a few clearly not-human breeds living in the parks or underground, but they were the minority. And when they had a problem, most of them dealt with it internally. In fact, most of the breeds dealt with their own shit. For one of them to come to us...

It could be good, or it could be seriously bad. The last time we'd gotten tangled in fatae business, we'd had to drag a ki-rin into disgrace. Never mind that the Ancient had brought it on itself; we were still the ones who had exposed it. The fact that the honored one had chosen suicide rather than live with the knowledge of what it had done...

Technically, and what passed for legally among the fatae, what happened wasn't our fault, nor our responsibility. But I still felt sick about it and suspected the others did, too. I didn't want to deal with a fatae case.

"Still." I was running through excuses and justifications in my head, if only for the practice. "Someone else could handle it. What about Sharon? She's good with delicate situations."

"You're the fatae specialist," Nick pointed out with damnable reasonableness. "Stosser will put you on it, if there's anything to be put on."

Right on cue, there was a touch of current against my awareness. *torres*

The feel of that ping was unmistakable. I sighed and got to my feet. "I hate it when you're right," I grumbled, shoved my lunch back into the fridge, and headed into the office to face my fate.

We had started two years ago with one suite, taking up a quarter of the seventh floor. About a year back the guys acquired the second suite of offices on our side of the building and combined the space, repurposing the original layout into a warren of rooms that gave the illusion of privacy without sacrificing an inch of workspace. Nice, except when you were doing the Tread of Dread, as Nifty had dubbed the walk from the break room to Stosser's office at the very end of the long hall.

I knocked once, and the door opened.

"Sir?"

Usually I'd have started with "you rang, oh great and mighty?" but what worked with humans could backfire spectacularly with fatae. The fact that I knew that—the result of years more experience interacting with the nonhuman members of the *Cosa* than anyone else in the office except possibly Venec—was why I'd been called here. Nick had it in one.

"Torres. Come in."

I came in, closing the door behind me, uncertain of where to go after that. The office was large enough to hold five people comfortably, seven if we all squeezed. Right then, there were only four—me, Stosser, and two figures, cloaked, with their backs to me—but it felt crowded as hell.

Then they turned around, and all the air left my lungs in a surprised, if hopefully discreet, whoosh.

Benjamin Venec took good care of his investigators. If they were stressed, he gave them something to snarl at. If they were worried, he could provide a sounding board. If they were pissed off, he was willing to fight with them. But he couldn't force them to relax; even if that had been his style, his pups were stubborn. They'd decide when they went down, not someone else, opponent or boss.

So he could have told Torres to go home and get some sleep. She might even have gone—or at least started to. But he knew her: something shiny would catch her attention, either a case or a person, and she'd be off again. That was just…Torres.

The fact that he had given up any right to be jealous of either things or people she deemed shiny didn't seem to help the slight burning sensation to the left of his gut when he felt her sudden rush of surprise, followed by a shimmer of glee and anticipation that was uniquely Bonita Torres.

Her signature was like coconut liquor, spicy and warm, and he let himself enjoy the taste—offsetting the burning sensation, or enhancing it, he wasn't sure.

The pleasure was balanced by a sense of moral discomfort, though. They'd agreed to stay out of each other's headspace unless invited. Bonnie had been scrupulous about maintaining that agreement. He hadn't. And claiming that it was part of his job, as her boss and teacher, nothing more than he did for the others, only went so far in justifying what his mentor would have called a blatant misuse of Talent.

Ben didn't even try to justify it, not to himself. He might be a bastard, but he was an honest one. He simply couldn't avoid the overlap: even with his walls up, he was hyperaware of every strong emotion that passed through Torres, and the girl never felt anything halfway. It should have been annoying to his more cynical, jaded self, the way she threw herself wholeheartedly into every step of her life and dragged him along, via the Merge, without even realizing it. Instead, the experience amused, exasperated, frustrated, and invigorated him, sometimes all at once.

He let it ride. The first rule of dealing with the Merge, they had discovered, was not dealing with the Merge, and so far, he had been able to ignore the other, totally unprofessional urges. Mostly.

The fact that Bonnie took other lovers had been established—by her—early on. Also established: it was none of his damn business. She kept her private life private, but the Merge… If she knew how much leaked, even when she thought her walls were up, she'd be horrified. And mortified. Thankfully, she was as particular as she was omnivorous, and they had been few and far between lately. He always knew, though.

He waited a minute, just letting the Merge-connection wash over him, and the sense of surprise and excitement faded, her thoughts settling into the focused hum that meant that whatever was making her quiver was work-related.

Work was within his purview. Ben tapped his pencil against the desk, resisting temptation for all of ten heartbeats.

new job? he queried his partner.

interesting problem Ian sent back, not so much words as a perception of something sharp and dark, versus Bonnie's sense of shiny.

Ben tapped the pencil harder.

too much he suggested, with just the sense of scales tilting too far to one side. The past few months they'd been getting a steady stream of work, from piddling jobs like the one they'd tested Farshad on to the more complicated blackmail-and-possible-murder case he'd given Sharon, Pietr, and Jenna.

There was silence from Ian, which could mean anything from disagreement to his being attacked at knifepoint by the supposed client.

No, if that were the case, even if Ian were his usual cool self, Torres would have reacted. So: he was being ignored.

In its own way, that was reassuring. Torres and Stosser both had the kind of focus that didn't miss much. Whatever was going on there, he could safely ignore it for now in favor of…

Ben paused his pencil-tapping. Actually, there was nothing pending on his desk. Lou, their office manager, had the day-to-day things running smoothly, and with the exception of Ian's new project, whatever it was, nothing new had come in needing his attention.

Ben exhaled, waiting for the other shoe to drop. Nothing did. Everyone was either out on a job or finishing up their paperwork. Nothing new needed to be evaluated and assigned. That meant he was free to pick up the job that had come across his desk this morning. Not a PUPI investigation; something from his previous line of work. He'd given up his sidelines while they got PUPI running, but not gotten out of the game entirely.

This project would only take a day or three, and it would be good to get out of Big Dog mode, use his other skills before they got rusty…and, he admitted, get himself out of Bonnie's immediate vicinity, give the connection between them time to cool off a bit. She'd been single for a couple-three months now, but every time she did hook up with someone, he could feel himself hovering between an all-out confrontation or sliding the knife in deep, in places only he knew about. He was capable of both, he knew. Both would end badly.

Yeah, time away would be a good thing.

taking a few days off he told his partner and got a distracted mmm-hmm back. Not that he needed permission, but with Ian it was better to clear the decks anyway, in case he had something tucked up his sleeve that Ben would be needed for.

Looking at the packet of papers on his desk again, he picked up the landline—an old-fashioned rotary, thrice-warded against random current-spikes—and dialed the number in the letterhead. He let it rotate through the phone-tree options until an actual operator came to see what the problem was.

"Extension 319, please."

He waited while he was clicked through, and a familiar voice picked up at the other end.

"Allen? It's Ben. Usual plus expenses, and I can be there this afternoon."

two

Holy mother of meatloaf, the atmosphere in Stosser's office didn't just hum—it fricking crackled.

The boss did the introductions. "This is Bonita Torres."

"The Torres is known to us."

It took me a second, then my manners flooded back and I made as graceful a salutation as I could. A properly elegant curtsy requires yards of skirts and a fitted corset, but I didn't think the Lord would be offended, so long as the proper respect was shown. How the hell was my name known to him? That wasn't good. Or it was very good. I wasn't sure.

The other unknown figure in the room laughed at my response, a low noise that sent a different kind of shiver down my neck. Oh, fuck. Stosser, damn him, looked utterly unaffected.

"She will be acceptable," the other, still-hooded figure said. Her voice was low, a smoky contralto, but not even remotely masculine. It was the voice that could lure otherwise sane men to their doom with a smile on their lips and a sparkle in their eye.

A thought passed through my head that it wasn't really a surprise Stosser was unaffected: he had already trooped merrily along to his doom, that being us, here, this.

I wanted very badly to know what the hell was going on, but also knew damn well to keep my mouth shut unless spoken to.

"Our guests have come to us about a child who has gone missing."

I turned my head slightly, to indicate that I was listening to the Big Dog, but I kept my gaze on the Lord. Not that I distrusted him, exactly, but I wanted to keep him in my sight at all times. The Lady didn't worry me—I might like guys and girls, but the Fey Folk kept it pure vanilla when they deigned to mess with mortals. At worst, she'd try to make me a lapdog, and my kinks didn't bend that way.

"A Fey child?" Even as I asked I knew that wasn't it. Not just because Fey children were rare and protected, but because the Fey would not involve mortals in their own business. While not nearly as arrogant as the angeli, the Fey were still about as insular as a breed could get, in the modern world. Which, in my opinion, was good for all concerned.

Every fairy tale you ever heard? The truth was worse.

"A mortal child." Stosser clarified the case. The Lord did not move away from my gaze, allowing me to watch him, and I knew damn well he was allowing me to do so. His cowl lay against his shoulders, and his face was clearly visible, a Rackham sketch come to life, but twice as vibrant and three times as dangerous, if he desired. "A seven-year-old girl, abducted from her bed during the dark of the moon."

Which had been last week. "Not quite seven, I bet." It wasn't a guess; a child past that birthday would be safe from the Fey; I didn't know if Catholicism set seven as the age of reason because the Fey stopped being interested in human children around then, implying that God had claimed them, or if the Fey stopped being interested because the child actually had developed a moral backbone. It didn't matter which came first so long as you could keep your offspring safe until then.

Someone hadn't.

"And you came to us because…you didn't take her? And her parents think you did?" That made no sense; they wouldn't care what mortals thought. Especially if nothing could be pinned to them.

"Our Troop abides under the Palisades Treaty," the Lord said. I was starting to get—not used to his gaze, but able to ignore it. Sort of.

"But you think someone slipped up, maybe couldn't resist?" Stosser asked.

No. Not that. It didn't feel right.

"Or another Troop is poaching?" he continued.

Poaching in their territory and letting them take the blame. Yes.

"That," the Lady said, and her voice was the growl of a sweet-tuned sports car, clearly annoyed that Stosser seemed oblivious, "is what you must discover."

"We must?" The words slipped out, even though I'd have sworn my mouth was shut. Oh, not smart, Bonita, not smart questioning one of the Fey. I didn't think they would do anything here—hell, I knew they wouldn't do anything here, not within our walls. That would be rude. But once I was out on the street, once I left the protection of human habitations… Being well over the age of reason didn't protect you from anything save abduction. There were far worse things the Fey could—and did—do to humans who crossed them. And they could make you like it.

The Lord seemed to be in command of these negotiations,

from the way he stepped in. Or maybe he just wanted to keep the Lady from saying anything more. "If the human child was taken within our Troop, we will deal with it. If she was taken by another, infringing on our lands and agreements... then we will deal with it." I did not like the sound of that, and from the way Stosser went even more still, neither did he. But neither of us said anything. "If she was taken by another, one not-Fey, and a trail was left to indicate that a Troop had done it, breaking the Treaty..."

The Lord looked me direct in the eye then, his gaze un-shadowed, and the tawny-gold of his irises was exactly like an owl's, just like legend claimed. "It was not so many turns of the moon past that this city was at shattering point, mortal and breed, *Cosa* and Null."

Understatement, that. The battle of Burning Bridge last winter had been a high point in human-fatae cooperation, but the before and after... I knew I didn't know how close to the brink the city had come and was pretty sure that I didn't want to know.

"We have no wish for that point to return."

No. Nobody did, not even the most rabid antihuman fatae. We'd scared ourselves sober, for once.

If someone was trying to set up the Fey, we needed to be on it, to prevent any more damage from being done. A PUP's word that the Fey were not guilty would be trusted; we'd earned that, at least.

"You have the best contacts within the fatae community," Stosser said to me. "If anyone knows anything, they'll tell you."

The boss knew better than to use his usual glamour of competence with not one but two Fey in the room, but he practically glowed with such utter confidence in my abilities, I almost believed it, too. Sure, not a problem, boss.

"It is done, then," the Lady said, her voice still disturbing but not so obviously fishing for bait. We weren't interesting enough for her to keep playing with, I guess. The Lord lifted his hood back over his head, making them a matched set, and they swept out of the room like the arrogant bastards they were. I was pretty sure I never saw either one of them touch the door; it opened for them like it was eager to do their bidding.

Or maybe just to be rid of them. I know I breathed a little easier once I sensed they had left the office entirely.

Only then did I turn to Stosser. "Who's on—"

"Just you."

"What?" We did not go out alone. That was the first rule, hammered into us from day one, by Venec. Pups worked in pairs, to make sure someone always had your back.

"I don't want this looking like an investigation. Not yet. Ideally not ever."

I tended toward the blunt—tactless, Venec said, often—but my mentor had been a politician to match Stosser, once upon a time, and I knew when a game was on. "You want me to solve it quietly, have them owe us without anyone knowing they owe us, and have them know that we kept them out of it, but without ever being tacky enough to say so." Shit. "We're doing this pro bono?"

Stosser's expression didn't change, which meant absolutely nothing. "For a fee to be determined later."

"Uh-huh. They're really worried, if they're agreeing to that." The Fey were the ones who gave the fatae some of the worst reps—even more than redcaps or angeli. Not because they were violent, but because they were sneaky to a level that would make a corporate lawyer jealous. Agreeing to a deal without having all the terms nailed down hard-and-fast and in their favor? That was the kind of mistake they anticipated mortals doing, not one they made themselves. I was immediately, worryingly suspicious.

"Um, boss?"

"Let me worry about that, Torres. You just do your job." There was a sudden sparkle in his eyes that I distrusted. "Manage this without getting anyone killed, and we'll make a Council schmoozer out of you yet."

On that threat, I turned and ran. Slowly, decorously even, but I ran.

The doors off the hallway at this end were all closed, but I could still feel the steady hum of activity throughout the office as I made my way back, pausing in the half-open doorway of the main conference room at the other end. There was a single pup in residence, working at the long, polished wood table.

"Kill me now, please."

Pietr made a gunlike shape with his right hand and mimed shooting me, even as he kept writing with his left.

My fellow investigator and sometimes lover had just finished a three-week-long investigation into a missing sculpture, an alleged magical Artifact that turned out to have been a spell-cast but otherwise ordinary figurine pawned by the owner's stepdaughter. I wasn't sure why the boring jobs generated the most paperwork, but it always seemed to be the case.

I stood in the doorway and watched him awhile longer. Pietr was the quiet one, among all of us. He thought first, and then thought again, and then when he did something he did it well and thoroughly. And yes, that included sex. He also had the interesting and occasionally useful, more often annoying, tendency to fade from sight, literally, when under stress. That little quirk made it problematic, at times, to work in the field with him. He was sharp and clear today, though.

He looked up at me, just then, as though suddenly realizing I was watching him. "New assignment? Need help? I'm just about done here."

Pietr would have been useful as backup, but Stosser's orders were, well, orders. I shook my head. "No. I'm good. Just some Q&A among the fatae the Big Dog wants done. One-person gig."

"Lucky you." He knew that was against standing procedure but didn't push.

"Yeah. Lucky me. We still on for dinner next week?"

"Assuming no last-minute disasters, yeah. Wear your dancing shoes."

I nodded and went the rest of the way to the break room, where there was no sign of Nicky. I eyed the coffeemaker on the kitchenette counter to my right, then decided that more caffeine wasn't what I needed. Sleep, now, that would have been nice. And I needed to re-source my current; I'd been too busy to dig deep recently, and I could feel a hollowness inside that had nothing to do with hunger.

Calories weren't the only thing we had to replenish after working. A Talent's core stored their current, and the longer it stayed there the more it conformed to that individual's signature, making it easier to use.

It also made it easier for us to track down the Talent who had used it, like matching fingerprints to fingers. So far, we'd kept that bit of info to ourselves. Trade secrets—no reason to give up what slight advantage we had over our criminally minded peers.

I thought about making a second try at lunch, but my appetite had fled. The Fey suspected someone was interfering with the Treaty and had given us the chance to stop it. If we couldn't...

Yeah. Suddenly, a sandwich wasn't so appetizing.

If I wasn't going to eat, and I wasn't going to tell Stosser where he could stick this job, it was time to get my ass out of the office. I'd always hated the "soonest begun, soonest ended" crap, but it had the nasty flavor of truth.

I went over to the small board that hung on the wall next to the main door and marked myself "out, on job." Lou had set the system up after one too many confusions about who was where, when, and god help the pup who forgot to check in or out. I left my work-kit in the closet; I wouldn't need the external tools of my trade for this—just my brain.

I hoped.

The external hallway was empty, as usual. There were two other offices on our floor, but it was rare that we saw anyone go in or out save the UPS guy. I paused a moment at the elevator and then told myself taking the stairs was exercise, nothing whatsoever to do with the lingering memory of the boy who had died there when the power failed, now almost two years ago. Nothing at all, nope.

The six flights down were easy, but the moment I hit the outside air, I felt sweat break out on my skin. It wasn't that hot outside yet, but the air still had the feel of an oven. I plucked at the fabric of my T-shirt and scowled. It was barely June. This was going to be a bitch of a summer, you could tell already. Great. Still, maybe a lot of people would take the summer off, go cool down somewhere else, which would mean fewer people rubbing raw nerves against each other, making life easier for the rest of us in the city.

Yeah, and cave dragons were suddenly going to start giving interest-free loans.

So. Scouting the fatae. Where, and how to begin? It's not like this gig came with a bunch of guidelines or clues…

Try acting like a trained professional, an acerbic voice in my head suggested. My own voice, this time.

Right. First things first. I dipped a mental hand into my

core, the pool of current all Talent carry within us as a matter of course, and tested my levels. Blue-and-green threads brushed against me like slender little snakes, sparking and snapping as they moved, crackling when they touched each other. Low, definitely low. Discretion would probably be the better part of valor, then. There was a power generator on the West Side I could dip into without inconveniencing anyone, while I made my plans.

Current—magic—liked to run alongside electricity. In the wild state, that meant ley lines, electrical storms, that sort of thing. For the modern Talent, though, the best, most reliable source of power was, well, a power plant. The trick was learning how to take enough to satisfy your needs, without draining so much you blew the source.

I grabbed the 1 train downtown, got off at 66th, and checked into the nearest 'bux for my latte. The place was doing the usual midafternoon traffic, so I grabbed the first empty chair I saw and sat back like I was just another poser killing time before a date.

Once I was sure nobody was going to approach me, I let myself relax a little, the outer awareness alert and upright while my core opened up and went in search of all the tasty current it could sense shimmering outside.

Compared to the faint hum of the wiring and overhead lights, the generator a few blocks away was like a sauna, warm and inviting. The temptation was there to slide into it and soak up all that was on offer, but that would have been bad manners, not only to any other Talent looking to use it, but for the folk whose rents paid for the power. "Take only what you need, and not all from one source, Bonita," I could hear J saying, like I was a wide-eyed eight-year-old again.

The current swirling inside the generator was a dark, clean blue, its lines sharp and delineated. Ask any five Talent what the colors meant, and you'd get six different answers, but a sharp-edge meant it was fresh, that there was no one else's signature already on it, softening the feel. I'd never been able to sense that, before becoming a PUP.

Lots of things I couldn't do, before. We all were the type to really look at things, not just accept what was on the surface; that was why Stosser hired us in the first place, because we didn't accept the first impression as truth. But two years of doing this day in and out had put us on another skill level entirely. The more you used, the more you could do. The thought of what we might be able to do five years from now...

"Bonita?"

Oh, hell. I brought myself back to the Starbucks, keeping the connection to the generator open, if narrowed, and looked to see who had approached me, who knew me well enough to use my name, but not so well to use the shorter version.

"Andrea. I didn't know you slummed in public coffee-houses."

The words were joking, the tone probably softer than I'd intended, because Andrea took it for an invite, sitting on the windowsill next to my table in lieu of an available chair.

Five foot ten, short blond hair, eyes the color of the Aegean Sea, and teeth as white and straight as money could make them. Andrea was Eastern Council, running at the same levels as my mentor used to.

Because of that, I was cautious about why she'd approached me. I doubted she was just happy to see a familiar face; we'd flirted a bit back when I was still living with J up in Boston, but she was in her thirties, and I'd been twenty, and nothing more than a few innuendos had been exchanged.

And now...now I was a PUP and had to think about things like why someone wanted to get to know me, rather than just enjoying their company. Even the Council people who supported Stosser's Great Experiment still saw us as tools for them to use rather than the impartial clearinghouse we were trying to become. So there was that.

"I heard that you were living in the city now, but I didn't think I'd run into you. I should have, of course. That's how it works—you think this is a huge place, but it's really such a small town." She leaned forward, her blue silk blouse open just enough at the collar that I could see the swell of her breasts and the gold chain that dropped between them, and part of my brain kicked into a different gear. Apparently, being out of college meant I was fair game now.

Huh. Andy was gorgeous, smart, ambitious, and potentially very useful to me, long-term, if I were going to think the way she did. And I was—modesty aside—smart, good-looking, and potentially very useful to her, both short- and long-term, if she had any ambitions in the Council, which I knew damn well she did. We would be, as the pundits like to say, a dream power couple.

And the sex would probably be a lot of fun.

There was just one damn problem. The Merge. Other than Pietr, who knew what the deal was and where he stood, all of my sexual relations for the past year had lasted two weeks, tops. Not that my sex drive had suddenly gone away—far from it. It had just... I need to be emotionally engaged with the person I'm sleeping with. Not love, but like-a-lot. And respect. And...

And every time I touched someone else, I knew that it wasn't enough. I wanted Venec. I wanted the spark-and-thump I got just touching him. Wanted to know if his eyes were as intense when he hit orgasm as they were when he was decoding an evidence tangle. Wanted...

I wanted him out of my head, out of my groin, and the last lingering scent of him out of my core, because it was just the damn Merge, and I did not like being directed by anything, least of all some obscure, magical hand-of-fate.

But I knew, by now, that he wasn't going anywhere. And neither was I. It just… I wasn't ready yet.

Andy touched my hand, her fingers soft and firm and smelling like very expensive sin. "I have to get to a meeting—I'm already running late—but can I ping you later, maybe have dinner?"

I didn't want to encourage her if there was nothing happening—I'm a flirt, not a tease—but Andy could be useful. And it wasn't like I wasn't glad to have someone to exchange friendly innuendo with who knew the rules and wasn't interested in a lifetime of devotion. And having a Council friend was never a bad thing, despite what my lonejack-raised co-workers believed.

I tested my conscience and came back with a quick response. "Sure. Ping me."

I watched her leave, enjoying the view her knee-length pencil skirt gave me, then brought myself back to the business at hand. My core hadn't quite topped off, but it was good enough. Time to get moving. Stosser would expect me to have something to report, come morning.

Not an answer: even the Big Dog wasn't that unreasonable. But a little girl was missing, and finding out who took her was my job. No fucking pressure, right.

I had a number of contacts among the fatae, both through my mentor and my own social circles. Bobo, the Meshaden who acted as my occasional bodyguard and gossip-bringer. Danny, the half-faun P.I. who did side work for us occasionally and had connections into just about every shadowed corner of the city. Madame, the Ancient dragon who lived in a penthouse cave high above the cityscape and had her talon on the pulse of everything scandalous in the society world, human and otherwise. But even as I ticked off names in my head, I knew that if I wanted the most up-to-date details that other people wouldn't want known, if time was of the essence and cost not really an object, there was one place to go and two people to talk to.

For various interpretations of "people," anyway.

I didn't have the patience to deal with the stop-and-start motion of a cross-town bus, so I hailed a cab. Stosser would damn well approve the expense, even if we were doing this pro bono.

Once upon a time, meeting up with The Wren had been a thing of awe—after all, she was The Retriever, at least in the States—the most talented (and Talented) of current-thieves. Then we'd become building-mates, and friends, and I almost stopped thinking of her in a professional manner.

Almost. Not quite.

The past year or so, we'd lived in the same building— she'd gotten me my apartment, in fact. But about a month ago, when the planned condo conversion of our building fell through, she'd moved uptown. I didn't blame her—our building was cozy and had a sense of living energy in the actual construction that made Talent feel comfortable, but it was also kinda cramped and rundown, and her sweetie lived uptown anyway, so...

It wasn't like we saw each other every day, anyway.

I gave the cabbie Wren's new address and leaned against the seat as the car jolted forward, moving into traffic. Pulling the file Stosser had given me out of my bag, I opened the folder and studied the report in more detail, putting aside what the Lord said and concentrating only on the established facts. Kids sometimes went missing with no supernatural elements involved, and I'd learned the hard way about not checking every-damn-possibility. Especially if anything contradicted what the client gave us. But the notes didn't give me anything new, or even problematic. Parents still married, so not a custody battle. No other relatives who might be problems. Family decently middle-class, not the sort to be targeted for ransom. Both parents worked in academia, teachers, so it's not like there was the high probability of coercion or blackmail, either, unless PTA meetings had gotten a hell of a lot tougher since I was in school.

The cab dumped me out on the corner rather than fight the delivery van double-parked and blocking traffic, and I walked the half block to "The Westerly." I had laughed when I saw the name on the formal, cream-colored change-of-address card delivered in the mail a few weeks before. Seeing it, though— J's building was called Branderford. I wanted to live in a building that had a name. And a doorman. And...

And, pointless. I couldn't afford an apartment in a building with a name and a doorman. Not yet, anyway.

Doormen in New York City are more than guys—or women—who open doors and accept deliveries. They're the first line of security for the residents. So I was prepared to do the usual who-I'm-here-to-see routine—I was assuming Wren, being Talent, would not have bought into one of those places with the full electronic security systems. To my surprise, though, the doorman riding the simple but splashy marble counter merely looked up, nodded, and pressed a button, summoning the elevator. I let a slender tendril rise, and it was met by a similar one from the doorman.

Huh. Not so much a surprise that the doorman was a Talent—we tended to non-office jobs as a whole: less chance to current-spike the tech—but that Wren had apparently put me on an all-clear list. I guess she was hoping I'd still show up with lasagna every now and then.

The elevator was clean and well maintained, with pretty architectural touches that said the building was a prewar renovation. My estimate of how much she paid for the place went up, considerably. Ouch. But she could afford it: you didn't hire The Wren for cut-rate work.

The apartment was on the top floor—Wren liked not having anyone thumping above her, considering the odd hours she slept. Twenty-four J was at the end of the hallway, the fifth down, which meant she had a corner apartment. My estimate of the cost went up, again. Damn.

The door opened even before I got there, and the moment I saw two expectant faces, one brown-eyed and human, one red-eyed and ursine, staring at me, I apologized. "No food this time, sorry. Will you take a rain check?"

It wasn't as though I was such an amazing cook—they were just that bad at it. I wasn't sure Wren knew how to use her stove to do more than reheat pizza, and the demon…

PB had agile paws, but his short, black-padded fingers ended in sharp white nails that probably didn't make it too easy to cook. Certainly I'd never gotten any indication that he even had a kitchen, wherever he lived.

The first time I had seen the demon, it had been in an all-night diner, during the ki-rin job. He had been the first demon I'd ever encountered—maybe the only, since I still wasn't sure if the angular shadow that had passed me late one night had been a demon, despite the glimpse of pale red eyes under its slouch hat. There were a lot of strange and dangerous things in the *Cosa Nostradamus,* and a lot of them didn't care to be identified by humans.

My hosts let me in despite the lack of lasagna. I took a minute to case the joint, noting that, as expected, Wren hadn't done damn-all to decorate and that she needed curtains for that wall of windows, no matter how nice the view.

"Whatever it is, I didn't do it," Wren said, then added, "probably."

It was an old joke, or a year-old, anyway, which was as long as I'd known the thief well enough to have jokes. Wren Valere was not only a Retriever; to a lot of folk she was The Retriever. Like Pietr, she had the ability to disappear from sight, slide through barriers, and sneak into anywhere she wasn't supposed to be, only unlike Pietr she'd gone for a life of… I couldn't exactly call it crime, since a lot of the jobs I knew she'd taken involved reclaiming objects for their rightful owners. But she moved in a gray area I tried not to look too deeply in. We were friends, and I wanted to keep it that way.

Also, Wren and her partner, Sergei, and PB, had been responsible for keeping the city from going down in flames earlier this year. Everyone knew, even if nobody talked about it. Whatever forces had set us up to war, she had taken them on and won.

No matter what side of the law you were on, you did not want Wren Valere pissed at you. Thankfully, from the moment I'd met her, sent over by Stosser to check into things when her apartment had been bugged by forces unknown, we'd hit it off. Totally nonsexual—I have a useful sense for who's off the market, and Valere and her partner, Sergei, were like peanut and butter.

"Come on in," Wren said, even though I had already gone well past the door frame. She might have been ironic; it was tough to tell sometimes with her. "Sit down. I think there's furniture somewhere under all the boxes. You want coffee?"

"Yes, please."

I found a space on the dark green sofa, which was definitely new. Wren's old place had a sort of bedraggled assortment of furniture, like she'd never quite thought about the fact that guests would need a place to sit. This… I sensed PB's paw in this.

PB found a footstool under a garbage bag that looked like it was filled with pillows, and perched himself on top, tossing the bag onto the polished hardwood floor. He didn't say anything, just looked at me, his rounded, white-furred ears twitching ever so slightly, like a radarscope listening for something human ears would miss.

I looked back. If I'd ever been uneasy under that weirdly red gaze, it had faded a long time ago. Angeli were bastards, but demon, far as my experience went, were loyal and honest, if occasionally short-tempered. Trust the *Cosa* to screw up their naming conventions.

"It's a fatae thing," I said, to head off any concerns Valere might have had about my showing up unannounced.

"Of course it is," PB muttered. Wren handed me a plain white mug filled with caffeinated nirvana, and I took a deep sip. She might not be able to cook, but Valere could magic up a serious pot of coffee.

"And it's delicate," I added.

"Of course it is," the Retriever said.

I thought about how much to tell them, zipped through the best- and worst-case scenarios, and shrugged mentally. Delicate, and no-footprint, but Stosser had set me to this scent, and I'd follow it best I could, and that meant using my sources as best I could. And for these two, that meant telling them the truth.

Just not all the truth.

"A girl's gone missing. Baby girl. Seven years old."

They went the same place I did, hearing her age: just the right age for a Fey-snatch, if someone were willing to break the Treaty.

"The Fey say they don't have her." Let them think I already

checked that avenue, rather than taking it on faith from a client. I thought again of the Lord's expression, and restrained a shudder. No, clients lied, and the Fey lied even more, but not in this specific instance. They wanted to know who had her, enough to give Stosser a blank IOU in return.

PB humphed. "No chance she went willingly?"

That was the other way a breed could acquire humans: glamour them into coming of their own accord. We called it fairy-dusting, and it wasn't covered under any treaties.

"She's seven, PB. Doesn't matter what she wanted. She's still a baby. Babies can't go willingly." Wren sat on the hassock opposite me, looking thoughtful. "You've checked into the usual gossip spots, I assume, otherwise you wouldn't be going to me."

"Not yet."

That took them both aback, PB's ears going flat in surprise.

"The usual spots take time, and greasing. I need to know, hot and fast, if there's any gossip in the fatae community, about newcomers, maybe someone out to prove a point, or score a grudge." I hesitated, then unreeled a little more truth to hook them with. "It feels like a setup. Someone's trying to make it look like the Treaty's been broken."

These two knew better than anyone how bad a broken treaty could get—especially one between humans and fatae. If that was what was going on, it had to be stopped and fixed, before word got out.

Wren thought about it for a minute, and I watched. Looking at Wren was difficult; even when you stared right at her, she seemed to slip away from your eye. But Pietr and I had been lovers on and off for months, and I'd almost gotten the trick of looking-not-looking. Average height, average looks, average coloring—brown hair, brown eyes, a face that could have come from almost any genetic stew. Even without magic, Wren Valere didn't appear on your mental radar.

That—and a natural talent for larceny—was what made her a Retriever.

"Nothing," she said. "It's been quiet since… It's been quiet."

Since she'd taken out the organization that had been fucking with the *Cosa* and Nulls alike, she meant. Another thing nobody talked about but everyone knew.

"PB?" She turned to the demon, her head tilted. "You hang in lower sewers than I do. You hear anything?"

Every demon, Venec had told me once, looked different. Rumor had it they were artificial, created like Frankenstein's monster, their only shared characteristic those red eyes and a snarly disposition. PB looked like a pint-size polar bear, all thick white fur and powerful limbs, and a snout that was supremely made for frowning, which is what he was doing right now.

"Danny had some trouble a couple-three months ago, but that was a teenager. Nothing about a wee one. That screams of trooping fairies."

Despite myself, I cracked a grin. Only a demon would call them that, especially out loud. *Fey folk* was the preferred polite term, if you didn't want a Lady's gaze turned on you, which I desperately didn't. Demon, though—demon didn't care. There wasn't a Fey glamour in the universe that could hold a demon against his will. Some said it was because they had no soul. Me, I think they were just too stubborn.

"The Fey Lord says they did not. Swears it, in fact." Breaking a sworn statement had penalties I didn't think the Lord wanted to pay, not unless he was playing some deeper game than even Stosser could guess. And this…didn't feel like a game.

"And the Fey Lady?" Having PB's direct red gaze on you

was disconcerting as hell, even when you considered him a friend, like I did. It was a fair guess on his part: they came in pairs, like mittens.

"Noncommittal, but seemed very certain it was from outside her Troop."

We'd lost Wren from the conversation; she had gotten up and left the room without me even noticing. Retrievers were like that. PB shifted on the footstool, his toe-claws tapping quietly on the hardwood floor.

"So you want to know if there's news of a schism within the city's Troop, or if anyone outside's trying to poke holes into it. No. And trust me, *that* I would have heard about. Troop wars aren't as ugly as some things we've faced, but they're bad enough."

I wasn't surprised. "That was about what I'd figured, yeah." If it were that simple, the Fey would have figured it out for themselves and dealt with it already. We only got the tricky things.

"What does it feel like?"

Normally I didn't talk about this—job details—outside the pack. But PB was unarguably loyal to Wren, and Wren...

Was, technically, on the other side. Not all Retrievers were criminals—they worked for legitimate owners as often as not—but it was better not to think about how they did their job. That said, Wren could be trusted. Within reason.

"It feels like a mess," I admitted. "And maybe a wild-goose chase, with the Fey holding the feathers. But that's me, lead goose-chaser."

The phone rang in the kitchen, once, and Wren picked it up. I tried not to listen in, but even with her voice lowered, I could still pick up most of the words. From the way PB had gone all distracted, he could hear even more: demon senses were a hell of a lot better than puny human ones.

"Sergei," he said, neither of us pretending we weren't eaves-dropping. "He has a new job for her. And not a minute too soon—she was about to start stealing things out of boredom."

I shushed him, and her voice, slightly raised, carried into the living room.

"On a scale of one to ten?"

"Private or corporate?"

A groan: she hadn't liked the answer. "A shove-and-grab?"

A long pause: he was explaining something. PB's ears twitched: he was picking up more than me, but not sharing now. Just as well: I really didn't want to know the details.

"I should scoot," I said, getting up. "Tell Wren I said thanks, and I'll try to bring by a housewarming lasagna or something this weekend, okay?" I hadn't had much time to cook lately, which might have been half my problem: I de-stressed by feeding people. Taking an hour or two to myself would be a very good idea and keep the wheels here properly greased.

"You're not going to hang around and help me bully Valere into ordering curtains?" He held up one of the shelter maga-zines, with Post-it notes stuck all over the pages.

"Oh, hell, no. You're on your own for that one. If you hear anything…"

"Yeah, you got it. Go, before I start asking your opinion on carpets."

I laughed and left.

three

I'd walked out of Wren's apartment with no useful information but, thanks to PB's comments, with the beginnings of a plan: hit up Danny for details on what the smaller *Cosa*-fry were doing. It made sense that PB and Wren had come up dry, in retrospect: PB's main gig was as a courier who asked no questions and spilled no secrets. When he looked, he looked big picture, citywide. But a little girl might fall between the cracks, especially if there wasn't something Dire involved. A private eye who worked for whatever cases came along would be able to see the smaller details.

And I already knew that Danny, a former NYPD patrolman, had a weakness for kids in distress. He'd drop anything not-urgent, and maybe even a few things that were, to help me out.

I didn't feel good about using his soft spot that way, but I was going to do it, anyway. It helped to know that he'd do exactly the same thing if the situation were reversed.

The afternoon sun hit me a few steps down the street, like it was trying to coax me into taking the rest of the day off to sprawl on the Great Lawn and read the newspaper front to back. I couldn't remember the last time I'd actually had time to do something like that.

And today wasn't going to be that day, either. I ignored the siren call, intent on my destination, weaving around the slower-moving clumps with the agility of practice. Not that I was looking forward to going back down into the subway: three seasons of the year they were fine, but once we got into summer... Ugh. Manhattan was a relatively small city; why the hell couldn't everyone I needed to talk to be within a ten-block radius?

The 6 subway downtown to Danny's office wasn't bad, though; relatively uncrowded, and the air was flowing properly. And it took less time than a cab.

I leaned back against the plastic subway seat and tried to even out my breathing—and my thinking. Sometimes, kids get lost. The fact that I didn't want to think about it, that it made my gut hurt, didn't change that. If someone hadn't implied fatae involvement, this little girl would just be a poster on a cop-shop board somewhere, another Amber Alert on the wires. And if there wasn't anything to do with the *Cosa Nostradamus...*

PUPI's mission statement did not encompass the Null world, to quote directly from one of Stosser's usual "we are here to help you" speeches. Didn't matter. Even once the Fey were cleared, I knew already I wasn't going to let this case go. A dozen years ago I could have gotten lost, too. My dad had been loving but kinda loose about parenting, and if I hadn't found J, if he hadn't found me, been willing to mentor me...

Being Talent didn't mean you got a pass on the rest of the crap life could hand out. Mentorship was supposed to be a safety net and a lifeline, but it didn't always work out that way. And Null kids... They didn't even have that.

I got off at my stop, giving a hairy eyeball to the guy who tried to use the in/out crush at the door as an excuse to grab my ass, and made my way to Sylvan Investigations.

I didn't bother knocking, and the door, as usual, wasn't locked. Danny's office still looked like it was straight out of Dashiell Hammett, with a front room staged with a secretary's desk, padded guest chairs, and some anemic-looking potted plants, waiting for some bright but world-wise dame to answer the phone, while the detective slept off a bender in the back room.

Danny didn't have a receptionist, and he usually slept off his hangovers at home.

A weary voice called out, "What do you want?"

Or, maybe not.

I took myself all the way into the back room and shut the door behind me. "You look like hell." Danny was a good-looking guy, the product of an attractive woman—I'd seen pictures of his mom, stern but lovely in Navy blues—and an unknown, unlamented faun who, like all of his breed, had the strong, stocky body that Danny had inherited, along with the short, curved horns that were only barely hidden by his thick brown hair. Right now, though, Danny was slumped in the chair behind his desk, cowboy boots up on the afore-mentioned desk. His eyes were closed, and his face was lined and gray, like he hadn't slept in a week.

He might not have, for all I knew. We hadn't had a chance to schmooze lately, with the workload Stosser kept handing the pack. I felt a flare of bad-friend guilt.

"Are you okay?" I had no idea what a fever would feel like on a mixed-breed, but moved forward to touch his fore-head, anyway. He batted my hand away and opened one eye enough to glare.

"I'm fine, Torres. It's just been a crappy week. What do you want?"

I didn't want to lay anything more on him, but there wasn't any point in walking away without at least asking.

"I have a case I was hoping you could help with. It's about a missing kid."

Danny's boots hit the floor so fast and hard I didn't even see him move. "What kid? When? How old?"

Whoa, hadn't been expecting that. A bit of an overreaction, even for Danny's known soft spot. I stumbled my reply, then recovered. "Seven years old. Missing a week now."

"Oh." He settled back a bit then, his shoulders not exactly relaxing, but no longer looking like he was about to leap out the door at a full run. "Not mine, then."

Oh, fuck. The pain in my stomach got worse. "You have another missing kid?"

"Two, actually. Probably dusted."

That was slang for being lured by one of the more seductive fatae breeds—like Danny's.

"One almost fifteen, the other a legal adult, just turned twenty-one, but parents still worried."

The difference—and that they were older—made me feel slightly better, and I relaxed, too, pulling one of the client chairs around the desk so I could sit next to Danny, not be separated by the expanse of wooden desk. "Nope, mine's seven, like I said."

"Boy or girl?"

"Girl. Yours?"

"Girls, too."

That still didn't mean any connection. "Do boy-children or girl-children go missing more often?" I'd never wondered that before.

"NISMART numbers say slightly more males than females, out of about a million-plus reported every year. Most are runaways, teenagers, or known-adult abductions. Only a small but ugly percentage are nonfamily kidnappings." Of course Danny would know. "Most are white. Yours?"

"No. Mom's Asian, dad's Caucasian."

Danny frowned. "Mine are mixed, too. Statistically that's odd, although within range for New York."

I thought about that and let it go. "Even if we had a full-scale kid-snatch going on, which I doubt, I can't think of any fatae breed who would be looking for the full range of age and—"

Something ticked in my brain, and I pulled out the file again, flipping through. "Seven. Fourteen. Twenty-one..."

"What?" Danny was watching me intently now, his skin still tired-looking but his eyes alert and focused, his usual energy back.

"Magic." I said it like a curse word. It fit, damn it. It all fit....

"What?"

I forgot sometimes that Danny was fatae, not Talent. They looked at—and reacted to—things differently than we did. Also, they got told different stories as kids. "Old magic, pre-current." Before the modern age, before Founder Ben: when things were messy and magic was as much hope and prayer as science. "Seven was a magic number, really strong, potent. Even today, some people like to run things in sets of seven, hedge their bets. And here we've got my girl, seven. Yours, if fourteen, twice seven, and twenty-one, thrice seven. Three's a strong number, too. All gone missing in the same city, the same time, and you think there was *Cosa* involvement in your cases, too, otherwise you wouldn't have mentioned the fatae." Danny handled Null cases, too, but he wouldn't immediately have associated something I was working on with one of those.

By the time I'd finished, the words spilling out of my mouth, he was already reaching across his desk, pulling a pile of folders toward him. Being fatae, Danny could use computers, but he tended to do that stuff away from where Talent might drop by. He ran a shoestring operation, and we were hard on electronics, especially when we got emotional.

"Melinda, fourteen. Went missing two weeks ago. I've been on the case for three days, after the NYPD dumped her in with the runaways. Haven't turned up a whisper of anything. Started with the street kids, got nothing. Was starting to wonder if she'd skipped town or hooked with a dead-end john when Gail's parents called me. She's been missing almost a month, and all the stats are the same—smart, pretty, but not overwhelmingly brilliant or beautiful, everything to stay home for, suddenly up and gone between midnight and dawn."

He put his hand palm-down on the file, like he was trying to hold them safe, and turned his head to look sideways at me.

I stared at his hand. They were blunt-tipped, his fingers, strong and scattered with coarse brown hairs. Venec's hands were strong, too, but more tapered and smooth. I shook my head, dismissing the thought. "My girl's too young to be really slotted—but she's definitely cute. Smart... Unless they're genius level, how do you tell at that age?"

Danny snorted. "Don't ask me." He was an only child, and despite his breed's proclivities—or maybe because of them— he wasn't the type to sleep around. I'd sussed early on that Danny was looking for One True Love, god help him. "Talent family?"

I shook my head. "No."

"So how did they come to you?"

I hesitated, then went for broke. "They didn't."

That got me a closer look, squinty-eyed, like they must teach in the academy, the kind of look that makes you talk too much when a cop asks to see your ID. "Spill, Torres."

Stosser was going to kill me. But, damn it, Danny might have the info that broke the case. And he took discreet into artistic levels. And the Big Dogs had taught us to trust our gut instincts. "The Fey Folk asked us to look into it. Rumor is that they were responsible for my girl's disappearance. They say no. They don't want people claiming they've broken Treaty."

"An' if PSI says they're clean, most folk will stand by that." Danny nodded. "Sounds like Stosser's long-term plan to own the *Cosa* is working." He shook his head then, dismissing the boss's plans as unimportant, which, to him, they were. "Damn it, Bonnie, I think we're onto something. My girls are Null. Yours?"

One of the first things I'd checked. Talent kids tend to wander down slightly different rabbit holes, when they go missing. "Yeah."

It might not mean anything, all these facts. Sometimes, even the most suspicious of circumstances turned out to be flutterby, unrelated and unconnected. But there was a thick, heavy feeling in my core and a tingling of my kenning, the sense that sometimes, often unpredictably, hinted at the future, that told me otherwise. A full eighty percent of this job was listening to the facts and sorting the evidence, and then fitting them together. Sometimes it took logic; sometimes it took a wild leap. More often, it took both.

"If it's not the usual suspects, but the gossip points there…" I didn't want to say the word, but I had to. "You think it's the Silence, come back?"

For years, an organization called, ironically, the Silence

had been spreading enough lies and rumors around the city, enough to nearly destroy the *Cosa Nostradamus*. We'd taken to the streets to fight them, one snowy night last year, and they'd finally disappeared from the scene a few months ago, their office building still sitting vacant. Wren Valere had been elbows-deep in what was going on, then. If they'd come back, Wren would have known. She would have told me, us. Right?

"If they were back, the Dynamic Duo would have let us know," Danny said, echoing my thoughts. "Right?"

"Right."

I sounded convinced, but there was a low note of doubt in my stomach to go with everything else. Wren Valere was my friend. A genuine hero, although she'd scoff at the thought. She was also a Retriever, and like Danny, she took discretion to an art form when needed. Discretion that, to me, could translate as withholding evidence. How far could we trust her to share information? Yeah, hero, friend, etc., but...

I couldn't afford to be distracted by a maybebwhatif. Useless dithering, Torres. Focus on the facts. "I'll have Venec put a few feelers out, just in case." Ben had friends in seriously low places, even for the *Cosa,* and if the Silence were back, those friends would be scurrying for their lives. "But for now, we focus on the girls and work our way out to their captors, not the other way around."

"Right. Here." He pulled a handful of sheets from the folders and shuffled them together. "Copies of all the known facts on my girls. Okay to copy yours?"

"Yeah, go ahead." We'd hired Danny for side work before; Stosser and Venec trusted him. Besides, I'd already spilled the part I wasn't supposed to say; wasn't like his having hardcopy would change anything.

The copier machine was a tiny little thing, off in the corner of the room. Danny fed the sheets in, one at a time, while I grabbed one of the client chairs and draped myself into it.

Better to fess up now than get caught out later. But indirectly...

boss?

There was a slight lag in his response. Nothing that would have been noticeable with anyone else, but I'd become accustomed to Venec being just next to my thoughts at all times. Distance was a factor in pings; maybe it mattered here, too? If so, he wasn't in the city anymore. Huh.

what?

twist in the job Stosser gave me. taking Danny on. he has a case that might match it

A sense of acknowledgment, acceptance, and being busy somewhere else. Ben was leaving the city. Yeah, moving... I concentrated a little. Southward.

?

do your job, torres

And then he was gone. Okay, fine. There was absolutely no reason for me to feel like I'd been punched in the stomach, right? He was the boss, and I was the pup, and we'd agreed that was where we were and he had no obligation to tell me where he was going, any more than I checked in with him, off-hours.

I'd never been jealous before in my entire life. Not even when J, my mentor, went out to visit his first student, now a lawyer out in California, and didn't invite me to come along. I'd understood I shared J, and was okay with that. Not when lovers had moved on, or when a potential lover had chosen someone else. It just... I had never understood how you could resent someone spending time somewhere else, like only you had a claim on their life.

But I did now. And I didn't like how tightly I hugged that feeling, as though it should give me comfort instead of pain.

"Okay, here." Danny came back and handed over the originals. "You want to work this together or split up?"

Having something concrete to work on would keep Venec and his mysterious errand out of my mind. "Split up." Plausible deniability was key: Danny could be pretty bullheaded, and Stosser had told me to go gentle. "We can work more contacts that way. If you find something…" I paused. Danny couldn't ping me, and I didn't carry a cell phone, for obvious reasons. I'd gotten really spoiled, working only with Talent.

Luckily, Danny was used to it. "If I find anything, I'll call the office and they can ping you."

"Yeah." I paused, looking over the paperwork. My throat tightened at the black-and-white reproductions of those faces. Three girls, one of them only a few years younger than me, one of them still a baby. Missing for weeks now. "Danny."

"I have to believe they're alive," he said, somehow knowing what I didn't want to ask. "I couldn't do this job otherwise. You do the same, Bonnie. Believe."

I carried that with me, the belief in his voice, all the way back down to the street and the next stop along the gossip network. It didn't help shake the feeling of an onrushing train that had started prickling up and down my arms the moment I picked up all three files, though.

Kenning. It wasn't quite foresight or even precognition, nothing that precise or useful. But the weird shimmer of current let me know there was something building. Something that involved me. And it was rarely good.

On the train heading toward Philadelphia, Ben Venec felt a twinge of unease. Bonnie, he identified, and then frowned. No, not Bonnie. She was worried. The Merge and his own abilities told him that through their brief contact, but she was focused on the chase, whatever Ian had set her on earlier. It was something else prickling at him.

He touched the briefcase on the seat next to him, his unease making him need to confirm, physically, that it was there and safe. He didn't have even a touch of precog, or Bonnie's kenning, but his instincts were good, and something felt wrong, off. He just couldn't figure out what.

He ran down the mental list of possibilities. Ian? No, he was accounted for. It wasn't the pups themselves; when he'd left, the office was humming along at a mad but steady pace, and if anything had gone wrong, he would have heard the yelps. The job he was heading for? Unlikely. It was bog-standard, more a distraction than a challenge.

"All right. Apprehension noted and filed," he said out loud, as though that would make whatever it was shut up. Much to his surprise, it did, a palpable sense of the unease backing off, like a cat settling back on its haunches to watch, rather than leap.

Interesting. Possibly it was his own nerves, reacting to... something. There were a limited number of things—and beings—that could cause that reaction. He considered the idea of another trickster imp in town, and dismissed it. This was more personal, more...direct.

"Aden, what are you up to?"

Ian's little sister, Aden, had made it her personal mandate to shut PUPI down, to keep her precious Council from being held accountable for their actions. She had been banned from approaching them directly, after her earliest attempt got an innocent Null killed, but she hadn't given up. Not by a long shot.

Not too long ago they—he and Ian—had been the focus of a Push, a current-driven emotion, intended to doubt themselves into making mistakes. With a touch of the Push himself, Ben had recognized it easily enough, but not before it had done some damage they couldn't afford. Aden had been behind that, and while Ian said he had dealt with her...

"There's nothing more stubborn than a Stosser on a crusade. The only question is what level of crazy will she bring, and from what direction?"

Since this twinge seemed intent on being a helpful warning rather than a distraction, Ben was willing to let it sit there and wait. He would be alert—but he would have been on alert, anyway. That was his job.

Popping open the brown leather briefcase, he extracted the file marked Ravenwood in thick black lettering, took out a folded blueprint, and smoothed it open, settling himself in to study the outlines of the museum. He hadn't taken on a side job in almost two years, burdened with getting his pups trained and ready, and he was looking forward to the work. Allen's employers—a small private museum in downtown Philadelphia—wanted a security system that couldn't be beat? Ben felt a sliver of challenge rise up within him as he considered the specs. Old building, with all the newest tech added to bring it to modern-day standards. Adding current to that wasn't going to be an easy job...which was why Allen had recommended him.

Time to prove that he could still do more than herd pups.

"Please. Don't."

The voice was tired, flattened in the way that human voices should never be. The cave's walls were high, but there was no echo, no sound at all, his words swallowed by the vast presence around him.

The dragon hovered over him, eyes burning in the darkness, drawing all the light into their glittering gold depths. "Give me your treasure."

Again and again, that demand. You could not refuse a dragon, could not resist. But he had none, no more to spare. No gold, no cash, no worldly possessions: he had offered them all, hours ago, and the dragon would not be sated. Even his core had been drained, the current sucked away so swiftly he had gone from full to empty in a heartbeat. Who knew dragons could do such a thing? Who knew they would?

Another slash of its claws, agony burning through his abdomen, and he was too tired to scream again. There was nothing left. No hope of rescue, no hope of survival. No hope of explanations: Why me? What did I do?

Please, his lips formed, but no sound emerged.

When the next blow came, he fell into it, the only escape he had. The last thing he heard, echoing down into oblivion, was the dragon's howl of rage.

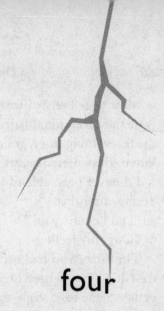

four

"Ow! Damn it, I just wanted to talk to you!"

The brownie didn't let go of my wrist, its blunt teeth digging in more firmly. The little bastard was about the size of a French bulldog and just as solid, so this was really beginning to hurt, not to mention being annoying as hell. If I tried to shake him off, I'd probably snap my wrist.

"Og, let the lady go."

Og rolled his eyes up at me, the whites yellowed and sick-looking, and I hoped to hell I wasn't going to need a tetanus shot after all this. Or rabies.

"You heard the man, Og," I said, sugar-sweet. "Lemme go. Or I will zap you with enough current to make your whiskers curl around your ears."

Brownies don't actually have ears, just little pinholes like dolphins, but the threat sounded scary enough that he unhinged his jaw and let go. I refused to step back or check the skin to see if it was broken, but stared down at the little bastard until it cast that yellowed gaze to the wooden floor, sulky but cowed.

Most fatae breeds I treat with cautious respect. Brownies were the exception: I hated them, and they seemed to return the favor. Long story, going back to me, age five, and a stray kitten. Brownies love cats, too—but not quite the same way.

I'd never been able to look at Girl Scouts without shuddering, after that.

"Did he hurt you?"

"Only my feelings."

The fatae who had ordered Og to loose the teeth was a da-esh, a close-related breed. They tended to pal around together. Same basic shape and coloring—imagine if the stereotypical alien silhouette had put on twenty pounds and filed its head to a smooth, round shape—but about a foot taller and with better social skills.

"You'll survive," he diagnosed. "What did you come down here to ask about?"

"Down here" was more figurative than literal: we were in a tiny café on the Upper West Side, dimly lit, with an old TV muted in the corner and a waitress who looked like she'd escaped from a high school for the permanently don't-give-a-damn doing her nails at the only other occupied table. I'd only just sat at their table when Og decided I'd make a good appetizer.

"You know we make good on useful data," I said, not quite answering. It paid to remind informants about that: PSI appreciated free info, especially when solving the case benefited everyone, but we didn't expect our informants to put themselves on the line without some kind of compensation. It was also a reminder to my companions that I wasn't a private citizen, as it were: if they screwed with me, it wouldn't be just me pissed off with them. Stosser and Venec had reputations both independently and together that would make anyone seriously reconsider trying to scam their people.

"I can't tell you shit until you ask a question, puppy." The da-esh looked me up and down, while Og climbed back into his chair and glared at me from across the table, brave again now that its pack leader had taken control. "You're Torres, right?"

"Right." There were enough of us in the office now that it could get confusing to fatae, I supposed. Not like when we started, and there were only five of us, and nobody ever mistook me for Sharon, more's the pity.

"Huh."

I had absolutely no idea how to decode that, so I just waited.

It took three sips of whatever the da-esh was drinking for him to decide. "You pups have done fair by us so far. If I know anything useful, and it don't get me killed to tell, I'll share."

That was a better offer than most I got. I nodded agreement of the terms. Unlike the others I'd spoken to today, he only got the driest of details. "Missing-persons case. Three persons. Child, teenager, and a young adult—all female, all missing from the city in the past month. Null, or at least non-declared." Sometimes Talent popped up out of nowhere, and the two youngest were young enough to be uncertain. "I'm looking for trace of any of them." I reached—carefully, with an eye on Og—into my bag and pulled out three photographs. Spread out on the table in the dim light, I could barely see the details, but brownies and their kin make up for their lack of external ears by having rather spectacular night vision.

"Human. Two overtly Caucasian, one with a definite Asian parent. No similarity in coloring or in face shape. They are all coddled little brats, but no meanness in them."

My jaw might have dropped open just a little bit, because Og chuckled, a nasty little sound.

"We are not, how do they call it, apex predators," my informant said, ignoring his companion. "Survival often involves being able to read information quickly, off limited data. That is why you came to me, isn't it?"

It was. I just hadn't expected it to be quite so detailed.

"Have you heard anything about missing females, human, or anyone who might have an interest in them?" I was choosing my words carefully, something you had to do when dealing even with the most friendly of fatae. "Interest either in having them, having them harmed, or having harm come to them." The last two weren't the same thing, and you could hide a lot of malice in the space between.

"You mean other than the usual steal, molest, eat, and otherwise do evil with?"

I sighed. "Yeah, other than that."

The da-esh showed his teeth in a grin, and I really wished he hadn't. Their kind were carrion-eaters, when they couldn't get fresh cat, and not much on hygiene. "There was a case a while back, of gnomes dusting teenage girls. I guess they couldn't get dates for the prom. But nothing else. Mostly when someone's little girl goes missing, she does it of her own free will. My pretty unicorn or elf-prince of something." The scorn practically dropped off his words. I really couldn't blame him.

"Now, if it were boys gone missing, that would be unusual. Unless an elf-wench's gone hunting, they tend to be safe."

Elf-wench. That was even worse than "trooping fairies." I was so never going to use that in a Lady's hearing. In fact, I was never even going to think it.

"And nobody's been talking trash about humans again?"

The da-esh paused, then looked over at Og. I guessed he would be more likely to hear—and maybe partake of—any such trash-talking.

Og looked sulky, his mouth drawn in a tight little frown. "Nobody dare trash-talk," he said, and his tone was that of a ten-year-old grounded for the first time. "Not since The Wren do what she did."

What had The Wren done? Was this tied into... No, didn't know, didn't want to know, didn't want to have to take any notice, official or otherwise. If Wren had won us goodwill among the fatae—or at least put the fear of Talent into them— then I'd use it and be glad.

"But," Og went on, and it was like the words were getting pulled with pliers from his throat, "there is a thing."

"A thing?" I was prepared to bribe, if needed—we had a slush fund for that, not all of it in cash—but the da-esh beat me to it, placing one large hand square on the top of Og's head and pushing down with obvious threat. "Talk, or I eat your brains for breakfast," he said.

I was pretty sure that wasn't an idle threat. From the way Og's eyes rolled up into his head, he was, too.

"Whispers. Not even whispers. Loud thinking, maybe." He squirmed a little under the weight of the hand, then shrugged, all pretense of resistance going out of him. "I hear talk in the Greening Space. The piskies talk. Humans, too many humans, pissing off fatae already there. All hours, sleeping and eating and shitting there."

"A full campsite?" I was suspecting they didn't have official permits, but Central Park was large, and a few people could probably disappear for a while, especially in warmer weather. A settled camp, though, would be harder to hide.

It's tough to shrug when you're being squished from above, but Og did his best. "Whispers. They hide, but they are not good enough to hide from piskies."

Piskies were the *Cosa Nostradamus*'s official gossips—tiny, inquisitive, borderline-rude pranksters who didn't understand the meaning of the word *privacy* and wouldn't have cared if they did. They looked a bit like one of those old-style Kewpie dolls crossed with a squirrel, or maybe a mouse lemur—big eyes, grasping claws, fluffy tail, and a topknot of hair that came in colors that should not be seen in nature. Most of the *Cosa Nostradamus* despised them, but people I respected—namely Wren Valere and Ian Stosser—listened very carefully if a piskie spoke to them.

"A campsite of humans in Central Park," I repeated, to make sure that I wasn't misunderstanding.

"Children-humans," Og corrected me. "That was why the piskies whispered. Young humans. They thought they might play with them but they threw pinecones and rocks and drove them away, instead."

The pronoun abuse in that sentence nearly gave me a headache, but I was able to follow it. "The children drove the piskies away. They didn't want to be found."

That meant that there had to be at least one Talent in the group, or someone familiar enough with the fatae to know that either the piskies weren't a hallucination—a common enough belief—or that if you were trying to keep a low profile, you did not invite piskies to hang around.

"Human-children…" In fatae-terms, that meant teens, not little kids. "And no adults?"

Og rolled his yellowing eyes up at me again. "How should I know? I only know what piskies whisper and they're piskies."

Valid point. The fact that they liked to gossip did not mean that they got the facts straight, or wouldn't embellish or pare down to make the story more interesting.

"Enough?" the da-esh asked, and I nodded. He lifted his hand, and Og popped up like a cork, glaring at me like it was all my fault his rounded scalp had gotten polished.

My mentor had spent his entire adult life walking vari-

ous halls of power, putting a word in one ear, a hand on another shoulder, coaxing and pulling events and people into
patterns he approved and could use. I was starting to see—
on a far more crude and after-the-fact fashion—why it was
so appealing.

"My thanks," I said, and my hand moved off the table,
leaving a suitable donation to the da-esh's bar tab. Before Og
could grab at it, I had turned and left.

Out on the street, I got out of the pedestrian flow, leaned
my back against a building, and called the team.

hey A tight ping, but broad enough to reach the original Five—Pietr, Sharon, Nifty, Nick, and myself. Nobody
else needed in on this—they hadn't time yet to build up useful contacts.

Sharon and Nifty came back right away, clear question
marks forming in my awareness, with Nick's query half a
second later. Nothing from Pietr. He must be busy.

*anyone hear any chatter along the rat-line the past week
or so?* The actual ping was less actual words than a query
and a feel for what I wanted. Group-pings were hard enough
to maintain without wasting the extra energy trying to shape
words, too.

piskies? Nifty was dubious.

nothing here Sharon came back, and Nick echoed that.

what's up? That came from all three of them, in varying degrees.

job for Stosser. tell ya later

Their awareness faded from mine, and I was alone in my
head. Pings weren't really communication, the way you would
talk to someone, and it wasn't telepathy, either: there was, so
far as anyone could tell, no such thing as real telepathy, although the incredibly tight, almost verbal pings Venec and
I could manage might come close. That said, pings were

damned convenient, and I could not understand my mentor's reluctance to use them more—it was very definitely a generational divide. I had long suspected that J would probably still be using a wand if he thought it wouldn't get him laughed out of the bar.

I started walking again, not really having a direction, but I thought better when I could pace. So. Piskies. I had been casting a wide net, hoping to pull in something that would give me a specific direction. Now that I had it...I wasn't quite sure what to do. Investigate immediately? Gather more information and see if there was backup for what was—admittedly—a vague mention by an unreliable source? Go back to the office and report on my morning's work, and ask Stosser for further instructions?

That third choice wasn't even an option. Ian was a brilliant people-shmoozer and politician, and the driving force behind PSI, absolutely. As an investigator, though? Not so much. In point of fact, he sucked at tight-focus detail work. I could ask Venec, but he'd sounded occupied with his own shit, whatever it was, and anyway, even if he was here he'd just give me one of those Looks. And he'd be right to do so. I was dithering, and that was so unlike me I had to stop in the middle of the sidewalk—earning dirty looks from the people who had to swerve around me—and wonder what the hell was going on.

"Y'know, I really don't like this job."

I took a step, frowning. The words had come out of me, driven by kenning-chill I could still feel shivering in my bones. Maybe it was time to stop and explore that a bit. Talk it out, Torres. Ignore the nice people carefully not-staring at me, and talk it out. Pretend you've got an ear-thingy on and there's someone on the other end of the line...

Venec. His eyes half-closed, leaning against a wall like his shoulder bones grew out of it, listening to everything I said and everything I wasn't saying.

"This job… We have so many other things going on, everyone's working flat-out, and I'm doing pro bono work for the Fey, trying to clear up their problem so Stosser can maybe yank their leash later…"

So I felt put-upon. That wasn't enough to explain the shivery unhappy-feeling in my bones. A little girl, seven years old, was missing. And maybe others, too, if Danny's girls were related somehow. Even if they had just run away to join a bunch of would-be park-dwellers, my job was to find out and bring at least one of them safely home.

I started walking again, briskly, as though to leave the unease behind simply by outpacing it. "Torres, get your head out of your ass, your self-pity back in its box, and get to work."

The kenning was never wrong—but it was always vague. The unease might be related to this case. It might not. I had no way of telling, without more info, and even if the kenning was related, it would hardly be the first time one of our cases ran us into trouble. So. I would check up on the lead, reconnoiter a bit, and see if there was anything actually going down in the Park. If not, well, checking on leads was part of the game. If yes…then I could go on from there.

The one thing I couldn't do was let my feeling of being shunted off into a low-importance case interfere with my ability to kick ass.

Central Park is large. If you don't live in New York City, you may not realize that, or think that the small portion that you see is all there is, just a breath of greenery in the middle of the concrete jungle.

The truth is, Central Park is more than eight hundred acres of lawns, woods, lakes, playgrounds, fields, and rambling paths that never actually go in a straight line. There are bridges and underpasses, tunnels and suddenly-appearing gazebos, restaurants and castles, and god knows what else tucked into the utterly artificial and incredibly lovely grounds. Something like thirty thousand trees, according to the stats, and rumors of coyotes to go with the birds and rabbits and squirrels and occasional seriously confused deer.

And there are fatae. Exactly how many *Cosa*-cousins live in the Park is unknown—even if we tried to run a census, they'd either refuse to answer or lie. Piskies, flocks of them nestling in the trees and building, their nests tangled in the roots. Dryads, not as many as we might wish, but enough to help keep the rooted trees healthy and well. Some of Danny's full-blooded faun cousins, and at least one centaur. I didn't think the lakes were deep enough to support any of the aquatic fatae, but I've been wrong a lot before, enough that I'd be very careful leaning too far over a watery surface. City fatae tended to abide by the Treaty…but water-sprites were changeable and moody and saw most humans as annoyances at best. Venec and Stosser would be peeved if they had to ransom me from the bottom of a lake.

The moment I entered the Park at West 77th Street, I knew that I was being watched. Fatae don't use magic the way we do, but they're part of it, and they know it when it walks by. I could pretend I wasn't aware of the surveillance, make like I was just out for a nice afternoon stroll, or I could stop and deal with it now.

I stopped.

The closest person to me was a woman pushing a stroller a few yards ahead of me. Other than that, the walkway I was on appeared deserted. I waited until she was out of earshot, then cocked my hip and addressed the air around me.

"If you've got something to say, say it. I'm listening."

Silence. Not even a rustle or a giggle, which meant that it probably wasn't piskies. When no pinecones or other shot hit the back of my neck, I decided it definitely wasn't piskies.

"Come on, this is boring. You have a question? Ask. Got a warning? Go ahead. But don't just skulk silently. It's creepy as hell."

The sense of being watched didn't go away, and I was starting to get annoyed. "You know who I am." It wasn't a question this time; last I'd gone hunting in the Park I'd almost managed to set off an interspecies incident, riling a Schiera to the point that it spat poison at me. That was the kind of thing that got retold. And I wasn't exactly subdued in my appearance—I didn't dye my hair the extreme colors I used to, after being told in no uncertain terms it wasn't a good look for an investigator, but the naturally white-blond puff of curls, matched to my normal urban goth-gear, was easily identifiable. Lot of Talent in the city, but the combo of Talent, appearance, and showing up to poke my nose directly into things that other folk looked away from? Savvy fatae knew who I was, and unsavvy or ignorant fatae wouldn't have lingered once I called them out.

"Come on. Seriously?"

"Seriously."

My heart went into my throat and my eyes probably bugged out, and I resisted—barely—the urge to drop to my knees and apologize for every thoughtless, stupid, or mean thing I'd ever done. The woman standing in front of me tilted her long, solemn face to one side and lifted one long, gnarled hand to my hair, touching it as gently as sun touches a leaf.

"I startled you. That was not my intent."

"M'lady—" And unlike with the Lady this morning, the title came easily to my mouth, without resentment. "You do not startle but amaze."

Rorani. Not merely a dryad but The Dryad. It was rumored that her tree predated the Park itself, making her well over three hundred years old. Nobody had ever seen her tree, at least not and spoken about it, but Rorani was always there, moving through the Park the closest thing to a guardian spirit it had. If the fatae in New York had any leader at all, or one soul they would listen to without hesitation, it was Rorani. Her willowy green-and-brown presence could stop a bar fight in progress, halt a bellow midsound, and make edged weapons disappear as though they'd been magicked into fog.

"You are here about the children."

"What, everyone knows about this except us?" I sighed and dragged a hand across my face as though to erase the words. "I am sorry. I just…"

"I have been watching them," she said, accepting my apology without acknowledging either it or my rudeness. "I worry. But I did not know who to speak to, or even if I should. Humans…are difficult sometimes."

"As opposed to the logical, tractable, and obedient fatae?"

At that, she smiled, a small, almost-shy grin that could break your heart. "Even so."

That grin didn't mask her concern, or soothe my unease, but it put paid to my thinking this job wasn't worth my skills. Even if this had nothing to do with my case, I was glad I'd come. Anything that worried the Lady of The Greening, Stosser would want to know about.

"These children. Show me?"

I was surprised when the dryad hailed a pedicab. I don't know why—even dryads must get tired of walking, eventually. I always felt guilty using a pedicab—I was in better shape than a lot of the drivers—but Rorani stepped as gracefully into the carriage as a queen into her coach, me the awkward lackey trailing at her heels.

"To the Meer, please," Rorani said, and the pedicab headed northeast.

My first thought was to be thankful that I had encountered Rorani the moment I entered the Park, saving me probably hours of searching...and that thought led me to the suspicion that it hadn't entirely been coincidental. Accusing a dryad of collusion with a da-esh, though, took cojones I did not have. And it changed nothing, save that the fatae of the city were helping in an investigation without being prodded, coerced, or paid, and that was...new.

I had no expectation that we were all going to join hands and sing "Kumbaya" anytime soon; we might have stepped back from the edge regarding human-fatae relations, but there were still generations of tension built into every encounter. If Rorani had given word that we were to be helped...that was a very good sign.

We skirted the Reservoir and got off a little while after 102nd street, vaguely on the east side of the Park. Rorani waited, and I belatedly dug into my bag for cash to pay the cabbie. He sneered at my request for a receipt.

"This way," she said, as he pedaled away. We walked past the Lasker Pool and off the roadway, down a worn path, and into surprisingly deep woods.

This part of the Park had been designed to mimic a natural forest, and once within it, you could not see—or hear—any hint of the city around us, not even the tallest skyscrapers. I was pretty sure that a slender beech winked at me as we passed, but I didn't have time to stop and say hello—and I might have imagined it, anyway.

We walked down the deer path, single file, until Rorani stopped, waiting for me to see whatever it was she wanted me to see.

There was a decline, sloping gradually into a little flat-bottomed valley, with another higher, rocky rise on the other side. The floor was covered in grass and ground cover, the trees midheight and leafy, and—then the scene shifted, the way some paintings do when you stare at them too long.

I saw the bedrolls first. They were tucked under a clump of thick-trunked trees, concealed under tarps painted to mimic the ground, but the shapes were wrong, jumping out at me like they were splashed with bright orange paint. The storage container was harder to find; they'd found one the same gray as the rocks and cluttered it up so that the lines resembled a small boulder. I was impressed.

Once I saw that, the bodies came into focus. Three skinny forms in dark hoodies and jeans, curled up against each other like kittens, and another higher up on a rock, his or her legs hanging over the side, reading a book. It was a quiet, peaceful scene, and I couldn't see a thing about it that would have worried Rorani, other than the fact that all four were young enough to be living at home, not out here on their own. But that was a human concern, not a fatae one.

The campsite, now that I was aware of it, looked well established. Without using magic to hide it, I was amazed they'd been able to keep it from being discovered even a week, much less a month or more. I guess if nobody's looking, it's easier to hide.

Had anyone been looking for these girls, before us? The cops had…but in a city this size, kids go missing at such a rate it must be impossible to keep up, even on a purely Null basis. Add in the fatae, and the risk of being dusted or—well, nobody had been eaten in years. That we knew about, anyway.

"How many are there?" I spoke softly, although I was pretty sure that they couldn't hear us from up here.

"I'm not sure," she said, equally as quiet. "They come and go, and I cannot stay to watch them as I might. I have seen as many as a dozen gathered. A dozen, and their leader." She paused, and her hand touched my shoulder, the fingers folding around my skin. "Their leader. She...worries me."

Ah. I had thought Rorani would not mind teenagers gathering peacefully among her trees; there was something else going on. "An adult?"

"Yes. A Null. And yet there is magic there. She holds them in sway. A glamour, save she has none. She speaks, and they gather around. She points, and they scatter."

I chewed on my lower lip, listening. What Rorani was describing was a charismatic, like Stosser. Take a charismatic, Talent or Null, add a bunch of under-twenty-somethings, and put them out here, with no other distractions? You have a cult.

Most cult leaders were male, from what I'd ever read, but *most* doesn't ever mean *all*. A females-only cult? If they were religious, I'd lay money on Dianic—or Artemic—or any of the other mythological interpretations. No stag to hunt here, though.

"What do you—" I started to ask, when something caught Rorani's attention. "Oh, dear," she said, in a tone of voice that put every nerve I had on edge. There was "oh, dear, that's too bad," and then there's "oh, dear, this is very bad," and hers was the latter.

We weren't alone. Out of the stillness, a dozen creatures flowed over the hill behind the campsite. They were long and lean and shimmered a pale silver like sunlight on water, and I had no idea what the hell I was looking at except I was pretty sure they weren't bringing milk and cookies. As we watched, the first one started picking a careful, silent route down the hill.

The kids below had no idea they were about to have company.

"Landvættir," Rorani said. Her fingers moved restlessly, her lovely face grave, but she remained still by my side, merely watching. "They claimed this area before the humans came. I tried to warn them, but they did not hear me."

I wasn't sure if she had tried to warn the humans or the breed, but it didn't matter. Dryads were negotiators, not fighters; she wasn't about to get involved in what was about to happen. I'm not much of a fighter, either. Every time I'm near a fight—any kind, even a scuffle—my heart starts to pound and my stomach hurts. But I couldn't stand by and watch someone get hurt, either.

Any faint hope that the fatae meant no harm was dashed when—the moment they hit ground—they attacked. The humans were caught off guard, but rallied in a way that suggested they'd been taught at least some fighting moves: they rolled away from the first attackers, then went back-to-back in pairs, grabbing whatever was nearest to hand as weapons.

My move into the clearing was more hasty than graceful, but a few bruises and dirt on my clothes were the least of my worries. The fatae had sharp claws and blunted snouts that still looked like they could do some harm, and the four humans had what looked like pocket knives, a baseball bat, and a large rock. That wasn't going to do it, even if they had the first idea where the fatae were vulnerable.

I had no idea, either—I'd never encountered these lan-whatevers before. But I had a trick these Nulls didn't; one that any fatae would recognize and respect.

I hoped.

Reaching up with my current-sense—the thing that makes your hairs stand on end and your skin vibrate when there's an electrical storm overhead—I grabbed the first bit of wild current I could find and dragged it down into my core. I'm normally not much for wild-sourcing, but in this place and this instance, it seemed the right thing to do.

The new current sizzled hot and fierce, and I didn't give it time to settle into my core before I was pulling it up and out again. Thin, sharp blue lines sparked along my skin, like electric veins, and crackled and popped in the air around my hands.

Most of what we did these days was careful, regulated, and always, always thought out in advance. I had absolutely no idea what I was going to do right then, except it involved keeping anyone—human or fatae—from getting killed.

One of the girls saw me, and I could tell from her body language that she wasn't sure if I was friend or foe. Trying to reassure her, without catching the fataes' attention, I nearly fell over one of the camouflaged lumps and kicked aside something small and shiny. A metal tent peg. I grabbed it instinctively, and the moment the cool metal hit my palm, I had a plan.

I ignored the individual scuffles, dodged around a fatae who tried to grab at me, and made it to the center of the scrum. Holding the spike up over my head, I gathered all of that wild current and sent it into the metal, wrapping it tight with hot blue threads of my own core-current, forcing it to my will.

"Sit *down*," I yelled and put all my annoyance, my frustration, my worry, and my sheer irritation at wasting time with this crap into those two words.

The magic echoed like a thunderclap under the tree branches, and I swear I heard some of the granite behind me calve off and splinter in response. The effect on the fatae was gratifying. They weren't built to actually sit down, but they dropped to the ground anyway, bellies low and clawed hands down. The humans went down like someone had cut their strings, in at least one instance falling over her erstwhile opponent.

"*Stay* down," I said, still annoyed, when one of the humans tried to get back up, and she subsided. A fierce looking *chica*, maybe midteens, with dirty blond hair in a braid and a pair of brown eyes that were currently trying to glare me in half. She was pissed and wanted to get back into the fight. Despite myself, I started to grin and had to force it back. Now was not the time to admire her scruff.

The magic, amplified through the metal spike, had hit the ground hard, hard enough that there were still sparks in the dirt, moving like miniature whirlwinds. When one of the fatae shifted, it sparked him—her, it?—hard enough that it uttered a clear yelp and turned to glare at me with the pained expression of its human counterpart.

Apparently, I had ruined their party.

"Life sucks, kids," I said to both of them.

There was a scuffling noise behind me, somehow managing to sound graceful, and I knew even before the fatae all looked in that direction that Rorani had decided to join us.

"This will not do," she said. "This is not acceptable."

The human children—and this close I could see that they were in fact all children, none of them past fourteen, probably—went wide-eyed in astonishment and fear. The fatae were just very attentive. I'd never seen—hell, I'd never even heard of a dryad losing her temper, but that was very much what was happening next to me. It took every bit of control I had not to step away.

Rorani wasn't sparking, or yelling, or waving her arms. She had, in fact, gone very still and very tall, and the impression was not of a delicate, willowy lady but an ancient tree, deep-rooted and stern, standing beside me.

"Sweet Dog of Mercy," I whispered, barely audible even to myself. Rorani was an American Chestnut.

To survive the blight, to live so long after her tree-kin had died out and been replaced by lesser trees... There was a lot about the Lady of the Greening, and the way the fatae reacted to her, that made more sense now.

"The Greening is large. Treaties exist. Even if these humans did not know, you did." She was talking to the fatae then. "You knew, and were warned to behave, and yet... this? This attack?"

The pissy-looking fatae shifted its gaze, and the others all looked down at the ground. In that moment I realized something: these fatae were teenagers, too. Or whatever passed for it, in their lifecycle.

We'd interrupted the equivalent of a teenage gang turf war.

"You." I pivoted slowly and took on the brown-eyed human. "Where are the rest of your folk?"

She glared at me, utterly defiant. She'd get up in an instant and start the fight again, not cowed by the magic show I'd just put on or the fact that her opponents looked like something from a high-budget sci-fi flick. She might be Null, but magic didn't impress her much. If I were a high-res user, or could make with the mojo, I'd change that, fast, but I'd always been brutally honest about my capabilities. I was smarter, faster, and able to outthink most other Talent, thanks to J's and Venec's training, but I would get blown off the curb in a real power-off. And pulling all that wild current, without warning, had given me the start of a serious stomachache.

"I'm not the enemy here," I said impatiently. "In fact, I just saved your asses. You might have won this fight, but you might not have, and even if you did, you're outnumbered here. You know that, right?"

"We're protected."

That was from another of the girls, the one who had been reading up on the rock. She was about the same age, still skinny, still looking like someone needed to tuck her into bed, not toss her into the street.

"Protected?" Rorani had said that their leader was a Null. Was Rorani wrong? Or was another person, a Talent, protecting them? If so, why? I held up a hand, the current still sparking under my skin, making it look like it was wreathed in bright blue smoke, and showed it to her. "Like this?"

She glanced at my hand, swallowed, and looked away. Not scared, but…disturbed? They definitely knew magic, same as they knew fatae; enough to deal with it, but not anywhere enough to be comfortable. Or, probably, understand exactly what they were dealing with.

Their leader had taught them, but not well. That probably meant they weren't as protected as they thought, either.

I looked at Rorani, whose lovely face was still set in stern lines that would have made me quake if it was directed at me. The fatae certainly knew they were in deep shit, the way they were still flat on their bellies.

"You," she said now. "Take your fellows and be gone. This place is now mine."

The lead fatae actually had the cojones to try and protest. "We…"

"I have spoken."

And that was that. It and its fellows got up, moving slow and careful, and slid back out the way they came.

"Will they cause trouble later?" I asked her, watching them go.

"They will not. Their elders…possibly. It will depend." She looked over the remaining humans and sighed, the sound of wind through leaves. "These are your people. You will be able to manage it?"

To most fatae, humans were all one breed: Talent or Null, lonejack or Council. I'd expected more of Rorani, but it wasn't as though I could hand these idiots over to her. And I still had my own case to follow up on, something I'd nearly forgotten in the current-rush and the confusion of the fight.

My stomachache got worse. The thought of my girl being somewhere among these would-be toughs meant there might be others stolen away, too. Maybe all of them.

Even if babygirl wasn't here, I couldn't walk away from this, not without knowing who was teaching them and who was—allegedly—protecting them.

"Yeah, I've got it," I told Rorani.

"Then I shall leave you to your work, and I shall manage mine." She offered me her hand, and I took it. The flesh was hard but soft at the same time, like velvet over bone, and I had the moment's thought that I should bow over it, not shake it.

Then the moment passed. Rorani turned away, blending into the landscape the same way she'd appeared, and I was left with four uncowed, unbiddable teenage girls who clearly saw no reason to answer any of my questions.

five

"You say you're protected." I had settled with my butt on an outcrop of rock, giving me the double advantage of covering my back and making it look like I was just lounging, totally in control of the situation. The first rule of interrogation, as per Benjamin Venec, was to proceed as though you were utterly certain that you would be given all the answers you wanted, in time. Let the perp worry about how you planned to get those answers.

"You can't make us talk," the third girl said, all spitfire defiance. Oh, darling, I just did. But I only smiled and nodded my head. "You're right, I can't. Well, I could, but that would be messy and you'd probably lie, anyway. At first."

I let that sink in for half a breath.

"Seriously," I continued, girl-to-girl. "You're not dumb. You know what I am—you weren't surprised by the magic—so you know I can do stuff you can't."

There was a twitch at that, just the slightest twitch, but I caught it. Rorani had said these girls were all Nulls, hadn't she? I tried to remember. The missing girls were all Nulls, mine and Danny's. Did they think they could do magic, too? Had their protector gathered them here to be some kind of modern hedge-witch coven? Well, stranger things than that had happened in the Park before, the past few hundred years, but…

It always happened during a case, that click click click moment when a few pieces just snapped into place. Not a cult: a coven.

That would explain the transits of seven: like I'd thought, it was an attempt at old-ways magic. The ability to manage current was born in you; it could be trained, but not taught. But there were always people who tried, using all the old ways—sacrifices and potions, prayers and bargains—and all too often listening to fatae happy to take advantage of gullible humans.

The old ways had been unreliable and variable and failed more than they succeeded, but if you had the right place and the right words and did the right things, even Nulls—those who weren't entirely current-blind—could summon a wisp of natural power. Just enough to make them want more.

"Did your protector teach you about magic? Did she promise to teach you?" A charismatic, luring girls—young girls, almost-brilliant, almost-pretty, wanting to be special—with the promise of learning magic. How could they resist?

"She said—" one of them started.

"Shut up!" That was my fierce *chica,* trying to regain control.

Now all four glared at me, upset and angry and, in at least one case, about to cry. I was such utter crap at interrogation. Sharon would have had them spilling everything from the name of their first Barbie to who they fantasized about at night, by now.

They would have been fourteen when they were taken, assuming they weren't originally in a seven-year-old bunch. No, Rorani would have said if they'd been here that long. I tried to remember being fourteen—okay. Yeah.

"I don't care," I said, playing it jaded and way tougher-than-thou. "I really don't. You can play circle-the-pole and play at hedge-witchery until you're forty. Have fun. I'm looking for someone." Three someones, actually, but one they might be willing to give up; three would be too much.

"A little girl named Molly," I went on. "A baby, next to you guys, and she's too young to be out here. You know that." They were nearly adults, after all, my tone said. Old enough to make decisions, choose for themselves. But a little one like that?

There was silence, then my fierce *chica* with the tough brown eyes nodded, trying to match my tough 'tude. "I said she was too young. But…"

Normally, the "her parents want her home" line would have been my next line, but something warned me that might be the wrong card to play. Huh. No, not me. That was Venec's experience, lingering through the Merge. I'd gotten better at scenting out that particular flavor, although it still freaked me out a little, the way it got through every wall we put up.

Like kenning. Damned annoying, and damned useful.

"She's out here with you? She's with the others now?" Rorani had implied a largish group, so it was a calculated assumption, that there were at least three others, to make it ten, and probably more.

"They're training. We alternate, so nobody gets worn-out." The girl who had been silent until now spoke up, shaking off the look of disgust my *chica* gave her. "Oh, give it up, Steph. She knows. And she's not going to drag us home, are you?"

I wanted to. I really did. Drag them home and make sure

their parents spanked them for being such brats. But they weren't Talent, and I wasn't a social worker. "No. You guys are here of your own free will, you're not being mistreated… so, no. I'm not."

I might mention it to Danny, though. And their leader? Oh, I was so going to check her out. Even without the kenning telling me this was trouble, anyone dragging teenagers out into the woods—or what passed for woods—to teach them magic was something we needed to know about. If she was a harmless witch-wannabe, whatever her actual intentions, then it would be a matter for the cops. But if she were a Talent, then it was our responsibility—ours meaning the *Cosa* in general, not PSI specifically. And a Talent luring Nulls? Oh, that could be potentially so very bad. The Burning had been a long time ago, but we were never allowed to forget what could—and did—happen when Nulls got scared.

But first, get the missing girl home and the Fey Folk off our backs.

"It's all right, Steph," I said, keeping my body relaxed, although the stone was beginning to dig into my back. "All I want to do is make sure the little'un is okay."

"Why? Why do you care? It's not like anyone's paid attention to any of us before. Nobody told us—" Steph's jaw clamped shut, hard, on whatever she was about to say.

Damn it, I'd just gotten her mad enough… And then I realized we weren't alone in the ravine anymore. I turned slowly, pivoting toward my left, and saw a handful of girls standing there, staring at me. All teenagers or a little older. None of them, I knew immediately, were the unnamed leader: too young. And none of them were Danny's missing two.

I finally did what I should have the moment they mentioned magic, if I hadn't been distracted by the fight: I pulled a tendril of current from my core and let it waft over the new arrivals. Among Talent, it's the polite way of asking if anyone's there. Even if they're trying to pass as Null for some reason, there would be a response, an instinctive reaction to current being offered to them. Nulls wouldn't even notice, would be as oblivious to it as they would a dog whistle.

All five of the newcomers stiffened as though I'd slapped them, and I could feel current stir, but not a single one of them responded; I couldn't even feel them restraining it, just a sense of it being there, but at the same time, not.

And that, in a day of odd, was seriously odd.

"Keep your cool, guys," I said, trying to remember every lesson Venec had ever given about keeping body language nonthreatening but not weak. Shoulders down, chin up, gaze steady, palms forward, check…don't sweat…not so much with the check. "I just helped your friends avoid an attack by other Park locals, so that makes me a friendly."

"It's cool," Steph said, surprising the hell out of me. "Relax."

"She's one of them." A girl in the back of the newcomers, her skin the color of blackstrap molasses and her voice the clean-edged, fast-spoken rhythm of a native New Yorker, set her chin and glared at me. What was with all the glaring these girls did? Had I been like that at fourteen?

Inner honesty made me say, yes, I had.

"She's not like that. I mean, she's…" The third girl from what I was starting to think of as "my" group trailed off, looking at Steph uncertainly. I needed another set of eyes to track everything that was happening, because there was no way I was taking more than ten percent of my attention off the newcomers, not yet.

"She wants to know about Mollywog," Steph said.

"Mollywog's ours," the third girl said, possessively.

"Molly's too young for this. All the little'uns are. You know that, no matter what she said."

A lanky brunette crossed her arms over her chest and looked incredulous. "You're challenging her?"

Steph looked down at the ground, her mouth tight with unhappiness. No, she wasn't going to challenge their leader, even if she didn't feel good about something. Was that the natural inclination of a beta-dog in the pack, or was there something more going on here?

Not my worry, not right now, anyway. I was an investigator, not a social worker, damn it.

"Let me talk to Molly," I said. "Assure myself that she's okay. Can I do that, at least? Is she nearby?"

Silence.

I took a deep breath, then let it out in a long swoosh. *All right, then.*

"I've been helpful, and I've been gentle. Now I'm starting to get annoyed." The difference between Talent and Null isn't will, or brains, or fairy dust. It's a purely physical ability to recognize and manipulate the natural power generated around us, running alongside electricity. Some of that power is manmade…but the original current, the most powerful current, is wild.

Central Park, home to not one but three ley lines, practically seethed with it. I'd already pulled from it once, to stop the fight, so it was easy enough to tap the nearest line again and gather its energy to me.

"Spirits, gather. Hear my call.

Tree and dell, rock and pond;

Invaders come

Defend your land!"

The speechifying was all utter crap, of course, but the way the current swirled to me was very real, the electric-neon sparks visible—and enough to make just about any Null shit their pants.

Raw current was impressive-looking but useless: I shaped the current into the first thing that came to mind: a thick-bladed bastard sword like the one J had in his study. His was an antique gag gift, not capable of doing anything more than knocking you unconscious with a concussion. But mine was sharp and deadly, shimmering with power, poised in mid-air with the blade up and tilted over my shoulder as though awaiting my command.

The girls didn't look quite scared enough, although there was a lot of nervous body movement, so I added a little over-the-top flash.

"Intruders. Mortal fools…"

The voice was straight out of central casting, a low, hollow-sounding voice, gender neutral and one hundred percent unnerving. I think I'd remembered it from some god-awful scream-queen movie Nick made me watch one night last winter.

Two of the girls shrieked, and out of the corner of my eye I saw one of them sink to her knees, whether in prayer or terror I'm not sure. I kept my attention on the de facto leaders of each group, though, tough-*chica* Steph and the dark-skinned girl in back, who was still glaring at me like I'd done everything wrong in her entire life. Steph had started, but otherwise not reacted. They both knew it was magic, but they weren't entirely sure if it was me or I'd really called up the spirits of the Park.

The sword tilted a little more, and—feeling the surprising weight on my shoulder—I briefly wondered the same thing. As Farshad learned that morning—god, only this morning?— just because you call up A, that doesn't mean B isn't also listening.

Well, if I did have some help with this, so much the better.

"This Park was created for all," I said, trying to pick my way through words that would both accomplish what I needed and not piss off any magic, old or otherwise, that might have come to watch. What did I know about the Park? Not much. Built in the 1800s, it had been mostly unusable land, but there had been people living here, hadn't there? Poor folk who'd been kicked out, and…I tried to remember anything I'd ever been told, anything I'd ever read, thankful again for my near-perfect recall. There had been an African-American community somewhere near here, yeah. Freedmen and their families. Family bonds. Okay.

"It was created for all, claimed by all. You have every right to be here…but not to take a child from her parents. Her parents miss her."

I actually had no idea if they did or not—the Fey had come to us to save their reps, not out of any concern for the child—but I could only imagine J's reaction if I'd disappeared, or even Zaki's, casual a dad as he'd been. Panic, fear, anguish…yeah.

"We were chosen." The unnamed girl pushed her way past her cronies, giving the one on her knees a disdainful look. "All of us, including the little'uns. We have no other family now."

Charismatic leader. Cutting ties to the family. Loyalty to the group over all. Uh-huh.

"Bullshit." I emphasized my words with the release of more current, snapping in the air, the sharp bits of light clearly visible to all but the Nullest of humans. The blade over my shoulder started to glow, too. I definitely hadn't done that. "You all have families. They may not be much, but you have 'em. And Mollywog's too young to decide that she doesn't want 'em. You know that."

Right now, if the Merge had given me access to Venec's skill with the Push, the ability to influence thoughts, I would have taken it, and gladly. But it didn't seem to work that way. I had to rely on my own powers of persuasion…and the time-honored tradition of scare tactics.

The sword, as though sensing my thoughts, lifted off my shoulder and flew through the air, stopping with its point pressing into Steph's neck. I guess I, or it, or some combination had decided that she would be the one more likely to crack. Her eyes practically crossed, trying to look at both the blade and me, but she didn't flinch.

"There's a difference between loyalty and stupidity," I said. "You're pretty sure I won't kill you…but you're not entirely certain." The current crawled up and down my bare arms, thin lines of neon-blue and green drawing their attention, even away from the sword. "The one thing you know is that I'm more powerful than you, more powerful than you ever dreamed of being. I might even, you're thinking, be more powerful than your leader."

I let a slow smile grow on my face. It wasn't a nice smile, either; I knew because I'd copied it from Stosser at his most evil-minded.

"I am."

I raised my left hand, and the sword flew back into my hand, just heavy enough for me to grip it, nowhere near as heavy as an actual blade of that size might be. There was a shock of contact; I had been right, there was something other than me animating it, although the form was made from my current. Weird, unnerving, and not the point right now. I lowered the blade again to her throat.

"Stop it!"

The voice was strong and female, and I tilted my head,

half expecting to see the Mysterious Leader come to rally her troops. But Steph reacted not with respect or fear, but disdain.

"Why are you even still here?" she asked the girl who had shouted, as though I didn't have a cold steel blade to her neck. "You didn't make the cut, and you're too old."

The newcomer scrambled down over the rocks, wincing a little as she slipped; she was not graceful, that was for certain. Older than the others, although I couldn't tell by how much— three years? Five? Tall, almost bulky, and awkward with it, she still had a presence to her, although the overall impression was of diffidence, not strength. "Please don't kill her."

She was talking to me, not them.

The force in the blade wanted to address this new challenger: I told it to stand down, at least for a moment. The game had changed.

"Please. I can't bear… Not anymore."

I had no idea what this girl was talking about, but there was no way I was going to add to the pain in her voice. The sword lowered, slowly, and Steph fell backward, still glaring at me but not quite daring to attack again—or run away.

"Molly," I said. "Bring her to me, and I can forget I ever saw you." I would, but I had the distinct impression that the spirit who had come along for the ride wouldn't. I saw no need to tell them that, though.

Steph nodded once, realizing that was the best deal she was going to get, and all the girls fled, leaving me with a current-sword in my hands and the newcomer, who sagged down onto the grass as though arriving had taken all the strength she had.

The hilt of the blade shimmied once in my hands, to get my attention, and then faded back into loose current, disappearing on the breeze. The newcomer's gaze watched it disappear, her expression caught between fear and wonder.

Talent. Not just current-aware Null, like those girls, but

an actual Talent. I could feel the difference, like skim milk to cream.

"You came for the Mollywog?" she asked me.

"Yeah."

"Good. She doesn't deserve to be out here."

Okay, something was weird. This girl… She was maybe my age, if the other girls said she was too old, and she'd been part of their group but…failed? Hadn't passed the initiation? But she was an actual Talent!

"What's your name?"

She glared at me, then sighed, like it was all too heavy to hold in anymore. "Ellen."

Not Danny's missing girl, but someone else. Somebody else's missing daughter.

"There was another girl, a little younger than you, maybe…?"

"Zette. You're looking for her, too?" Ellen shook her head. "Forget it. You might get Mollywog back, but they're keeping Zette. She's part of the Plan."

Anything that had a capital-*P* plan, involving current, yeah, we needed to know about that. But it could be Stosser's headache. Right now, I was more interested in the girl in front of me. "And you're not part of the Plan?"

Ellen shivered, and I realized suddenly that for all that she was solidly built—a few inches taller than me, but twice the bulk, which admittedly wasn't difficult—she still managed to look too skinny. Healthy on her would be another ten pounds, and a layer of muscle. Her hair was a crop of curls, like mine, but black as sin, and her eyes were large and round and just as dark, over a nose that managed to be both hawklike and cute at the same time, matching cheekbones that could probably slice cheese. Not pretty, but fierce, that face. The expression on it, of fear and hesitation, didn't fit, at all.

Every single one of my instincts said that this girl had been hurt somehow. Not physically, but emotionally. Psychologically, and by more than her current situation.

And yet, she had leaped into the fight, rather than hiding.

The sensation I had, of another force in the Park with me, returned. Softly this time, almost curious. Ellen's expression twitched, like someone had touched the tip of her nose.

As gently as I could, I pulled a strand of current from my core, imbued it with as much of my signature as I could, consciously, and wafted it toward her, just to see what she could do.

She saw it, or felt it, there was no doubt about that—and no doubt, to my mind, that she didn't have a clue what it was.

Talent. Untrained. Utterly, absolutely untrained. It unraveled in front of me without her having to say a word: born into a Null family, probably, had no Talent around, no experience, no nothing, and so no mentor to guide her when she needed training. No idea that what she felt, what she did, was totally normal, for *Cosa Nostradamus* standards of normal.

These girls, gathered by their mysterious leader… I'd eat my boots if they weren't all of them sensitive Nulls, playing at magic, feeding their leader's fantasies with their own desires to be different, special. This girl Ellen… She was the real thing. And they had rejected her. I would have laughed if I didn't know she would take it the wrong way.

Also, if it hadn't been scary-serious. Ellen needed training, and she needed it fast. And not just from anyone, either. Matching a teen with a mentor was tough enough, but an adult starting from scratch? An adult without the first clue, who had no reason, I could tell already, to trust anyone worth a damn?

My first instinct was to take her to Stosser.

First instinct gave way to basic fact: Stosser, while, yeah, strong enough, would be one of the world's crappiest mentors. Too brilliant, too sharp, already overworked and no patience whatsoever.

J? No. I loved my mentor, but he had done his time twice, and he was in his late seventies now. I couldn't ask him to do that, not again, not with someone with absolutely no idea what she was. J, much as I love him, lives entirely in the world of the *Cosa*. This girl needed someone who understood both worlds, who lived in them, and wasn't the sort of get-in-your-face...

And then it hit me.

"Hold here a second," I said, taking a chance and putting a hand on her bare arm. Her skin was chilled, but she didn't flinch away from me. Good. I tried to exude a little of Stosser's sense of everything-is-under-control, even as I was reaching out to find my pack.

nicky

wazzup?

need you here

I didn't give him any more information, just a picture of where we were and a sense that he should arrive out of sight, not showboat. All I needed was someone Translocating in three inches from Ellen's nose. She might hurt him. Or pass out.

"This...crew," I said to her, as gently as I could. "You didn't fit in." It wasn't a question. "Why didn't you go home?"

"Home?" The word, in her mouth, broke my heart. "My mother said..." Ellen shrugged, a helpless, broken-winged gesture. "She said to go, and be damned. They already thought I was crazy, all the..." She stopped and looked at me, like I was about to pass judgment, too.

"All the things you saw? The things you felt? The crackle under your skin sometimes and the way your blood tingled during a thunderstorm?" If she'd been giving off current the way we tend to when we're pre-mentorship, then her family must have been freaked out of their minds and not known why. Wasn't the Council supposed to be alert to this kind of shit? Hadn't there been a single lonejack within a mile, when all this was happening?

"The things I saw..." She was whispering now, talking to herself, not me. "They said I was crazy. They were going to put me away, somewhere I couldn't hurt myself or anyone else. But those things were real. I know that now. They're everywhere, here in the Park..."

Fatae.

"Yes." I put as much reassurance as I could into my voice. "They're..." Saying they were harmless was a lie, but... "They're just like us. Some good, some bad, mostly they'll just leave you alone if you don't bother them."

"Fairies."

"Some. We call them fatae, as a whole. It's from the Latin. It means, well, fairies." I cracked a grin, and she almost reluctantly mirrored it. *Fatae* actually refers to the Fates, or a greater supernatural whole, but no need to freak her out with that particular bit.

"You're a Talent," I said. "Like me."

"Like..." And one of her square-tipped fingers waved almost helplessly, trying to describe something she wasn't supposed to talk about.

"Like your leader?" I guessed. "I don't know. Maybe. But not like those other girls. They don't have it. You do."

That made her eyes go even wider. "They said..."

"They were wrong."

Ellen didn't look convinced. I guess, in her place, I would be skeptical, too. I didn't know what she'd been through, although I could make a guess, but having me tell her—skinny, scrawny, close-to-her-own-age Bonnie—wasn't going to do the trick. And she hadn't really seen what I'd done with the others, only their reactions. Even the sword had faded away quietly.

"Hey, Bonnie, what's the emergency?"

Nicky walked out from the tree line like he'd just strolled in from Fifth Avenue and gave Ellen an almost involuntary onceover. Not offensively, just "okay, new girl, must look" sort of thing. Ellen blushed but didn't startle.

That was why I'd called Nicky, instead of one of the others. Sharon was too sharp, too quick to judge. Nifty was just too damn intimidating, on first sight. Pietr might have done the job, but he was too good-looking, in his quiet way. Lou… We called her *"mami,"* but I had no idea how she'd react to this. And Stosser was Right Out, despite the thought of it giving me a wicked amusement. Nicky slipped in under your guard, and you could go your entire life never knowing how dangerous he could be.

"I need you to do me a favor," I said and gave him a very brief rundown of my assignment, pinging him underneath with the need to keep it all very low-key. "So the girls have promised to bring her back here. I need you to wait and take possession."

"Of a baby?" Nick's obvious distress was pretty funny, actually.

"She's seven," Ellen said. "Not a baby."

"And she'll go with me? I'm a stranger."

"You tell her you're taking her home to her parents," I said. "That should do it." I couldn't imagine being seven and stuck among strangers was all that much fun, despite what a fourteen-year-old might enjoy.

"And where are you going?"

"I need Ellen to meet someone," I said.

Nicky still didn't look happy, but he settled down on a rock and pulled a book out, prepared to wait for as long as it took.

"If they don't show up," I said, hazarding a look at the sky to gauge time, "in an hour, then let me know." I had a feeling they'd show up, though. I'd looked into Steph's eyes: she didn't want me coming after her. The kid didn't mean enough to her to deal with that. So long as they avoided their leader, still the unknown in all this…

"And take the kid to Stosser?"

"Right."

"On the bus or…?"

"Take a cab. It's billable time." I had heard of people—Nulls—being Translocated without damage, but I'd never met anyone who did it, and the thought of what could happen… Oh, hell, no. Current acted like electricity in a lot of ways, and one of those is what it could do to untrained, ungrounded Null flesh.

As I led Ellen out of the Park, putting up my hand to hail one of the cabs that cruised down Fifth Avenue, I remembered how we had pinched every penny the first year. The subway was still transport of choice, but cabs weren't verboten any longer.

What I was about to do wasn't on company billing-time, technically, but I didn't care. There was no way I was taking this girl—and never mind that she was maybe a year younger than me, she was a kid—on a convoluted bus trip across town, when a cab would cost twice as much but take half the time.

"Where are we going?"

It took her almost three blocks into the trip to ask.

"There's a lot that you need to learn," I said, watching the meter tick off each increase. "Mostly, usually, we learn it when we're teenagers, when we're first starting to…see and feel all that. Someone should have trained you but they didn't, and now we're going to fix that."

A mentor was more than a teacher. They were a guide to the ins and outs of current, and the *Cosa Nostradamus* as a whole, and generally just how to survive without losing your shit. It was one-on-one, no set guidelines or textbooks. You learned what your mentor thought that you should learn, how she had learned it, and all the side notes that came with; lines of mentorship were damned important to Talent interactions and politics, even if some folk insisted they weren't.

Ellen was going to need not only good training, but someone who understood how Nulls thought. More, she was going to need a mentor who, when named, elicited respect, to get Ellen through the inevitable missteps she was going to make.

All that had gone through my head when I first realized how helpless Ellen was, and led us to this place.

I just hoped that PB wasn't there. That might be too much, right away.

"Bonnie." Wren didn't look unhappy to see me twice in a day, which was nice, although her gaze did drop down to my hands first, looking for her lasagna. Nice to know she loved me for a reason.

"Genevieve Valere, this is Ellen…" I realized suddenly I didn't know her last name.

"Just Ellen."

All right, then.

If Wren was taken aback at being introduced by her real name, she didn't show it, offering her hand to Ellen and shaking it—and then giving me a startled, quizzical look as she felt what I had, the fizzing, ungrounded core of a Talent who had no idea what she was or what to do with herself.

"Bonnie…" There was a faint, panicked tinge to her tone.

"It's time, Wren," I said firmly. "And Ellen needs you."

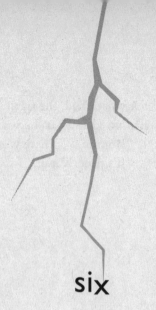

six

Handoff accomplished, I ran. I'm not afraid to admit it. Wren knew damn well why I'd brought the girl to her, and Ellen…

I had no idea what Ellen thought or wanted or wished for. Honestly, it didn't matter. She needed training, for her own sake and the safety of people around her. Right now she was beat down and depressed, not angry. If she did get angry, or frustrated, she could do damage. If she grabbed too much current, without knowing how to ground herself properly…

Overrush. Current ran through our systems, trained or not, and the fact that she hadn't used it yet was surprising—maybe she had, and it scared her so much she'd shut it down. That only made it more urgent that she learn what she was and how to manage it. Until then, she could short herself out, fry not only her body but her brains, maybe kill people around her, too. That's why we're taught control before any-thing else, early enough that we don't have much current in our core yet.

I'd never seen anyone overrush, but I'd heard stories. We all heard the stories.

I made it to the bus stop without Wren pinging me to get my ass back there, and decided, cautiously, that it was safe to relax. Wren could handle Ellen. She was used to working with Nulls, through her partner, and knew all about control, and…

And she knew about being overlooked and misunderstood, too. Valere never talked about her childhood, but she didn't have to. She was a Retriever. Like Pietr, people didn't notice her, even when she wanted them to. Being a Retriever was as much self-defense as it was a career choice.

The bus came, and I got on, sliding my card and holding my breath, as usual, that the magnetic strip still worked. It did. Credit cards lasted about a day near me now, but Metrocards survived. Thank you, universe.

So, what was the life-lesson in all that—we are what our Talent makes us? Magic is destiny? Before, I would have scoffed at the idea: J had taught me that we make our own destiny from the materials we're given or acquire. But the Merge was making me rethink that. Not that I believed I was predestined to a single lifetime forsaking-all-others soul-mate crap with Venec, because I wasn't going to go there. Nor was I going to turn into an obedient little breeding machine, if that's what it wanted.

But the Merge had changed me. There was no getting around that fact. Or we'd changed ourselves, because of it. When we attracted the attention of the Roblin earlier this year, Venec and I had let down our walls to draw the mischief imp in, giving it a situation where it could potentially cause the most damage, focusing its attention on us so it didn't bother anyone else. I'd worried then that those walls wouldn't ever go back up again, not entirely.

I'd been right.

The thought was enough to lift a whisper of awareness deep in my core, the scent of his signature wafting through my bones. If I pushed, I would know exactly where he was—within a reasonable distance—and what he was feeling. His thoughts were still a mystery, unless he let down his walls intentionally, for which I was deeply thankful. I had enough in my brain without his, too. Also, I got the feeling that Ben had some seriously scary thoughts.

okay?

yeah

The exchange was so brief, so instinctive, it was over before I realized it was happening. Somewhere wherever Ben was, he'd felt my roil of emotions and roused himself long enough to make sure everything was all right.

I didn't like the rush of warm satisfaction that went through me at that, but I didn't dislike it, either. And that was the weirdest thing of all about the Merge. There was no sense of anticipation or anxiety, no emotional highs or lows. I had no doubt at all what Ben was thinking, what he was feeling, at least in regard to me.

The bus turned the corner, jolting me slightly in my seat, and I realized that we were almost at my stop. I hit the tape to alert the driver and got to my feet. Hopefully Nick had collected Mollywog from her erstwhile would-be sisters and deposited her with Stosser, who would have passed her along to the parents, and the Fey Lord and Lady would then be off our back and owe us a favor.

No, owe Stosser a favor. I didn't want to have anything to do with that.

I took the stairs up to our office two at a time, hearing my boots make a satisfying echo with each stomp, and hit the seventh floor not even breathing hard. Yay, me.

"Hey." Nicky was in the break room, pulling a soda out of the fridge, when I came in.

I scanned the room quickly for anyone pint-size. "Everything okay?"

"Yeah, although I had to do some quick talking and fancy footwork to get those wannabe Amazons to hand over the kid to me, when you weren't there. Thanks a lot, by the way. I owe you."

I took the sarcasm in stride—Nicky really wasn't all that good at it. "And the kid?"

"Molly—who is, by the way, the most talkative little kid I have ever met, and I've met a lot—is fine and happy and thinks she's been on an adventure and is now off to see her folks again. Not a bruise on her, no obvious trauma in her sparkly little self."

I hadn't even known I'd been worried about that until a weight slid off my neck.

"Thanks."

"Yeah, well, you may not thank me after Stosser gets through with you. He was not happy you handed the job over to me, for some reason."

Oh, swell. "The, um, clients weren't there?"

"Don't know. Stosser met me at the door." He frowned. "We weren't hired by Molly's parents?"

Stosser had said to keep it quiet, but I'd already told Danny, and hell, Nicky had been the one to tell me that there were fatae in with Stosser....

"Nope. Rumor had been that the Fey were kidsnatching again. They wanted the rumors put down."

"We were hired by the Fey?" Nick's pale brown eyes went wide, and not much surprised him anymore. That was who was in the office?

"Mmm." Say neither yes nor no, and you have plausible if not moral deniability.

"So who was the snatcher?" The Fey, identified and placed,

were immediately of less interest. The PUPI mindset kicking in.

"That…may be something we should keep an eye on. A woman, identity unknown, is luring girls, taking seven-year-olds, anyway, and luring older girls to join her. She's a charismatic, possibly Talent, using current as bait."

Nicky narrowed his eyes. "Molly isn't Talent, I don't think." You couldn't really be sure until puberty, but he was probably right.

"None of the girls are." Except Ellen, who they'd rejected. "Sensitive Nulls, but not Talent. That's what makes it so weird. I promised I wouldn't squeal on them, if they handed Molly over, but…"

"But." Nicky shared my own apprehension, which made me feel both better and worse.

"Rorani is concerned." I decided not to say anything about the spirit of Central Park that might or might not have helped me out. A dryad was a real, solid thing. Ghosts…not so much. And I wasn't really sure, anyway. I could have done it myself and stress-imagined the feeling of "otherness."

"You saw Rorani?" Thick envy in his voice, there. Nicky had gone from fanboy to blasé about the fatae overall, but Rorani was…special.

"She's the one who showed me where they were living. I would have found them eventually, but…"

"Uh-huh." He let the sop to my ego go. "Normally I'd say none of our business, until we're called in—" we were supposed to be the tools of investigation, not the instigator of same— "but this isn't good. If this woman's Talent… Bonnie, you gotta tell Stosser, get him to do something, or tell someone who can do something."

"Yeah, I know." I looked, involuntarily, down the hallway. It was quiet, all the doors shut. "But not until I know for a fact our clients are out of the office. I'd just as soon not run into them again. Ever."

Nick looked at me like I'd grown another head, the soda bottle paused halfway to his mouth.

"Bonnie, I've seen you mouth off to a dragon."

"A dragon can only eat you." The Fey could do far, far worse, if they wanted.

He didn't look convinced, but didn't argue the point. I kept getting the feeling that, despite constant urgings, Nicky still hadn't boned up on his fairy tales. I have no idea what his mentor had been thinking.

"Nick?" I jumped: Lou could be as quiet as Pietr sometimes, and I'd swear she hadn't been in the hallway when I'd just looked, nor had I heard any doors open.

"There you are." Our office manager grabbed him by the nearest elbow and pulled him toward the hallway. "Sharon needs your particular skill set on something."

Something electronic, that meant. Nick, for all his scrawny exterior, was one of the more unusual of Talents, born with the ability to actually use current on electronics. Even rarer than a Retriever, and three times as dangerous—and for us, invaluable.

"What's up?" I asked, starting to follow, and Lou let go of him and grabbed me by the shoulder, swinging me around. "Not so fast, wonder girl."

"What?"

"Bonnie, *chica,* I know that we all think we're superheroes, but seriously? When was the last time you took more than a day off?"

I started to protest, and she shook her head at me, all MamaLou. "Without being ordered to."

"Okay, that's not fair. We've been busy as hell." Never

mind that I'd been begging for time off. I'd wanted off baby-sitting, not work.

"Yeah, we have." Lou kept track of who was scheduled to what case, so she knew exactly how busy we were. "And we will be again. But right now? We've got it under control. And you're not assigned to anything pending. So, please? Go away."

Lou's tone was light, but the look in her eyes was serious. And, worse, she was right. We all took one day off every six, no matter what we were working on, but all that meant was that we weren't actively working a case. The last time I let go of the job and just relaxed was…

I couldn't remember.

Lou must have seen something change in my expression, because her stance softened a little. "Go play, Bonita. Before you forget how."

In things like this, Lou outranked even Stosser, so I wasn't going to fight her. Only… "One last thing I gotta do, first."

Once Lou assured me the coast was clear, I marched down to Stosser's office and reported in.

The Big Dog heard me out without comment. His hair was sleeked back in its usual ponytail, but he was wearing a crunchy-granola outfit now, rather than the earlier suit. I didn't know if it had been for the Fey's benefit, or something else was going on, and I didn't ask.

"You never saw this woman?"

"Didn't get a name, either. I thought it more important to bring the girl back than to risk antagonizing them."

"No, you were right." He looked at me then, his gaze way too direct and thinky for my comfort. "And you took this… Ellen to Wren Valere."

It wasn't a question, so I didn't answer it.

"You've got a good eye for diplomacy, despite yourself," he said, and my entire body tensed.

"No." The word fell from my lips before I knew I was going to say anything.

"What?"

"No. Look, boss… Yeah, I can think on my feet, and I can plan ahead, and I'm good at making sure things go where they're supposed to, but don't even go there. You have Lou to run the office, and Venec to run us, and please, will someone just let me get back to doing what I do best? I would be horribly unhappy as your third in command."

I had ego, yeah, but I could see in his face I'd been right about what he was thinking, where he wanted to lead me. It wasn't the first time something like this had come up.

I could also see that he hadn't let go of the idea, even as he nodded.

"You working a live case?"

"No." I waited. That really hadn't been a question, either.

I don't know if he'd overheard Lou, or they were just thinking along the same tracks, but he nodded again and then looked away, dismissing me, his mind obviously already ranging onto the next problem. "Go home, take some downtime. Don't come back for—" and he hesitated "—three days. Four. Hell, I don't want to see you again until next Monday, all right?"

That definitely wasn't a question.

Home for me was a brownstone apartment building in the West Village. Wren might have moved out, but I was staying put. Besides the fact that it was all I could afford, I'd fallen in love with the apartment, despite its rundown and somewhat creaky bones. There were no ley lines anywhere near the building, but something inside the bricks it was made from, or the bedrock it was built on, carried its own magic, and like knew like.

Now, though…I still loved it, but it wasn't the same. Wren had moved out, gone uptown to her shiny new condo and taken PB with her, and with them went the stream of fatae who used to tromp to her apartment, eating the lasagna or stew I'd shoved into her freezer so she didn't starve, a steady source of gossip and companionship on the nights when I didn't want to be alone, a comforting, distant hum of energy overhead when I did.

A Null couple now lived on the top floor. Nice people, but not *my* people. And the irony of that made me smile, because they were in many ways exactly my kind of people— free-living club kids who'd gotten out of the house and were making careers for themselves. But…

Not *Cosa*.

I hated it, that I thought that way. But the few times recently I'd gone to hang out with old friends from college or tried to meet someone who wasn't a Talent, I ran out of things to say. I couldn't talk about my job, not really, and…

And Lou was right. I didn't have anything else going on in my life. Or, I had a lot of things going on, but none of it was going anywhere.

I dropped my coat and case by the door and stared at the antique red lacquered Chinese chest, not even noticing its usually soothing gaudiness. Me, who'd been direct like an arrow my entire life, now treading water. Feeling sorry for myself. Lonely. Oh, hell. When had I turned into this?

trouble?

Venec again, and this time I was caught so off guard I didn't shunt away my frustration or confusion but let it flow through the Merge, answering him not with words or even emotions but the utter sense of helplessness.

I was never helpless. Ever.

His response was immediate and totally unexpected: *come down here*

Wren Valere was not often stumped. Her entire career was based on three things: the ability to move without being seen, the ability to plan every move down to the last detail, and the ability to think on her feet when the details went sideways.

Now she was faced with a young woman who watched her the way a mouse would a cat, never blinking, never losing track of where she, Wren, was. She had been given no time to plan, and she had absolutely no idea what to do with her life suddenly turned sideways.

It wasn't that Wren didn't have sympathy for the girl: she did. Lured away from her home by a would-be cult leader and discarded when she didn't fit their parameters for creating a coven…because she already *had* magic… It would be funny, if it wasn't so sad. And if she weren't so obviously in desperate need of a mentor.

Not six months ago, Wren had told Sergei that she might consider being a mentor. In the aftermath of retrieving the Talent the Silence had stolen, looking at those brave, terrified teenagers and knowing that she could make a difference…

Not every Talent mentored. Nobody would think less of her if she didn't: she had given more than enough to the *Cosa* already. But…her mentor had saved her life. That was no exaggeration; he had taken in a scared, criminally minded child and given her guidance, understanding, and the strength to deal with the hand Life had dealt her. Her mother, a total Null, had never been able to understand her daughter; her father had never been in the picture: there was only John Ebenezer.

The day Neezer had disappeared, Wren thought her life

was over. She had learned, years later, that he was alive, wizzed beyond recall to human society, that if he saw her again he would be driven by his madness to kill her...and he still protected her. Because that's what a mentor did.

And none of those thoughts helped with the present-day scenario. Ellen sat quietly on her sofa, her knees carefully together, her shoulders back but somehow still managing to give the impression that she was hunched over, as though she were expecting a blow. And yet, her expression wasn't that of someone who had been abused; Wren had seen enough of those over the years. No, Ellen was...watchful, careful, but not afraid. Not of The Wren, anyway.

"So. What the hell am I going to do with you?"

"Bonnie said I needed to be trained. That I was dangerous." Ellen sounded as if she wasn't sure what she thought of that idea, trying to decide if being dangerous was a bad thing or a good thing.

"Bonnie's right. Last time I was around someone untrained, they set fire to the restaurant we were in."

Ellen's round eyes got even wider at that, but she didn't scoff or even ask how. She might not know anything about current, Wren decided, but she'd seen enough to know that more was possible than she'd been told.

That was as good a place as any to start.

Only not just right now. Not when Sergei had just handed her a job that needed to be done right away.

"All right. If we're going to do this, we're doing it. Do you have a place to stay?"

Ellen shook her head.

"Anything other than the clothing on your back?"

A slight hesitation, as though she were considering something, then another shake of the head.

"Anyone you need to tell where you are?" Wren already

knew the answer to that, but she wanted to hear Ellen say it. Or shake it, as the case may be. Another head shake, this one immediate and definite.

"Right. The only problem is, I was about to head out on a job when you showed up, and no, I can't take you with me," she said, although Ellen hadn't shown any signs of asking that—or, indeed, anything.

Bonnie hadn't told her much, but Wren could tell that the girl in front of her was already on overload. Ellen had to be kept calm, and ideally far away from the casual use of current until she could deal with it—and herself—better.

"I can't just leave you here," she said, running through her options. If this had been a normal situation, a Null girl sitting on her sofa with those lost, unblinking eyes, Wren would have called her mother. Marguerite Valere was at her best with someone to fuss over. Unfortunately, she was use-less when it came to the *Cosa,* being unable to see the faint glimmer of supernatural even when it stood directly in front of her—as PB had, on occasion, trying not to be hurt that his best friend's mother didn't acknowledge him.

How anyone could manage to say good-morning to a four-foot tall, white-furred, red-eyed demon and not actually see it, Wren could not comprehend, but her mother had done so, more than once. That meant that while there would be no current-use there, there would also be no understanding or compassion for Ellen's fears. Not good.

She might have called Bonnie, but Bonnie had been the one to hand the problem over. And there wasn't anyone else she felt confident enough to ask: her job tended to bring her around unsavory sorts, not trustworthy. Tree-taller would have been exactly the person, but—the pain of his death still haunted Wren, years later. And his widow wanted nothing to do with the *Cosa,* after that.

Trustworthy...

Wren eyed Ellen again, thinking hard. "Oh, hell, you're going to have to meet him at some point, anyway."

"Who?"

The first question she'd asked, and she didn't hesitate in asking. Wren thought that was a good sign.

"My partner."

It was Monday, so he would be doing inventory at the gallery—the second gallery, she corrected herself. The larger one downtown was now being handled by his assistant, and Sergei had rented a space uptown, featuring smaller, three-dimensional art, rather than the large paintings and sculptures Didier Gallery Downtown showcased.

"He's...like us?"

Wren laughed. "Not hardly. He's a Null—without magic—but he can sense it, and he knows all about the fatae, about all the *Cosa Nostradamus*. He came to it late in life, though—" when he was in his twenties, recruited by the anti-magic group the Silence, which he had later helped destroy "—and he knows what it's like to be utterly...confused."

"Confused." Ellen smiled, and Wren was struck by what a sweet smile it was, not at all cynical or bitter. "Yeah, confused about sums it up, right now."

Wren smiled back at her, unable to not. "Well, we can take care of some of that, anyway. And you'll like Sergei. Everyone does. That's part of his annoying charm."

They would get along fine; Sergei would make sure of that, and keep her away from current without dismissing her fears. And then, when Wren got back from Philadelphia, she'd figure out how the hell she was going to teach a totally untrained twenty-something everything she should have learned when she was thirteen.

seven

"Come down here."

That suggestion—order?—had left me flat-footed and a little taken aback. That voice had been Ben, not Venec. I didn't know how I knew, but I did. And it was a really important distinction. We had been doing this dance for so long, keeping work and personal separate, trying not to screw a really good working relationship with, well, screwing.

Except that excuse hadn't been valid for a while now. The rest of the pack knew. Venec had never once slipped in favoritism, and nobody seemed to expect that he would. So the only thing holding us back was, well, us.

Venec wasn't in the city, he wasn't working, and I had time off, and he was doing something not PUPI-related and…

And I didn't know what any of it meant, or if this was incredibly stupid or finally smart, but there was a little giddy feeling at the base of my spine that I hadn't felt in too damn long, and I knew better than to poke at it like it was trace. It wasn't trace. It wasn't job-related. This wasn't the Merge—or, okay, it was always the Merge between us. But it was us, too. Making our own decisions, without the usual urgency or stress of the job to complicate our reactions.

I could have said no. The Bonnie of— Hell, half an hour ago, I would have said no. Caught up in that perfect storm of self-pity and frustration and helplessness, my practical, pragmatic side didn't stand a chance.

I threw a change of clothes, my toiletry kit, and my notebook into my overnight bag before I could change my mind, and headed for Penn Station.

An hour later I was on a train down to Philly, grabbing a window seat so I could watch the Jersey landscape go by, alternating stretches of greenery and Metroparks. The car I was in was only three-quarters full, and I was able to keep the seat next to me clear—no risking some unsuspecting businessman's laptop or cell phone, or having to deflect unwanted conversation. The feel of electricity humming through the train soothed, letting my brain generate the mental equivalent of white noise: not thinking, not learning or doing, just being.

I was almost asleep when the first tremor of kenning shivered down my spine, invading my brain.

A dragon, circling overhead, tarnished pewter against a purple-black sky. Fire, raining down like meteors, falling past a metal structure ringed with St. Elmo's fire....

That was past. I let the memory-image go, my heartbeat not changing, my thoughts undisturbed. The dragon had been on our side, nominally, and we'd all survived the Battle of Burning Bridge, cooled the flames that threatened to destroy the city last year. It was all good.

The kenning wasn't done with me, yet.

Dragons, three of them now, circling in a pattern that I should recognize against a sky the bruised purple of a tornado warning. The pattern left faint traces against the sky, etching itself and then fading

before I could grasp it. I had no idea what it was, no sense of famil-
iarity and yet I knew I should know it.

Then my awareness slipped, a dizzying dive into fire, burning deep and low this time, a forge that could smelt the earth's
heart. A splattering of red…blood? *Blood everywhere, thick and*
heavy, coating the flames, dripping down slowly, drying in impos-
sible shapes, pulsing like a heart…

Somewhere in the depths of my mind I was disturbed by
the surreal intensity of the visuals, but most of me was still
caught in the fuguelike calm, unable to do more than watch,
observe, let the kenning wash through me however it would.

too late A whisper like dry leaves and rattling shells,
the scraping of talons gently across a chalkboard, a threat—
or a regret—implicit in the words. Awareness shifted again,
a dragon's wings coming down with a gust of fetid air, en-
folding, releasing. The flash of something moving out of the
corner of my eye, unseen, the rattle of bones, and a wisp of
fog like congealing unease.

And then it was gone.

I hadn't realized my eyes closed until they opened again,
looking out at the sidings of whatever station we were pulling out of. Princeton Junction flashed by on an old-fashioned
wooden sign. Across the aisle, a man with a square, open-
looking face had turned to look at me, his expression caught
between worry and hesitation, like he thought I needed help,
but wasn't sure he wanted to get involved.

I looked away, not sure what to tell him.

An hour left until Philadelphia, the conductor announced,
while I wiped a crust of sweat off the ridge of my nose and
reached for the bottle of water on the pull-down tray in front
of me. My throat tasted like ash and sour lemon, and my eyes
itched, like I'd been staring into smoke.

I didn't like this. I didn't like it at all. Kenning was so damn vague, but I knew better than to dismiss it. Something was coming. But the signals were so cloudy and confused, shaped by my past fears. Was the warning aimed at me specifically, or was I only one of many affected? Should I be warning others? Were the dragons real or a metaphor?

Without my scrying crystals—packed in their box at home—or any way to focus myself that wouldn't draw way too much attention in public, I couldn't do anything except accept the warning and keep on keeping on. Carefully.

Out of habit, I reached for my notebook and started writing as much as I could remember. It wasn't much, a few paragraphs of images and feelings, but when I looked at it, done, I got the same sense of quavery unease I'd felt at the start of the kenning. Something was coming. Something dangerous, probably bad—because the kenning never bothered to bring me good news, damn it—and soon. Near me. Involving me.

If I hadn't been on the train, I might have gone into fugue state and reached for more, but if I were responsible for the third rail splurting out, even if none of my fellow passengers knew, I'd feel guilty all week. Plus, god knows how long it would take them to fix things.

I stared at my notebook, then slapped it shut. So much for relaxing. The rest of the trip I sat, my muscles tense, staring out the window at the darkening landscape but not really seeing anything. When the train finally arrived at 30th Street Station, I grabbed my bag and got off the train, moving with the flow of humanity, be-suited business folk and knapsack-slung teenagers, and me somewhere in-between.

And then Ben was there, leaning against a wall, waiting for me, and it was utter instinct that made me drop my bag and wrap my arms around him, feeling his arms pull me in closer, hearing his heart thumping inside his chest, feeling his sense of welcome and comfort enfold me, the Merge humming in satisfaction, and I couldn't even bring myself to be annoyed because it felt so right.

I knew why we'd fought it. I knew why we'd fight it again, eventually. But right now…I needed this. So I took it.

"Do we need to talk about whatever it was?" His voice was a low growl, felt as much as heard, and I shook my head, knowing he would pick up on my reluctance even if he didn't feel the gesture.

"Not yet."

It was coming. It involved me, if not us. But, selfishly, right then, I wanted to be off-duty. I didn't want to be Venec and Torres, just Bonnie and Ben.

Venec would have pushed. Ben let it be.

The last time I'd been in Philadelphia I'd been fourteen: J and I meeting one of his old friends for dinner. I suppose I should have been playing tourist, gawking out the window of the cab we'd gotten outside the station, but Ben had his arm around my shoulders and I turned my head into his chest and listened to his heartbeat until we got to the hotel. It was nice—not fancy, just a basic chain hotel, but clean and well decorated. Ben took my bag—a leather carry-all I'd had since I was in high school—and handed it over to a bellhop with instructions to take it up to his room. Huh.

Well, yeah.

"You need to eat something."

It wasn't a question, and—testing the shakiness of my knees—he wasn't wrong. After this morning's adventure I felt like a wrung-out rag. I'd forgotten to eat. Again.

He took my arm and headed toward the little restaurant off to the side of the lobby, where Ben ordered a pot of cof-fee and the sandwich special from a waitress who looked like she was killing time before Hollywood called. I stared at him across the table, resisting the urge to fiddle with the napkins or count the cubes of sugar in the little bowl next to a small vase of real flowers, something with tiny pink-and-white petals.

I'd come down here not really thinking about why I was coming, telling myself that I was getting away from the city so I didn't spend my time off sulking in my apartment or prowling areas that would only remind me that I wasn't working, but the realization that there was only one hotel room brought it all back in a rush. Benjamin Venec. My boss. The other side of the Merge. Guy who could set my entire body to thrumming at the worst moment, and whether it was the Merge or just natural hormones really didn't matter anymore, because it was going to happen no matter what.

The guy who had invited me down here, for reasons of his own.

And all I kept wondering was "If we have sex, and satisfy the Merge, will it stop?"

I wasn't sure what I wanted the answer to be.

"So. Why are you down here?" I was sort of embarrassed I hadn't asked him that in the first place, or when I got off the train, but in my defense the kenning had distracted me, and then the feel of his arm around my shoulders had distracted me further. But now he was on the opposite side of the table, and I was suddenly curious as hell.

His body language was calm and collected, but the buzz I was picking up told me he was about half an inch from playing with the napkins, too. Good. I'd hate to think I was the only one nervous here.

"A side job. I'm working with a local museum, training their people how to detect and avoid a current-based heist."

"Oh. Cool." If he did his job right, that would be one less eventual case that PUPI would get, but I couldn't really see anything wrong with that. It wasn't like there wasn't enough crap that we did get called in on.

The waitress delivered our sandwiches, and I stared at the plate, not sure if I was actually hungry or not. I decided I was and took a bite. A second later, I was ravenous, and all other thoughts were pushed to the side while I cleaned my plate.

Ben ate about half his sandwich but kept talking. "The guy I'm working for, he's smart, one of the best security experts I know. He worked for an insurance company for years. That's where I met him. They just got funding to upgrade, and he wants to do it right. A museum with an aging security system is one that doesn't get offered topnotch collections on loan."

The fact that Ben was actually letting me in on his life outside the office…working on the stuff he'd done before… Yeah, I wasn't going to say anything that might screw that up or shut him down. "You do a lot of work like that?"

He shrugged, a casual gesture that said nothing. "Used to. Safer than tracking down bail-jumpers and runaways, and pays better. Museums are pretty savvy about this sort of thing. Most of them have been hit more than once by thieves working with current. They may not know what it is, exactly, but their boards want it dealt with, and so someone, somewhere, knows enough to call a specialist."

"And that would be you."

"Among a few others, yeah." He looked at me then, and the crooked grin I'd come to know too well appeared, and the awkwardness disappeared. "And you. Wanna learn the trade?"

Oh, hell, yeah.

Not too far away, a black sedan car slid to the curb on a street off Logan Square. As a woman emerged from the backseat, the sky changed, the quality of light darkening slightly as though a shadow had passed overhead, although the sky remained clear. She looked up, her dark eyes squinting as she tried to decipher some invisible shape, sense the form of the thing shadowing her as the sun set.

The man who had gotten out with her stopped, waiting. "Is something wrong?"

She shook her head, not bothering to look at her companion. If she could not sense anything, he would be unlikely to do so. Aden Stosser was not one to suffer from apprehension or second thoughts, but it did occur to her that the shadow overhead could simply be hesitation over what she was about to do.

"This is your fault, Ian," she said quietly. "If you hadn't gotten in so deep, if you'd listened to me, instead of insisting that the world dance to your tune, I wouldn't be here now."

"Ms. Aden." Her companion waited, patient. "If you are having second thoughts, now would be the time to act on them. Once we enter the building, the—"

"The die is cast, the Rubicon crossed. Yes, I know." Sorcerers awaited her. Even the thought made her gut clench. The name they chose might be pretentious, but their power was not. She would not be taking on an ally of equal or lesser power, but making supplication to a stronger force—one that might ask much of her in return.

Yet, sorcerers policed themselves, allowing none outside their group to have a say in their doings. Surely such Talent would be sympathetic to her cause, be willing to put some small amount of their power at her disposal?

She had tried to talk Ian out of this madness and failed. She had tried to stop them and failed. More than half the Councils had given their approval, and even overseas, they were beginning to rumble with talk of a similar organization.

Already, the fabric of their society was shredding. If these sorcerers agreed to cage Ian, take away his glamour, his persuasive abilities…she could talk sense back into the Council and stem the tide.

She firmed her jaw and smoothed back her dark red hair. "Let's go."

eight

Several hours later, that cheesesteak sandwich sitting heavy in my stomach, my nerves nicely awake, I was standing in the brightly lit hallway of the Ravenwood Museum. The museum was closed, so we had the paintings and sculptures in the dozen or so small galleries to ourselves. The Met, it wasn't, but the stuff was quality; I'd spent enough years living with J to recognize art, even if it wasn't a familiar brushstroke.

"They specialize in American painters," Ben told me when we came in. "Private funding. The Board is highly paranoid and slightly panicky about security. Smaller museums tend to be more attractive targets, since they have less funding, and often their works are easier to fence."

It made sense: disposing of a Degas or Picasso—or an O'Keefe or Cassatt—took some doing. A Reid or Gilbert, grabbing names off two of the pieces we'd passed, probably less work, even if less money.

The what, I thought, was less interesting to me than the how. I had a blueprint in one hand, my other hand flat on the wall nearest me, and Ben was lecturing me on how to sense the electrical wires and to tell the difference between the lines, identifying and "plucking" at the ones that connected to the alarm system. This was more to my taste than babysitting newbies or facing down sullen teenagers.

"The trick is to sensitize them without actually setting them off. That way, when someone else touches them with current, trying to overload them, a warning is set off."

A warning that was tied to a batch of elementals lurking in the walls, tiny semisentient creatures drawn by the excess of electricity the building provided. I'd encountered them once before, on a site, but using them this way, as part of a system rather than merely relying on their reaction to an intrusion, was new to me.

It sounded simple, and it was…but simple didn't mean easy. Ben had let me try, just a single unconnected strand, and I'd broken it with my lightest, most delicate touch.

"How long did it take you to learn how to do this?"

Another shrug, but this one was too casual.

"Dammit, you invented this, didn't you?" I was torn between irritation and admiration, and just a hint of…

Wow. I almost stopped, shocked once I identified the emotion. Pride. For him, in him. Not the sort of attaboy feeling I got when one of my fellow pups did something smart, either. It was…

"Bonnie. You still with me?"

"Yeah, right, sorry." I tucked that soft, warm thing away carefully and focused on my hand on the wall. "So you make, like, a really fine thread and needle?" I asked, envisioning a thread of current so fine I could barely see it, only sense it.

"Yeah, I guess." I suspected any attempt Ben made at sewing had involved surgical thread, not embroidery floss, but you picked the image that worked for you. I let the thread spin out, snaking from my palm down into the wall, reaching…

Something hard and sharp slammed into me, like a dozen icy-cold needles. "Holy mother of fu— What the hell was that?"

Ben was already moving, grabbing at one of the security guards who had been watching us without trying to be obvious. "There's a breach. Call the security desk now!"

Holy shit. So now I knew what it felt like when the alarm was triggered. I swallowed, still feeling the sharp sting that had jagged its way through my flesh, and then started running after Ben, damning the vanity that had made me wear my pretty, utterly-impractical-for-running boots. They made a nice clattering noise on the floor, though, as I followed the constant tug that told me where Ben was, his annoyance and glee clear to my oversensitive awareness. Glee because he had proof the system worked. Annoyance...

I could feel my ears burn, clear sign that I was blushing. Annoyance because his rather carefully detailed plans for tonight involving a bottle of wine, a very nice meal, and maybe some skin-to-skin had been disrupted.

Whatever I'd maybe, possibly had in mind coming down here, Ben was a step ahead of me. Maybe two. Guess I wasn't the only one tired of treading water.

All that was shelved for now, though.

I caught up with him as he hit the staff elevator, slipping in as the doors closed, his hand reaching out to hold them for me.

"Run faster next time," he said. I would have stuck my tongue out if I weren't breathing so heavily. He, of course, was barely breathing hard. Bastard.

The moment the door opened onto a sparse basement floor, Venec was already talking. "What's going on, people?"

"There's nothing on the monitors."

The man talking was about the size and shape of a troll, with one of the loveliest voices I'd ever heard. Even the fact that he was clearly pissed off didn't lessen the beauty of his tenor.

"What about the tripwires?" Venec asked.

"Nothing. We didn't have a clue until the alarm went off."

Concerned satisfaction hummed from Ben: he was in his element, proven right and in control of the situation. I studied him, slightly disturbed at how much of a turn-on that arrogance was.

"Someone tried to make a play on the museum here." His finger traced a line over the digital display, not getting any closer to it than he had to. Even so, several of the displays were breaking up into static. I moved back a few paces so I could still hear what was going on but was out of immediate range of what looked like a massive amount of very expensive technology.

Usually, unless we were under a lot of stress, or pulling down a lot of current, it took extended exposure to wreck electronics. But I didn't want to be the one who exceptioned the rule. Ben was on the payroll; let him worry about it.

His attention was focused on "listening" to the current. "Whoever it is, they've backed off. They must have realized that they tripped a wire somewhere."

"So you think that's it?" The troll frowned, and his voice deepened, sending involuntary shivers along my back. I'd always been a sucker for smooth, dark voices, even in the most inappropriate time and place.

"It depends on who it was and what they were trying for. Some thieves, yeah, they'll stand down now. There's no point to them overreaching and getting caught—no score is worth that to a professional." Implied, if unsaid, was the fact that no amateur could have gotten that far. Not against one of his systems. Arrogance again; definitely hot. Also, kinda cute.

"Some thieves. But not all?" Troll was staring at him, expecting an answer, pronto.

Ben looked thoughtful, but I couldn't read anything from him at all now. He wasn't keeping me out; he was just so focused on this, there wasn't room for anything else. I suspected I got like that, too.

"Not all," he agreed. "And then there are those who will take my system as a personal affront and keep trying until they break it."

Well. I guess I knew what we were doing tonight.

A few blocks away from the museum, Wren Valere wrapped her hands around a mug of tea and scowled into the tepid liquid. The initial approach had gone smoothly, slipping through the front ring of security without them even having a whisker-twitch of alarm. Any Retriever worth their name could bypass Null guards—The Wren could tap-dance naked, painted purple, and clapping castanets, and they shouldn't even blink.

And they hadn't. But she'd not gotten cocky; even the best could get caught. The next stage had been the basic alarms, the motion detectors and tripwires every modern museum set up to keep patrons from getting too close. She'd made it through to the staff-only areas without anyone seeing her, much less asking what she was doing there, without a security badge or escort, when suddenly there had been...

Fingers on her.

Not physical, actual fingers, but the sense of being touched, patted down, like being pushed through some weird, magical combination of a security gate and a car wash. It was similar to the sensation she had when encountering elementals, tiny semi-aware creatures that gathered in current-streams and could sometimes be used as a basic alarm system, but...

Less excited, more controlled. Elementals were random, even when you got them set in one place: they reacted randomly. This had been a specific reaction, a security lock using a level of magic, of sophistication, that Wren hadn't run into before.

And the moment she became aware of it, she knew that whoever had set up the system was aware of her, too.

What she didn't know was if they knew that she knew that they were aware of her.

Wren parsed that sentence in her head and scowled more deeply at the tea. The waitress at the diner a few blocks from the museum where she'd taken refuge approached her, thinking she needed more hot water, and then backed off, warned by some job-honed sense that this wasn't a customer who wanted to be disturbed.

Wren didn't even like tea; that was Sergei's drink. But it comforted her to hold the warmth and smell its scent, as though her partner was there to advise her.

Not that it took much thinking. The Wren always followed through, always completed the job. That was why Sergei could ask for—and get—such high fees: discretion and success were a potent combination for the majority of her clients. Plus, this one, with its potential double paycheck of getting paid once to steal the artwork and then again to sell it, was too profitable to screw up. That would be Sergei's take, anyway.

Wren just couldn't stand being beaten.

nine

Luisa Novoa had once dreamed of being something special, someone admired and imitated. She had no skill at singing or painting or acting, so had thrown herself into the business world, only to discover that she was merely competent there, as well.

PUPI had been her last hope; when Ian Stosser had recruited her, she had thought that now, finally, she would excel...

"Come on. Give me something."

"I can't re-create something out of nothing." Lou wasn't the smartest of the pups. She wasn't the most skilled or the highest res. She wasn't even the most inventive, or the best at spotting evidence or trace. But she had discovered that there was one way that she did, finally, shine. More, it made her indispensable.

Ian Stosser let the charming, coaxing, charismatic tone drop from his voice, which was a relief to both of them. "All this information, and you can't find anything?"

Lou could compile data. All the information that PUPI

cleaned, or learned, or put together, and used to solve a case—or discarded as being irrelevant to the case—she gathered, and ordered, and made sense out of. And she could find it, later, when it was needed.

"I can't find what doesn't exist, boss."

He didn't swear or scowl, or prod her into trying again, the way Venec did. He simply stared at her, those pale eyes cold and unnervingly keen. "It has to."

When Ian Stosser got something in his head, it was impossible to dislodge it. He was determined that Lou had facts at her disposal, and therefore she needed only to find them.

"Seriously, boss. Before Bonnie told us, I'd never even heard about the Merge. None of us had—not even you. And the only stuff I've gotten since then—" and she had researched, because that was what she did "—just repeats the same thing over and over again, that the Merge is meant to draw two Talent together, to create something greater."

She held up a hand to stop him before he could even open his mouth. "And the only places I have found that are in texts that are, like, a hundred years old. If it's happened since then, nobody's talking about it. At all."

She shook her head, stretching her fingers out, palms down over the table, and stared at them as though the answer was there. "Hell, I don't even know that it ever happened before, either. It's all…theory and claims, not any specifics."

"It's happening now, which means it's happened before. Venec and Torres are special, but they're not that special. I don't like operating blind. It's too much of a variable, and we can't afford it, not now." Stosser wasn't the sort to show worry by anything as obvious as chewing his nails or pacing, but there was a certain level of anxiety under the surface that—if you knew him well enough—you could pick up.

Lou hadn't been a pup long, but she had been working

with Stosser every day since she started. At this point, she could read him better than anyone else, except Venec. What she didn't understand was why he was anxious.

"Boss...it's their lives. Not a case. Why don't you just let them deal with it? They've got it under control." She thought about the sparks that still simmered whenever the two of them sat next to each other, which was more often these days, and amended that. "Mostly." Then she tilted her head and gave him a stern look that rivaled his own. "Unless you're thinking about trying to use this somehow. Because if you are, Ian Stosser, that is right out. *De ninguna manera, no se cómo.* You don't do that to your own people. You don't do that to anyone. It's not right."

"Yes, *mami*."

She studied him, not appeased by his apparent meekness nor his attempt at humor. "I am serious, boss. You screw with one of us, we assume you will screw with any of us, and you lose us. You know that, right? And I'm not talking about your charisma enchantment cantrips *de mierda*—that's the job. You mess with our heads, or our hearts...and not a single pup will ever trust you again."

Stosser held his hands up as though making a vow. "I solemnly swear I am not going to nor am I contemplating using the Merge in any way." The anxiety slipped through, just a hint more, with a whiff of exhaustion that worried Lou more than anything else. "But I want to know what it is, every detail, to make sure that nobody else can use it, either. Because eventually, somebody's going to slip, somebody's going to notice. And if the wrong person does...it goes from being their own business to ours. *Tu entiende?*"

Their gazes held, and neither of them blinked. "*Sí. Entiendo.*"

"Good. Keep at it."

★ ★ ★

Whatever Ben had originally planned for dinner, my expectations had been…well, non-expectant. If I'd guessed where we'd end up for dinner, it could have been anywhere from a five-star restaurant to a burger dive to a Tibetan soup kitchen. Benjamin Venec was a man of varied tastes, all of them intriguing.

I would not, however, have guessed that I'd end up sitting on an overturned crate, eating pizza in a mostly empty storeroom in the museum's subbasement, with not only Venec but his friend Allen, who was the spectacularly ugly man I'd met earlier. Allen not only had a lovely speaking voice, but he could sing, too, as he kept proving by breaking out into improvised, completely rude riffs on Gilbert and Sullivan that made me fall off my crate laughing—twice.

The laughter was a welcome break, considering the intensity of what we were doing. The crate next to our makeshift table was covered with layers of blueprints, far more complicated than the one I'd been using earlier. Most of them detailed the physical layouts of the building, but two of them were electronic schemata, and one, on incredibly fine onionskin, was the hand-drawn plans for Venec's security system. When you placed it over the schemata, you could see the entire security picture, Null- and current-based. We'd been going over every inch, determining what had been broken by our would-be thief, and how, and how to prevent it from happening again.

And the clock was ticking: whoever it was had to try again soon or risk us closing all the potential windows.

"So you think that they're going to come in here?" Allen jabbed one gnarled finger at the topmost sheet, the grease from his pizza leaving a smudge.

"It's the weak spot, so if they know their job, yeah, they will."

"You left me a weak spot? In the security system I am paying you massive sums of money for?"

"Your idea of massive is like a john's measurement of his own sex appeal. And, yes, there's a weak spot. So anyone who takes a go at your museum will go there, and they can be trapped easier. Christ, you hired me—trust me to do my thing, willya?"

Someone who came down looking for a romantic wooing—or at least some hot and heavy sexing—might have felt cheated at being cooped up in a dank subbasement listening to two guys bicker as they worked. I was, god help me, enchanted. Venec, fierce and growly and smart, was sexy as hell. Benjamin, the off-duty side, had a surprisingly deep reservoir of compassion and kindness that always made me melt.

Benjy, as apparently only Allen was allowed to call him, was just as intense and engaged and fucking adorable.

He looked up and caught me watching him, and grinned. No guards up, no reserve, no hesitation, just this arrogant "I know you're watching me, I know you think I'm hot" grin. I wasn't sure if I wanted to hit him or kiss him.

Probably both. I settled for grabbing another slice of pizza. It wasn't as good as what we got back home, but this chicken-pizza thing wasn't entirely an abomination. Maybe.

"All right, fine." Allen took a hit off his soda and let out a soft belch. "'Scuse me. And you were going to tell me about this sticky spot before you finished up?"

"Of course."

"Of course. Bah. I—"

Whatever he was going to say was cut off by the sound of something beeping. He grabbed at his belt, already unfolding his legs and walking away from us as he answered the cell phone. He might be willing to risk us near the security console, apparently, but not his phone.

"What? How'd you know? I— Yeah, yeah, he's with me."

He shot a glance over his shoulder at us, clearly worried. We both went on alert, immediately: Who was calling him, and why were they asking after Venec?

"Yeah. All right. I'll bring them down. What? Oh, ah, one of his people is here, too. I assume you'll want both of 'em for this."

Business, not social. I put the remains of my slice down, half-eaten. Sometimes it was better to have an empty stomach when you went out on a scene.

Allen listened to a few more sentences, then closed the phone and put it back on his belt without saying goodbye to whoever it was. Or maybe they hadn't said goodbye to him.

"I'm sorry, but that was my friend Charles, down at the station. He heard you were here, and…"

"And?" Ben's voice was guardedly curious, not committing to anything.

"He wondered if you'd come down and take a look at something. Officially."

"The Philly P.D. is hiring us?"

Allen shrugged. "I guess so."

"Well, then." And that quickly, Benjy disappeared, and Venec showed up. I was, weirdly, relieved. Benjy might be adorable, but I knew Venec.

Allen piled us into his car and drove us, not to the nearest precinct house, but to a more modern-looking building, set on the corner of a busy, tree-lined street. The morgue.

I was going to behave, I swear I was, but while we were waiting in the soothingly bland waiting area for someone to come get us, the words just slipped out. "I see dead people."

"Yeah, we get that a lot."

I turned around to face the voice, and looked up. And up.

"Chuck, this is Ben Venec and Bonita Torres."

Charles Andrulis was the tallest, darkest man I had ever met. Taller than Venec, he had to be at least six four, and three feet wide at the shoulder, and skin you could lose current in, with a clean-shaved head and, I quickly discovered, a handshake like the slap of god. It was like running into Nifty's big brother, emphasis on *big*.

Having done the introductions, Allen left us, muttering something about getting back to work that didn't involve the smell of formaldehyde. Andrulis looked at Venec and then looked back at me, and I could practically feel him sizing us up. Venec went totally still, the way he did, and we waited.

"All right." Whatever he'd decided, I guess we'd passed muster, because he went into his spiel, even as he was ushering us past the security desk and into the Holy of Holies. He spoke directly to Venec, but I didn't take offense. Ben was, in Ian Stosser's absence, the official face of PUPI. Being ignored meant I had a better chance of being left alone to do my job, rather than peppered with questions or told useless info a Null thought I'd need.

"We have a corpse here, came in from a murder scene. Name of Warren Shultz. Upstanding citizen, no record, no slander, no foul. But somebody wanted him very much slabbed, to the point where they not only killed him, they scraped out his insides."

"Beg pardon?" Venec actually sounded surprised. I wasn't used to that happening.

Andrulis was leading us along a narrow hallway that was clearly not for public use: the walls needed repainting, and the tile underfoot was cracked. He pushed open a single swinging door and held it with one arm for us to enter. "You'll see."

I'd never actually been in a morgue before; my dead bodies had all been fresh, so to speak, or reconstructed through
current-trace back in the office. I didn't know what to
expect—some sense of death, all the grubby, messy, emotional bits of it, being present, maybe.

Instead, I could have been back in college, hanging out in
the chem lab watching two of my more insane friends mix
concoctions just to hear them go *boom*. I'd been more on
the humanities side of things, but chem majors knew how
to party.

"Over here." He gestured to the young man who had
turned when we came in. "Joey, we need Shultz. Number
32, I think."

The tech nodded like Andrulis had just ordered a double
cheeseburger, then pulled out a gurney and brought it over
to us. He pulled aside the sheet and stepped back.

It was a body. Not gruesome, or scary, just sort of cold
and clean and kind of sad. There were ugly-looking incisions
along the arms and legs and torso, and you could tell that it
had been done with something really sharp. The seams on
the limbs, unlike the torso, didn't quite match up perfectly.
Curious, I lifted my hand over the body.

"Hey!" Andrulis protested, stepping forward as though to
knock my hand away.

"It's okay." Venec. "Bonnie?"

I let my hand rest a few inches over the flesh, feeling the
coolness of not-life between us. It was just flesh. Meat, or-
gans, skin, bone, same as me, and all of it was made up of
the same atoms, whirling really fast, and if one was living
and one was dead, the only difference was a matter of time.

I'd never been what Nicky would call a delicate flower.

There wasn't any visible dirt or markings, but the skin was

off-color, and there wasn't even the hint of current on his skin. Had he been washed?

"Was the body hosed down?"

I heard the rustle of paper: Andrulis checking his notes? "No. Not even a sponge-bath."

So there should be some trace…but there wasn't. Huh.

"He was a Talent," I said.

"Yeah, we know." Andrulis didn't sound impressed. "That's why we brought you here."

"But he wasn't killed by current."

"You sure?" Andrulis again; Venec knew if I said something like that, it was because I was sure.

"Yeah." If he had been, there would have been some trace of it in the tissue, even now. So long as the body hadn't been hosed down—running water could wash away current-trace same as it did everything else. But the flesh was quiet.

"Damn. That would have…"

He stopped, but I could fill it in—"simplified things." The police generally abandoned cases where cause of death was current—abandoned officially, that was. Unofficially they handed them over to us. Or that was the long-term plan, anyway. For now, most of 'em went into cardboard boxes marked "unresolved."

I left my hand where it was, concentrating.

"Bonnie?"

"Hang on a sec, boss."

I wasn't gleaning, exactly. Gleaning was pulling trace from a scene, to be used in reconstructing it later, under controlled—and less fraught—circumstances. I didn't want to collect anything, right now—I just wanted to see it.

Or, more specifically, I wanted to see whatever it was what I thought I'd sensed.

careful Venec warned me.

I didn't need the reminder. Death-related emotions were verboten, in a gleaning. Not just because they were too easily manipulated and distorted, both on the scene and afterward, but because emotions could drag you in, if they were too strong, make the gleaner relive the moment—and, when that moment was death…well, we'd learned not to do that the hard way.

"There's something there…" I was talking directly to Venec now, barely verbalizing, but I knew that he heard me. He always heard me. "Under the surface…in the cuts. The first ones, I mean, not the autopsy.…"

"The ME didn't find anything."

Good ears on the tall guy. "Not physical. Not magical, exactly. I'm not sure. There was something…" I didn't want to go any farther down: quiet or not, this was still a recent murder victim. But I would, if that's what it took. "Huh. Under the cuts… The knife he used, did they find it?"

"No."

Damn. That really would have made everything so much simpler. Something the killer held, used… "I think the weapon's important. There's something about whatever made those cuts. It left the faintest trace—too faint to glean, but I can feel it." Like a splinter under the skin, too fine to catch, but enough to be an irritant.

Venec sighed. "Tell me we don't have another god-damned Excalibur on our hands."

I wasn't even tempted to laugh at that. "Smaller. Like a scalpel, probably, or a fillet knife." Magical? Maybe, probably not. But there was something about it. Something that fit well in the hand and turned with a twitch of muscle, cutting and sliding, searching under the skin. I might have been projecting, but I didn't think so. "The weapon was made by the killer? Or he's had it for a long time—maybe he thinks the blade is like an extension of himself." I was reaching, try-ing to figure out why the blade felt important to me. Huh, male? Default reflex, no reason to think otherwise right now. Roll with it, Bonnie. "Metal conducts, but it also imprints, especially used to kill someone." Stone, metal—go anywhere there had been ritual sacrifices over a long period of time, and ask a Talent what they felt. We weren't much for visiting the really gory historical sites.

"If you find the blade we can find the killer, I think. There's a connection between them. Other than that..."

"Think you could get more from the other body?"

Whoa. I turned to Andrulis at the same time as Venec, and we spoke in unison. "There's two?"

There were two. Both male, both in their mid-forties, both Talent. Both of them had been cut open the same way, and both of them had been cut open, as nearly as I could tell, by the same instrument, leaving that same tickle of current-residue.

I left my hand fall to my side, aware of an ache in my shoul-der and neck that was going to turn into a headache real soon now, if I wasn't careful. I looked at Venec, who had been watching me work. "Do you want to back-check my work?"

Normally I wouldn't ask—and he would never think to offer. But we were on unfamiliar territory—this was the first time we'd been called in by the Philadelphia P.D., and they were looking to Benjamin Venec for answers, not an un-known female. It sucked like a Hoover on steroids, but that was the deal, and I represented PUPI here, not myself. My ego would survive.

Venec stepped forward, placing his hand over the body the way he'd seen me do. "The deep-read spell or Low Swing?"

"Low Swing." Low Swing was a specific cantrip that looked hard at a particular area, but didn't dig for as much specific info as a deep read. Really, at this point, we could just think about what we wanted to learn, and the current would shape to that desire—that's all a spell was, force of will and desire shaping the magic to do what you wanted—but using the same framework made it easier for us to ensure mostly consistent results no matter who worked it.

Mostly, because everyone's current was slightly different, and everyone's training was slightly different, but working together to develop the spells offset that.

While Venec slipped into fugue state to check my impressions, I turned back to Andrulis, who was waiting a few paces behind us, our technician off in the corner doing something that looked science-y and official—if it wasn't so obvious he was watching us. Not suspiciously: more like he was fascinated by the show. I guess even death could get routine, after a while.

A quick current-check told me the tech was Talent, if not high-res, so I included both of them in my question. "Is there any record of anything like this before? These particular cuts, this kind of killing?"

The tech shook his head and shrugged. He wasn't going to step on Andrulis's toes, clearly.

"Not here." Andrulis paused, like he was expecting me to suddenly summon the answers out of thin air.

I waited. I still wasn't as good at it as Pietr or Sharon, but if you concentrated on a particular spot just below their left ear and breathed steadily, people assumed you were willing to wait until everyone died of old age, and gave in. Andrulis was no exception.

"There were a few murders that might have been similar. In San Diego, about ten years ago. I've requested the full files, on the off chance that they're the same, but nothing's come in yet."

"Let us know when they do?" It wasn't a request, really, and he knew it, but the uptick at the end of the sentence made it sound more polite. My dad had taught me that. *"You can get away with being a demanding brat if they don't realize you're a brat, brat."* I could still hear him say it, his hands working on a piece of wood he was carving, slow, steady strokes with the planer, ninety percent of his focus on the work, five percent on me, and five percent in that place only Zaki ever went and he never really came back from.

My mother must have been one seriously hardheaded pragmatist and passed those genes on, because my dad had been born a dreamer.

"Of course," Andrulis said, bringing me back from that snippet of long-ago memory. My attention flickered from below his ear to his eyes, and I realized, uneasily, that Andrulis was watching Venec with an intensity that made me slightly uneasy. Had he studied me with that same hungry expression? Did he even know he was doing it? I looked sideways back at the tech, and he gave me just the slightest upturn of his lips in a wry smile and a flicker of his own core-current, to reassure me. He saw, he knew, and he wasn't worried, so I relaxed.

Most Nulls didn't even notice current. Some, though, could almost feel it, and Talent-envy could turn into Talent-hate, easily. But sometimes it was just casual gee-wish-I-could-do-that, the same as I felt listening to someone sing or play an instrument.

Big Dog chose that moment to come back into the conversation. "Definitely a current-forged instrument. There are vibrations in the flesh that don't come from anything else."

Venec had finished pretty fast, making me wonder if he'd just done it for show. The thought made me feel better, which made me realize I had been kind of hurt by his willingness to back-check me, like he thought I might have screwed something up.

idiot

The Merge-ping was a honeyed, slow rebuke, barely vocalized, and didn't distract Venec from picking up the conversation as though he'd been part of it all along.

"We're done here," Andrulis said, and the tech came forward to cover up both bodies, returning them to their resting places. He moved with an economy of motion, but not brusque or uncaring. I hadn't known either of the corpses, but it made me feel better to know that they were being cared for, even now.

Venec ignored him. "You said there were similar murders?"

"I went through the national database the moment I realized there were two with similar characteristics, trying to match up the descriptions. It's sketchy—not everything's been uploaded yet, and not all departments are even online—but that's what kicked back. Getting off-line records will take a while longer."

Computers. Whatever envy Andrulis had for magic, I was developing for computers. They would make our job so damn much easier, if we could only use them without blowing their little innards—and memory—on a regular basis.

"I think it's time to bring Ian in on this," Venec said. "Is there an office we can use? One without any tech you might want to use, later?"

Most of the NYPD precincts had a broom closet they set aside for that kind of thing. Turned out that morgues in Philadelphia had much the same. Actually, it was a really nice broom closet, with chairs that were padded and a coffeemaker that looked like it might actually work and a jumble of heavy white mugs that looked like they could be used to subdue a corpse-turned-zombie, if things got out of hand.

Andrulis turned us loose and left us there, closing the door behind him.

Venec stared at the room like he was taking inventory, but I got the distinct feeling he wasn't seeing any of it. "This wasn't exactly what I'd hoped for, when I told you to come down. You were supposed to be taking time off."

"Yeah. You owe me," I said, and if I put a twist of innuendo into my tone, there wasn't anyone there but us to hear it.

"Hold that thought." He sat at the table, pushing the chair back slightly so he could extend his legs, and let his eyes glaze over while he focused on reaching Ian. I unbuilt my wall just enough that I could hear the steady, low hum that was Benjamin Venec, the current coiled up in his core, smooth and controlled like a masterwork. The feeling of someone else that close, that unguarded, still freaked me out a little. The fact that he knew I was there and didn't mind—much—was even freakier. Your core was as private as your thoughts and shouldn't be that easily observed.

But the Merge made it not only possible, but actively difficult to avoid.

ian

yes? Even in his pings, Ian Stosser's tone was cool, controlled, and precise. If I hadn't seen the man angry, worried, and sad—sometimes in quick succession—I'd assume he had no deep emotions at all. What he had was control, a level impressive even among Council-trained Talent.

And then there was a burst of information, like a high-speed train roaring past, and the only reason I knew what it was about was because I already knew what it was about.

An endless second of silence, then another, while Stosser digested the update.

that…sounds familiar He hesitated, and I got the feeling that Venec thought there was something he wanted to say, but wasn't going to. ★will investigate★

Then, silence, and Ben's eyes slowly refocused on the room.

"That's it?" Even after two years, I wasn't quite used to Stosser's mad swings between control-freak and hands-off management.

"That's enough," Venec said. "All right, the bodies. Theorize."

Classic Venec management. No time to stop and second-guess yourself: decide and deliver.

"Two men, both middle-aged. Both Talent. One was white, the other probably Latino." The files would confirm that, but right now he was asking what I'd seen. "Physically fit, but not athletes." I hadn't looked at their faces long, so I didn't know if they had any physical resemblance. "The killer left their heads alone, far as I could tell. The stitches on the head and the Y incision on the torso were neatly done, unlike the ones on the limbs and down the sternum and spine." A fair assumption that the killer had made the messy stitches, cleaning up after his work. "Why would you cut someone open and then stitch them back together? Right, I know—no questions yet." I took a deep breath and went on to the things I knew for certain.

"The instrument that was used to carve them up—probably a knife, certainly a sharp edge. Metal...maybe stone or ceramic, but I don't think so. It was delicate, like I said. A scalpel or a filleting knife." J had a row of knives lined up on the wall of his kitchen, glinting in the light. One of them was about six inches long, narrow, the blade surprisingly flexible, with just a slight curve to the shape. I pictured the knife, imagined holding it in my hand, how I would have to hold it in order to make those cuts, to slip into human flesh...

"The blade would have to be very strong and very flex-

ible to avoid the bones but still be able to scrape the flesh…
What was the killer trying to do? If I knew that…"

"If we knew that we'd be halfway to solved. So we'll get
there. What else about the blade?"

"Nothing. Sorry."

It was possible to re-create an image using the space it left
behind in the current, but there needed to be more buildup,
something that had been there a long time. The knife had
come and gone, and while I might have been able to pick
up an emotional trace based on its proximity to the dying…
We'd done that, once. The strength of the victims' dying
emotions had swamped us, nearly killed us. Gleaning the
emotions of murdered people was number one on the Do
Not Do list.

"The knife…definitely a feel of magic to it. But faint, so
it's not the knife itself. No Excalibur."

"Thank you for small blessings," Venec muttered. Arti-
facts were a headache in and of themselves, even without the
homicide.

"The killer's signature, maybe." Venec didn't sound too
hopeful, since signatures were only useful if you had something to match it against. Someday we were going to get that
database of magical signatures. Probably about the same time
we got a solid and lasting peace treaty in the Middle East.

I was certain the blade was metal. Stone could hold current, but it wasn't flexible, and ceramic was magically inert.

"There are easier ways to kill someone if you're Talent,
though." God knows, we'd seen enough of them, the past
two years. "The knife had a signature, but it wasn't… If it was
resonating from the killer, it should have been more definite.
The edges were all smudgy."

"If the killer wasn't Talent, then—"

The door opened, and Charles Andrulis stormed in—and

I mean stormed like a raging cloud wrapped up in wind and filled with hail.

"Just got an updated count. Ten years ago, in San Diego," Andrulis said, his words hitting like that cold hail I'd sensed. "Ten bodies."

"Ten in ten?" I didn't mean for it to sound funny. Nobody laughed.

"And ten years before that. In Montreal." He waved a folder in his hand, I guessed filled with the reports he'd been waiting for.

"It's happened twice before…these kind of killings?"

"Exactly the same, down to the knife strokes. And the fact that they were all Talent. Two cities…maybe more. I have them looking for anything thirty years before."

"You're saying we have a serial killer," Venec said.

"Maybe."

Another cop came in then, an older guy, balding with a paunch, and a cardboard box of pastries in his hand, like he knew we were going to be here awhile. I had a mournful thought for the night I'd half expected when I came down here, and let it go.

Andrulis took the box and nodded. "Thanks, Dave." Dave nodded in return, then glanced sideways at us, less out of curiosity than an ingrained habit of checking faces, and backed out again.

Andrulis was too big a guy to let himself lose control, but I could feel the tension in him, even without current. "Nobody's going to say anything officially, not yet, but…"

But that many bodies with such specific means of death probably meant one killer, and you didn't have to be a genius— or a cop—to know what that meant.

"There was no connection to the other bodies before," Andrulis went on, putting the box of doughnuts on the table.

"They were all different social strata, different neighborhoods, over a period of time, and the reports just said knife wounds as cause of death, not... It wasn't until the reports were entered into the database and the specifics subcategorized...and even then it took us asking for a specific string to give back a pattern. You people don't exactly advertise."

"A serial killer going after Talents." Venec reached into the box and pulled out a pastry that looked so sugar-laden it made my teeth ache. He ate it in two bites. "Why did nobody know there was a serial killer before?"

And by "nobody" Venec meant "us." Or maybe Council... He was lonejack-bred but had been around Ian long enough to assume the Council had their finger on everything one way or the other.

"Because we try not to see things like that," I said, and I meant Council. "Because we still, even now, want to pretend that we're better than the average bear, more adjusted, less prone to the usual level of maladjusted psycho crap. Like current somehow makes us superior."

"Dammit..." He knew I was right. He also know that pretense was utterly wrong. We'd seen enough to prove that.

"We need to tell Ian. And get some people down here." He looked at Andrulis and held out his hand. "Is that file for us?"

"It is now. I don't have the authority to offer you official status, beyond bringing you in to see the bodies, but unofficially, whatever help we can give is yours. Two bodies is bad enough. We do not want ten."

The idea of eating one of those Danish, weirdly, made me feel ill, despite the current I'd used earlier. It had been too long a day, the cheesesteak sandwich and the half-eaten pizza still sitting heavy in my stomach, and the windowless room was adding to my disorientation. It was still dark outside, wasn't it? Or was it already coming up on the morning?

How long had we been in here? Only the sense of Venec, solid and real next to me, kept me from thinking I'd fallen into some more-bizarre-than-usual rabbit hole.

Once I let my brain wander, I wondered about Ellen, and how she was faring with Wren, and if the little girl was happy being home, and if the Fey Lord planned to honor whatever promise he had made to Stosser in exchange for our help, and if those other girls in the Park had somewhere to take hot showers, after sleeping on the rocks, and what had their leader planned for them, when they got older? I'd had Lou call Danny and let him know to check the Park for his own missing girl. That didn't break my promise to leave them alone, technically, and if anyone could get those girls help, it was Danny. Hopefully he'd get backup before tackling the leader.

The threads tangled in my head, kicking back odd associations and nonexistent connections. There was the instinctive urge to find correlations, and never mind that they were all different cases. No wonder Lou and Stosser had wanted me out of the office for a while; pity it hadn't worked out quite the way they'd planned.

"What's going to happen to the bodies now?" I asked suddenly. "The ones in the morgue."

"The ME's signed off on the autopsies, so normally we'd release them to the next of kin. Do you have a reason for us to hold on to them?"

Not really, no. It was rare that a second visit told you more than the first, gleaning-wise. Current weakened, signatures faded, and the inevitable decay wouldn't help matters, either. But I had the feeling that I'd missed something.

"I'd like the others to take a look, if you can wait another day or two. We all have different strengths…. Sharon should come down. And…" I paused, running through the pack in my mind. None of the newbies, not for something like this.

"Pietr." Nifty wasn't as good at gleaning, and Nicky's specialization meant we kept him in reserve, when we could. Pietr also had the strongest stomach: if the bodies did start to turn, it wouldn't bother him.

"Right." Andrulis looked unhappy, but I couldn't tell if it was because I was bringing in more people or the thought of having to deal with more Talent specifically.

Or maybe he was thinking about the same thing I was, about the eight other people who might be next, if this was a serial killer looking to rack up ten kills before he was done.

ten

It turned out to be a little after 1:00 a.m. when we finally left the precinct house, let out the back door into a warm, sticky night. Philadelphia not having the cruising taxi-sharks we were used to, we'd asked the guy at the desk to call us a cab back to the hotel, and despite the sugar high, we'd no sooner made it into the room—large, with a king-size bed prominent in it—than we collapsed. I had a vague memory of taking off my shoes and rummaging in my bag for a toothbrush, but only the fact that I woke up shoeless and without that horrible morning-after feel in my mouth proved I'd done either.

I also woke up fully dressed, tangled around a likewise fully-dressed Venec. My hand was numb from where it had been tucked under his ribcage, and his knee had slid between my legs, cradling me in a way that would have been erotic if we hadn't both been so flustered.

Not from waking up that way but from the way we'd woken up, with an alarm ringing in our ears. Not physical; magical. The museum.

"Damn it, I forgot to reset it after the last attempt," Venec muttered, sitting upright and scrubbing at his face. "I hope to hell someone's paying attention there." He leaned over to reach for the phone half a beat before it rang.

"Yeah. Yeah, I know, I...They got in? That fast? Damn it. But they didn't...Okay, good, yeah. All right, no, no, I'll be over."

Two attempts within twelve hours, and on the second time they got all the way past before Ben's alarm noticed the thief?

I had a sudden sinking feeling in my gut that I knew who had triggered the alarm.

"Go back to sleep, Bonnie," he said, leaning over to grab his shoes from the floor where he'd kicked them off last night. "I'm going to have to rebuild the blasted thing, it sounds like, and that could take an hour or two. No reason we both should be exhausted when the others get here."

"Yeah." My voice sounded even less awake than I felt, and I let myself sink back onto the too-soft mattress, watching him reach for his jacket and wallet. His hair was sticking up a little at the top of his skull, and his skin was a little soft and pouchy under the eyes, exactly like a guy woken at 5:00 a.m. by the sound of alarms chiming through his bones. "You..."

"Yeah?" He turned, but I could see—hell, I could feel—that he was already out of the room and gone.

"Never mind. Mmm, gonna keep the bed warm. Have fun."

He gave me a tight, fierce grin. "I will."

I watched him leave and then closed my eyes but didn't drift back into sleep. Instead, my mind followed the patterns of the system the way Venec had shown me, mentally ticking off each trap and wondering how Wren had managed to bypass them.

Because it had to be her. The only thief—the only Retriever—I knew who could match Venec for trickiness, for speed, and for sheer determination to come back for a second try so quickly and succeed.

Almost succeed, I reminded myself. But I wasn't sure who I'd put money on, third time around. And there would be a third: Wren had her entire career resting on the fact that she always got the job done.

I'd worried about this, from the first. The day that Wren Valere and PUPI went head-to-head. Now that it was here... With the memory of the corpses in the morgue not hours old, a museum break-in seemed such a minor thing. Nobody would die over this: let them have their fun. May the sneaki-est mind win.

With the scent of Venec's body on the pillow under my cheek, I let my thoughts drift into sleepy mist and then into sleep itself.

The phone woke me about two hours later. Those two hours were incredibly important: this time my eyes opened easily, my body stretched lazily, feeling things crackle nicely into place, and I felt amazing.

The phone rang again, and I rolled over and snagged it. "Allo?"

Once, not so long ago, I'd taken phones for granted. I couldn't carry a cell phone, no, but a landline hadn't taken damage from the current in my core, beyond the occasional crackle in the line. Two years working with PUPI, using current every day, had changed that. Phones, credit cards, all the accoutrements of modern life, were not for the likes of us. I was just thankful that mass transit, for the most part, was larger than any single core, and we didn't seem to impact trains or subways without specific effort.

Most of us didn't fly much, though.

"Bonnie." Sharon, her voice sharp and clear through the receiver. "We're here."

"Here?" My brain, still sleep-fogged, didn't quite compute.

"In the lobby. They won't give us your room number, though." She sounded deeply annoyed, and I focused enough on the clock to realize that they must have left New York at Oh Hell Early to get here by now.

"Why didn't you just Transloc?" A simple ping would have gotten our location, and there wasn't any risk of being seen arriving, if they came straight to the room.

There was a long silence, and I started to laugh. Oh.

"I'm fully dressed. And alone. Room 722. Come on up."

I hung up the phone and started the little coffeemaker, hoping that I'd have time for a shower before we met with Venec.

The moment the coffee started to burble, there was a knock on the door and the faint stirring of something at the back of my awareness. I opened the door without looking out the security pinhole, letting Sharon and Pietr in, and went back to monitoring the coffee. The stirring in my head pushed a little harder.

yeah?

Venec's sense-of-self came through: exhausted but satisfied. He'd managed to retrofit the alarm system enough that he was satisfied it would hold up against another attempt, and transferred the alert from himself to whoever was their designated alarmee. I didn't envy the bastard that job one bit.

they're here I sent back. *meet you there or you here?*

A sense of intense hunger, a feeling of urgency, and an address came into my thoughts. A diner, halfway between the hotel and the museum. A safe place for discussion—Talent-owned, then. Or at least Talent-friendly. Also, the sense of where to Translocate in, to avoid appearing on top of anyone. Very Talent-friendly, then, if they had a place specifically set aside.

I poured myself a cup of coffee and went into the bathroom, leaving the other two to contemplate the fact that there was only one bed in the room.

When I came out, showered and ready to go, they both looked smugly satisfied but didn't say anything.

I didn't have the heart to tell them that nothing had happened.

Okay, nothing like that had happened, anyway.

I watched them trying not to watch me, smiling a little. Sharon was still the same as ever: lush curves and blond hair in a simple but stylish coif. I knew for a fact that she had an entire closet of tailored suits, but today she was wearing a knee-length skirt and heels under a lightweight cotton sweater that should have looked casual, but on her were still stylish. Pietr was slender and sleek in chinos and a cream button-down, with gray eyes that when I first met him had been filled with mischief but now were tempered with a sort of amused skepticism. I wondered sometimes what my pack mates saw in my eyes, but I never wondered enough to actually ask. I knew what I saw, and that was hard enough.

"Right. We're supposed to meet Venec downtown. How much did Stosser tell you?"

"Two dead bodies, both Talent, same cause of death, get our asses down here in a way that does not raise any eyebrows but do it now." Sharon recited the words as we headed down the hallway to the elevator bank. "He seems really intent on there not being any notice taken of our being here. Technically we're not even on a job—we're here on vacation, same as you. So what the hell is going on?"

Big Dog was playing this one tight. Weird, this and the missing-kid case—usually Stosser was all about making us visible. But from an investigative angle, it made sense: we stumbled onto this case, and so far there had been no chatter at all—which meant that, right now, nobody should know about the potential back history except us and Allen's cop-friend Charles. That meant that we had a chance for a totally clean investigation. More, we had a chance to figure out what was going on before anyone else twigged to the fact that someone was hunting—and killing—Talent, and had been for maybe thirty years, without being caught.

All that boiled down to one immediate fact: we probably should take the old-fashioned route to the diner, rather than Translocating. Low-key. Minimal current-use and no flashing of our kits. Which was good, since I hadn't even brought mine down.

"We don't know anything about the two victims," I said, listening to the hum of the elevator around us. Thankfully we were the only ones in it, and I was pretty sure that while hotel security might monitor with cameras, they weren't eavesdropping, too. Pretty sure.

Venec might want to teach us how to short out a recording device, next training session. I wasn't going to try it on my own, though, and sure as hell not in a moving elevator car. We all still had bad memories of an elevator car plummeting through the shaft, even though none of us had been in it.

"Okay, that's not true," I corrected myself. "We know the basics—both male, mid-forties, so pretty much prime of life. Both in excellent condition, according to the ME's report. They should have made it to their eighties at least. Standard height, standard weight, no distinguishing features or factors… They were pretty much factory-setting ordinary guys, who also happened to be Talent."

"Names?"

I handed Sharon the file, which Venec had thankfully left

by the side of the bed when he headed out this morning. I noted that they hadn't asked where he was. Not that that was unusual: we normally handled this stuff on our own.

"Warren Schultz and Ed Brock. Both unmarried, no kids. Schultz worked out of a home office, so nobody even noticed he was missing until he didn't show up for a meeting.

"The ME says he was dead for a few days when they found him." I didn't want to think about what the body had looked like before he was cleaned up. The killer restitched the cuts, but so sloppily…why sew the body up at all? Was he rushed, or uncertain, or just bad with a needle? Was the resewing a clue to finding the killer or just a useless quirk?

There are no useless pieces of information. The echo of a long-ago training session.

Yes, boss, I thought obediently. But if we don't know what it means, for now, it's useless.

"They found Brock the next morning, though," Pietr said, reading over Sharon's shoulder.

"Cause of death wasn't anything magical, but…knife wounds?" Sharon frowned.

"That's a delicate way of putting it. They were taken apart very carefully with a sharp-edged instrument. Not a scalpel but something like it."

We stopped talking as the elevator opened onto the lobby. There were only a handful of people milling about, checking in or out, but it seemed prudent to shut up until we were outside.

I'd once spent months living in a hotel, so while the others looked up and down the street for a cab—none of us were willing to risk an unfamiliar city's mass transit, that morning—I turned to the doorman and smiled. "Can you get us a cab for three, please?"

One sharp whistle-blast later, and we were being tucked

into a very clean cab with a driver who, despite appearances, spoke perfectly enunciated English. A smile and a "please" can get you far in the world. He also had a privacy board between his seat and ours, and after giving him the address, we made use of it.

"When you say taken apart, you mean...?" Pietr had the file now, having taken it from Sharon when we were in public and she couldn't make a fuss. But instead of looking through it—and there were pictures, unfortunately—he turned to me, waiting for an answer.

I thought about making him look at the photos for himself, but there was no point.

"I mean, they were taken apart. With a knife that had a definite current-signature, although I suppose that could be from something as basic as a sharp-edge spell." I said it, but I didn't believe it. What Venec and I had sensed was something different, less identifiable. "The bodies were sliced open deliberately, like the guy was cutting on the dotted line. The entire body, neck to ankles, and their insides scraped around under the skin."

"Cut open?" Sharon wasn't getting it. Pietr did.

"Vivisection." The word was flat and hard, and the hand holding the file tightened so much his knuckles went white.

"Yeah." I'd been trying not to think about that, avoiding the word. About the one bit of info I'd only discovered in the file, not during my examination. According to the ME's report, they'd been cut open, dissected, while they were still alive.

We'd seen a lot, the past two years. Murder for money. Fraud. Obsession and betrayal and just out-and-out meanness. But this...this was something new.

I was suddenly very glad I hadn't ditched the rules and tried to glean for emotions.

"Vivisection is a scientific pro—" Sharon started, then stopped. "Ugh."

Yeah.

"And someone did that to them...." Sharon, interestingly, was having trouble dealing with it. Usually she was the least squeamish of us all. "I'm guessing he did it without anesthesia."

I was guessing that, too. "Generally, the kind of person who does this, I'm thinking they don't worry much about the suffering they're inflicting. In fact, that may be the point."

"So it's not just a serial killer. It's a sadistic serial killer who likes sharp, shiny things. Joy." Pietr was still the king of deadpan, out of all of us.

"And the number ten," Sharon added. "Ten bodies, ten years between...which probably brings in a whole 'nother level of pathology to the discussion. I don't know about you, but I'm not qualified to even talk about that."

"Venec will find someone who is." If he hadn't been distracted by the alarm system, he would have already, I suspected. I made a mental note to mention it to him, discreetly, when we got to the diner.

"So what do you want us to do? You're lead on this."

The cab turned a corner and stopped. Apparently, we had arrived. Pietr paid the guy, and we piled out, the question put on hold for the moment. Which was good, because I still wasn't sure how to answer it.

The place was a classic diner, from the metallic front to the old guy sitting on a stool behind the glass-countered register and the harassed-looking waitress who took us to the back booth, where Venec was waiting.

He looked tired and rumpled, and I felt the immediate urge to go sit next to him, to let my presence be a comfort.

And for the first time since the Merge hit us, that's exactly what I did. He didn't seem to react to my sitting next to him on the booth's bench, but there was a slight, barely notice-able easing of his body tension. Anyone else I'd have said they weren't aware of it, but this was Benjamin Venec, so I knew he'd noticed. But he didn't comment on it, didn't look at me, didn't even let his elbow brush against me.

I felt welcomed, anyway.

"Glad you two made it. Has Bonnie briefed you?"

Pietr put the folder on the table, next to the pot of coffee that was already waiting. "Yeah. But let me see if I have it down. Two bodies, killed within a week of each other, sliced up like lab animals, and we think this is the work of a guy who has done it at least to ten others before in two different cities, which means if he holds to pattern we have another eight bodies waiting to be found before he moves on?"

"Conjecture and theory," Venec said. "But, yes, that about sums it up. Except the fact, which you omitted, that the vic-tims were all Talent."

Pietr's expression didn't change, but the fingers of the hand resting on the folder twitched. Venec still had a way of mak-ing us feel like rookies sometimes.

"How strong were they?" That was one thing that wasn't in the examiner's report. There was no way to tell that after someone was dead. When all the other electrical impulses powering the human body stopped, so did the ability to power current. It took a little longer to fade entirely than, say, a heartbeat, but nothing lasted once the corpse was cold. My mentor used to say that he thought the myth of vampires came from that idea that there were some who could hold current even after death, keep their hearts pumping postmortem.

"You think that's connected to their deaths?" He wasn't questioning my assumption, just asking if that was my as-sumption.

"I don't know." I reached for the coffeepot, pouring a dose into one of the heavy white mugs that bore a startling resemblance to the ones at the cop shop. A liberal splash of milk and two sugars, and my tongue started to forgive me for the hotel-room crap. "I was just thinking about the girls in the Park."

"The what?" Sharon looked up, at that.

"Oh, right." It seemed like a week ago to me, but it had only been, god, twenty-four hours? "Stosser had me track down a missing girl. It ended up being almost stupid-easy, mainly because the fatae seemed to have an interest in getting her home, too. Rorani took me to where she was—yeah, I know, but believe me, that's almost the least weird part of it. The girl-child, she was part of a bunch of girls, most of them older—seven and fourteen and twenty-one were the points. And, yeah, you're thinking what I thought—old magic." I lifted my left hand palm up, indicating that I didn't have any definite proof, one way or the other. "I didn't stick around to get the details, but there's a woman living in the Park who's gathering these girls into a coven, telling them that if they clap their hands hard enough or some crap, she'll be able to turn them into magic users."

Sharon looked puzzled. "And this connects to the case down here…how?"

"It doesn't. But I guess it's been in the back of my head, about how we look at each other not by money or looks, at least not all the time, but about power." Not consciously, but one of those things that only comes to the surface when you have enough data points to make a picture. "A woman approached me this week back home. Someone I've known for years. She's Council, high up. She might have been flirting with me—god knows she did that before. But when I thought about responding I also thought about power and leverage and usefulness. And it was all based on the fact that she's pretty high-res and respected, and we could use that. And I know, not for a fact but a pretty good suss, that she's interested in me not just because I'm cute, but because I've gotten stronger since she knew me before. Both in current-use and in allies."

Sharon shook her head, shifting in her seat, crossing one leg over the other and, from Pietr's grimace, kicking him in the process. "Sorry. I'm still not seeing the connection."

I tried to find the words to explain why these things kept crisscrossing in my brain, but couldn't.

"There may not be one. I don't know. I just keep flicking back to it, and when my brain does that—"

"There's usually a good reason," Pietr finished. "Yeah, all right."

"I think it's important that we know how good the dead guys were. And the ten dead in San Diego, too, if we can."

I didn't even mention Montreal. The Canadian Talents were…not organized would be a kind way of putting it. I doubted, twenty years later, if there was any record at all, beyond what a friend or relative remembered, and getting information through traditional channels, across international borders… By the time we got anything, the killer would have moved on already.

"If the killer is targeting based on their skill level, that would be useful to know," Venec agreed. "Sharon, your research skills are best—you work with that. And get Nicky on it, too."

So much for me being point. Then it struck me: Venec had called Nick, Nicky. He never did that. But I did, all the time.

It wasn't enough to make me smile, not with a killer on the loose, but I did file the fact away for later teasing.

"Pietr, Bonnie wanted you to look at the bodies."

He grimaced and added more sugar to his coffee. "Gee, thanks."

"Relax, we've seen worse. I just want to see if you pick up anything more than what I did, which is why—before you ask—I haven't told you what I picked up." He knew they were cut open with a knife, but just looking at the bodies would have told him that. I wanted to know if he sensed anything beyond the physical, either about the victims…or the killer. Or the knife, for that matter. The knife still bothered me. Why were Venec and I both picking up a sense of current from the knife, when all other trace was wiped clean?

"What kind of a timeline are we working with here? If this is the same killer—and we don't know that for certain—then how long did he stretch his spree? Are we talking one a day, or…?"

"I spoke with Andrulis this morning," Venec said, ignoring the fact that it was barely 8:00 a.m. right then. "The previous murders were committed over a period of nine weeks. Time of death for our two was estimated to be five days apart, and the last body's been in the morgue for a day, so if we don't move fast…"

"We're going to have another body on the slab by the end of the week," Sharon finished.

Suddenly, my coffee tasted metallic in my throat, and I put the mug down. Sharon's blond head dipped slightly, her chin toward her chest, and Pietr's body didn't move, but there was an audible sense of slumping in his presence.

"Stop it." Venec's voice was hard but not harsh. "None of that is your fault. I know you people are good, damn good, but you can't stop a killer you didn't even know about twenty-four hours ago from killing twenty-four hours ago."

The fact that he was right didn't change anything.

"Fine. If guilt will make you work harder, then use it. If not, dump it now. Cholis, Torres, get in gear—they're expecting you at the morgue. The sooner you get that done, the sooner the families can have their deceased back."

When he used our last names like that, it was like a switch flicked in our brains, and the guilt was replaced by determination. Or it did in mine, anyway, and from the way Pietr stood up, I think it did for him, too. I wasn't sure if it was psychological manipulation or just good management—or if there was any real difference—but it worked and that was good.

Venec was right. We couldn't do anything for those who were already dead except make sure nobody else joined them.

We left Sharon sitting at the table with Venec—leaving them with the bill for the coffee we didn't finish.

I still had my ID badge from the earlier visit shoved into my pocket, but we had to stop and check in, anyway, to get Pietr cleared. Once his name was checked off against the list, we went on into the main area, where a white-coated lab tech waited for us, looking both impatient and bored.

"This way."

No *please* in that request. We fell in behind her without comment, walking not through the back hallway but the main corridor, filled with people in lab coats, people in ordinary office-wear, and the occasional uniformed cops, all intent on being somewhere else, and not paying us a bit of attention.

Pietr looked around, his forehead scrunching up a little. "What?"

"I thought it would be more…"

I waited, then prompted, "A little more…?"

"I don't know. More something other than what it is."

I knew exactly what he meant. "It's an office."

"Where dead people are."

"Well, yeah. You saw the sign that said County Morgue?"

Our escort ignored us: I got the feeling that she was used

to people nattering uncomfortably as they were being led past rooms filled with dead bodies.

We were brought into the same room as before, only this time there were no bodies in the open: everything was locked away. My imagination pictured a walk-in freezer with bodies stacked in permafrost, even though I knew—now, anyway—that there was no such thing.

"Shultz and Brock, right?"

"Yes, please." I hoped so, anyway. The thought of them wheeling out the wrong bodies was too close to farce for me to handle right now. The coffee was sitting badly in my stomach, and my gut let out an embarrassing gurgle that echoed too loudly in the empty room.

"Here." Pietr handed me something; I took it automatically, not even looking. It was a cylinder pack of Tums, already opened.

"My stomach's been crap the past six months."

I hadn't known. Once, we'd known everything about each other, the original five. We'd lived in each other's pockets, gotten drunk together, bitched about cases, and cried on each other's shoulders…even after Lou joined us and we started getting busy…but not so much, these days. I suddenly, jarringly, missed those days.

"You okay?" I asked now.

"Yeah. Doc says I need to eat more roughage and reduce the stress in my life."

I wasn't sure if you were supposed to laugh in a morgue. "Yeah. Good luck with that."

The clattering of wheels brought me back to the moment, and our escort came back with a body on a gurney. It was still covered with a sheet, the edges hanging just far enough over the side to hide the flesh but not disguising the metallic coldness of the gurney below.

"Brock," she announced.

"Thank you."

Pietr hesitated, as though expecting something to happen—a more formal introduction? a list of instructions?—then stepped forward and drew the sheet down, gently, starting at the face and moving the sheet all the way to its knees. I chewed on two antacid tablets, concentrating on the gritty chalk between my teeth, and tried not to think about the fact that the db's skin color had changed enough in twenty-four hours for me to notice the difference.

"Male. Mid-forties, maybe. In decent shape before death, based on what the muscle tissue looks like. Not heavily built but not a little guy, either. Subduing him long enough to… Hard to tell if there were any restraint marks on hands or legs… Bonnie?"

My memory supplied the details of the report without having to think about it. "Marks on the shoulders and upper arms indicated restraint of some sort, although it was impossible to indicate the form. Bruising around the ankles suggest that some form of soft restraint was used on the legs." Not rope: maybe cloth tape.

"If current had been used to hold them down, there would be signs of it," Pietr said, looking more carefully at the skin. "No bruising, no indication of burst blood vessels or any kind of scorch marks." Current, like electricity, burns. We can handle it—that's what makes us Talent—but when it's used as a restraint, there are always traces left behind.

I realized, uneasily, that I'd gotten used to the antiseptic, over-cleaned smell of the air inside the building, so much so that when a waft of fresh air came in from an open door or window somewhere, my stomach roiled at that, not the tang of disinfectants that had clogged my sinuses a moment before.

"Two different series of cuts. The examiner's work here—"

his hand moved over the torso, hovering inches above the skin "—and the killer's work here. The examiner's hand was steadier, which would make sense since his subject was already dead. Less likely to struggle or resist, even with restraints. But also…" He paused, then finished, "Also, the examiner was just doing a job. He knew what he was looking for and what he was probably going to find."

"The killer…wasn't?" He'd picked up more than I had, although I'd been drawn more to the knife than the bodies.

"Gut feeling," Pietr replied. "Just…gut feeling."

There was a deep sigh, the sound of him going into fugue state, and I waited, slipping the antacids into my jacket pocket. The tang of fresh air faded, and I was aware again of the smells layering one on top of each other, like a strata of stink.

"Our killer…was…not excited. Not anticipating." His hand moved lower, and I could feel his current relax, which seemed contradictory, but that was how Pietr worked: the more he focused, the less you noticed him. "He was…hopeful."

"Hopeful of what?" I kept my voice even, not wanting to break him from his concentration. Emotional gleaning was verboten, but Pietr, of all of us, could keep his distance, not get caught up in it. And he wasn't going after the victim, so that should save him from any death throes. I hoped.

I stayed alert, anyway.

The woman who had led us in had disappeared; I hadn't even noticed her leaving. That let us talk more openly: unlike Andrulis, we had no idea if she knew what we were or about the *Cosa* at all. It was strange interacting with people on the job where that was an issue….

"I don't know. I can't even tell what kind of hope it was."

That surprised me, although I wasn't sure why. "There are different kinds of hope?"

Pietr moved his hands down the corpse's legs, then back

up, hovering over the stomach. "Of course there are. There's joyful and painful and the sort of sick hope when you're expecting bad news...."

It made sense when he explained it that way. But I was still trying to figure out why someone would be hopeful when he cut into someone living...

"Like a surgeon, maybe, hoping to... No, that doesn't make any sense. What—"

"Hey!"

We both turned at the shout, since it had clearly been directed at us. A woman stood there, dressed in the kind of suit that, to me, labeled her "midlevel admin and self-conscious of status." I groaned inwardly. Here came trouble.

stay quiet I pinged to Pietr. Probably needlessly: from the way her gaze refocused on me, he had already faded from sight.

"What are you doing here? Who let you in?"

"We have passes," I started to say, showing her the plastic bit hanging around my neck.

"Of course you do. You couldn't have gotten down here without one. But why are you here? Who gave you permission to inspect a body?" She picked up my pass between two fingers and inspected it, but since it was legitimate, she couldn't find anything wrong.

She peered over my shoulder at the body we had been examining and made a reproving sound. "You need to leave now."

Our very first case, we'd been looking over a piece of evidence when security came to kick us out. Then, Nick had made with the Jedi mind tricks and convinced the man what we were supposed to be there, that we were legitimate, and we got out without being arrested. I was crap at that sort of thing, and Pietr was effectively useless right now, so despite the fact that we were legitimate and we did have permission to be there, I merely ducked my head under the woman's wrath and let her escort us out.

Andrulis could explain to her later why he put two civilians on the visitors' list. That wasn't my headache.

"We didn't get to see the other body."

I leaned against the wall of the building, out of the direct flow of traffic, and watched people going about their business, seemingly oblivious to the death behind the building's facade. I couldn't decide if it was a good thing or not that people could accept the presence of the dead so easily.

"It was a few days older—odds are you wouldn't have gotten anything more from it." Although it had been the first—

"Oh, god."

"What?"

"We've been assuming that these are the first. What if they're not, and they just haven't found the others yet?"

"Jesus. Torres."

He leaned against the wall next to me, his arms crossed over his chest, and we stared out at the street. It was greener here than in New York, and the streets were less crowded. Or maybe it just felt that way to us, here and now.

"Y'know, it doesn't matter," I decided. "The cops are looking, and we can put the word out about anyone going missing, but we need to look at the evidence we have, not what might still be out there. Like Venec said, we can't do anything about what might already have happened."

"So." Pietr drummed his fingers absently on his knee, as though he were counting off. "Hopefulness. And a scalpel with an unknown current-signature that gives you the wiggies. That's what we've got that the police don't."

As evidence went, that wasn't much. But it was what we had.

"The knife... The trace was part of it, not just a smudge

from the person using it." The more I thought about it, the more certain I was about that. "My first thought had been current-forged, but it could be a sharpening spell that's been maintained long enough to work its way into the metal." Metal took to current the way a pole called down lightning, only current tended to stick.

"Are there metalsmiths who make knives with current?" Pietr hummed under his breath. "They'd be lonejack or gypsy, then, probably." Pietr's family were gypsy—more clannish than lonejacks, but not willing to toe the Council line. "I'll check on that. I'd like a current-blade myself."

"Yeah, so the cops can frisk and arrest you?" The banter made me feel a little better, distancing myself from the contents of the rooms behind us, the tables and boxes filled with bodies unclaimed, unnamed, or just waiting to be stamped "officially deceased."

"There are so many reasons a weapon could pick up a signature. I'm more concerned about the emotions I picked up. Hoping…what?"

"If we knew that, we'd know motivation," I said. My nose caught the scent of a grease truck down the block, and my stomach rumbled. A little too early for cart food, probably. But I'd have to eat and remind Pietr to, too. If they'd had breakfast, it had been hours ago.

"We know that all the victims have been Talent. But we don't know if the killer was. Even a Null can use a knife that's been spell-cast, with or without knowing it. Hell, we don't even know if the killer's human!"

I thought about the idea that a fatae could be doing this. It was certainly possible—and had historical precedent. "God, what a mess that would be." Rorani and the Fey might be willing to work with us now, but if we accused a fatae of going wholesale on humans…everyone would be protecting their own backsides and leaving ours out to hang. "You're the one who gleaned emotion—what do you think?"

Pietr signed, a long, slow exhale, as he ran over the memory. "Human," he said finally. "It felt human."

I thought about the sensation I'd picked up from the cuts and agreed. Which was disturbing, actually. I'd rather someone who could do that to another living being—many living beings—would feel a little less human.

"Is there a spell that would be able to show him?"

I had a nearly perfect memory, so the pack tended to use me as a portable library for spells and research. I let my brain ponder the question for a minute. "Every spell and cantrip I know requires that we have something with a connection to the subject. If we had the weapon, we could force something out of it. But if we had the weapon…"

Every Talent put their own mark on their magic, called a signature. The longer they held current in their core, the stronger the signature. If our killer was a Talent and had been intensely emotional while killing…it was almost inevitable that trace would be left on the weapon, too.

But we didn't have the weapon, only the small bit I'd been able to feel of it, and that…hadn't felt right. A signature was… like a scent. You could take the same perfume, and it would smell different on each person, becoming distinct, so you could pick it out of a dark room full of other smells. The feeling I'd picked up under the cuts had been…more like a low rumble of noise, not distinct enough to identify.

"Damn it." Pietr wasn't much for cursing, so the swear caught me by surprise. "He's out there. He's still killing. And we're just sitting here…."

I felt his frustration myself, too. By now we should have had something tangible, something we could use to pin down the next step, find the next clue. We didn't always win, but damn it, we didn't just sit around and wait!

anything? I reached out to Venec, hoping to hear that Sharon and Nick had better luck with their research, or come up with something that would slot into what Pietr and I had and give us some kind of a lead. There was an echoing sort of silence, which was unusual between the two of us, these days, and then a response. But not the sort I was expecting.

get back here. now

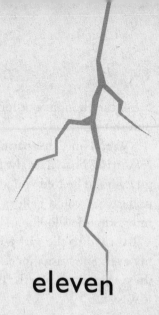

eleven

A summons like that, you don't screw around with finding a cab and risking city traffic. We found a quiet space behind one of the pillars guarding the entrance, out of direct sight of anyone passing on the street, and waited until the entrance itself was clear. With a quick visual confirm from Venec that the inner hallway was also clear, we Translocated back to the one place we knew well enough: the hotel.

The room was surprisingly crowded. Venec, as usual, was holding up a wall, his arms crossed against his chest. He was utterly still in a way that meant something was wrong, but I'd known that from the feel of his ping. Sharon was perched on the desk, her shoes off and legs swinging gently. When she was calm, she was utterly still. She wasn't calm now.

The surprise guests were a tall, handsome man with dark hair liberally shot with gray and an equally tall, dark-skinned girl.

I knew them both.

"Sergei. Is Wren all right? Is—" Had trying to run through Venec's security wall gotten her hurt? I thought it but didn't

speak the thought out loud. If Ben's system had hurt her...
Shit shit shit.

"Wren's fine," her partner told me, his gaze the same warm,
reassuring brown as always. Sergei Didier was the kind of
guy who, if he told you it would be okay as the Titanic sank
under you, you'd believe him. "But we seem to have an...
interesting development."

I turned to the girl with him. "Ellen?" She didn't meet
my eyes. She wasn't meeting anyone's eyes, in fact, staring at
the carpet like it was the most fascinating thing in the room.
It wasn't.

I checked her over once, visually, looking for any injuries,
anything that might explain her behavior, then looked at
Venec, who shook his head slightly, meaning that he didn't
know what was going on, either.

That meant Sergei had brought Ellen down here himself.
He was a Null, and Wren was crap at Translocating—and
Ellen didn't have a clue about Talent, much less any training,
so there was no way she'd done it.

That meant they'd taken the train—or driven. Knowing
Sergei, I was pretty sure he could drive, New Yorker or not.

And they'd come to us, not Wren, who was still somewhere in the area. Had known to come to us...how? More
to the point, why?

I shook off my dithering and just asked. "What happened?"

"It would seem, if I have my terminology right," Sergei
said, his voice slow and deliberate and just a little too aware of
the show he was making, "that our girl here is a storm-seer."

You know that old saying about being able to hear a pin
drop? It's not true. When it gets that quiet, all you can hear
is the sound of the blood in your skull, thump-thump-
thumping.

"Bloody hell," Pietr said in a whisper, his voice somewhere

between disbelief and awe, and then the sound came back, cranked to eleven.

"There hasn't been a certified aeromancer in…" My memory failed me. "Fifty years, maybe. Maybe more."

"Yes. That's what I was told, too." Sergei's voice was still dry, still enjoying the show a little too much, but there was an undercurrent of worry there, too.

"What happened? And why bring her to us?" Venec tried to take back control of the situation, uncrossing his arms and stepping away from the wall.

"I saw Wren." Ellen lifted her head and looked at me. Her eyes were filled with misery that made my heart—admittedly an easy target—hurt for her. "I saw Wren, and I saw another man. Tall, pale, with hair like a night-candle.

"They were both dead."

An aeromancer is the fancy name for a storm-seer, someone who sees the past—and the future—through pure current. I could scry reasonably well and had more than a touch of the kenning that told me when things were happening, but those were just trickles, faint awareness of the patterns that were flowing through our present, hitting the immediate past and future. I couldn't actually see anything, and not very far into the future—and not really into the past at all.

Ellen had seen Wren, whom she knew, and a man who could only be our other Big Dog, the flame-headed, pale-as-a-satanic-candle himself, Ian Stosser.

And they were, she claimed, dead.

"Not yet." It wasn't a question Pietr was asking, but Ellen shook her head, anyway. "Not yet. But soon. I don't know how I know, but I know."

Her voice was shaking, and she still wouldn't look at anyone except me, but the certainty was in her voice like bed-rock. You could ground yourself in it.

Venec already had that gone-away look on his face that meant he was pinging Ian. "Where's Wren?" I asked Sergei. "No, don't give me bullshit. I know she's down here—she's making a run on the museum."

Sergei opened his mouth to deny everything, and then I could see the pieces start to click in his brain.

I headed off any questions he might have, while Venec was preoccupied. "Not me, not us officially. A side project of Venec's. Which is all fun and games when it was just them butting heads but not now." Not if someone was kenning her and the Big Dog being dead. "You need to call her in now."

"I tried." His voice was a growl of frustration. "I left a message for her the minute Ellen had her—" he was about to say *fit,* I could sense it, then changed it to "—vision. But she didn't respond, and…"

And he was a Null and couldn't ping her, and she was Talent and working, so wouldn't have any electronics on her, certainly not a cell phone. So he came to us.

"How did you know where to find us?"

"Your office manager."

Lou. Of course.

"She didn't know where Stosser was but said that Venec was down here. I would have called the hotel, but…" He sat down now at the desk chair that had been pulled away from where Sharon was sitting. "I thought this was something that needed to be dealt with in person."

Emotions caused current-spike. Phones were durable, in the short-term, but, no, he was right. This… And Lou would have thought it better to hear it from him, not her, so she hadn't told us anything. I wasn't sure I agreed with that, and I was pretty sure Venec was pissed.

"A storm-seer." Sharon didn't know Wren and had a supreme confidence that Ian could beat even death itself, I guess, because she was more stuck on Ellen's ability than anything else. "And we— Nobody knew about her until now?"

"She didn't know about herself until now," I said. "Ellen, are you okay?"

I guess nobody had thought to ask her that before, because she just crumbled like a cookie, her face scrunching up and her body collapsing in on itself, falling to her knees on the carpet before anyone could react.

"Oh, shit." I was next to her before anyone else: when I looked up, expecting help, my brave cohorts were staring at us like we'd just grown wings or something. Only Sergei came forward, kneeling and putting a gentle hand on Ellen's shoulder. But his expression, turned to me, said plainly he had no idea what to do.

Hell, neither did I. Bad enough Ellen had grown up not knowing what she was or why things happened around her. Then to be abandoned, the way her family obviously had abandoned her, and not wanted by the group where you were supposed to fit in… All that could sucker-punch anyone. But then suddenly to learn that you were not only special but rare?

The scullery-maid-turned-princess story might sound like a fairy tale, but I could see where it came with its own special hell.

"Ellen. Ellen, look at me."

Dammit, she was one of those women who looked good when they cried. I'd hate her if I didn't feel so bad for her.

"I know this is all tough, and confusing, and things I can't even begin to understand. But I promised you we'd see you through this, remember?"

"You left, and then Wren left, and he…" She sniffled and

her words were lost, but I had a pretty good idea what she was saying.

"He's not one of us, no, but he knows us. And he knows what it's like to be surrounded by people like us and not know what the hell is going on." I was guessing there, actually, but it was an educated guess.

"I don't want this. I thought I did but I don't. I just want… I want…" Her voice trailed off into messy hiccups. I looked up and tried to catch Sharon's eye—she had way more of a capable mom mode than I did. But she shook her head and pulled away, backing up without actually moving, her eyes wide with a sort of nuh-uh denial. Pietr looked like he wanted to help but didn't know what to do any more than I did.

Venec was behind me, but I could feel him through the Merge, as though he were whispering in my ear.

we need her. we need to know what she saw. if it's anything we really need to worry about or not

Because it might not be. If she was a storm-seer, she was totally untrained, and that meant she could have misinterpreted what she saw, or seen it wrong, or…

I'm purely incapable of telling comforting lies to myself. Storm-seers didn't see things "wrong," and they didn't misinterpret. They couldn't. That's what made them seers.

"Ellen, I know this is hard. Believe me, I know. I've got a touch of it myself, so I know how scary it can be."

That got her attention.

"But you have a gift, a lot stronger than mine, and it's maybe given us a warning that could save lives. So we need to know everything you saw, okay? Even if it doesn't make any sense to you, it might to us."

I waited for her to take all that in. "Can you do that?"

A long, shuddery breath, and out of somewhere the glint of steel shone through. "Yeah. Yeah, I can do that."

She found her way back to her feet, and I followed her every inch, ready if she needed me but not touching her. Not because I thought that was the right thing to do, but because I was terrified of doing the wrong thing.

"Water?"

She took the glass from Pietr's hand gratefully, chugging it down like she was parched. It was probably going to give her a stomachache, but we'd worry about that later.

"All right. Tell me what you remember, in as much detail as you can. Don't worry about it making sense. Just talk it through."

"I was sitting in Sergei's living room. Drinking tea."

Of course she was. Sergei made tea like pups made coffee: instinctively in times of both relaxation and stress.

"I was looking at the pattern of the cup," Ellen said, her voice already calmer, more meditative. "It looked fragile, but it felt sturdy, strong. And I was going to ask him about it, where it was made, how old it was, because it felt maybe old, and there was a surge in the building."

"They were running tests on the alarm system that morning," Sergei said quietly, so quietly I barely heard it, but each word clear in my ears. Neat trick, that, for a Null.

"And then I saw them. Not doing anything, not anywhere, just standing there. Wren and the man. They weren't looking at each other. I don't think they were even aware of each other... No, they were looking away from each other. And I knew...I knew that they were dead.

"And then I dropped the cup. And it broke, and they were gone."

"That's it?" Sharon sounded disappointed.

"Sometimes that's all you get," I said, but I was a little surprised, too. Scrying could give you vague shit and suggestions, yeah, but I'd thought a seer would have something more...

specific. Maybe it was because she was so new to it all—or maybe the trigger, the current-rush in his building, hadn't been strong enough or wasn't clean enough. Aeromancers traditionally sourced wild. Of course, "traditional" meant over a hundred years ago, with less shaped current available, so who knew…

"It doesn't help, does it?" Ellen sounded like she was going to cry again.

"What was he wearing? The man, what kind of clothing was he wearing?" Venec's question made her close her eyes and think back.

"Dark clothing. They made his hair look brighter, like it was backlit. And it was…it was moving, like there was a breeze."

"It was loose?"

"Mmm-hmm. No. Part of it was tied back, but strands were loose. Dark pants and a jacket, tailored, and a shirt…a white shirt? Not white, no, but pale-colored. He looked annoyed."

Stosser had three clothing styles: crunchy-granola jeans and flannel, when he was thinking hard; casual metro-chic for normal days; and obscenely expensive suit-and-tie. This sounded like the third, and that meant he had been dealing with the Council. The fact that his hair was moving meant not that it was windy, but that his core was up. Ian Stosser was a powerhouse on a good day. When he was upset… Yeah, suit and annoyed equaled Council. Or his sister. Oh, hell.

"Ben?"

"No Council meetings, not that I knew about. But you know he doesn't tell me everything. Last I heard from him, you two were closeted with the new clients. I have no idea what he's up to right now. What about Valere? Where's she?"

Sergei coughed into his fist, and I bit back an utterly inappropriate giggle.

Never let it be said that Benjamin Venec wasn't quick on the uptake, even half-exhausted and worrying about other things. "Goddammit." He ran a hand through his hair, ruffling it even more, and glared at me. "And you knew? Were you going to tell me this little fact anytime soon?"

As always, when we got into it, everyone else in the room disappeared. I felt an answering flicker of current rise out of my core—not offensive or defensive but definitely reactive. "Would it have made a difference? And, anyway, you were having fun. Knowing who it was would be cheating."

"That's not cheating. It's…" He looked irritated and sounded annoyed, but I could feel the resigned amusement simmering in him, so I just waited. "Next time, if I happen to be going up against The Wren, please let me know, all right?"

"Gotcha." Next time, I intended to know nothing and say less.

"If you two are quite done?" Sharon asked, impatient, and the connection broke, and we were in a room filled with people again.

"So you can get hold of Wren, or no?" I asked Sergei.

"No. Not until she contacts me. And she won't until the job is done—particularly if she's got to restructure her plans. She'll hole up until she figures it out."

They'd been partners for a long time, according to gossip, since Wren was a teenager. Whatever scenario they'd worked out, I wasn't going to question it. "And if I were to ping her?"

"She might listen…or she might block you out. It depends on what she's doing and if she knows that your…that Venec here is the one defending the museum."

"Damn." But it made sense. We weren't friends and former building-mates now, but the competition—the ones trying

to ruin her perfect record. She wouldn't listen to us, suspecting a trap, or at very least, a distraction.

And normally, she'd be right.

"Is there anyone she'd listen to?"

"Is there ever?"

"What about PB?"

Sergei sighed. "He left for South America yesterday."

Really? Huh. I thought he'd given up on couriering, but
maybe not. "All right. For now, we just have to trust to her
own native suspicion and caution. I assume Lou's already trying to find Stosser?"

"I suggested that would be a good idea, yes. If she's actually doing it…"

"She is." Pietr, who had gone silent during most of this,
had apparently been busy. "She and Nick are hunting him
down, while Nifty covers the ongoing assignments and deals
with everything else. As soon as he resurfaces enough to hear
a ping, we'll have him."

You weren't supposed to ignore a ping, but Stosser was the
Big Dog, and rules Venec made to keep us in line didn't seem
to apply to him. If he wasn't responding to Ben, he wasn't
going to respond to a pup, not unless we all mobbed him.

"Boss?"

Sharon looked at Venec, asking the same question I'd come
to: Was it time to mob Stosser?

"We don't know enough," he said. "He's better off undis-
tracted, whatever he's doing."

She had called him, and he had gone. He always did, and
he always would. But it was becoming tiresome.

"You're acting like a spoiled five-year-old, upset because
she didn't get a pony on her birthday."

She sat comfortably in her chair, in the town house that was clearly not hers; the decor was all wrong for her usual tastes, too exotic and crowded with knickknacks. It had a decidedly masculine feel. Masculine and magical. And darker than Ian Stosser was comfortable associating with his baby sister.

"I am acting like an adult, determined to do what is necessary to prevent something terrible from happening."

He tore his attention away from a particularly fierce African mask on the wall and looked at her. "You've been saying that for three years now. No, four. Tell me, Aden—what terrible things have happened? When has the sky fallen?"

Her face moved through a variety of emotions, settling on scorn. "It's a joke to you, isn't it?"

"No, Aden. Never a joke. You've seen the good we can do. You were part of it!" She had helped him corral the trickster imp, setting up the capture and punishment of a man who had imprisoned his wife and son for years with magic.

"That was different."

Different: because it had involved a nonhuman and a Null. She had no problem with them being tracked down, identified, and punished by external sources. Only Talent should be exempt. Only Council should be allowed to judge Council.

"We're not special, Aden. We're just human. And we need to be held liable for what we do—to everyone, not just a star chamber. You knew that once."

"No, that was always your folly. I interpret a jury of her peers differently."

It was an old disagreement, and one they were unlikely to settle now, if ever. But the new twist in her argument had him particularly concerned.

He picked up the folders that were on the desk, the simple silver sigil pressed into the paper unmistakable, and waved them at her, feeling frustration build. "Aden, you can't, you didn't... Aden, sorcerers? Using their town house—what deal have you made, Aden? Why? They're extreme even by Council standards!"

She didn't even glance at the folders. "Use the tools that come to hand. Isn't that what we were taught?"

They had been. The Stossers were pragmatic, practical, and focused at all times. It was their inheritance, their destiny. Not to lead—they had no desire for the spotlight, his gift of charisma notwithstanding—but to guide, to take whatever form was needed and shape the future into the history they desired. They, meaning Council. The Stossers had been Council since the first generation on American soil.

Ian might have changed his desires but not his means. For him to take offense at Aden's actions would be to be offended at his own, to find the way he had manipulated and shoved his PUPs offensive, disgusting.

Self-disgust was nothing new to Ian Stosser.

"Ian, I know you're struggling."

His spine stiffened, although his face remained as much a mask as the objects on the wall.

"There's no shame attached if you let it go. As you say, you did good. You can take what you've learned and put it to better use. I'll help you...."

"More acceptable to your usage, you mean. Aden, do you really think shame, fear of admitting failure, is what keeps me going?"

Of course she did. She couldn't imagine what else might drive him so hard.

The faint touch of a ping slid across his awareness, searching for him, sliding off his walls, and was gone. Lou. Whatever it was, it could wait.

"Aden." His entire world had narrowed to her, this woman who was still, to him, a little girl, looking for her big brother to somehow save the day. "Don't do this. We've just put the

Cosa back together—what you're doing could destroy it forever."

"Destroy it? Or remake it into what it should have been? I'm not a monster, Ian. Despite what you're thinking. I don't want to rule the world or cast down others...but there's no reason to let others rule us. Not when they cannot understand what we do, what we are. I want to protect that, too. Ian."

He stalked to the far end of the room and stared out the window at the city below. She must hate it here, the Schuylkill River barely visible in the distance. Aden always returned to the water, either a lake large enough you couldn't see across or the ocean. Endless waves, washing away at the shore. Patience and the long view. He, on the other hand, saw all too well what happened in the short-term, the immediate world.

Two sides of the same coin, and therefore unable to ever see a problem the same way.

"These people..." He gestured around him, indicating the owners of this town house and everything it represented, "if they are allowed to win, it will be Chicago all over again."

"What happened in Chicago was the proper order of things."

"No, it was not." But he said it without heat: had she agreed with him, ever, she would have been on his side, supporting what he did with PUPI, not trying to stop him at every turn.

"We allowed killers to walk free, Aden. Not just killers— coldblooded murderers. Whatever you might think about our origins, our destiny..." His voice dropped. "They murdered children, Aden."

A shudder went through her slender body, and her head, crowned with red hair a darker auburn than his own, dipped toward her chest. "It was an accident, a terrible accident. Allowing others to judge, dragging the story out into the public eye, would not have changed a thing."

His jaw hurt from not clenching his teeth, from biting back the words he wanted to say, from not taking her and shaking her until some decency, some compassion broken open in her brilliant mind. "It was murder. And I will never stop until I can prove it and force them to justice. No matter how many years have passed."

"And when you do that, you will destroy the Council that absolved them, as well. You will shatter the Council itself, to defend those who are already dead."

The crux of their argument, finally out and spoken. "If it comes to that. Yes."

If she could strike him down now, she would. If she could bind him somehow, stop him, she would. She had tried; tried and failed. She had tried to strike at him through his pups, the embodiment of his goal, and failed there, as well—and in the failing, been censured by the very organization she fought so hard to protect.

His heart broke for her, a little. But only a little.

He had only one defense left. "If you stand with these people, Aden, these sorcerers. If you stand with them and their goals...I do not know you. You are no sister of mine."

"It's too late, Ian. You're going to have to be the one who yields."

He stared at her, serene again. "I won't."

"I know."

Two sides of the coin; but only one could come out on top. He kissed her on the cheek, a caress she allowed, and let himself out, back onto the street.

He did not look up to see if she watched him walk away.

twelve

Two years ago, the news that a storm-seer had foreseen the deaths of both my boss and my friend might have freaked me out. After those two years, seeing what we had seen, I was still freaked out but functional.

"So, we have two cases. Find a serial killer before anyone else dies, and figure out who wants to kill the boss, and stop it." And Wren. Who would want to kill a Retriever? Hire them, fire them, scare them off, yeah. But kill? Okay, this was Wren—that was a more complicated question. But the fact that Ellen saw them both in the same vision suggested they were connected. Didn't it?

Venec lifted three fingers, then folded one down halfway. "Two and a half cases, really. If we're counting Valere's attempted break-in in progress."

He was still cranky about that. Not that Wren was involved, but that I'd known and not told him.

"Being hired to prevent it is not the same as being hired to solve it. Anyway, that wasn't a PUPI case. And I only suspected." A potential serial killer I could handle. The boss in danger I could handle. Setting myself up against Wren had the potential to get messy. Especially if we were supposed to be finding out what was gunning for her, too. What if something we did caused her to get hurt or die? Oh, god, was that the connection? I felt queasy.

"It's my reputation on the line as much as it is hers." Venec sounded miffed, like he thought I was trying to avoid investigating. I wasn't. Okay, I was.

"I know," I said out loud, pitched just enough to carry to him and not be heard by any of the others in the room, who were ostentatiously ignoring us. Ellen and Sharon had settled in on the far side of the room; they were talking quietly, intently. Pietr, meanwhile, was going over a map spread out on the table, sticking pins into locations and then moving them around. He could have been performing a spell or trying to map out Starbucks locations, for all I could tell. "I just... really hoped we wouldn't have to deal with this and especially not in the middle of *this*."

"Oh, you mean because you hoped something would be easy?"

And there, in the middle of stress and complications and worries, surrounded by coworkers and near-strangers: the touch of warmth and affection, core to core.

I'd been fighting against the Merge for a year now; we both had. Even when we gave way for the sake of work, we still fought, resisting any external force that tried to make us dance to its tune. We'd fought so hard, we'd refused to see the benefits, too.

Knowing someone had your back and actually feeling them at your back, the rock-solid assurance that they weren't going anywhere; the difference between the two was chalk and cheese. I don't know why Ben had changed his mind, but for me—well, once I admitted I was being dumb, I didn't want to be dumb any longer.

For now, though, I accepted the touch, returned it, and then shut the connection down. It was still there; if we wanted it, it would be there. But it wasn't needed right now.

"Can we at least table the question until she actually breaks in and steals whatever it is she's stealing?"

"Yeah. About that."

I'd sensed Sergei standing there, waiting, but his intrusion into the conversation still startled me.

"About that?" Venec prompted the older man.

"I don't think the museum directors will authorize hiring anyone competent to regain whatever is stolen."

They stared at each other a long while, and I was shut out entirely of whatever was going on, either through XY connection or something else.

"They hired you." Venec sounded resigned, as though it were merely a confirmation of something he'd long suspected about the world.

"Classic case of the left hand having no idea what the right is doing." Sergei was being suavely consoling, which he did annoyingly well. "Security wanted the best protection they could manage, to placate the Board, so they hired you. The Board, for reasons of their own I'm not at liberty to discuss, wanted something to disappear without a trace—so they hired Wren. If you ever speak of this, I will break your jaw."

He was talking to both of us now.

"You can try," Ben said, and he was speaking for both of us, then, his lips pulled back in something that wasn't quite a smile.

"Children," I said, breaking into the moment before they started actually bumping chests. "We're all professionals here, remember. Ben, he wasn't threatening me. At least, not that way. And if he was, I could defend myself quite well, thank you. And, Sergei?" I looked up at him—and then up again, because he was a tall bastard. "Don't ever threaten me. Wren might be able to steal anything, but I know how to make you disappear."

And then I smiled, a real smile, so that he knew we were all friends together. He smiled back. There was an awful lot of teeth-baring going on in that room.

The moment might have gone somewhere, but Ellen's voice, raised into almost a wail, broke in.

"But then where does it come from?"

"We don't know." Sharon's voice had the same tone my mentor's used to get, when I was being particularly intense about something that had no answer, or at least no satisfying one.

"But if we don't know what causes it or where it comes from, then why did Denise say... She promised them!"

I left the boys to their teeth-baring and went across the room. Pietr had seemingly disappeared. Upset women weren't usually enough to stress him, but maybe it was just a cumulative overload.

"What did Denise promise?" Densie, I was guessing, was the mysterious charismatic in the Park.

"She said... When she came to us, she said that we were special, that we had abilities..." Ellen made a noise like a snort, full of disgust, and the diffident, worried girl disappeared for a moment under a flash of fire. "The younger girls ate it up. When you're fourteen, you want someone to come and tell you that you're special, that you have a destiny. I should have known better. But I was so tired, so bored of being different, of having weird things happen and nobody could tell me why, nobody would believe me... I fell, same as the younger ones. But she was as full of shit as the doctors who told me I was just making things up...."

Hah. I'd been right. "What else did she say, Ellen?"

push her Venec in my brain, although he stayed at the other side of the room, not wanting to crowd Ellen.

back off I sent, with a wash of irritation that he was trying to tell me how to do my job. The irony of that hit me a second later, with the backwash of his own amusement.

"What else did Denise tell you?"

"That together we could become something stronger, a force that nobody would be able to ignore." The words had the weight of a speech to them, rehearsed and often repeated, until they were embedded in Ellen's memory. "That if we all worked together, with her as the center, we could do anything. That nobody would ever doubt us or overlook us again."

"She was trying to use them as signal boosters." Sharon sounded incredulous.

"Low-res, probably." Pietr had joined us at some point, and it became a three-way conversation, not so much excluding Ellen as flowing over her. "The woman, I mean. Most covens were originally formed that way, a strong Talent gathering lesser ones or sensitive Nulls, their abilities layering to create a more powerful community."

Back in the back-when, before Founder Ben discovered the actual basis of Talent, how to best channel and use current. When we were called witches or warlocks or sorcerers and magic was something uncertain and unpredictable.

"That's why only girls?" It made sense, in that crazy makes-no-sense kind of way. "I bet she insisted they all be virgins, too." Sexuality had been big in the bad old days. There were still some people who insisted purity—or lack thereof—

enhanced your abilities, but I'd never seen proof one way or the other.

"Did she really think she'd be able to take their ability somehow?" Sharon was incredulous. "Is that even possible?"

"No. Not that I've ever heard, anyway." And between the bunch of us, we'd heard almost everything, at this point. Stosser might know more, but we didn't know where he was, to ask.

"So how the hell…?" I could practically see the activity inside Pietr's head. It wasn't really the point, and way down on the priority list right now, but we were trained to figure things out and ferret out information, and we had an actual source here. Like a three-headed hound, we all turned to Ellen, who looked like she wanted to run into the bathroom and slam the door but was too scared to move.

"How did Denise say she was going to strengthen you?"

Venec's question, his voice low but still carrying easily across the room, seemed to prod her into a response.

"She taught us how to meditate, to let our magic flow into her, like rivers going into the ocean, and then she'd send it back to us, stronger…."

Sharon made an impatient sound, a cross between a tsk and a harrumph. "It doesn't work that way."

That got our rabbit's dander up. "How do you know? How do you know that she couldn't do it?"

Sharon looked like she was going to launch into a lecture on what was and wasn't possible, but I shook my head slightly and, thankfully, she caught it. She'd forgotten that Ellen hadn't been trained the way we had, so to her, anything was as impossible as the other.

"The rules of current are pretty well-known by now," Pietr said. "Have been for a couple hundred years. We're learning how to pool our abilities, more effectively and consistently than the way they did in covens, but actually taking ability from one person and putting it into another? Can't be done. And from Nulls? You can't develop what's not there."

Our rabbit had a stubborn streak, because his words just made her set herself more firmly in defense of the woman who had lured and abandoned her. "Just because you haven't seen it before doesn't mean it's not true."

Since that's pretty much the basis of all investigation—facts, not theories—Ellen had us there. The feeling of amused pride was a surprise, until I realized that it was coming from Venec, not me, and he was proud of Ellen, not us.

shut up I thought at him crossly.

"All this is fascinating," Sergei said in a dry enough voice that it was clear he didn't find it fascinating at all. "But I'm not seeing where it gets us any closer to finding out who may be gunning for your boss and my partner, or how to stop it."

"Tall, Dark and Null over there is right," I said, using a nickname I'd heard PB use once or twice. "Focus, people. Sergei, thanks for the info. We're on the job. Can you take Ellen somewhere and feed her?" And keep both of them out of our way, I really meant. "And if you hear from Wren, anything at all, let us know the minute you hang up the phone, okay?"

He looked like he was going to say something sarcastic, then just nodded and stood up, reaching out a hand for Ellen. She took it with a kind of relief that confirmed what I'd been thinking; she was finding being around Talent unnerving, never mind she was one.

It might be too late to do anything other than teach her basic control and put her back into the Null world. But that was someone else's problem. Right now, our job was to stop anyone else—known or unknown—from getting killed.

Once the two outsiders were gone, Venec took control of the show.

"Priority goes to the case we actually have information on. Pietr, you be the conduit back to the office." Pietr nodded, and his eyes took on the slightly hazy look of someone in fugue state. It wasn't a direct line, the way a conference call would be, but it distracted fewer of us, and whoever was in the office would be able to hear what we were saying, even if they couldn't respond directly.

"All right. What do we know about our Decade Killer?"

He'd given the vivisectionist a name. I wasn't sure if that was good or bad, but it simplified things, differentiating him from Stosser and Wren's maybe-killer still out there.

I reeled off the known facts. "Kills Talent. Males, between the ages of thirty and sixty. Mostly but not all white—that could just be the logistics of where he's killing—Montreal, San Diego…"

"We'll see a difference in Philly, then. More mixed community."

"Maybe, maybe not," Venec said. "San Diego's a vastly different population pool than Montreal. Financial background of the victims?"

The details of the file came back to me, on command. "Blue-collar to white, running a gamut similar to that of ages…nothing extreme in either end. Lonejack and Council, both. Steady citizens. Although there could have been homeless people thrown into the mix and they'd never been found or reported."

We weren't the police or the Feds; even with our contacts and the local help, we still didn't have the resources they did. I could feel the tension in the room rise, humming through everyone's core, as we considered the magnitude of information we didn't have. Pietr was right; these two might not be the first, only the found.

"One thing that's bothering me," Sharon said.

"Only one?" Pietr looked surprised.

"Shut up. Thirty years from the first killings we know about until now. Either our guy started young, or he's no spring chicken now."

"No age-enforced retirement in that field," Venec said. "Killers might pause—for whatever reason—but they don't stop. Not guys like this. Not unless they're stopped."

"Yes, but—"

"What about my kenning?" I said to Venec, suddenly. In all this, I'd almost—not forgotten, because you didn't forget something like that, or at least I didn't, but pushed aside. But now that the thought rose up again, I could feel/taste/smell the vision all over again.

I hadn't seen death, no, but kenning was like tarot cards— what you thought you saw might not be what it actually meant. I did know that something was coming. Something dangerous, probably bad—because the kenning never bothered to bring me good news—and soon. Near me. Involving me. Did this qualify?

"You had a kenning? What did you see?" Sharon practically quivered to attention, and even Venec leaned forward. I hadn't told him the details, had brushed it off as not belonging on this time away from the job. I wouldn't make that mistake again, ever.

"Dragons." I closed my eyes and the visuals returned fresh as new. "Three dragons, circling. Fire, dark and deep, like a forge, like the core of the earth. A splattering of red…blood? Thick and heavy, dripping down slowly, drying in impossible shapes, pulsing off the wall…and it said something."

"What?"

I shook my head. "I don't remember. I wrote it down, though. Something...some warning, but really vague. But I remember—whatever it was, it knew me."

I'd been, in that split second, terrified.

"You've seen dragons before," Venec said.

In visions and in person. But the dragon I'd seen in my vision hadn't been like anything else, and certainly not like Madame...

I opened my eyes. Madame, the Great Worm of Manhattan. Ancient, magnificent, an old family friend and terrible gossip. She claimed Manhattan as her territory, so if another dragon, great or minor, had been looking for me, Madame would know. Would she tell me, if I didn't ask her directly?

I didn't know.

"It might not have anything to do with this case." It might involve Stosser and Wren—the fatae weren't always friendly to them. I wasn't sure that thought made me feel any better. No, it definitely didn't make me feel better. On the other hand, I hadn't had the kenning—

"You had the kenning on the way down here." And there was Venec, sharing my thoughts in his own brain. "Once you left New York?"

"Yeah." Damn. If there was a dragon down here looking for me, Madame might take no interest in it at all.

"Proximity could be a trigger—there was nothing to worry about until you came down here. That would suggest it was tied to this case."

"Wren's down here," I pointed out. "And I was coming down to interact with the museum."

"But Ian isn't here and has nothing to do with the museum," he countered. "But since you have connections to both Ian and Valere, your point's taken. And dragons are never anything to ignore. Pietr."

Pietr's eyes remained unfocused, but he lifted his head and nodded, indicating he was still transmitting to the main office.

"Have Lou run a search for anything involving dragons, greater or lesser, in the past thirty—no, fifty years. North America only. Don't let's get the Old World involved in this unless we have cause to."

Asian dragons were a different sort from the European ones, anyway, and Americans different again. No less dangerous, just…different. This had felt Western, at least: all dry air and ice and brimstone.

"Keep the focus on the cities we know about, once you have a baseline," I added, speaking directly to Lou rather than the formality of addressing Pietr. "That should narrow it down." If nothing came up, then we'd worry about metaphorical dragons.

"You really think there's that much dragon activity in North America?" Pietr asked; it could have been him or Lou with the actual question.

I remembered the feel of being trapped with a cave dragon when I was a teenager, and shrugged. "I think…we'd be surprised how much goes on that we don't know about. The Council—hell, nobody wants to talk about the bad stuff. You know that."

Most of our cases, especially the early ones, had been cleaning up messes nobody wanted to talk about, finding culprits nobody wanted to acknowledge. If human beings were ostriches, the *Cosa Nostradamus* was right there with their heads in the sand.

The Decade Killer was human; we'd ascertained that much. Did he or she have a connection to a greater or lesser worm? If it was just a metaphor, for what? That was the damnable thing about kennings: no way to know for certain until after the fact.

The phone rang then, the sharp noise startling us enough that we all jumped. Nobody even tried to pretend they hadn't.

"Room's in your name," I said to Venec, when nobody went to pick it up. It might be Sergei, with news about Wren…but I didn't think so.

He gave me a look, then walked across the room and picked up the plastic receiver like it was a snake that might bite him. "Hello? Yeah, this is…Okay. What's…Oh, hell."

It was a resigned, annoyed "oh, hell," not an alarmed one. But the look on his face was of an incoming headache, so we waited until he'd finished mmm-hmming and scribbling notes on the pad of paper the hotel had left by the phone, and placed the receiver back into the cradle.

"Whatever's going on with Ian—and The Wren—is officially back-burnered. Someone talked. Word's out on the current that we've got a killer and that he's targeting Talent."

"Details?" Sharon meant if details of the killings had gotten out: how they were done specifically.

"None yet, but it's just a matter of time. And god help us if they discover he's done it before. There will be a damned panic that won't be restricted to this city."

"Screw you."

He wasn't pleading; he'd stopped pleading the moment he read his killer's intention. It didn't take magic: the eyes said it all. Not dead, the way you'd think, but filled with a dreadful vigor, the pupils enlarged over the white mask, the breathing too quick, but controlled. Those eyes, that breathing, all filled with an overwhelming, possessive sense of *wanting*. Of *greed*.

He had seen those eyes, brighter then, come out of the shadows. It had been so swift—a blitz attack, the cop shows called it, he thought—all the karate he'd taken, that had made him feel secure walking through even the dubious neighborhoods, had been utterly useless. He'd tried to fight, tried to run, and then something sickly sweet, like sugared sulfur, like garbage had filled his nostrils, and he'd passed out.

Now there was a weight on his shoulders, pinning him to the table, the metal cold against his skin, chafing his buttocks. No clothing, not even his underwear. His left knee ached where he'd been hit with a stick of some kind that sent him facedown on the pavement; his ribs a mass of sharp bruises where he'd been kicked, when he tried to get up; his throat and nose itchy from whatever they'd held over his mouth.

Stripped bare, his skin was pebbled with goose bumps, his balls so far withdrawn he might as well be neutered, sweat cold and clammy even though the room they were in was comfortably warm, with the occasional whirring noise of an air conditioner working somewhere.

"Screw you," he said again. Not "I don't want to die" because he knew he was going to, eventually, inevitably. Not even "please don't hurt me" because he knew it was going to hurt. "Screw you" for his daughters, who would never hug him again, and his partner, who would remember the fights, and not the good times, and his clients, who would be cast onto some other lawyer's mercy, without warning.

The killer moved forward, his breath rising like steam, his skin rough and blotched over the mask. Near-hallucinating from the pain, for a moment the skin looked like scales.

A shadow passed over him, cast from behind: something else in the room, watching. Waiting. He could feel the greedy hunger, sliding like hot fingers through his brain, demanding entrance.

"Screw you," he whispered, as the knife touched the skin

of his shoulder, scoring the flesh like claws, opening him like a wallet, sliding inside.

"Give it to me," the killer said, his voice hot, flat, hissing like a flame. "Give it to me, and you can live."

Even if he knew what they wanted, he'd seen killers' eyes before. He knew when they lied.

thirteen

We'd called it a day around ten Tuesday night, and extra hotel rooms had been hustled up, the keys handed around. Sharon took one, Pietr took the other, and everyone looked at me. Standard would be for the girls to bunk together, but it wasn't a secret that Pietr and I had shared sheets a few times. I rolled my eyes and told them both to get the hell out of my room.

"That was subtle."

"My stuff's already in the bathroom." And subtle had never really been my thing. I'd never apologized for my sexual behavior before. I sure as hell wasn't going to start now.

"You want me to sleep in the armchair?" It was comfortable enough, and I'd done worse. I knew he was standing just behind me; what I didn't know was what he was going to say. His walls were up, and his breathing was too calm to read.

Then his hand touched my shoulder, slid down my arm, and covered my hand, turning so that our fingers tangled. It was kind of awkward, but I didn't mind. We just stood there, breathing together.

"I'm glad you stayed."

That was it, that was all he said, and then he let go of my hand and walked past me into the bathroom, shutting the door carefully.

As sweet nothings went, it wasn't all that. Good thing I'd never been a traditional sort of girl.

The next morning when we met up for breakfast, neither Sharon nor Pietr were giving me the side-eye. They might have been giving Venec the side-eye, but if so, that was his problem.

I didn't have the heart to tell them that, once again, we'd curled up together in bed, spooned together just enough to let the usual sparks of current crackle and pop between us... and gone to sleep. Neither of us was going anywhere; we had time. And right now, with everything on our minds... wasn't the time.

"Did anyone have any brilliant revelations or flashes of insight overnight?"

"Not a thing," Pietr said. "You?"

"Venec snores." It honestly was all I had, but the stunned silence—and then faint snickers—were worth the dirty look Venec gave me.

And he really did snore. It didn't take kenning to foresee a pair of earplugs for me in my near future.

Once the coffee was consumed and plates cleared, we went back upstairs and went back to work. Thankfully, the housekeeping staff had already been through. I did catch Sharon giving the bed a side-eye once or twice, then they got over it—the way they'd promised me, months ago, they would—and we settled back into harness.

"Recap," Venec said, taking up his usual position holding up the wall with his shoulders.

I let Sharon do the honors, sitting on the desk with my legs dangling, letting the information flow over me. Sometimes, if I just let myself drift and the right key word hit… Not this time, though. The kenning had apparently given me everything it had, already.

I supposed that was good: it meant nothing had changed, and by changed I meant gotten worse.

Lacking the whiteboard we usually used, we laid out sheets of hotel stationery to chart the things we knew, versus the things we suspected. It took us about an hour and was a pretty sad display. But, unlike a normal case, we had no idea where to even start looking.

And Sergei hadn't called, so Wren was still in the wind. He and Ellen were checking out off-the-path hotels and rooms, trying to figure out where she holed up.

The rest of the morning was spent moving those slips of paper around, arguing over theories, and trying not to think about the fact that every minute that went by, someone got closer to another vivisection

"Enough, people. You've been at this all day, and break-fast alone does not a pup feed. Go down to the restaurant, get some decent food in you. A salad, Bonnie. Protein, Sharon."

"What about you, boss?" Pietr asked. And how come his eating habits didn't get critiqued?

"I want to check in with the museum, make sure everything's okay there. I'll join you later."

I should have known he wouldn't—couldn't—let that go.

The same waitress from my first meal there was back again. She didn't seem to recognize me. I passed on the sandwich this time and went for a bowl of chicken noodle soup with a green salad, instead. It came with a short loaf of French bread, and I spent the entire meal dunking the end into my bowl and then eating that, rather than actually putting a spoon into the soup. I ate the salad, though. Sharon had a salad, too, and one of the most disgustingly juicy hamburgers I'd ever seen, while Pietr ordered the sandwich special and, unlike me, finished every scrap.

I toyed with my spoon and looked around, letting myself scan for entrances, exits, possible ambush points—all the things Venec was constantly trying to hammer into our heads. It was hard, though: the restaurant and the lobby had taken on the air of odd familiarity you get when you're someplace new that looks like places you've been before. Had I really first eaten here just the day before—surely it had been a week, already? No, it was only Wednesday.

Venec joined us just as I was scraping the bottom of my bowl, sliding in next to me. There wasn't the usual sharp snap of a spark that happened when we touched, just a warm sparkle, like fairy dust tingling on my skin. Weird. Interesting. I filed that away for further investigation—later. When we weren't on the job.

He didn't say anything about Ian, either success or failure, or about the museum break-in. "I spoke with the hotel management. They have a space downstairs we can use, while we're here."

That was good, because it had been starting to get a little close in that hotel room. What seems like a lovely, large space when it's just two of you becomes damned crowded when it's suddenly four, and the detritus of an investigation piles up fast. If we were on the case, we needed proper space to work.

"A conference room?" This wasn't a business hotel; they didn't seem to have a lot of event space advertised.

Venec snorted. "Not exactly."

"Not exactly" turned out to be an understatement. We found ourselves—using the service elevator—in a cheerless, dingily lit room near the boiler room. With a single rickety table and plastic chairs, this was clearly the place they lectured incoming chambermaids. That said, it was larger than the hotel room, and the AC worked, and there was a bank of vending machines in the hallway outside, so if the walls were reminiscent of a down-at-its-heels high school and my nose kept picking up trails of chlorine and bleach and a nastier undertone of what might have been mold, we could live with that.

Sharon kept sneezing, so it probably was mold.

Lacking a whiteboard, someone on staff had dragged out a rickety chalkboard on wheels, like the kind they used to use in classrooms, and half leaned it against the wall. It wobbled, but it didn't fall over, and there was chalk, so we were in business.

Proper tools at hand, we got back to work.

There were two timelines: Schultz and Brock. Time of disappearance, time of estimated death, time of discovery. A side chart listed their various attributes, as we knew them: hair, height, weight, age, marital status, etc. There were a few overlaps, but nothing that Sharon, our stats expert, said were notable.

"And there's absolutely nothing in their personal or work lives that overlaps. Brock is—was—an associate at a law firm—Kale, Whittier and Stovel. I don't know anyone there, but I've put out feelers for anyone who does." Sharon had worked as a paralegal at a Talent-heavy law firm before she joined PUPI and still kept her contacts shiny. "Someone will have the dirt on him, if there's dirt to be found.

"Schultz, on the other hand, was a soloist. Older, more established. He left a group practice about five years ago and had his own storefront."

"He's a CPA?"

"He was, anyway."

"Right. Was."

I flipped through the folder marked San Diego. "The pre-

vious victims, ten years ago, were all over the place. A dock-
worker, a nurse, a grad student—philosophy, a carpenter, a
dentist, a livery car driver, two stay-at-home dads, a retired
teacher, and an airline pilot."

"A nurse? I thought you said all the victims were guys."

Pietr got there before I could: "And the winner of the Nifty
Award for Shameless Sexism goes to…"

Sharon looked startled, then held up her hands in a gesture of surrender. "All right, point made. But is there any
hundred-percent overlap at all, with those ten?"

"Other than male, middle-aged, Talent, and living in the
same city?" I shook my head. "Nothing that is in these records. No idea if they were Council or lonejack, though.
That might be useful."

"Any chance we could get that out of their local Councils?"

My laugh was answer enough, I guess, because Sharon
made a face and went back to work.

The records we had were piled in the center of the table, for
somewhat scattered definitions of a pile. Andrulis had sent a
car over with the boxes while we were eating. It was only fair,
I thought, since he'd been the one to drag us into this. But
that was probably all the official help we were going to get.

Venec had disappeared an hour or so ago, muttering something about using his contacts to track down our missing cats,
by which I assumed he meant both Stosser and Wren. I'd suggested that he include Sergei in his search, but he'd just given
me A Look and left.

Ben could work with Stosser, but apparently any other
alpha male was right out. Good to know.

"They were all… No, damn, one lefty in Montreal, and
Brock is a lefty, too. Damn. I thought I had something." I
stared at the scratchpad in front of me, then glared at the
chalkboard like it was somehow at fault.

"We're starting with more information than we usually have—actual bodies, historical evidence, cooperation, kinda, of the local cops...so why does it feel like we've got nothing?"

"Because we've got nothing," Sharon said. "Nothing useful. And because we're waiting for the word to come that they've found another body."

The three of us all turned to look at the door, expecting someone to burst in and say "wait no longer."

The door stayed closed. I wasn't sure if I was relieved or not.

"Talent." Sharon got up and swung the chalkboard around, top-to-bottom, with a dramatic gesture, and wrote the word on the clean surface with large, slanting letters.

"That's what we know, that's the consistent pattern. All three cities, all twenty-two men. Male, middle-aged, and Talent. Everything else, for now, is unimportant."

Pietr shoved the file he was looking through back onto the pile and leaned back in his chair, making it creak in an unnerving fashion.

"Okay," he said. "So...which do we deal with first?"

"Gender." It was instinct, but I'd always trusted my instincts. "Talent is a broader category, with both genders. And the age range is too wide for specifics, except that he wanted them strong and healthy. So why only male?"

"You might as well ask why Talent." Sharon shrugged. "Six of one, six of another. Gender it is. Why would a killer focus on men, as opposed to women, or both?"

"Machismo." Pietr spoke first. "A real man, someone secure, doesn't hurt a woman, and a guy who has something to prove isn't going to attack someone obviously weaker. That's the opposite of proving something."

"Weaker?" I raised an eyebrow at that.

"Bonnie, I don't care how strong you are or how dirty you

fight—and I know you fight plenty dirty. Pound for pound even an out-of-shape guy can probably take down the average female. It's just genetics."

I hated the fact that he was right.

"So which is it?" Sharon asked. "Secure or looking for a challenge?"

"Secure," Pietr and I both said at the same time. I looked at him, and he made a "go ahead" gesture.

"The victims were bruised, but not showing any abrasions that would indicate that they were tied down. The records from earlier deaths didn't mention any bruising at all. However he's catching them or restraining them while he…does what he does, it's not violent."

I stopped and cocked my head, considering that statement. "Right. You know what I mean. They're not fighting back, so either he's drugging them or somehow convincing them to stay put. No violence is suggested by the evidence. It's not about the thrill of the victory or about taking down more powerful prey—the act of cutting into them is what our guy's after. Causing very specific, controlled pain."

I swallowed, aware of how clinical I was being and how uncomfortable I was with that. This guy was a monster, and I…

"We need a profiler," I said. "Somebody who actually knows what they're doing. We're just guessing here. He could be doing this for a thousand reasons, half of which we can't even begin to guess."

"We don't have a profiler." Yet, I could hear Sharon thinking. "So we're all we've got. We're all his next victim has."

I shoved away from the table, the chair's wheels squeaking against the floor, and started to pace.

"Male. All strong guys, none of them injured or handicapped prior to the attack. So, yeah, he's not cutting out the weakest, and he's not going after athletes or professional fighters, either. Ordinary Joes. Cutting into them. Vivisecting them. Ugh." I clenched my toes inside my stompy boots and reached instinctively for my current. Despite my emotional upset, the pool of current coiled inside me was smooth and calm.

ben

It was instinctive, not even a mental vocalization, and I felt the touch of his core against mine, a cat's whisker of a touch, and then he was gone. I was on my own.

"What if we're looking at this the wrong way?" Sharon said suddenly, her blue eyes bright, and while her body might do a centerfold justice, it was her mind that had gotten hired. She had something.

I wasn't on my own. I had my pack.

"Spill." Pietr swung his chair around to face her, and I went back to my chair, resting my elbows on the table and cupping my chin in my hands. "Come on," I said when she hesitated. "What did you just stub your toe on?"

"I don't think we should be looking at who or the how. I think we should be looking at what and why."

"But we don't know either of those things."

"Maybe…maybe we do." She started to say something else, then lifted her fingers to her mouth and pressed them to her lips, as though silencing herself while her brain thought things through. "Vivisection. The reports were all clear on that. This guy wasn't carving them up like a turkey or slashing—he was cutting them open in the same exact way, with nearly surgical precision. All males, all within an age range… What does that sound like?"

"A control group," Pietr said.

"Yeah. Exactly."

★ ★ ★

ben

He felt Bonnie reaching for him; the touch-back was instinctive, unthinking, and more than he could afford to give just then. He shut it down and went back to the chore at hand. Literally.

"Don't piss me off, Sparky." Benjamin Venec cultivated a veneer of calm control, but nobody who had ever pissed him off underestimated his temper.

"I swear, I don't know. I don't know anything. I mean, sure, I know who has it in for your partner—bloody well everyone, that's who. Anyone who doesn't have it in for you, anyway. But that ain't news!"

No, it wasn't. He and Ian had managed to make a great number of people—and not-people—unhappy in recent years, even without direct contact. The fact that they existed was enough of an affront. The PUPs, for now, were seen as their tools, rather than individual threats in and of themselves. Ben was determined to keep it that way as long as possible, and no matter that their feelings might be hurt if they realized it. But that thought, too, was a distraction.

"Someone specific. Someone who's been mouthing off more than usual or gotten quieter than usual?"

The human shook his head. "I swear, Venec. I don't like you much, but I'm not going to lie to your face, not when you're in that kinda mood. You've got too long a memory."

"You're a smart man, Sparky."

He was. He was also the front for a euphemistically named "greeting service" that hired out fatae as exotic escorts—and Venec suspected that not all the fatae had gotten into the gig of their own free will. Someday, the company would do something demonstrably over the line, and things would get interesting. But this wasn't that day.

"If you hear anything...it will be worthwhile for you to come to me first. And fast." Flash the stick and then show 'em the carrot. It wasn't smooth, but it worked.

"Yeah. Yeah, I will."

Ben left the plush office, nodding at the mer-girl lounging in the massive tank in the waiting room. She opened her sea-green eyes and watched him go, not bothering to wave: he clearly wasn't a potential client.

"Damn it, Ian, where are you?" His partner was ignoring him, and that never, ever boded well. *IAN!*

what? The mental sensation was so calm, almost puzzled, exactly like a little kid who had no idea the adults all thought he was missing and didn't understand what all the shouting was about, that Ben stopped dead in his tracks, not sure if he wanted to laugh or scream.

get your ass over here he said instead.

When you didn't have windows or a clock—and none of us carried watches anymore, since even wind-up ones went kerflooey after a while—time could get away from you. So it wasn't until Sharon's back made an audible crack when she straightened up that we realized we'd been at it well past dinnertime, and the tension in the room was starting to become an almost palpable stink.

Pietr had gone through his gypsy contacts and found nothing on the knife, and Lou's research on dragons had turned up nothing useful to our current case.

"We're spinning our wheels," Pietr said in disgust, and I was forced to agree. The more we looked at the facts we did have, the more Pietr's theory seemed laughably obvious: our killer was choosing the same victim, over and over again, and doing the same thing, over and over again.

"But what the hell does he want?" Sharon asked.

And that was where we'd been stuck.

Sharon reached up to undo and rebraid her hair. The braid had been perfect until then; it was just a frustrated twitch. Pietr's was to disappear from sight. I…had no idea what mine was.

"If it was just for torture, then I'd think there would be more damage done, yeah? Something that inflicted more pain, before they died." I thought back to what I'd felt, under the cuts, and how the ME's report had said things were… missing. "Why was he scraping under the skin, and what happened to the scrapings?"

"Lunch?"

The fact that we had to consider that possibility made me, for an instant, really hate my job.

"Maybe he's reliving something that was done to him, some trauma he saw." Sharon tapped her fingers against the table. "Trying to understand it, maybe, or get back what was taken? And, no, I have no idea what or how."

"That makes as much sense as anything else. If we had access to the bodies…"

"We don't. We got kicked out once already, and without any kind of official standing I doubt we'll get back in." Not without pulling strings that might be too expensive, in terms of favors owed. "Anyway, corpses only last so long, and even a preservation cantrip won't keep decay from coming to visit eventually."

"Nice image, thanks." Pietr looked a little green. Apparently he was okay with cannibalism but not decay. "What about from the photos? I know, it's 2-D and mostly useless, but…"

Sharon and Pietr both looked at me: they were good field techs, but I was better at re-crafting existing spells to suit our specific needs.

"There's an old spell that hunters used to use," I said slowly, trying to chase down the memory. Sitting in the library of J's apartment, Rupert still a puppy, all tail and fur, sleeping at J's feet; me curled into the leather armchair across from them, listening while J told me about the change from old magic to current and how spells were adapted...and some fell by the wayside. "To appease the spirits of the animals they killed."

"That's religion, not magic. Or what passed for it, back then." Sharon, Lou, and Farshad were the only ones in our pack who could be considered religious: I guess Shar was a bit of a snob about deism.

"Old magic is all about faith. For our purposes, it counts." Sharon's mentor had advocated a less-is-better mode of current use; she had a bunch of blocks in her history, too. Or maybe, just as likely, I was overstuffed with details nobody else cared about.

Until we needed them, anyway.

"Faith like a priest would define it, or...?"

Yeah, a snob. And annoyed at having her snobbery called out. She'd done it to me often enough; we both survived.

"That the animal spirits would hear them, and understand that their lives were not taken lightly, and be appeased—and not scare away game in the next hunt. I think. The point is, the spell I'm thinking of used cave paintings. Flat, two-dimensional paintings..."

"Like crime-scene photographs." Pietr nodded. "You think you can use the photos to...what? Link the killer to the evidence somehow?"

"I don't know. Maybe."

There were a handful of ways to re-create a scene from the evidence, depending on what kind of evidence you had. But I'd never—none of us had ever tried doing it from secondhand evidence like a photograph, mainly because our few attempts at using cameras ended up in dead cameras and overexposed film. The digital experiment had ended even worse.

"You're going to need to eat before you do anything," Sharon said, her momentary pique forgotten. "And I'm starving. Think the hotel will let us order a pizza down here?"

The moment she said that I realized how hungry I was, and Pietr's stomach, almost on cue, let out a growl.

"Right. I'm going to go up to the front desk and call in an order. Bonnie, go take a walk, clear your lungs, and see if the hotel has a backup power source you can draw down on because I know damn well you're running half-loaded."

She was right, so I didn't bother to complain about her being bossy. It wouldn't have helped, anyway.

Pietr came with me, down the dreary hallway and out the service door. There was a little courtyard behind the hotel that you could only access from there: guests could look out at the greenery but not get down into it. The noise of the generator was muted, but for a Talent, it might as well have been ringing bells to announce its location.

"There's a bench over there," Pietr said, steering me toward it. It was small, wooden, obviously more to look at than use, but I sat, anyway. I could go into fugue state standing up, but it was easier not to.

I tilted my head and looked up at the sky. Buildings rose around us, but there was a square patch of blue just overhead, and I let myself focus on the impossible depth of it. Some people's cores are in a constant roil, snapping and sparking every time they get upset. I tend to run cool, more core coiling around itself in layers. It wasn't good or bad, just who I was, like my memory recall and my kenning. But right now, with the situation with Venec starting to simmer, and a killer on the loose, and my boss and a friend maybe going to end up dead soon, I almost wished that my current mirrored the uncertainty in my life, just once.

The call of the generator reached out to me, and I slid a mental hand into its warmth, letting electricity run through my fingers the way someone might test bathwater. I really didn't need a lot: contrary to Sharon's assumption, I wasn't low, but it was soothing to top off.

Creating a spell from scratch was hard work, but relatively simple. Adapting an existing one was trickier. Adapting an old spell thousands of years old, off a retold memory?

Venec and Stosser didn't allow false modesty in their pups. I was good enough to do it. But it wasn't going to be easy.

I cupped those mental hands and scooped out current from the electrical power, letting it slide into my own core and settle. It was a little like drinking soup on a rainy day: smooth and warm and comforting.

I opened my eyes—not having even realized I'd shut them—and brought my head forward, wincing a little as my neck protested. I must have been sitting there longer than I thought.

Pietr was holding a yoga pose that made my knees hurt just looking at it, his arms lifted, one leg raised and bent. As I watched, he bent, slowly, carefully, and placed his palms on the ground, his raised leg steady, as though he were carved from stone.

"I could really hate you for that," I said.

"It's a question of regular practice. You're too lazy to do it, that's all." His voice was muffled until he raised himself out of the folded pose, as graceful—and boneless—as a snake. His muscles were both strong and supple, I knew that from first-hand experience, but it was still impressive to watch.

"Let's go see if the pizza's en route," he said. "And then we can get started."

"We?" I stood up and tried to raise one eyebrow at him.

"What, you think you were going in alone? Oh, hell, no. I'll shadow, Sharon will spot. I have no desire to get another lecture from Venec about one of us hotdogging it."

And Venec would know, too, if I tried. I swear, I couldn't decide if the Merge was a royal pain in my ass with occasional benefits or just a royal pain in the ass.

We retraced our steps, only to discover that the door had swung shut and needed a key to get in. We both stared at it in disbelief, like that would be enough to make it swing back open.

It wasn't.

"Oh, for..." I was ready to ping Sharon, have her come and let us in—and deal with the inevitable ribbing—when Pietr merely reached down and touched his index finger to the lock, then with his other hand turned the handle and opened the door.

"I hang out with the thief, and you can lock-pick without tools. It figures."

"It's not lock-picking. It's alternative keying."

"Uh-huh."

Sharon came out of the bathroom and saw us. She started down the hallway when at the same exact moment the service elevator pinged and the door opened, and I felt Venec's touch slipping against my walls.

"Hey."

Sharon turned on her heel, and she and Pietr both gawked at the new arrival.

"He doesn't have our pizza," Pietr said, focused on the obvious.

"That's because he's not the delivery guy. Charles Andrulis, Philly P.D." I made the introductions quickly: "Sharon

Mendelssohn, Pietr Cholis." I glanced at the file in his hand and made a logical leap: "More info on the case?"

"Not the way you're thinking." If possible, Andrulis's dark features got even more locked-down. "We've got another body."

Expecting it didn't make the gut-jolt any easier to bear.

"You might want to poke or prong or whatever it is you do to get Ben down here."

That had been the gist of Venec's touch. "They're on their way."

"They?"

There was a faint crackle of energy, and Andrulis stepped back instinctively, just as Ian Stosser Translocated in, his long orange-red hair loose and static-y. Whatever Big Dog had been doing, he was not in a good mood. Venec appeared a second after, looking only slightly less grumpy.

Andrulis handed Venec the files without blinking: if he hadn't seen someone Transloc before, he was a damn good poker player. "I wasn't here. Everything we know so far's in there."

"If we need anything more," Stosser started to say, and Andrulis shook his head. "Don't call me. Two's bad luck. Three's about to become a media event. The moment the press picks up on the fact that this guy's killed before? All hell breaks loose. And we can't even release the single thing they all have in common, other than being middle-aged males...."

The rest of the world, some of them know about Talent, some of them suspect, but mostly they like being ignorant of anything they're not part of. Mostly that was a good thing—most humans shouldn't know about the fatae. Like the man says, they can't handle the truth. But that means the risk of someone like Ellen, utterly lost. And sometimes...sometimes it would be really nice to be able to go on the TV and announce that non-Talent need not fear, but look out for any-one sniffing at power lines...

Wishes were horses, but nobody knew how to ride, my dad used to say. Of course, Zaki—my dad—had been noto-rious for wishing his way through most of life. My mentor had trained me better.

"Good luck," Venec said, and Andrulis nodded, glum. "Yeah. You, too. If you do find the guy..." There was a pause, then his massive shoulders lifted in something that wasn't quite a shrug. "I don't think the taxpayers would mind too much if he never comes up for trial, you know?"

"We only investigate. We don't prosecute," Stosser said sharply.

"Yeah, okay, whatever." Andrulis clearly didn't believe the disclaimer. Looking over the past year, I wasn't sure I did, either.

"Remember—I was never here, and you never got any of this from me."

Taking him at his word, I guess, Stosser turned and went into the room we'd been using without saying goodbye or thanks, and Sharon and Pietr followed on his heels. I looked at Venec, then turned and left, too.

Ben came in a minute later, walls up and not meeting my eyes. Something was up. I didn't pry: he'd either share it with me later, or he wouldn't. Neither of them said anything about Ellen's vision, but I was assuming Stosser knew. If not, I sure as hell wasn't going to be the one to say anything.

Sharon, uncharacteristically, looked uncertain. "Should we still go ahead with the spell, Bonnie, or...?"

"Yeah." Then with more determination, "Yeah. The new info, whatever it is, will help. Two points are okay but three points of reference are better."

I hadn't even looked once at the new file, and already the

body was not a person, not even a db, but a point of reference. The fact that it was necessary, that it was what allowed us to do our job and keep someone else, hopefully, from being a point of reference…well, it helped, some. And I tried not to think about the rest.

"Spell? Did you put it in the book?"

For all that Venec worked directly with us while Stosser handled the front-man gig, both Big Dogs kept a close eye on the spells we were crafting. In theory, you didn't really need a spell to direct current: it was a question of Talent and focus, and the words were just an aid to the focus. But forensic spellwork, as Venec tagged it, needed to be consistent. When we did A it had to result in B, every single time, or our results could be challenged, and a single challenge could make it—and us—useless. So once we figured out how to do something effectively, we codified the wording in the book— an old-fashioned grimoire—and made sure everyone had it memorized, so that there was no margin for oops.

"Still in the figuring-it-out stage, boss," I said. "It's still theory." Theory, unlike fieldwork where he was useless, was something Stosser was good at.

He took the bait. "All right. Talk me through it."

While I ran through the basics of my idea for the Big Dog, I watched out of the corner of my eye as Sharon and Pietr spread the file on the table, keeping it separate, for now, from the rest of the materials. New info, then compare and contrast: that was how you built a case. My stomach rumbled, reminding me that the pizza still hadn't gotten here, and now we were going to have to share with the Big Dogs, too. I hoped Sharon had ordered enough.

"I don't think it's going to work," Stosser said. He had commandeered one of the chairs and was sitting back, his hands steepled under his chin, his long legs stretched out in front of him. Dressed all in black today, his long orange-red hair now pulled back again, he could have been a beatnik escaped from a different decade—or a classic wizard updated by way of Prada.

The fact that my slacks and silk T-shirt probably cost almost as much as his outfit failed to make me look or feel anywhere near as sleek. Fluffy blond curls and a delicate bone structure do not make one sleek. Nicky calls me "dandelion," not "iris" or "lily."

"Why not?" I asked, affronted. "We have all the elements—the image of the victims, the continued hunt…"

"You didn't kill the victims, didn't know them or need them. Without the emotional impact, there's no real connection, the way there was between hunter and prey."

"Oh." I slumped into my own chair and thought about that for a minute. "Damn." He was right, of course. Ian Stosser was usually right with things like this. That made him both useful and damned annoying, and I could understand how he got up a lot of people's noses. Okay, that and his insistence that we be held accountable for the actions we—Talent—take with magic. That was particularly irksome to a lot of people, including his own sister. Somehow I didn't think they were going to object to us taking on this particular case, though, since…

"Guys?"

All four of them looked up, with varying expressions of "what?"

"All the victims are Talent," I said. "We know that. But we have no confirmation about the killer."

"You said that you picked up something from the blade?" Venec asked.

"There was something under the cuts, yeah, but I told

you, it felt like the knife itself leaving a trace, not the user. And there wasn't any trace of external current on the victims, either caught in the wounds or left on the skin." That didn't disprove Talent, but it made it less likely.

"Could the killer have washed the bodies himself, before dumping them? To remove any trace?" Pietr asked.

"Possible—but why?" Until we'd come on the scene, only a Talent cop would have noticed evidence like that, and there were few enough of those that the odds of them being on the case were low to start. We were getting known, yeah, but the specifics of what we did were still vague—and we kept them that way intentionally. And we didn't normally work in Philly.

"Because…" Pietr stopped and second-guessed himself. "Because I was assuming only another Talent would be able to catch and bind a Talent to this extent, without physical restraints. Which isn't true."

"It's mostly true," Venec said. "If the Talent in question was willing to use current to defend himself. But these guys… Most of them were in good shape, and not so active in the community that their deaths made much of a ripple in the gossip."

If there was one thing that united the *Cosa Nostradamus,* it was gossip. We'd called around on some of the biggest gossips, but no one had info to share on these kills—especially as we were still trying to keep the current kills a secret, to avoid a nationwide panic breaking out. We just didn't have enough information yet.

"So odds are, they relied on physical strength, same as Nulls would. And it wasn't enough—by the time they were panicked enough to use current, it was too late. But Torres is right, that doesn't tell us one way or the other about the killer."

Except that, if he was Talent and the lack of signature was

deliberate, he thought about being traced-back, which meant he was aware of us, or at least the possibility of us being called in. That made our job tougher.

"If this is the same guy as was in Montreal and San Diego, I bet he was more careless back then. We weren't around to hunt him."

"If he is aware of us, though, your spell might be able to work," Stosser said. "Think at it a different way."

"Huh?"

I was at a loss, but thankfully Sharon got it. "Not hunter to prey, but hunter to hunter?"

"Oh." I swung my brain around and tried to see where he was pointing. "Use the photos not as a connection to the victims, but the killer...and see what he saw when he left the bodies?" One hunter to another, with the same mind-set, the emotional need to stop him? Huh. If we could make that work...

"Not go into his mind, though, right? Because, um, crazy sociopath vivisectionist?" Sharon waved her hand around, as though to emphasize that this might be a bad thing.

"It's like the negative-space cantrip," I said. "Not to get inside, but to show what was around." To see the space where the victim fit. And the knife—if I could get a decent idea of the weapon...then we could identify that sense of current. Maybe. I could feel the pieces start to slot into place, my mind pulling forward bits of other spells and fitting them in with the original idea.

"Is there anything other than the photographs you can use?" Pietr asked, sorting through the piles. "There's some decent scene reports...."

"No. Nobody else's interpretation. Just the visuals, the last thing the killer saw before he left them." I was on the right track now, I could feel it, the way current was shivering through my skin, gathering itself even before I called it. Sharon was a great investigator, Nicky was a current-hacker, Nifty could probably match current-for-current with Venec, if not Stosser, and Pietr was the sneakiest thinker I'd ever met, but when it came to lab work and crafting cantrips...I was the top dog, and everyone knew it.

Someone had pulled the relevant photos out of the files and laid them on the table in a sort of triangle.

"Do you want the older photos, too?" That was Venec, not quite hovering, but steady at my shoulder. His presence was so familiar now, I hadn't even been aware of him standing there.

"Not yet. Let me see if this works, first." More than three points would be good, but too many and too old... I was worried that it might dilute, rather than enhance, the connection.

First step: fugue state. Lean back, breathe. Let everyone else, everything else, fade from my conscious awareness. It was all still there, still noted: fugue state enhanced your awareness rather than limiting it, but you were so aware you could ignore it without endangering yourself. Sharon: bright and sharp. Pietr: deeper tones, fading into mist at the edges but fierce and strong. Stosser was, as always, like a pillar of current-fire, tight-wrapped with control like barbed wire around a tornado.

I wished I could take credit for that line, but it was Pietr's. And Venec.

I could feel him just underneath my skin, even when I wasn't in fugue state. It wasn't sexual—well, mostly it wasn't sexual. In fugue state, the walls might as well not even be there: we overlapped, our cores not snapping and sparking the way current should, but tangling into thicker, more complicated knots.

★??★

Not so much question, or worry, as the awareness of a

question and worry and reassurance and support. Someone else—some other person—might have embraced the Merge, welcomed the way it tied us together. Venec and I fought it at first, each for our own reasons, but he had come to terms with the reality much better than I.

I guess it wasn't surprising that he had made the first move toward truce.

My father had been functionally useless as a parent; my mother had abandoned us before I could walk. J had been an excellent mentor, as much a father as Zaki couldn't manage, but I'd always known I was one of many people he loved. And my lovers—I had loved them all, just never enough to give myself over to them. Not deep down. Not at core-level.

I suspected Ben had, once. And the experience had taught him something I still didn't know. But I thought maybe I could learn.

focus

yes, sir I sent back and let go of even the awareness of Venec behind me, narrowing the universe down to the three photographs in front of me. Seeing them as images, but also seeing them as more, connectors to the bodies themselves. Current flickered inside my core, like a miniature lightning storm amid swirling black-and-green clouds.

The old spell tied hunter to prey, based on the element of respect and need. I wasn't able to muster respect—this person was a sick bastard—but need, that I could do. On the strands of current, I wove not a net but a rope, a cord that pulsed with the need, first from me and then, carefully braided in, from everyone else in the room. They felt me touch, ask, and gave, a silent opening of themselves that was a hallmark of what we did, who we were.

This was what Stosser and Venec had created. I felt a momentary flash of awe and pride, and let it go, focusing on that braided cord. When it felt ready I reached through the images, pulling on the emotional representation of the violence the victims suffered, adding that to our need, reinforcing it, hunting for what lingered on the other end.

"Hunter, favor us."

The original chant had talked about feeding familie, and allowing the spirits of the prey to return in the spring. I hadn't thought specifically of how to adapt those words to my modern needs, but once I started, it seemed to rise naturally, as though the words had always been there.

Maybe they had.

"Hunter, favor us. Guide my hand to the hand that binds, the hand that bleeds, the hand that cuts, the hand that kills. Guide my spell to the one who hunts."

Tricky here. The current flowed under my touch, linking me to the photographs, and I had to be careful to work this just right. Too vague, and it would dissipate. Too specific, and...

Too specific and I might get nothing, missing the mark— or I could be pulled into my quarry's thoughts, his emotions; his core, if he was Talent. And in the pulling, I could be lost.

got your back

Pietr this time, like a warm hand between my shoulder blades. Less backup—I didn't need anyone watching my back here in our own space—and more reassurance that anything I needed was there for the asking.

Venec might be current's Merge-picked match for me, but Pietr and I had been lovers and were friends, and the connection, in some ways, was stronger.

"Go," I told the current-spell, releasing all but a single strand, curled in the center of my palm. It slipped away, draining my core to the point that I actually noticed it—and noticed something else as well: every two notches I slipped, half a notch refilled.

Ben.

Not even noticing, just reacting.

I took it, stirred it into my core, and made a mental note to thank him later. And then I waited for the spell to boomerang back to me.

Breathing. Holding the fugue state. Letting the others move around me, their voices not-quite-distinguishable as words, merely color-blocks of noise, their intent not-threatening and therefore ignorable.

I didn't know what to expect, so I expected nothing. Waiting, open, trusting Pietr to protect me if anything went wrong, trusting my pack to have my back, that anything that meant to harm me would have to go through them, first.

Because they were doing other things did not mean they were not also watching me.

That was Venec's gift to us, breaking us to harness, teaching us how to work independently and together at the same time, without fuss or resistance until it was as natural as breathing, as—

The spell boomeranged back and slammed me in the gut. I bent over instinctively, even though the hit was magical, not physical, and felt the spell break and scatter around me. Two years of experience was barely enough to let me catch the shards, fitting them together instinctively, quick-panic movements like handling forge-hot shards of glass. A picture formed, and I poured more current into it, turning up the depth and brightness until it was visible to everyone in the room.

"Holy…" Pietr saw it take form first, but I could tell when I had everyone's attention. As dramatic pauses went, it was pretty damn fine.

"That's the murder weapon."

"Yeah." Once I was sure I'd secured the image, I rose up from fugue state and refocused my eyes on the Null world. Usually it seemed drab and flat after being so hyperaware of current, but my attention was focused—like everyone else's—on the image floating a foot above the table.

"I thought you were going to reach the killer himself?" Stosser didn't sound disapproving but a little surprised.

"I did." The gut-punch made me sound oddly breathless, but I was certain of my result—and why. "The killer was so focused on his cuts, on making each one perfect, focusing on what he wanted, this is all he saw. Not the victim. Not himself. Just the knife."

It wasn't a scalpel; too large, and too long, for all that it had a surgical precision to it. Like a filleting knife, if you were deboning a Jurassic flounder.

"He doesn't see the people," Pietr said, as the spell-knife flashed down and up again, all the more disturbing for the fact that it stayed clean and shiny. Where was the blood that had to speckle it in real time? "They're not important to him."

"What is important to him? What is he trying to do? Is it their pain? Their screams?" Stosser was talking to himself; we were just there to listen along. But I answered anyway, like an idiot.

"He wants something. I don't know what. I'd have to do a deeper—"

"No." Venec, with Sharon a half-second behind him. Not that it mattered; I wasn't going to volunteer. The idea of intentionally going into a serial vivisectionist's emotions was not high on my to-do list, even without the PUPI-wide ban on it. If we needed to do it to catch the guy… We'd do it as a team, and Venec would be lead dog.

That wasn't my decision but his, solid and unquestionable.

"No," Stosser agreed, and I could feel everyone exhale in relief.

"We have the weapon," Venec said, turning everyone's attention back to the display. "And, therefore, by extension, we have the killer."

He had his teaching-dog voice on.

"But there's nothing attached to it," Pietr said. "We can't—"

"Look at how the blade is held. What does that tell us?"

"The cuts are precise, but...weird." Sharon walked around the table, studying the motions closely. "He's holding it like a paintbrush, not a kitchen knife."

"He's right-handed," I said. It figured: a lefty might have been easier to find. "The angle he's coming down at, that's from the right side of the body, not the left."

I'd taken self-defense classes as a kid, at J's insistence, but that knowledge came from fight class with Nick, who was a surprisingly dirty fighter—and had trained us all to be the same.

"There's something about the way he's moving." Venec had stepped closer to the table, almost bending over into the range of the gleaning, and I pinged him with a faint warning; he stepped back before I could even finish sending. You didn't want to tangle in someone else's spellwork, even as tuned-in to each other as we were.

"He's moving around. Like the body is on a table, which would make sense."

"The bodies were found in alleys, in every case," I said. "Near trash cans, not hidden."

"A dump site. They are just trash to him, when he's done."

"But he has a table to work on, not the floor. That suggests a specific place, where he has tools. And privacy." Sharon was sorting through her thoughts like file cards.

"And soundproofing," Pietr added

"Current could do that. Or keep the victim from scream-ing."

"Would he bother? If he doesn't see them, literally or emo-tionally..."

"He's pausing," Venec said. "A cut and a cut and a cut and then a pause. What is he waiting for?"

"Listening?" That felt right to me somehow.

"Maybe." But he didn't sound convinced.

"Watching," Stosser said. "He's watching. It's not the sound that he's getting off on. It's the body language. Maybe the expression. He probably did silence each victim, because the inability to scream for help—or express the pain—probably intensified the agony."

It was seriously creepy how carefully Stosser enunciated each word, so precise in his assessment, almost like he was enjoying it. He wasn't, not exactly, but his brain tended to be more analytical and occasionally forget that there was a person dying under those blows.

Well, dead already now.

"Boss," Sharon said. "You're seriously creepy sometimes."

I loved my coworkers. A lot.

"So he's a sadist who thinks he's an artist, making each strike just so over and over again—trying to create a masterpiece?"

"Or re-create one, maybe." Pietr had not quite disappeared, but he was definitely fading a bit at the edges. What fasci-nated Stosser was stressing him.

okay?

no And a sense of having seen it all before, unvoiced, unformed but present in his ping. Suddenly, a lot about my coworker/once-lover clicked into place, and I felt my gorge rise.

stop

I stopped. He didn't want sympathy, he didn't want under-standing, he just wanted to let it go. So we let it go.

"That would explain why he doesn't see them," Sharon said, oblivious to the undercurrents. "They're just his clay."

"The same strokes, over and over again." The fact that we'd already identified it as a control group—a scientific experi-ment—made it worse, not better; confirming the fact that, unless we stopped it, he'd keep going.

The pattern was seriously bugging me, as I watched the knife rise and fall. "We need more detail on the actual deaths. That's what will turn the lock—understanding what he's doing, why."

Venec shook his head. "We don't have access to the local cops anymore, and bringing anyone else up to speed would take too long, too many channels to wade through. Pietr—"

"Already on it. Nick's going to fire up his scrying machine and see what he can do."

I should offer to deep-scry, too. I didn't want to. I wanted to not look at this anymore, turn away, forget that anyone could do this not just once, or twice, but so many times.

PUPI didn't turn away. We didn't forget. Not until we had all the facts.

"All right, then," Stosser said, "we need to—"

"Someone order a pizza?"

The smell hit my nose the same instant the unfamiliar voice did. I was pretty sure I didn't lunge at the poor hotel secu-rity guy holding our dinner, but it was a close thing. Venec moved in front of the table, his build sort of blocking the guy's view of the table, should he happen to wonder what the hell was going on, while Sharon pulled her wallet from her purse slung over the chair and tried to pay the guy.

"Nah, they put it on your master room charge," the guy said, waving her off. "And the tip. Manager's orders."

They were probably afraid we'd stiff them or something. Venec had worked some fast-talking to get us this room but I had no idea what he'd said. The manager was a Null—most of the staff were, too. No idea if the pizza guy was, but nobody wanted to risk him asking questions about what he might or might not see down here.

I took the boxes from the guy and body checked him gently out the door, making sure he went straight to the elevator before looking around for a place to put the pies. Even if the display hadn't been off-putting for dinner, there were still piles of paper scattered over the surface that would not be improved by grease stains.

"Over here." Sharon pulled forward a battered metal stool from the corner of the room, even as Pietr rescued the plastic bag of sodas from the top of the pizzas. "I hope they gave us napkins."

They had. And then there was silence, save for the sound of soda fizzing and jaws chewing, while five hungry Talent refueled, the scalpel lifting and cutting in pantomime behind us.

After pizza, Stosser had pulled rank and told us all to call it quits for the night. Another one of the Rules: we didn't pull all-nighters. We might not sleep, but we needed to rest our brains for a few hours every twelve, for them to work effectively.

Resting your brains didn't mean turning them off, though.

Sharon raised one perfectly waxed eyebrow when I showed up at her door, bags in hand, but let me in, anyway.

"So. You and Venec."

I sighed, aware I wasn't going to be able to dodge, this time. "He and Stosser are having a Big Dog talk. I decided discretion was the better part of not getting bit."

"Should I be flattered?"

That I'd decided to crash with her, rather than Pietr, she meant. I thought that was what she meant, anyway.

"Life…has gotten a little complicated," I admitted.

"Good." Sharon sounded disgustingly smug and relieved at the same time. "You two were going past cute and into annoying, and we were about to draw lots to see who had to lock the two of you into a room until this got settled."

While I tried to decide if I even wanted to respond to that, Sharon went back to sitting on the edge of her bed, brushing out her hair. She had utterly gorgeous blond hair, thick and silky, and it was a shame that she always kept it pulled back, even though I totally understood not wanting to have to fuss with it during the day: it was the same reason I kept my curls short and simple.

"So, the museum thing. The one The Wren's involved in?"

"A side job Venec took on, invited me down to watch and learn."

"Mmm–hmm."

"Oh, shut up. Lou told me to take a break, and he invited. That's all."

"That's all?"

"Isn't that enough?"

I guess my exasperation showed, because she laughed and put down her brush, turning to look at me. Sharon was not only a straight shooter, but she also had the ability to tell when someone was not telling her the truth. It made her an excellent PUP—and a pain in the ass when you were playing poker.

"So, the fact that you guys only had the one room—with the one bed?"

"The first night, we came back to the room after midnight and fell asleep on top of the covers, fully dressed, surrounded by files. And last night…we were on a case."

"Uh-huh." She watched me; that perfectly sculpted face no

longer a disguise for the equally sculpted brain inside. "And if Valere hadn't tried to break in, while you were there?"

I made a face but didn't dodge. "I don't know."

I didn't. I didn't think Ben knew, either. We'd tried denial; we'd tried running parallel. They'd all worked—for a while. But it wasn't going away, and neither were we, so… The fact that we'd both given way at the same time might have been coincidence, or the Merge, but it happened. No point in poking at it now; time to move on.

"So we're still at status quo," Sharon said, standing up to put her brush back on the dresser.

"Why, your call-date coming up?" I knew that the pack had started betting on when we'd break—even before they knew about the Merge, they'd money on it.

"I'm playing the odds," Sharon said. "Spread my cash around. Feel free to take your time. I think Nifty's got next week, though."

"Gee, thanks." I layered the sarcasm extra heavy, there.

Sharon had a lovely laugh, and I didn't hear it anywhere near enough. She went to use the bathroom, and I lay on the second bed and contemplated the ceiling. No, I decided, it didn't bother me that the question of what we were going to do had been tabled by the job: we'd taken the first step toward wherever we were going, and we'd get there, eventually. At our own pace, though, not according to whatever agenda the Merge might have.

The thought of the Merge—some mystical matchmaking force—as a little old woman scowling at us because we were making her wait made me smile. And on that note, listening to the sound of water running in the bathroom, I fell asleep.

Dragons

Not again, part of my mind thought. I've already gotten the message. And then the dream took over, and the giant claw wrapped around my midsection squeezed out any thoughts other than *I can't breathe.*

A swoop, and we were airborne, the world falling away too quickly below me like a parachute drop in reverse. I squirmed, tucked against the scaled belly of the beast, and my flesh flowed and reformed around the claws, giving me room to wiggle. My rib cage adjusted to the pressure, so I was able to breathe, and once I was able to breathe I could look around.

Or rather, look down. The back of my head was cradled against the warm scales of the beast, and the view to either side was obstructed by the great wings, rising and declining like a heartbeat. The dragons I'd seen before, in person, soared more like raptors. But then, I'd never been this close to one in flight.

All of which was my dream-brain's way of not-looking down. I risked a quick glance and closed my eyes again, my dream-stomach roiling. Too high up now, too dizzy-making.

Look.

It was a command, rumbling through the bones of my head, and I knew that it came from the dragon above me. Since you did not refuse a dragon, I swallowed hard and opened my eyes.

We were over a great body of water now, which was somehow easier to look at. It was the view most people saw from an airplane, I supposed—J and I had always Translocated when we traveled, since he, like most high-res Talent, didn't trust any machine that relied on electrical equipment to stay in the air. The dragon dropped several hundred feet, leaving my stomach behind, and we were close enough to see the individual waves, tiny white caplets breaking and re-forming in a restless tangle that reminded me—in a more monochrome way—of the threads of current within my own core. Then a pod of sleek gray dolphins broke the surface, and I forgot everything else, in the sheer joy of watching them fly.

Look.

I was looking, but the feeling came that I wasn't looking the right way. Gathering faith that the dragon would not drop me, at least not until I had seen what it wanted to show me, I exhaled against the scaled restraints and slipped into fugue state.

And then I looked again.

Current. Everywhere. Slipping through the waves… No, it was the waves. The creatures within the waves. I could see through the gray-green water into the depths and beyond, where slow-moving, coldblooded creatures glowed with life, an endless routine of swim and eat and swim and eat and breed and swim and die. Fish and octopuses and whales and things I had no name for, ancient and terrifying. Merfolk, the deep-sea cousins no human ever encountered and lived, more vicious than their coastal kin, bared teeth at me, seeing me as I saw them, but not daring to attack, not while the dragon carried me.

And then the dragon rose and I realized we had dipped to skim the water, so close that my face was wet with salt-spray, my clothing soaked and hanging heavy off my limbs, even as we were rising and banking, turning over a coastline now, and with fugue-sight, magesight, I saw the power in the earth itself, the ley lines clearly visible, following fissures in the world, tracing veins across the rock, the entire world bound up by it, bound by it.

The immensity of it all was too much, and I closed my eyes, but the mage-sight remained.

Look.

I looked.

Remember.

And then the dragon released me, and I fell.

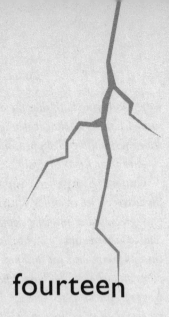

fourteen

"Bonnie! Bonnie!"

The sound came from too far away, and then it was right in my face, no transition whatsoever from dreamspace and waking. I sat upright, the sweat already drying on my skin, and stared blankly at Sharon. "What?" Had I woken her with my dreaming? Except it was too clear, too sharp in my head, and I knew damn well it hadn't been a dream. Not the way Nulls call it, anyway.

What had the dragon wanted me to see?

"Was I... What's wrong?" I might be awake but I wasn't coherent. Sharon didn't seem to notice.

"Come on. Get dressed."

"What?"

"I don't know. Pietr pinged me, woke me up. I guess he couldn't reach you."

The kenning-dream had taken me too far to reach, even by Pietr. Maybe Venec could have, but—

"Is Pietr okay? Venec?" I had already grabbed my pants

off the chair and was pulling them on, trying to remember where my boots had ended up.

"They're fine. It's Stosser."

I guess somehow we always thought that Ian Stosser was indestructible. He just kind of absorbed what the world tried to hit him with and...I don't know, ignored it. Even when his own sister took current-shots at us, he'd shaken it off and gone on with the job.

We knew better, of course. Ian Stosser might not show weakness to the world, not even to us, but he was only human, and he could be hurt.

The sight of the blood on his skin and clothing was still a shock. I wasn't sure, but I thought he was even paler than usual, which meant he was practically translucent.

"What happened?" Sharon, who had gotten her EMT certification last year, was our default medic. She immediately took the dampened towel away from Pietr and started clearing away the mess from Stosser's hands. The fact that he let her was proof that something was terribly wrong.

"God, did you wake the entire hotel?" Stosser might have been passive but he was not polite.

"Don't start with me, Ian. I swear to god, do not start with me right now. You knew you were at risk, and you went walking. In Philadelphia. Alone. At two in the goddamned morning." It would have been less frightening if Venec had been yelling, the way he yelled at us when we fucked up, instead of the cold, low, too-calm voice he was using.

"What happened?" I asked, since Sharon was too busy to insist on an answer.

"Stosser decided to take a walk to clear his head." After they'd finished arguing or during? I didn't ask.

Normally, Stosser wandering alone at night wouldn't be

an issue. It wasn't like he couldn't handle a mugger or even a gang of unruly bikers looking to pick on the metrosexual redhead. Except it looked like he hadn't been able to handle it.

Since Venec was still fuming, I turned to the other Big Dog. "I'm assuming the other guys look worse?"

That earned me a tight smile. "Much."

Venec was pacing the confines of the room, which—with all of us gathered—meant he was constantly having to turn around. It was making me dizzy, but stopping him would have been worse.

"I swear to god, Ian. You knew—you knew someone was going to be gunning for you, and still you went out alone." So he had been warned about Ellen's vision. Good. Not that it seemed to have had much impact on him.

"I am supposed to spend the rest of my life wrapped in current and locked away, then?"

"No. Just until we have some idea of who plans to make you dead."

If this was how they'd been arguing before, I was almost sorry I'd decamped. They sounded like an old married couple. It was serious—maybe deadly serious—but I had the terrible urge to giggle.

"Did you ever think that maybe nobody does? That maybe what the girl saw, if she really saw it, was the result of some natural demise? And that maybe it isn't going to be for another ten years?"

"That's not how it works, boss." I'd been quiet until now, keeping out of the line of potential fire, but this was something I knew about. And Stosser, for all his brilliance, apparently didn't. "If she's a true storm-seer, even untrained, then what she sees is tied up in possibilities and violence, not a peaceful and inevitable conclusion. Both you and Wren... Something you're doing now is going to get you killed. Soon."

It might not be tied together—Ellen knew Wren, and she knew me and I was tied to Stosser, so the connection might be that vague—but the threat was real.

Stosser looked away, only the tightness of his neck giving away the fact that he was in any discomfort under Sharon's competent ministrations. Or maybe it was just having to admit that he might have been wrong. "If so, then I should be safe so long as the Retriever isn't around, correct?"

"Or the same person kills you at different-but-close times, thereby establishing a connection. Or if the only connection is the fact that Ellen knows Bonnie." That was Sharon, making the same connections probably everyone else was, too. Ironic, really, since Stosser was the one who had set me on the missing-kid case, which led me to Ellen, which led to her having a vision about Stosser being dead.

"This seer would be a lot more useful if she could give specifics, the way you do when you scry," Stosser grumbled.

Proof that the boss wasn't as unshook as he claimed: my scrying was about as specific as a fortune cookie. You had to have details before it made sense. We were just really good at ferreting out the details.

"Yeah, well, if it was easy, anyone could do it, right?"

He was smart enough not to respond to that.

Sharon finished with the towel and was inspecting the cuts on his hands. From the way her forehead scrunched I could tell that she was worried about something, but sending him to a hospital... Even if Venec bodily put him into an ambulance, an MRI would probably short out under Stosser's current, anyway—intentionally or not. So she contented herself with wiping away the blood and making sure the cuts were clean before she bandaged them up. You could heal with current, but there was always a real risk of current screwing with the body's natural electrical system, rather than fixing it.

Ben might have been able to make a difference, but he wasn't going to do Stosser any favors, right now. Venec was old-fashioned that way: you earned a bruise, you got to live with it. Especially if you made him worry.

"All right," Stosser said, finally, clearly no longer talking to me. "Yes. It was careless of me."

I would have said stupid, but I wasn't going to. Ben's fury, and his fear, were obvious to everyone, and from the looks Pietr kept shooting me when he thought nobody was looking, he thought I should do something about it, before a real argument broke out.

I wanted to tell him that wasn't how it worked; just because you could reach someone more deeply, maybe even without them realizing it, didn't mean you had the right to do so. If he was angry and worried, he had cause to be, and it wasn't my place to tell him to calm down. Or, worse, make him calm down. That was not what the Merge was for.

Okay, technically and best we'd been able to determine from the few really old texts that mentioned it, the Merge was only interested in two people with strongly connecting current-cores creating new babies. And maybe Pietr was right, although not the way he thought he was. This might not be what the Merge had intended, but nothing said we couldn't use what it offered for our own purposes. Ben had refilled me when I needed it; what could I do, while still respecting his sense-of-self? Not to calm his rightful anger down but to ease the pressure of it.

I didn't so much take down my walls as let them soften; become permeable. If something unwanted pushed at them, they'd react by snapping back, but for now, things could come and go freely, if not easily.

And through that I could feel Ben, letting my core reach out and brush against his. Not an invasion, not even a push, merely the awareness that I was there. He would either ignore me or…

Let me in, with a sensation not of falling but sinking, softly and smoothly, without any panic or fear, the way your skin melts when a lover touches you with intent. I did not push, did not reach, but simply settled into the space given. I was still me, still within my own awareness—the loss-of-self I'd feared when the Merge first appeared had been beaten off with the club of my own strong self-image—but I could touch Ben's core, share his feelings, the occasional stray wisp of thought or action-to-be. If I focused I could "hear" his heart beat, although it was more the echo of electrical action through his own current than the actual noise.

let me I offered and felt him shift inside, letting me carry some of his distraction. It was like holding a scrying crystal, a massive one, and then passing over a ley line while you tried to scry: the bits that were cloudy came clear, and the things that had seemed clear before were now so sharp they sliced the sky.

Dragons

what?

nothing. later

While I was holding down the fort, so to speak, Venec continued the interrogation. "You drove them off?"

"I told you that already."

"How many were there? How did they get a drop on you? I'm assuming they used current, that you didn't get jumped by a bunch of Null hoods."

Venec's voice had gone sharp, goading, and Stosser reacted perfectly, even though he had to know that he was being goaded.

"I could handle Nulls and not even get dusty," he said, annoyed. "They used a current-net to stick me, then came down. Four of them, a nicely organized ambush. And, no, I don't know who they were, and, no, I don't need to know. Let it alone, Ben. Those aren't the droids we're looking for."

"You do know." Pietr had been quiet, but he broke in now and then looked as surprised as anyone that he'd said anything. "You know who they were…and they knew who you were, which means they jumped you for a reason. But this isn't a case anyone should want to scare us away from, so it's not that…"

"What are you tangled in, Ian?" Ben's voice, cooled from his earlier anger under my touch, but still intense. "What's going on?"

"Nothing we need to worry about."

"The last time you said that—the last three times you said that—it was Aden, and it was something we needed to worry about. No more, Ian. Not with a death vision hanging over your head and a serial killer running around not exactly waiting for us to catch him. I can't be distracted like that. None of us can be distracted like that."

The air pressure increased, and the damp strands of Stosser's hair lifted just enough off where it hit his shoulders that you'd think a storm front had just hit town. Which it had.

I eased off a little more from Ben's core, sliding my own sense of calm and rightness into the space left behind. And, oddly enough, I was calm. Normally, two high-res Talent start with a stare-down, you duck and ground and hope to hell none of the current hits you. But these were the Big Dogs, and they would never let any of their internal conflict touch us.

I was pretty sure of that, anyway. Maybe the Merge was shielding me: Pietr and Sharon were still as mice, their attention carefully not on either Stosser or Venec, waiting to see how the storm would break.

"Sonofabitch." It was an exhalation of sound more than

actual words out of Stosser's mouth, but the current-pressure retreated, and we could breathe again.

The Big Dog got up, pushing Sharon aside gently, and stalked to the door. The way he was walking, I could tell his ribs hurt. I also knew better than to suggest he have someone look at them.

"It's Chicago," he said, his hand on the door. "Just Chicago." And then he was gone, leaving the four of us standing, abandoned, in his hotel room.

"Boss?"

A multitude of questions in that one word. What just happened? What happened in Chicago? What should we do? What could we do?

I'd been shoved out. Venec was as walled-up and tied down as I'd ever felt him: I couldn't get the slightest read, not without digging, and that was the very last thing I wanted to do, right then. Not because it would be rude, but because one wrong tap, and he might explode.

He answered Pietr with another question. "Can you follow him without being seen?"

"What will he do to me if he sees me?"

"Bad things."

"I'll keep that in mind." Pietr waited a beat and then left the room, already beginning to fade around the edges. They'd been working on getting his tendency to disappear under stress under control—it made a belated kind of sense that they'd want ways to induce it, as well as reduce it.

"I am… I'm going to get rid of these rags—" Sharon held up the bloodstained washcloths "—and then, um, go back to sleep. Because there's nothing else to do right now, right?"

"Right," Venec agreed, but he sounded like he had barely heard her and had no idea what he was responding to. That was very much not Benjamin Venec. Sharon shot me a very pointed look and beat feet out the door. Her silent comment had been totally unnecessary: I wasn't going to leave Ben alone.

Not in any sense of the word.

"What happened? In Chicago?"

Venec had never lied to me. Not ever. He had refused to tell me things and expected me to respect that—and I had. But not this time. We couldn't afford to be working blind. Not with everything else that was going on.

"It's not—"

"Don't give me that shit." Suddenly, looking at his drawn and tired face, at wheneverthehell in the morning it was, I was furious. I don't get mad often but when I do, I don't hold back. "Somebody just hauled down on Stosser, hard enough to draw blood. And I don't see any new smoking craters on the sidewalk, so that means he didn't fight back. Not really, not the way he could, if somebody he didn't know attacked him, or if he felt he could let go. Pietr was right." And there was only one possible answer to that. "Was it her? Was it his bitch of a sister?"

Aden Stosser, who hated everything we were, everything we stood for—and hated her brother for creating us.

"No. Aden...would never attack directly, not like that. And I don't think she's capable of physically hurting Ian, any more than he would hurt her."

Personally, I thought that Ben was giving both Stossers more credit than they deserved...or maybe less. I didn't say that.

"Then what? Who? We need to know. For our own safety, as well as his, we need to know who else in this damned city is maybe aiming a smackdown on us. And that means knowing what happened in Chicago."

If it was related to Chicago, then odds were Ellen's seeing

both Stosser and Wren dead were unrelated to this attack. But somehow…I didn't think so. The fact that Venec wasn't shutting me down entirely meant he didn't think so, either. There were too many threads, and they were all tangling here, in a city not our own.

"Benjamin."

"Jesus. My mother used that exact same tone. Don't do that."

He got up and stared out the window. I knew damn well he wasn't seeing the view, though. I sat on the bed and waited.

"Ian was your age, maybe a year older. His mother was seated chair, Midwest Council."

One of the most powerful pooh-bahs, even in a council of overachievers. I'd known that, at one point, before Ian Stosser just became Stosser-the-boss.

"His father… God, Michael was one of those people, the hair on your arms stood up just being in the same room with him. I think he was born with core. And the kindest, softest voice. I don't think he ever raised his voice once."

Carrying that much power, he probably never needed to.

"What happened?" Because you could feel it coming, the way a story has an inevitable ending.

"He was a researcher. Not just theory—he was trained as a doctor."

Rare—current use and hard science didn't go well together, because of all the tech used. Something like an electron microscope or an X-ray machine….

"He did most of his work in the field, before Ian was born—working in South America, where they didn't have tech, just whatever they could do with what they packed in. Tiny towns, up in the mountains and hidden in jungles. Then he came back and married Sofia and spent the rest of his life researching. He had a theory. He believed that current was a genetic inheritance, but one that all humans had, in varying degrees. That it could be enhanced, built up…."

"Like the woman in the Park."

"What?" I'd jolted him from his memories, and he looked at me blankly.

"The woman in the Park, the one who lured all the girls to her, told them they'd be able to pool their abilities. We think she was trying to use them to enhance her own."

"Like a coven. That wasn't Uncle Mike's theory, but yeah, it's on the same sort of principle, that the use could be enhanced."

"So what happened?" Because, yeah, this was not going to have a good ending.

"Michael…" Not Uncle Mike now, I noted. "He started to become obsessed with the idea. That it wasn't so much Nulls and Talent, but a sliding scale. He thought that if we could just find some way to test, early on… If we could find them before they started to manifest, encourage even the latent skill sets, we'd increase the population significantly."

He paused.

"He thought that would be a wonderful thing."

"And someone else didn't."

"Council. They're jealous of their status. Not all of them, not even most of them, but enough. They have this idea that current makes them special, that they need answer only to their exact peers." He swallowed, and now I could feel him, still filled with sorrow and rage and confusion, still bright despite the years he'd stored them.

I knew what he was talking about: I'd been raised Council, even though my dad had been pure lonejack. That was the heart of Aden Stosser's accusations against us, that we would take that answerability away, open it to public scrutiny. True enough; that was exactly what we wanted to do. "They killed him?"

"Worse. They destroyed his records. Years of research, files and notes and…they turned them to ash."

Current-blast. It took a lot out of you, but it couldn't be put out, not without a matching current-blast, the way smoke-jumpers matched fire with fire. But there was worse coming. I could feel it.

"They also… Nobody could swear it was deliberate, but they also killed the kids he was working with. Four kids. The oldest wasn't even thirteen yet."

God. "His dad tried to stop them." Of course he did: any man Ben called "Uncle" would have died to protect children, no matter what his other personal flaws.

"Heart attack was the official verdict."

In other words, he drew so much current from his core, he drained his entire body—enough to damage the natural electrical surges of his body—and his heart stopped.

"They killed him. Standing there, never touching him, never doing anything directly, but they killed him and four innocent children."

"And Ian demanded that they be punished."

"No." Ben let out a noise that might have been trying for a laugh. "Aden did."

I didn't remember moving, but I was across the room, my arms around his torso, palms flat against his chest, feeling the reassuring rise and fall of his breathing, the steady beat of his heart. "What happened?"

"She went after the leader with a knife, as I recall. She's always been…emotional. Ian stopped her. I think…in some ways she has never forgiven him for that. She's very much eye for an eye."

"And instead he went in front of the Council and demanded a formal hearing, didn't he? To determine their guilt publicly, hold them responsible for his father's death?"

"You know Ian. He likes things…clear-cut, duly processed. He wanted them to have to admit their guilt in front of witnesses, so there would be no doubt, no second-guessing. So the verdict would be clean—and the blood not on his baby sister's hand."

"The Council disagreed?" There was Council, which meant anyone who agreed to live within their structure, and then there was the Council, the Talent who determined that structure and ruled their region with a mostly invisible but always-felt hand. In theory, it was of the members by the members. In practice…not always so much.

"I don't know what happened. Nobody talks about it, ever. But nobody was punished. All I know for sure is that Ian came out of that Council room determined to create a structure by which even the highest of the holies would not be able to evade responsibility. And the rest you know."

The rest, I was part of.

"None of which explains why someone related to that would come after him now. I mean, other than the Bitch. Or why he would let them."

Ben sighed, and it felt like a shudder. "The only thing that Ian holds more dearly than justice is honor. Whatever this is, it's tied to that. How? God knows. If you can figure out how Ian Stosser's brain works…"

All right. Good point.

I rested my cheek against Ben's shoulder, letting his breathing settle my own thoughts. The Merge seemed to hum like a generator, the connection between the two of us smooth and deep, almost effortless. The invasion of privacy I'd been afraid of for so long… Yeah, he knew more about me, could predict me in ways I wasn't comfortable with. And probably—definitely, he felt the same about me. But there were moments maybe it didn't feel like such a terrible thing, after all. Right now, at oh-dog-early in the morning, exhausted and worried, having someone who was totally there was…nice. Like bracing yourself for cold water and instead sliding into a nice warm gel.…

"Gel."

"What?"

His body was almost relaxed under my hands, but I could feel Venec come alert when I said that single word, his core reacting to me.

"Gel. That theory that Talent is actually just better insulation, allowing us to channel current rather than it slipping out of our bodies?"

"Yeah." That one word was not so much agreement as waiting to see where I was going with this.

"The theory that it can maybe be enhanced, added to. What Ian's dad was working on. The idea that woman in the Park had, that even those without Talent can maybe add to it. The idea of a sliding scale's been around for a while, in one form or other. So odds are, other Talent have thought it, right?"

"That would seem logical. Also, intuitive. There's no idea ever held by only a single mind."

That sounded like a quote, but I didn't recognize the source.

"So maybe…maybe our killer had it, too?"

He turned within my hold, putting his hands on my shoulders and moving me a little bit away; not a dismissal but reasserting the difference between Ben and Bonnie, and Venec and Torres. I was good with that.

"You think he was performing a scientific experiment… the vivisection not to cause pain, or ritual, but…"

"I think maybe he was trying to find the source of the insulation. Maybe…" I shuddered. "Maybe to scrape it out, and test it, or find some way, oh, god, some way to add it to himself. A transplant to increase his abilities. Or, if he's a Null, to, god, to steal them somehow."

"That's…"

"Gross."

"Brilliant."

"Also gross."

Venec swallowed hard and nodded. "Yes, also gross."

"If he used the same blade each time, trying to scrape the goo, all their current…" A shudder ran through my body this time. "God, can you imagine how many signatures must have touched it? How many layers… As they died, being conducted through the metal… It's taken on a life of its own, almost like an Artifact. That's what I was sensing." I was desperately thankful I'd never touched the actual weapon.

"It's just a theory." He paused. "A good one, though."

"I guess I should go wake Sharon up, huh?"

"No." Venec shook his head and sighed, then drew me toward him again, his hands slipping over my shoulders to the small of my back, pressing me against him. It wasn't sexual, in any way, but it was, too. Comfort and sex were linked in my mind, but this was that and a level of something else. A pause before battle, a gathering of forces.

And the kiss that followed was pure heat, even for us. Neither of us were novices at the game, and we'd gotten past the awkward who-does-what-where stage months ago. So just warmth and pressure and a hint of teeth and tongue, our bodies pressed against each other without any need to do more or go further.

We had time. We had all the time we had.

"Let her get a few more hours of sleep," he said, drawing

back just enough to speak, his breath warm and a little bit stale, which was weirdly…intimate. No rush to prep with mouthwash or breath mints, just him.

I could talk all I wanted about being on the job and dividing up personal from work, but the truth of the matter was that we lived our jobs, and there was never going to be a day—or night—where one or both of us wasn't going to be working.

And here we were, two consenting adults, in private, with a few hours to ourselves, and an itch that very badly needed to be scratched.

"Sleep, huh?" I managed, and felt his smile more than saw it, a glow of amusement tinged with smugness, and just a hint of uncertainty, wrapped in anticipation.

"She should sleep," he agreed. "You, not so much."

All right, then.

The thing about sex is, most of the time it's just a confirmation of what you already know: I like you, you like me, we can make each other feel good. Nothing wrong with that, at all. But when you delay, when you build up the tension, the anticipation, you run the risk of letdown, that the "feel good" isn't as good as you'd expected.

We didn't talk about it. We didn't think about it. Hands and fingers and mouths roamed freely, clothing sliding off, piece by piece, a slow discovery. That made him shiver. This made me giggle and buck. Naked, the air-conditioning barely able to keep us cool, I took a step backward, pulling him with me, and then turned even as I fell, so that he landed underneath me.

"Nice trick."

"I'm full of nice," I said, and he laughed, so I had to prove it to him.

Even when I was a teenager, sex was more than just in-and-out, to be crude. I was glad, but not surprised, to find out that Venec agreed. The Merge might have given us a fast track, but there was still so much to learn; no point in rushing things. We were sweaty but not sated, and it was enough. For now.

We ended up spooned together on the bed, his arms wrapped around me, one knee between mine, his lips pressed against the back of my neck, and slept.

If dragons flew overhead, in that hour before dawn, I didn't dream of them.

Ian knew that Pietr was behind him. He might not have had the training of the PUPs, the way Ben had, but he knew the signature of everyone who worked for him, invisible or not.

He also could not fault the way the boy handled himself: no less than fifteen paces behind, maintaining an unobstructed line of sight, not enough to crowd or insult, but were there to be trouble, able to come to immediate assistance—or, knowing his PUPs, to note the details for a later report, leaving the boss to handle it himself.

Ben had sent him. No doubt: not even the most aggressive PUP would follow a Big Dog without orders. And Ben was not wrong to worry. The fact that he had allowed his attackers to do as much damage as they had was proof that he, Ian, was not thinking clearly, taking too many risks. Drawing his enemies into a false sense of confidence that might, in fact, be truth; more a trap for himself than them.

Ben would scold him. Ben, who had been the original lone wolf before Ian made him the lead dog of the pack, knew how risky, how stupid it was to use oneself as bait and trap alike. Knew, because Ian had told him, over and over again.

The irony amused Ian. He did not think it would amuse

his partner. So he allowed Pietr to stay within sight, even as he sensed his attackers drawing near again.

The scrabble of claws was his first warning. Then the beasts were on him, with barely enough time to throw up a current-wall of protection.

stay back he warned Pietr. *do not interfere* At best, the boy would get hurt. At worst, he might actually damage the beasts before they could finish taking payment.

That was his last thought, before a claw reached through the current and struck him a blow across the back of his head.

fifteen

"A what?"

"I swear, boss, I don't know. They came out of nowhere, I swear, the air was clear and then suddenly they were on him."

"That's why you didn't fight back," I said. "They knew you wouldn't risk hurting them."

Venec looked at me, then back at Stosser, not used to being outside the loop. "What were they?"

I didn't answer, staring at Stosser, who had somehow managed to avoid getting cut open this time, although he had a serious goose egg swelling on the back of his head and a nasty bruise on his face where he'd hit the pavement. Enough time had passed between the attack and when Pietr had knocked on the door, Ian in tow and Sharon hurrying down the hallway, that the colors had come out nicely.

"Bonnie?" Venec, dangerously close to annoyance, although the worry and anger of before had disappeared. My acceptance of Ian's reluctance to strike back was enough to make him accept it, too.

"Why is this your debt, Ian?" It was none of my business… but I was the only one who knew to ask.

"Blood money. It seemed…appropriate."

I was utterly confused, and then things started to unravel, a little. "You're an idiot."

Big Dog didn't disagree with me. "It was my only option."

"Bonnie?"

"They're winglets," I said.

"Wing-baby dragons?" Pietr blinked at that.

"Not exactly. Cave dragons don't give birth—they're too ornery to even have a mating season, much less raise another creature. They…spawn. Split. Shake off winglets. Most of them get eaten, but if they can prove useful…they get to live."

I'd done research, after running into a loan-shark dragon myself, when I was younger. They were the loan sharks of the *Cosa Nostradamus,* and winglets were their collection agents.

Ben turned and looked at his partner. "They want your blood. Literally."

"Somewhat dramatic, Ben. They're merely…reminding me. If I can't give gold, they take blood."

"Any particular amount, or all of it?"

"I'm not sure. So far, they seem to be satisfied with small amounts. But they may decide to claw me dry and call the debt done." He wasn't, in my opinion, anywhere near worried enough about that possibility.

"You really need to find out the terms of repayment before you sign the contract, boss." I was trying for nonchalant, too, and not quite pulling it off.

"Wait—someone is repaying something with Ian's blood?" Pietr was utterly lost.

"Or Ian owes them something. That's it, isn't it?" Sharon was staring at Stosser as though she'd never seen him before. "You owe them…what?"

"The startup money. For us. Goddammit, Ian!" Ben was back to furious.

"It seemed like a good idea at the time. My life's work, given surety by my life's blood, if it didn't work."

"But it is working. We're making money. Why—"

"Because it takes money to keep us going," I said. "You put it back into the offices, into hiring new people, not paying back the original debt. And now the time's up."

"How much, Ben?"

"Two hundred."

"Thousand?" Pietr's voice almost squeaked.

"Is that the original loan, or—"

"All in. Two years' grace. I was supposed to start repayment last month."

Last month, when we'd hired new people to handle the workload, instead.

"All right." My voice was weirdly calm: I think Pietr was doing all the freak-out for all of us, his eyes wide and his mouth hanging open in a way that would be funny if it wasn't so serious. "We can do that."

"We can?" My fellow pups were clearly wondering where we'd lay hands on that sort of cash. So was I. But we'd manage it.

"No, Bonnie—"

"Shut up, Ian." Venec cut him off with a voice like ice. "We need you here, not bleeding out a week at a time, always waiting for the next attack. Dragons are stringent but not unreasonable, as loan sharks go, and it won't care where the repayment comes from, so long as it's made."

"If anyone finds out…" It would be a sign of weakness we couldn't afford, bad PR to kill all the good we'd done. Using a dragon's loan…defaulting on a dragon's loan? Even my father hadn't been idiot enough to do that, although the man who killed him had made it seem that way.

Had this been why I'd been dreaming of dragons? It made sense, but it didn't feel quite right. Not entirely. *Remember,* that fire-dry voice had whispered. But remember what? Something I had seen…but it was gone now, faded the way all kennings did.

Venec, meanwhile, was still lashing into his partner. "You'd rather bleed out than accept help? Don't be more of an idiot than you've already managed."

Stosser refused to look abashed—I don't think it was in his genetic makeup—but he nodded once and stopped protesting.

"Fine. We'll find the money and get them off your back— literally. We have something else to worry about right now," Venec went on, still radiating disgust at his partner's stubbornness. "Bonnie's figured out why our killer is doing what he does."

Everyone turned to look at me, even Stosser, dragons and debt not forgotten, but tabled for now. "Maybe," I said, switching gears, practically hearing everything go click. "I'm not a hundred percent sure, not even ninety percent. But it makes sense."

I outlined the basics, starting with the kids in Central Park and their charismatic, possibly Talented leader, the current trendy-if-contested theory of current-handling and genetics, and skipped over anything Venec had told me about Chicago, finishing with my thoughts about the knife, and saw the lights go on in everyone's eyes before I'd reached my conclusion.

"So we're looking for someone who knows about Talent, maybe is a low-level…?" I could see Pietr's brain-wheels turning.

"Or is high-res and wants more," Sharon said. "No way to tell."

"Logic. Think about the victims." I could visualize them all in my head, all the stats from the files, but knew the others lacked my particular recall. "None of the victims were particularly high-res themselves. I can't see him intentionally looking for low-end subjects, not if he wanted to gather more power to himself, or even just to see what made them strong. But he wouldn't go after anyone he wasn't sure he could take down. And since we already know that he's got to be at least forty, and probably older, unless he's a bodybuilder his physical strength isn't enough, so odds are he's low- or middling-res, but smart. And——"

"And not acting alone."

"What?" I stopped to look at Venec, who had broken into my presentation in a way he hadn't since I was a rookie.

"I just realized that was what I was seeing, with the knife, the restraints, the way the killer was moving—he kept going around in a three-quarter pattern, not a full circle. As though there was someone else at the head of the table, holding the victim down, keeping him calm. We're not looking for one killer, children. We're looking for two."

Sharon pretty much summed it up best, in her own everladylike manner.

"Oh, fuck."

Stosser made the decision to call in part of the team back in New York on this, full-time. Sharon, Pietr, and I stayed down in Philly, going over the physical files, while Lou and Nicky back in New York handled the research aspect, specifically Nicky doing some current-hacking on our past victims in San Diego and Montreal. Nifty, meanwhile, stepped up to handle the trainees, poor bastard. Although he seemed to enjoy it. I wondered if Farshad would still be in the office when we got back, and hoped so.

Part of me was curious about what Nick was up to; the other part remembered the few times I've been around when he worked his mojo, and was just as happy to avoid that particular headache.

Overall, I thought we'd gotten the better assignment. At least for the first three hours, until the photos and text started to swim in front of my eyes, and I was pretty sure I'd see that damn flashing knife in my dreams, even though I'd dismantled the display the night before.

"Come with me."

Ian appeared in the doorway of our makeshift office and crooked a finger, making it clear who he wanted. I was just as happy to get up and stretch my legs—and rest my eyes—a bit.

"What have you discovered?"

"Nothing." It burned to have to admit it. We were under a massive time-hammer: every hour that went by increased the risk that we'd have another body on our hands. "The ten-every-ten suggests that our perps have some kind of psychological fixation that's limiting them—or it could be a ritualistic thing. Lou is going over records to see if we have anything similar in the database."

A Null organization could have a computer that would sort and spit out this information in minutes. We had an old-fashioned, if incredibly complete, series of filing cabinets.

"Y'know, when we are flush again—" and it would happen, it had to happen "—we should think about hiring some trusty Nulls to set up an off-site database, so we could just call down a request and they could do the research. Hell of a lot faster, and time…time is the thing we never seem to have enough of."

"Nulls?" Stosser was momentarily diverted by the thought, and not in a good way. "I don't think that would be such a wise idea."

"Oh, don't you start. Not every Null is out to get us or use us, you know."

"Not every one, no," he agreed. "But enough are, and will, for me to be cautious about our existence spreading too far."

"Yeah, because no cop ever gossiped outside the *Cosa*." Sarcasm didn't so much drip from my words as gush.

"Gently, Torres. Leave the back talk to Ben. I need you to be obedient, right now."

I stopped, suddenly realizing that he had been leading me toward the elevator. "Where are we going? If you're taking a walk, boss, you need someone better in a fight or more—"

"I have a meeting."

"Boss, I am totally not dressed for a Council meeting." That was the only reason why he'd need me to be obedient. And why he was wearing one of his better suits, the one so plainly cut it had to cost a fortune.

Shit. Suit. The same thing he'd been wearing in Ellen's vision. I had the sudden urge to dig my heels in and refuse to go anywhere without backup—or at least telling everyone where we were going—but I knew that look on the Big Dog's face.

I could have reached for Venec, but by the time he got here… No. Play the cards, Bonnie. But stay ready.

"It's not formal." Like that was going to reassure me. "We're making a Statement."

"Oh." Nope, not reassured. We reached the elevator, and I took a moment to compose myself. It was only the elevator in the office that gave me the jeebies, not elevators in general, but I still had a moment of unease whenever I stepped into one, fully expecting the power to fail and us to plummet to the bottom of the shaft. Of course, being in the basement of the hotel, it couldn't plummet all that far.

"Why do you need me?"

"You're the one who figured it out. Also, you have a reputation."

"I have a reputation?"

Of course I did. I knew that—after two years with PUPI,
most of them out in the field, there were people who knew
me, knew what I did. And by "people" I meant both human
and not. But I hadn't exactly thought how that might translate to the Council.

Contemplating that, at least, distracted me. There are two
groups in the Talent population. Well, three, actually, but the
gypsies side with lonejacks when they bother to weigh in at
all. The lonejacks are independents, taking care of their own
shit, going their own way, and generally not getting in anyone's face until they have to. My dad had been a lonejack,
and so were most of the PUPs, including Venec. It was both
a philosophy and a culture, and hard to move from one to
the other, what we call crossing the river.

My mentor had been Council, though, and he'd pretty
much raised me from the time I was eight, Zaki being useless as a parental authority figure.

Council was all about rules and regulations, order and
authority. Not in a bad way, either, although most lonejacks
would disagree. There was a comfort and protection in being
Council, in knowing that you'd never be left to hang, never
abandoned, because there was a safety net underneath you.

The net came with a price, though: obedience to the seated
Council, the folk who made the rules. Ian Stosser had been
close enough to seated Council to burn himself—and he
had burned them, instead. Knowing what I did now, what
Ben had told me…a lot of things about the boss made more
sense now.

He'd started PUPI to ensure that nobody ever escaped
paying the price for crimes committed by magic—had ba-

sically told the Council to go fuck themselves. And they'd been trying to fuck us over ever since, even as they used our services. That's why they'd never done more than slap the Bitch's hand—why they would never do more.

"You really think they'll issue a Statement?"

"No." His voice was flat, and he stared at the elevator door in front of us, not wasting any of his legendary—and very real—charisma on me. "But we'll be on record as having tried."

A Statement was a warning and an APB and a request for information all in one, and every Council member who heard it would be bound by it. I assumed he was going to ask them to come to us with any information available on any of the murders, which, if they agreed, would be incredibly useful.

"If you don't think they will, why are we really going?"

Bastard wouldn't tell me.

We took a cab to a part of town I didn't recognize—not that I knew much outside of what I'd seen already—to a tiny little street and a tiny little town house. Ian paid off the cabbie and we got out.

The door opened: they'd obviously been watching for us. A young man stood there, wearing what had to be the Junior Edition of Stosser's suit. My black pants and dark green blouse, so nice when I packed them, were starting to get an inferiority complex.

"You could have Translocated," Junior said, ignoring me completely.

"Why?" Stosser said, with an air of such utter unconcern I wanted to stop and applaud. It could have been taken as the desire to not garner attention, to not use current frivolously—things the Council generally approved of. Or it could be read as simply not caring enough to spend the current—

a slap that the Council would not approve of but would not be able to prove he intended.

Stosser was a pain in the ass in many ways, but I was proud to study with him.

Junior escorted us into the house, which was just as small as it looked: a narrow living space with a kitchen beyond, and narrow stairs leading to the second floor. A safe house of some sort probably, from the decor, where they held meetings that should not be on official ground but were too sensitive to hold in public. J had told me about them; I'd never actually seen one myself. Had never thought I'd be in one.

"Ian."

The man who greeted the boss was old, older than J, even, with a bare scalp covered with age spots and a definite hitch in his step. The hair lifted on my arms when he came toward us, though, and I wasn't anywhere near foolish enough to dismiss him because of his age or infirmity.

"Uncle William. This is Bonita Torres, mentee of Joseph Cetala."

The mentor relationship was more binding than blood to Talent; who trained you set who you were, what you thought, and how you handled current. It didn't say anything about how skilled you were, officially, but certain lines tended to run more high-res than others.

J was a powerhouse, but that wasn't why Uncle William's silver eyebrow raised at the introduction. J had his fingers in a lot of Council pies, and I had a strong suspicion he'd helped bury a number of bodies, not all of them metaphorical. Stosser had just informed him that I was not only a PUP, but possibly a political player and to be trusted—at least as much as J was trusted.

I had a flashback to Andy approaching me in the Starbucks, and wondered if she'd hear about this, and what she'd think, and why I cared.

"Bonita was the investigator who determined the link between the killings."

"You think she will be persuasive enough to convince us to issue a Statement?"

No delicate games from Uncle William, apparently. If you didn't know Stosser, you wouldn't see the small start of surprise. Both Uncle William and I did know him, though.

"You thought we'd dicker while our people are being slaughtered?"

"Yes."

Me, too.

"Normally, you'd be right," William admitted, waving us to the waiting sofa. "But not this time."

"You will issue a Statement, then?"

"No."

All right, maybe he was playing games, after all.

"You must—"

"We must do nothing we do not believe to be in the best interests of the larger community," William said. Standard Council line.

Stosser, no surprise, wasn't buying that. "The ignorance of the many versus the safety of one?"

"A panic helps no one. Issuing a Statement without any more detail—without even an idea of who this man is or how to protect against him—would be foolish. We are all in agreement on this, Ian."

"We" meant all the national Councils, not merely our regional. I knew that simply from his inflection.

"So why did you even agree to this meeting, if you had already decided?" Stosser managed not to sound bitter, merely curious.

"In this discussion, some details were shared that it was determined that you should hear. Elements that may allow you to narrow your search—and if you are able to narrow it, to give us more detail. Then we will be able to reconsider the Statement."

Oh. Interesting.

"Information that you could not share before?" Stosser did not sound happy.

"Information that we did not have before. We have learned it and determined that it would be to the mutual benefit to share it."

A warning: behave, or we don't have to tell you anything. It didn't matter to this man that people might die, if Ian was going to sass him.

God, I really hated the Council some days.

"Fine." Stosser was sulky but polite, sitting down and folding his long legs under him with the grace of a gazelle come for tea. "Please. Inform us."

I had the passing thought that I was supposed to stand behind him and look menacing, like some kind of hench-thing, but I was able to identify that thought as a passing echo of Venec and not a serious consideration.

Ben could loom. From me, it would be laughable. So I sat on the sofa a careful distance from the boss, kept my spine straight, and listened.

"In Montreal, during the period you think this killer was operating there, a man fell under suspicion for murder. The victim—not one of your ten—was cut open, the muscle ignored and the bones of his body scraped dry in the same manner. But he was found not in an alley, but the house he and the suspected killer shared."

"He was Talent."

"Yes. Both the killer and the victim."

"And this was not entered into the public record, why?" Stosser was still polite, still calm, as though the Council covering up a murder wasn't exactly the sort of thing we were supposed to be fighting against. That wasn't justice; that was CYA.

"Because the victim was the suspect's mentor."

Oh.

And that was that. The Council lackey out front kindly— in other words, with obvious condescension that proved he was an idiot—offered to Translocate us back to our hotel, rather than having to slum it in a taxi.

"And you would deposit us, where? In a hotel room you've never seen? In front of a busy hotel, with no line of sight to ensure the space is cleared? Maybe a bathroom stall somewhere, that might or might not be occupied?" Stosser's scorn was magnificent. "Don't show off your ignorance quite so proudly."

"Way to win friends and influence enemies, boss," I said, as the flunky, flushed, flagged down the cab someone inside had—at our request—called for us. The rest of the ride back to the hotel was in silence, Stosser thinking his own thoughts, and me—well, mostly trying to nap. I was *tired*.

We got back to the hotel, and Venec was waiting out front, leaning up against the wall, talking to the doorman. A cigarette, unlit, was in one hand, like he'd taken it out of the pack and gotten distracted. I hadn't seen him smoke in months.

Venec stared into the air a moment and then tilted his head to look at Stosser. That subtle hum of current that told me they were communicating simmered in the air. As usual nobody else seemed to notice it. "Mouse and rat?"

Stosser's lean jaw clenched. Whatever "mouse and rat" was, he didn't like it. But he nodded once, a curt jerk of his chin. "Use your discretion. I assume you're not going to let me take part."

"You assume correctly. Go back to the office, Ian. Help Nifty keep the leash on the rest of our pups, before he quits in exhaustion."

Getting Stosser back into the office was an excellent idea. Even if Ellen hadn't seen him dead, just having him in the field made me uneasy. I had the misfortune to babysit him on a job once, and he almost ruined it, just by standing there. Ian Stosser was incredibly high-res and incredibly focused, and could—when he wanted to—be incredibly persuasive, but the boss had no ability whatsoever to dampen his core down. That's great when you want to overpower an enemy, but not so much when trying to glean a scattered scene—or whatever it was Venec had in mind.

The Big Dogs stared at each other, doing that quiet communication thing, and then Stosser nodded again.

"Torres..."

"I'll fill in the blanks for everyone, boss." Not everything that happened; Council politics didn't matter to the job. But everything else, yeah. "Moment we know anything, we'll report it."

Wren paced along the sidewalk, only half of her attention focused on walking a straight line and not bumping into people. She could feel the building, half a block away, as though it was literally glowing with heat, rather than simply exuding a faint trace of current, barely enough to register. Having tangled with the building twice already, though, it came through bright as a thunderstorm.

More, it came through with a recognizable signature.

She had known this would happen, eventually; although she had assumed it would be after she had retrieved something, not before. Still, now that she had identified it, there was no mistaking that dry, slightly smoky tang. She had felt it often enough, tangled in Bonnie's current.

Benjamin Venec was involved in the museum's security.

She felt a grin stretch across her face and suspected that it was an evil one. Easy jobs were, well, easy. The tough ones were *interesting*.

Still, she shouldn't rush into anything, especially where PUPI might be concerned. Especially after she'd been blocked on her first two approaches. She'd spent the time since then breaking down the defenses she'd encountered, using what she knew about Venec and his thought process—not enough, an oversight she would fix—and refining her attack, her entire focus on the job.

Wren thought she had the key now. But only an amateur rushed in the moment they finished prep. She needed to clear her head. It was also time—past time, really—to check in with Sergei, if for no other reason than she was curious as to how things were going with Ellen.

Turning left instead of right, she found a pay phone that, wonder of wonders, still worked.

"Hey."

Sergei didn't even bother to ask how she was doing or why she hadn't finished the job yet. "I'm at the Sofitel, in town. Get over here."

That was only a few blocks away. She hung up the phone, not bothering to ask why he was in town, and started walking. Fast.

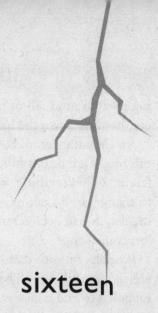

sixteen

The others hadn't gotten anywhere further, since I'd left. It was odd to realize we'd only been gone a little over an hour—my sense of time was starting to slip, which wasn't good. And the clock was still ticking: somewhere, our killer was stalking another victim—or maybe had already killed him.

I filled the others in, as I'd promised. None of them seemed much fussed about the Council; typical lonejacks, they didn't expect any help from that quarter, only interference. So far, they hadn't been wrong.

"So it started in Montreal?" Sharon added that to the notes.

"Sounds like it, yeah. A mentor-mentee slaying. Ugh." Pietr looked a little green. We all did, actually, even Venec.

"We need to get those files," Venec said. "And not wait for the Council to maybe-yes, maybe-no share them."

"Uh-huh. And how do you expect to do that?" Sharon did the eyebrow-raising thing, and Venec raised his hands in defeat. "Hell if I know."

Venec admitting he didn't have a plan. It would have been entertaining if it hadn't been so depressing. They started tossing ideas around, all of them utterly implausible. I slipped out, heading down the hallway for the little inner courtyard.

An eleventh victim. Despite what Uncle William had said, this might not be our killer at all—the dump was utterly different, and everything we'd learned said that was unlikely to change. It was entirely possible that this was a copycat, or the details had been scrambled and it wasn't the same at all, just coincidence.

Possible, but not damn likely. If it did start there, if this was the first killing… The mentor-mentee relationship wasn't supposed to end that way. What had gone wrong? If he was looking to add to his power…what had triggered it?

Not that it mattered to us. Our job was to find him and stop him, not to psychoanalyze him.

Just a minute in the fresh air, and I'd go back inside, I promised myself, sinking down onto the bench and leaning my head back. Just a few minutes.

"Hi."

I looked up, not surprised to see Wren standing there. I got the feeling that more than a few minutes had passed.

"Ellen saw you dead."

"Yeah, I know. Sergei just gave me the rundown."

She sat down next to me. I didn't know how she'd gotten into our basement retreat; she was The Wren—even crap at Translocation, she could still get in anywhere she wanted to.

"You being careful?"

"Yeah."

"Good."

I wanted to ask her if she was going to abandon her attempts on the museum, but I knew she wouldn't. And she wouldn't apologize for it, either.

Out of the corner of my eye, Wren Valere practically shimmered with magic, the way a heat mirage shimmered, making you wonder if you actually saw anything at all. The longer I knew her, the more I realized that her no-see-me was vastly different from Pietr's, although I couldn't have told you how or why, exactly.

"I was going to stop by the office later tonight to… explain," she said. "But then Sergei told me you were already down here."

"Explain?" Maybe I'd been wrong about that apology.

She sighed, tilting her head back to look up at the night sky. "The painting. It's part of a new exhibit they're about to open. But the painting itself, if it's shown…it could expose something the estate doesn't want known. And the Board wants to keep the estate happy. So they want the painting—and just that painting—to…go away."

"You're going to destroy it?" I couldn't imagine Sergei ever agreeing to that. A businessman, yeah, but he ran an art gallery in the Null world and was known for being kind of obsessive about it.

"Destroy it? Ha, no. Sergei has a buyer lined up. A Collector. Nobody will ever see it again."

I laughed; I couldn't help myself. "Paid to steal it, and then paid again to sell it? Nice way to double-dip a paycheck."

"Yeah. I thought so, too."

Wren Valere was a thief, but so was half the world, one way or the other. It wasn't going to be PSI's concern. Venec, on the other hand… Well, they could haggle that out themselves. I'd make popcorn.

Which meant one less problem to worry about, but two massive ones left on the table.

"Wren…have you pissed off any dragons, recently?"

"What?" She looked startled. "No. I don't even know any."

"Okay." My first dream had three dragons, circling. The winglets harassing Stosser, endangering PUPI? I'd thought there was some importance to the number three, but it was a risk interpreting too much in a kenning. Sometimes the message was straightforward: beware dragons. Or, if I wanted to dig a bit more, beware bargains made with dragons.

The second dream…a singular dragon, definitely a Greater Dragon, carrying me, showing me something important. I had forgotten, the details slipping out of reach, not even remembering that I had forgotten until now. Once remembered, the sensations slipped back in. Dragon-borne, surrounded by current skimming through the waves, snaking through bedrock, shimmering in the air. Less a threat or warning than a lesson, but of what?

Dragons. Cave dragons loan-sharked, sending their offshoots to call in debts. Greater Worms…hoarded. Madame, on her nest of gold, surrounded by things of beauty, gathering gossip and rumor. It's not about the value, but *what* we value.

What did we hoard? What did we covet? What did we fetch and claim?

My brain was moving almost too fast to keep up, sorting and sifting possibilities, clues, relevant and irrelevant thoughts. Why dragons specifically as an image? What did dragons want?

Power. You had it, you wanted it, you wanted more of it. Everyone always looking for an advantage, looking for an angle, looking for a way to add to their own hoard. Even people who said they didn't want power did, only under a different name. Looks. Friends. Skill. Money. It all came down to the same thing.

I couldn't think like a killer. It wasn't in me, I didn't want it in me. But I craved, I coveted. I was even learning to be possessive, like a dragon, to protect what was mine.

Click. Click. Click. The pieces didn't quite fit, not yet, but I could feel them shifting, in my head. If the eleventh murder was related… We already knew that we were looking for two killers. Mentor and mentee, chasing after their unholy grail? When one grew weak, did he sacrifice himself to the search? Or had it been as unwilling as all the other deaths? Mentor to mentee, the dragon's tail caught in its mouth, greed eating itself. The image stuck in my head, painfully clear.

Talent killing Talent, exactly what we'd been created to track down. A crime no Null cop would ever hear about, much less be able to solve.

"I need you to do something for me," I said.

"All right." That simple: she knew I wouldn't ask unless it was something only she could do.

"The Canadian Council has records we need. A killing that happened two decades ago. They won't give it to us."

"Do you have a name?"

"Nope. But it was… A mentor was killed, cut open. By his mentee."

"Jesus wept."

"Pretty much, yeah."

I was asking her to put herself into the line of fire, after she had been warned of her own death, to steal something that might not even be useful.

There was a long silence. I closed my eyes, breathing in the quiet.

"Bonnie?"

I looked up; Ben stood in front of me, outlined against the night air. I turned to my left: Wren had disappeared.

"It's late," he said. "Everyone's given up for the night. Come on. Time for bed."

I let him pull me up, and we stood there a long minute. There were things I could say…. Explanations of where I'd been when Stosser spirited me away, why I'd left the discussion, about what Wren had said and what I'd asked of her, ask what had been determined or decided while I hid out here…

But I didn't. I just let him lead me out of the garden and back into the hotel.

"Boss, go home."

"Yes, Mother."

Lou stood in the doorway and stared at Stosser until he looked up from the paperwork, spread out on the desk in front of him, and sighed. "I promise, Lou. As soon as I get all of this in order, I will."

"Uh-huh. And I will come in tomorrow morning, which by the way is only five hours from now, and find you still here, yes. And the paperwork still not done. Boss, go home."

Ian looked at the paperwork in front of him, well aware that he could have been done with all this hours ago. But fussing at it, letting the reminders poke at his conscience, made him aware of how close he had come to—what was the phrase Ben used? Screwing the pooch. His arrogance had saved him on more than one occasion, his refusal to give in and accept defeat or failure. But this time…

This could have cost him everything. More, it could have cost the PUPs everything, too. And that…that they would not allow. Not even to salve his ego.

Torres had been right.

The hint of a smile touched his narrow lips. "All right, Little Mother. All right. It will all be here in the morning, anyway."

As though hearing his words, the gentle, insistent sound of the carbon monoxide alarm went off again, and they both sighed.

"At least the fire alarm isn't going off, too," he said, tempting fate. But the louder siren stayed off.

"Someday there will be real trouble, and nobody's going to believe it," she muttered. "And then we're going to have to rescue an entire damn building of people."

"I'll deal with it," Ian said, standing up. "You go home. Yes, I promise, I'll leave as soon as I get it shut off." He meant it, too: if only because Lou would not hesitate to rat him out to Ben. Sometimes, he wondered who was actually running this agency.

"All right." She winced as the alarm started its cycle again, and headed down the hallway. "Give 'em hell this time!"

Ian, wincing at the noise, picked up the phone and dialed the building's main number. "Hi. This is Ian Stosser in 7C. You know the alarm's gone off again, right?"

There was a mumbled affirmative.

"And you're going to shut it off before I develop a migraine and have to get seriously cranky on your ass, yes?"

Getting another affirmative in response, he hung up the phone. As he did so, the alarm slowed and then cut off.

"Thank you, universe," he muttered. "We pay too much in rent for this crap to keep going on."

The thought of money made him look back at the paperwork. Having to rely on the others... He should have told Ben earlier. If Pietr had tried to interfere or if the winglets had tried to collect while they were on a case, distracting someone, it would have been his own fault.

"Time for an old Dog to learn new tricks," he said. His responsibilities had shifted in the past three years; it was time he accepted that. He would let others help keep the agency alive.

And Aden...Aden had chosen her path, foolish though it was. He shook his head, then rubbed the bridge of his nose, trying to fend off the sudden onslaught of the predicted headache. "Aden, you idiot. You don't bargain with sorcerers—they're worse than dragons." It was time to let her deal with her own karma and not interfere—not ride to her rescue or defense yet again. He would…probably fail miserably at both. But he would try.

If nothing else, the change in strategy would confuse his enemies, which would be entertaining. Ben would approve of that.

Ben. Ben and Bonnie, and her newfound aeromancer, and her visions of dragons. A tangle of associations he was too tired to deal with, right now. All that would have to be a different headache, for another day.

Turning off the overhead light, Ian closed the office door, took a single step down the darkened hallway, and fell forward, his knees buckling, even as he tried to pull enough current to Translocate.

Instead, he only had time for one urgent ping.

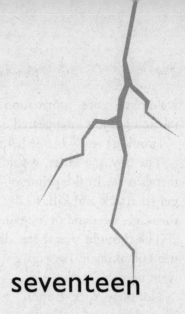

seventeen

I woke up before dawn, my muscles loose and sore and curled up against a warm body. That part wasn't unusual for me—although rarer in the past year than it had been since I hit puberty. The humming feeling deep in my core, though, was new.

"Forget about it," I whispered to it. "I'm on birth control."

Damned if the humming didn't sound smug. I allowed myself exactly twenty seconds to imagine a kid between us—strong-boned and willful, with a sharp mind and a sharper Talent—and then put that thought away. I wasn't ready to mentor, much less be a parent.

There was nothing more powerful in the *Cosa Nostradamus* than the mentor relationship. Nothing. The eleventh murder…weighed on me, even in my dreams, leaving me feeling uncertain and ill at ease. What could have driven him to that? Had it been the other way around, the older man killing his student… How much rage could a boy carry? What had happened between the two?

If we were lucky, and Wren was as good as she claimed,

we'd have more information. Assuming she had taken the job and not just disappeared on me.

I couldn't really blame her if she had.

The boy, the killer, would be, what—late thirties, early forties now. In the prime of his life, driven by some hunger to attack and kill, to dig and scrape men his mentor's then-age, over and over again.

The thought was there, dangling just out of reach. Instead of taking it, I got up, got dressed, and, closing my eyes, went home.

Not New York. Boston.

"Bonita."

J was never surprised at anything I did. Amused, often. Worried, occasionally—more now than when I was a teenager. But never surprised, even when I showed up in his kitchen at oh-dog-early, just the time I knew that he would be staggering into his gleaming, professional-quality kitchen to fix that first dose of coffee. He was wearing an old pair of gray sweatpants and an equally faded Red Sox sweatshirt: he had worn some variant of that every morning all the years of my mentorship. He would make coffee and fetch the newspaper from outside his door and settle in with Rupert to read it, front to back. When he—and Rupert—were both younger, a jog would have happened, too, but neither of them were young anymore.

Hell, neither of them were middle-aged anymore. The knowledge that I'd lose them was always present: J's worries about my job aside, I'd be the one left alone, sooner rather than later. To cause that pain intentionally, to strike at him… to kill him?

I think the bear hug I gave him surprised him. A little.

J had connections in high places, lines of gossip that could be useful. But I wasn't going to ask him to use them, not yet. Not unless all other lines failed. I didn't want him anywhere near this one. Thankfully, he didn't ask any questions.

I didn't talk about my job with J, at his request. Ask advice, yes. Come home for reassurances, definitely. Let him feed me, absolutely. But he didn't want to know what I was doing, anymore. He said he worried the same, knowing or not-knowing, but not having details allowed him to sleep better, once he was done worrying. So this morning he just accepted the hug, and then pushed my hair away from my face and said, simply, "You will have breakfast with me?"

"Please." Translocating back to Boston in the middle of a job wasn't the smartest thing I'd ever done, but they could do without me for an hour. And J would Transloc me back, if I asked him, so I wouldn't drain myself.

An hour, to spend making sure my mentor was well and healthy and knew I loved him. That was all I asked.

Venec woke up with a headache and an empty space next to him on the bed where he'd been sure there'd been a body. This had been a common occurrence once in his life, but not recently, so he took a minute to identify the details.

Bonnie, check. He could still feel the warmth of her body in the sheets, so she hadn't been gone long. He cracked open one eye and managed to see that there was no note. Not that he had expected one. The slightest tendril of current let into the world came back with a sense of well-being, and buttered toast and coffee. She was well and would be back soon.

The headache was harder to place. They hadn't been drinking, he hadn't eaten anything with peanuts, there wasn't a matching pain anywhere else to explain it. He let another tendril of current rise up through his body, moving along his veins from core to the front of his skull, delicately touching his own awareness for the cause. Healing yourself with current was a fool's game—it was too easy to overestimate the current needed and do more harm than good—but self-diagnosis was easier. But, no, there was nothing… There! He found the faintest twinge and followed it…outside his body.

Venec sat upright on the bed, the faint headache now a pounding migraine as the current-built door opened and the full alarm blared through. Someone—not someone, he knew damn well who—had gone after the museum again.

"Goddammit," he snarled. reaching for his clothing. "Goddammit."

By the time he Translocated to the museum, his shirt barely tucked in and his teeth unbrushed, the alarm had been cut off. Allen was waiting, his troll-like body radiating extreme annoyance.

"They got through. You said nobody could get through before the alarms would go off. We didn't catch anything on the cameras, nothing in any of the current-traps."

"No." Venec was grim. "No, you wouldn't. Damn it. What did she take?"

"She?" Allen knew about current, but he wasn't *Cosa,* wasn't hooked into the normal gossip channels.

"You were hit by The Wren. What did she take?"

"A single painting, from the new collection. It's not even particularly valuable, so I don't know why…"

"Don't try to figure it out," Venec advised him, carefully not grinding his jaw in annoyance, although he wanted to. "That's not your worry, and it will only give you a headache with no upside."

"But…the Board…"

"I'll deal with them. Give me a name."

The chairman of the board was not particularly surprised to have a man appear in his office without his secretary announcing anyone or buzzing them in. He did, however, have a pistol aimed directly at Venec's chest.

"Relax," Ben said in disgust. "I'm the good guy."

"You're the man who was hired to do our secondary security system." The guy was either very smart or a very good actor. Venec was betting on both. But not smart enough and not quite a good enough actor.

"I'm the guy who was hired to take the fall when something was stolen, you mean."

"I don't—"

"Cut the crap. I don't have time for it. The Wren doesn't steal for herself—she steals for other people. There's no reason for anyone to steal one painting from a new installation that hasn't even had previews yet—if a thief were going for this collection, they'd take more than one. This sort of cherry-pick shows something else is going on."

"And you think we arranged this robbery?" The man's voice was amused, but there was a tremor in his throat that said otherwise.

"I know you did." Didier had admitted the Board had hired Wren, but he'd assumed they were ignorant of who had been hired to do security. Ben was less trusting. All this pointed to the giant red button that said Setup. He had no time for this bullshit right now.

The man filled his chest with air and started to bluster. "I assure you—"

"I don't care. Whatever reason you had for it, whatever issues were involved, I don't care." He bit the words off, leaning forward and getting in the man's space. The gun rested in the man's hand, nearly forgotten and pointing at the floor. "But if you try to collect insurance on this, if you publicize this in any way shape or form, or attempt to punish anyone for this theft, I will take you down. You, personally."

They stared at each other, and something seemed to click in the man's head. He placed the gun gently on the desk and sat down again.

"Ah."

Venec waited. Ian was better at negotiation than he was, but he knew that the strongest stick was silence. Wait them out, and they usually begin to babble. This guy wasn't some alley hood, and he'd be tougher to crack—but he would crack. All Venec had to do was hold his cards close and let him assume there was a better hand underneath.

It took a few minutes, but the chairman cracked.

"If we stay silent about the theft, if we let it go, your reputation will not be damaged, for not building a sufficient defense. I see your point…but I'm not sure where there is a benefit to the museum."

Venec reached into his pocket, slowly, not wanting the man to suddenly think he was threatened again—at least not physically—and pulled out a slip of paper. He had pinged Nicky after talking to Allen and—after waking him out of a sound sleep—had gotten a few useful details.

"Whatever the motive, insurance is a secondary benefit. The painting wasn't insured for that much, as an individual piece. If you were really looking for a payoff, you would have had something else stolen. So there's something about that specific painting that you wanted gone. Am I right?"

The board member swallowed faintly, but otherwise his expression didn't change.

"Am I right?" Venec asked again and let just a flare of current rise from his core. The man in front of him was Null but not blind: he could feel the power rise and reacted to it in small ways that Venec was trained to spot: accelerated pulse, increased sweat production, and the tightening of muscles in

a preliminary fight-or-flight reaction. Back him into a corner, and he would stop thinking and merely react.

But a cornered man was also a dangerous man. Venec
showed him the stick, then offered a carrot.

"If you forego that insurance bonus, take your main ac-
complishment and let this all fade into never-happened-land,
then I will walk away. If you don't..."

Venec smiled without showing any teeth at all. "Then
your problems right now will suddenly seem very small. I
promise you that."

He walked out of the office feeling like things were almost under control.

And then they weren't.

I was just finishing my plate, sliding the last scraps to
Rupert under the table, while J as ever pretended not to notice, when the ping reached me.

bonnie

It took me half a second to identify Lou, the ping almost
too soft to hear, soft and tentative: two things I would never
have associated with her.

And in the next instant, I understood why.

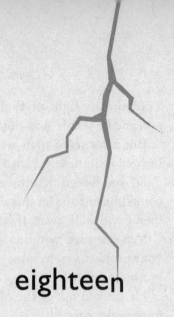

eighteen

Of all the scenarios I had ever run in my head, of all the worst-case possibilities, this one had never occurred to me. My kenning hadn't even given me a hint of this.

"The alarm was for real. We had them shut it off... because of all the false alarms, I guess..." Lou was shaking, the envelope of calm that had carried her through until now finally shredding.

The ambulance had come and gone, the report filed. If it had been an ordinary citizen, there wouldn't have been a lifted eye among the cops, but the brass knew who Ian Stosser was—had been—and the fact that it looked like an ordinary, stupid tragic accident still had them come out and poke around. The alarm was found to be honestly faulty—the false alarms we'd been having were the result of something funky in the main system. Not our fault, not job related. Just One of Those Things.

"No chance to Translocate out. No warning, no..." The laugh Ben gave raised the hair on the back of my neck, and not in a good way. "All the crap in his life, the high-placed tails he yanked, and a gas leak kills him. The indignity of it must be burning a hole in his gut, right now."

Lou, as office manager, had gotten the call from the police when they couldn't reach Ben at home. She in turn had summoned us all. The newbies hadn't been called in; they hadn't been here long enough to understand. The office was closed for the day, we told them. A day…probably no more.

They believed us.

The ambulance had taken the body away, and the office cleared, certified safe for us to go in. New detectors were in every room, temporary until the system could be overhauled. We were all supposed to go to the hospital, get checked out, make sure we hadn't been exposed to any long-term slow leak that might've done damage.

It happened every year. You read about it in the papers, saw it on the news. People leaving the stove on for warmth, during a winter's night, and never waking up. Batteries dying, or not having an alarm put in, and a leak…

It seemed so surreal, it couldn't be true.

It felt real.

Sharon was curled up on the sofa, Nicky next to her, his head resting on her shoulder. Nifty was on the floor at their feet—the most submissive pose I'd ever seen him in, ever, especially around Sharon. Lou had pulled in a straight-backed chair, turned it around and was sitting on it, her arms wrapped around the frame like it was all that kept her upright. She had been the last to see him; she blamed herself, even though there was no blame to be laid. She kept saying something in Spanish, too low for me to hear, but it sounded like a prayer.

Pietr had claimed the armchair, but you had to look closely to see him there, a mug of something held in both hands, his high cheekbones in such sharp profile I almost expected blood to seep through the skin.

Ian hadn't bled. The amount of carbon monoxide they'd found in the office, it killed him so quickly, there wasn't a chance for damage. He had looked peaceful when they wheeled him out, the sheet drawn back at our request, the EMTs impatient but not unkind.

How the hell had this happened? After so many false alarms, for the gas to come in, so much, so fast?

"She's gonna blame us for this," Nifty said, his voice too thin, as though the air had been sucked out of his broad chest, too.

She—Aden, Ian's sister. She had hated everything about her big brother's idea, had hated us as the embodiment of it...but she had loved Ian, as much as he had loved her. It had been majorly fucked up, that relationship, yeah.

"Let her. It doesn't matter." I felt like my body was made of lead; drained from the fight, the stress of the case. I should have been enjoying one last cup of coffee with J and then going back to work: instead, I'd come here, and found the rest of the team already on-site, and cops who wouldn't let us into the building until the all clear had been sounded.

Five hours ago, the world had made some kind of sense. Now...I felt gutted. And it wasn't just me.

"So what do we do now?" Nicky asked.

"About Aden? There's nothing to be done, unless she makes a move. And I'm not sure she will." Venec frowned deeper, his face caught in the pained expression he'd worn since we arrived. "Whatever their differences, whatever drove them apart, there was still such a bond between them, I'm not sure she'll have the heart to destroy the last thing he left."

"No, I mean...what now?" Nick waved a hand around the room, indicating us, it...everything. "What do we do now?"

Venec's arm was heavy around my neck, his breathing warm and steady beside me, but he didn't say anything.

None of us did.

PUPI had been Ian Stosser's dream. His idea, his drive, his vision that made any of this, any of us possible. He had argued in front of the Councils to make us legitimate, had faced down the lonejack doubters who challenged us. Had chosen us, shaped us, even Ben, into visions of what he wanted—what he needed us to be.

But we had been the ones who made it real.

"Now we find a killer," Venec said, finally. "Before anyone else dies."

Sharon exhaled and reached up to ruffle Nick's shaggy hair, exactly the way he hated. As though that broke some kind of stasis spell, Nifty stretched his arms out in front of him and got up in a supple move that someone half his bulk would have envied. "We need to eat, then. Pizza?"

Pizza. Food. Fuel to keep moving. Right. Someone's stomach growled.

"Anchovies," I said, anticipating the sounds of disgust from Pietr and Sharon.

"Half plain, half fishies. We'll split it."

"Gross." Sharon's fine features scrunched into a moue of distaste "Tell them to put up a barrier between the fishies, and maybe I'll consider it."

We weren't back to normal; we were going to have to redefine whatever the hell "normal" was. But we were moving again.

"His death doesn't wipe out the loan," I said to Ben, softly, turning halfway into his chest. "Cave-dragon loans don't work that way." His hand stroked my hair, tangling his fingers in the curls.

"I know. He'd already signed the paperwork to bring me into the deal, so it should…"

With that paperwork done, the burden would land on Ben,

not Aden as the next of kin. The irony of it amused me: she would have had to either pay up and keep us in business or default and pay the penalty. Much as I hated the Bitch... No, this was our responsibility.

It would just be a matter of getting the cash together. We could do it. His death might make things more difficult, but it could also work to our advantage. I could work on that later. Later would be soon enough.

I rested my face against Ben's chest, breathing in the musky, slightly smoky smell that always lingered on his skin, finding an unbearable comfort in it. The Merge shifted inside us, adjusting, and we let it.

Grief, I knew too well, took its own damn time. For now... we went on.

Later that day, the three of us were back in Philadelphia. Nobody wanted to be there—but we weren't going to give up, and somehow, it seemed easier to work here, in this basement room, than the office. Here, we could focus. Here, we didn't have to remember. Not yet.

A storm front had rolled in while we were in New York, and everyone had shivery-skin even with the thick walls of concrete and steel between us and the weather. We could feel the storm building, getting ready to hit. The first distant boom of thunder was almost a release, as though giving us permission to start breathing again.

Venec hadn't come down with us: I couldn't feel him, and I didn't want to push.

bonnie

There was a painful leap of hope, then I identified the ping: Wren. I took a step away from the others and acknowledged her.

i heard. i'm so sorry

I acknowledged the sympathy and waited.

there's no file

I had almost been expecting that. Council might have kept it for years just in case, but the moment more killings emerged, and they might be held accountable…

recent purge, or…?

long time ago. i found a reference to it in a logbook, both the crime and the decision to pretend it had never happened

There was a smugness in her tone that made me think that one, she'd gotten the logbook through particularly satisfying ways, and two, there was more in that logbook she wasn't planning on sharing. If it had nothing to do with the case, I was okay with that.

The Council hadn't even kept the records; they'd been covering their asses years ago. Why had I hoped for anything else?

thanks anyway. and…be careful Ian was dead, and nothing to do with dragons, but Ellen had seen them both in her vision.

you too

I blinked and came back to the group to find both Venec and Pietr watching me. I shook my head: nothing new to report.

Thunder crashed overhead, and we all jumped, then laughed. Of all the things that could spook a Talent, a thunderstorm should not be on the list.

The noise of the storm covered the sound of the elevator opening down the hall, so the first we knew we had a visitor was the squeaking of wet shoes on the linoleum tile outside our room.

She was soaked through, the water glistening on her skin, her hair plastered flat against her skull. She should have looked pitiful, or sad, or like a large, drowned rat, and she was all of those things but you couldn't remember it for long, under the sheer current rippling under her skin.

Thunder slammed outside, directly overhead this time, and I'd swear I saw her skin tremble in resonance.

Storm-seer. I had known the term since forever, had understood what it meant…but I hadn't, really. The way Ellen moved and looked—the girl I'd met in the Park was still there, but something else was, too. Not just current but wild current, streaming through her like a massive flock of birds, a murder of crows, rising and swooping in the air, like they were all controlled by one single brain, one single thought. Power that was only barely under control.

"Wha—" Sharon started to ask, and I slapped her arm, hard, almost instinctively trying to make her shut up. You didn't interrupt a seer; you didn't even think about interrupting a seer, even if she hadn't started to talk yet. God, was I the only one with a mentor versed in the classics? Sharon glared at me, those glorious blue eyes narrowed, but I couldn't give her my full attention right now, and after a second or two she gave up. I knew that Pietr was on the other side of me, but when I made a reflexive check for him, he was gone.

No, not gone. With practice and familiarity, I could feel him next to me. But visually, he had disappeared.

ben Not even a ping; a tight-focused tendril of awareness, reaching out and telling him something was happening—not dangerous, don't bull in, but come quietly. And quickly.

There was a snap of understanding, a brush of reassurance, and then I was a hundred percent in my own head, walls up and ready for anything our untrained seer might do. I hoped.

"I saw him again. Not her. His skin was blue with current and his eyes were black and there was a smell of burning around him." She shook a little, like a dog waking from a dream, and her pupils narrowed again like coming into the light, and she looked at me—and saw me, this time.

"Why do I keep seeing him? Isn't it enough that I warned him?"

The others, cowards, looked to me.

"Ellen."

Her eyes focused on me, and I guess my face was enough.

"He's dead." Her voice had gone flat and terrible.

"This morning. It was an accident, Ellen. A gas leak. There was nothing… No warning would have been enough." I hoped. I hoped to hell that there was nothing anyone could have done. Even the hint of it would gnaw at us forever.

"Nothing…" She stared at me, and I could see a hint of that hot-tempered girl moving underneath the shock. "Then why? Why do I see any of this? What's the point?"

If I knew that…I'd know what to say to her.

"We don't know enough to say what you're really seeing. When you learn how to control it— Where's Sergei?" He should not have let her come here alone. What the hell was the man thinking?

She swallowed, looked nervous. "I didn't tell him I was coming. He doesn't think… He thinks I should just stay quiet, that no good comes from anyone knowing when they're going to die. But it's not my fault I saw them, keep seeing them. He doesn't like me. Because I saw her dead. But she's alive, still, and he's dead, and that doesn't make any sense, either."

"You're new and still learning," Sharon said, shaking off whatever paralysis I'd put on her tongue. "You might not be seeing things right, or misinterpreting them. That happens."

"Maybe." She didn't look convinced. "I just wanted—"

I don't know what she wanted, because a clap of thunder hit the air over the building so hard and so loud that even our basement fortress shuddered slightly.

"Oh."

Ellen's eyes had gone dark again, and she swayed. I took a step forward to help her, then hesitated. Yeah, she was green as guacamole and maybe in distress, but she was also filled with an unknown, potentially active current, and there was an electrical storm over us. Basic training taught us how to ground and center so's not to be overrushed by a wild storm like this, how to pull down only what we needed and ignore the rest, but…she was full-grown and ignorant and a storm-seer.

And any one of those things could backlash on me, on any of us, if we touched her or even went near her at the wrong time. That she'd be sad and sorry afterward wouldn't help, if we were crisped in a defensive backlash.

Or, worse, if she tried to pull it back, too late, and hurt herself. As pups, we could handle backlash, even though it was never nice, like getting on a roller coaster right after a massive meal when you already had a stomach virus kind of not-nice.

"Ellen."

Pietr, stepping forward, his voice soft and smooth. Once upon a time he would have watched and waited, protected himself. Where working with the PUPs had toughed me, it had softened Pietr, allowed him to show the gentleness inside to strangers. How had I never seen that before?

"Ellen, it's okay. Nobody's upset, nobody's blaming you. We understand. It's not your fault. You saw it, you didn't cause it. We know how it works. You're among family now, and we're going to take care of you and teach you how to take care of yourself, so you understand all this." He talked her down like you would a junkie, no sudden moves, no raised voices, and not even the hint of current escaping him. In fact, I was pretty sure that he was absorbing some of hers, sliding it off her skin and enclosing it within his own core, which had to be giving him a serious case of the itches. But whatever he was doing, it worked: she stopped shuddering, and her entire body collapsed a little on her frame, like someone let half a squeak of air out.

Sharon half turned to me. "You should ping The Wren, tell her Ellen's here."

"Yeah." Except Wren was currently up in Canada, and Translocating had never been her best skill.

I suddenly remembered Wren's words to me, in the courtyard garden last night. "I was going to go to the office tonight, but…" If she had gone, would she have been in the building when the alarm went off? Had my sending her into danger, trying to steal from the Council, saved her life? If so, the irony was more than I could appreciate.

Sergei unnerved Ellen, Wren wasn't around—maybe hooking her with Wren hadn't been the best idea, after all.

"You want to stay here with us today?" It was a terrible idea, but the look of sudden, cautious hope in Ellen's eyes made it seem workable. "You'll need to stay out of the way, but—"

"I can do that," she said, sounding like a five-year-old hoping to get a bedtime extension, and something in my chest hurt.

bonnie?

Sharon, asking me if I was certain. I just shrugged, and while her mouth set in the flat line that meant she didn't approve, she didn't say anything out loud.

"Check in with the others, see if they've uncovered anything we can use, yet." Lou and Nicky were still in New York, working off-site, but Nick's netbook could work its magic anywhere.

"I hate working split up like this," Sharon muttered but nodded, heading into the hallway where the current-levels wouldn't be tainted by Ellen's display. As she did so, yet another bolt of thunder hit, close enough that we could hear windows rattling, and the hair along my arms and on my scalp lifted slightly. This was a doozy of a storm, and the thunder was bringing lightning with it. Pure, wild current in its natural form. I wasn't much for sourcing wild, but in a storm like this knocking on our door, shoving current into the air above us until we were practically breathing it in...

"Sharon!" I yelled, startling both Pietr and Ellen. "Forget about that. Get back in here." I had an idea.

"This is the craziest idea you've ever had, and that's saying something," Sharon said. She was muttering, but she wasn't refusing, which meant it was either crazy but brilliant, or we were really that much at a shithole dead end with time running out.

It had been a few days since the third body was found. If our boy was on schedule, another Talent was going to be taken, held, tortured, and killed before we knew who was doing it. I took a quick read of the room: we were worn to shreds already; another body might break us.

"I don't think I can do this," Ellen said.

"You're not doing it alone," I said. I was trying for patience, but her uncertainty was starting to get on my nerves. I was in no way shape or form decent mentor material. "We're with you. We'll guide and protect you."

I'd have felt better—we all would have—if Venec had come back. But he was still gone and still had his walls up thick enough that I knew better than to try to knock through them, and the others knew better than to ask me.

And no Stosser to call in. Damn it. No, I thought fiercely. Don't think. Work.

The little garden space was deserted—not surprising, considering the rain pelting down. You could barely look up without your vision being destroyed by water, but none of us needed to look up to know that there were thick, dark clouds filling the sky, turning it near-black, or that there were bolts of lightning crackling within those clouds, occasionally exploding between them or slamming down into the ground. We felt it, inside us, like the shiver of too-cold ice cream on your teeth, painful and kinda sexy-hot at the same time.

"Hold hands," Sharon said, taking up Ellen's left even as Pietr took her right. I completed the circle, the four of us looking like some kind of demented ring-around-the-rosy, if anyone staying in the hotel happened to look out the window.

"We'll ground you," I heard Sharon say. "Just, whatever you do, don't let go. Okay?"

Ellen nodded. Her eyes were bright, and she was looking less worried and more excited. I had a sudden glimpse at the girl who wanted so badly to be part of the Park coven and the pain she must have felt, to be rejected....

"You're part of this now," I said. She looked up at me, even though I wasn't sure she'd heard me, and smiled. Totally, absolutely not my type, not even a whisper of interest, but my heart almost melted and burst, seeing that smile.

"Ready...steady..." Pietr was barely whispering, but we all heard him even over the storm. I flexed my toes against the ground—we'd left our shoes back in the conference room—and felt for the rock, deep below. Grounding was more a mental and magical thing than it was physical, but it never hurt to remember that we were meat and bone, too.

The photographs were tucked inside my shirt, shoved under my bra strap. They were sharp and uncomfortable, digging into my skin, but that was sort of the point: close to the heart, the electrical pump that fueled us all, Talent and Null, digging into the flesh that formed us, the urge and the desire for more power singing through the storm-raddled air and connecting me...not to the victims, but to the hunters.

If they were hunting tonight, the photos, the sense of their methods, the image of their blow... Add in Ellen's particular skills channeling this storm to *see,* and it should all lead us to them.

Cave paintings in the rain. Cave paintings in current. The oldest magic, in the newest time...

I slipped into fugue state even as thunder rumbled overhead. The familiar hum of current slipped through me as they slid into fugue state as well, practice making perfect in a way that the would-be leader of the coven might have envied.

steady

Pietr, taking lead. Then Sharon's brightness, and the darker spark I could already identify as Ellen, muted but strong. I matched them, fit into them, and slid into the storm.

Hunger. Need. Power. Curiosity. Those were the threads we were reaching for, the current-bubble-bond between us stretching over the city, using the storm as a power source and a highway, moving up and down in-between lightning bolts.

It was incredibly, stupidly dangerous. Alone, we could never have done it. Without Ellen and her natural affinity for storms, I would never have suggested trying it. As current crackled in my bones, and the smell of burnt hair and skin filled my nostrils, I understood addiction for the first time.

focus

We followed each hint of those emotions, using my scrying to find them, and Sharon's truth-sensing to discard them, Pietr our anchor to the ground and Ellen our tie to the storm. It was slow, painstaking work that took only seconds per dive.

there?

there

here

And we dived, following another hint. The closer we got, the more the sensation grew, until part of me wanted to pull out, pull away, back off, but it was too late, and anyway, that wasn't the job, to run away.

Lightning flashed down, and we followed it, riding current into the source of the hint: a small cement building where lightning should not have hit. It was low to the ground and lacked nearly anything but the most basic of electronics: more a garage or warehouse than anything else.

Normally, riding current required that you have someone on-site to see through. Ideally, that someone was strong enough to corral and control the other awarenesses riding him: Stosser had done it the first time we tried this, and Venec after that in training. With only the four of us here, we had to scatter and improvise.

I didn't want to let go of anyone, but so long as we held onto each other, back in our flesh, it should be all right. "Should" being, as always, the operative term. Even when you'd codified a spell, there were still external events that could change the results.

The smell of bitter copper and musk refocused me, and I opened my "eyes" with mage-sight, looking out over the space. The shock made me aware of my physical body, bent over double and gagging, only the death-tight grip on my hands keeping me part of the circle.

The space was dimly lit to human eyes, but mage-sight saw things differently. No people, alive or dead, just an open space with high ceilings and thick walls painted a drab beige over the cement. The only electricity was being used to power the lights that hung from the ceiling at regular intervals, flickering dimly. A large slab table, at least three feet wide and six feet long, made of wood, polished...no, not polished. Worn down with use and stained a dark reddish-brown that I knew, instinctively, even without the stink, was not the original color of the grain. There were objects next to it, tall and skinny, and covered with tarps. I sent a finger of current toward them, gently, and was rewarded with a twitch of electricity: battery-operated floodlights.

The floor below was tile, either ceramic or something like, and it was too clean to belong with this cement-block warehouse—it had been washed down, and recently.

There was nothing that could wash down the air itself, thick with the scent of sweat, blood, and fear…and an even more disturbing excitement. Not sexual, thank god; I'd had to investigate that once, at a torture scene, and once was twice too much. This was cleaner, if you could use that word, and…colder.

But there was something else in the space, too. Even if you looked with mage-sight, you could barely see them, a faint buzzing glow that shimmered and moved like tiny hummingbirds.

Elementals, the same things Venec used in his security-net spell, only utterly disorganized here. They were drawn to current, the more intense the better, and normally swarmed inside major power lines, like cats sleeping in sunlight. So why were they here, in this cold, empty place?

I reached out, carefully, not wanting to spook and scatter them, and felt my pack mates doing the same.

corral I suggested, the image of horses penned inside a fence, and felt instant assent. It would be easier if we were still working as one entity, but we'd practiced this before, although on larger creatures. Moving slowly in a nearly choreographed dance, out current swirled inward, not so much boxing the elementals in as removing the space they could roam, encouraging their natural inclination to crowd together.

gently…

Like I didn't know that, I thought irritably, and my Self had another flash of my physical body, soaking wet and sour-mouthed from vomit, wanting only to be warm and dry and not here...

Focus. The body was the anchor but Self was the sail, the wheel, the... I gave up with the bad metaphors—I'd never been good with them—and did the thing I'd been avoiding. I touched the outer ring of elementals and asked them what they'd seen.

You don't get actual answers from elementals, of course. You don't even really get visuals, since they have no eyes, no sense of "seeing." It's all current, all impressions and... textures is the best way any of us were able to describe it.

Textures of screams and silence. The shiver of skin parting and silence falling, of the scrape of steel against bone and the slush of a wet mop on tile. The sensations of an abattoir.

We'd found it.

Coming back into your body is painful at best, even when you're in a controlled situation, comfortably arranged somewhere, dry and safe and knowing you had backup in case something went wrong. Dropping from a thunderstorm knowing it's about to leave the area, feeling the power drain from you and crashing into a body that's already trauma-tized, coming aware again knees-down in the mud and your hands covered with vomit, your throat sore like you'd been screaming—or sobbing?

That purely sucked.

"Oh, shit. Oh, holy shit." Ellen, muttering over and over to herself. I looked up, wiping my hands uselessly on my sod-den jeans, and saw that she was sitting on her haunches, her face held up to the sky, her eyes closed.

"You okay?"

"Yeah." Her voice was steady, not shaking, but there was a note in it that I couldn't recognize. "You people do that shit all the time?"

"Not all the time, no."

"Holy shit." She shuddered. "That... What we saw... That was real. Someone...did all that."

"Yeah."

She turned her head then, and her eyes gleamed even in the darkness, like whatever was left of the storm had snugged deep inside her. "Catch him."

"We will."

I looked up at the new voice, not at all surprised to see Venec there. He'd had the sense to wear a coat, a dark slicker of some kind, and a wide-brimmed hat kept the rain off his face, so he was really just a looming black shadow in the background, but I'd have known him even without the voice. Now that I was back in my body, as disgusting as it felt, my awareness of him returned, as well. Or rather, my awareness of my awareness. Thinking about it made everything hurt, so I stopped.

He was furious—we'd risked ourselves, and his wounds were still too raw to accept that. But he knew why we'd done it, why we'd had to. They'd trained us to finish the hunt.

"You all need showers. And a drink."

"We found them, boss." Sharon, already on her feet, although she looked like muddy hell. "Or, we found where... we found where the killings took place. I took soundings. We can find it again easy, and—"

"Showers. Dry clothing. Food. Then we discuss." The Big Dog wasn't open to discussion.

"They weren't there."

Just as well: we hadn't actually thought through what we'd

do once we found them. None of us were thinking as clearly as we'd thought. Venec didn't bother pointing that out.

"But this is where they do their killings?" He wanted us to be absolutely sure. Fortunately, there wasn't a hint of doubt in anyone's mind.

"That table, that wasn't just thrown together. It's old, at least a decade, and probably more. They've used it before. And they're not going to abandon it. It's..." I hesitated, looking for the right word. "Not fetishized, exactly, but I think there's something about that table that's important to our killer."

"Consistency. He keeps moving cities, but the table remains the same. We already know that he likes patterns, so this might be part of that. Boss—" and Pietr was shaking his head "—we need to hire a psychologist next, because this is way above our pay grade."

"So noted. Do your best."

That was all we were ever asked to do, and being the massive overachieving obsessionists we were, we could do no less. But I wasn't sure that it was going to be enough this time.

"We need to find them. But there's... The place was washed clean. Bastard is either obsessively clean, or he knew enough to wash his own trace off, same as he did with the bodies before dumping them. Even if we went in with a fine-tooth comb, I don't think we'd find anything to use for trace. Not unless someone's figured out how to get trace off an elemental."

They all looked at me, and I held up my hands, shaking my head. "Oh, hell, no. I'm good, but nobody's that good."

"Time's running out," Venec said, saying what we all knew. "There's going to be another body—they still have seven more to go, to satisfy the pattern, and short of watching over that place night and day until they bring someone back..."

"We could. I mean, now that we know where it is...we

could just tell the cops." Sharon, speaking reluctantly. It made perfect sense: Talent were being killed by Talent, but it wasn't a magical killing, as such. The cops could handle it.

"On what evidence?" Pietr held up his hand, fingers curled into his palm, and then lifted his index. "One wooden table that might or might not still have useful DNA after being hosed down, and might not even be there by the time the cops show up. If they've used it in other cities, they can move it—and won't willingly abandon it if threatened. Two—" and his middle finger joined the index "—the collective impressions of a bunch of elementals confirming that there was magic and violence done where. Yeah. That will go over well."

He had a point. Even among the *Cosa,* there were a lot of people who thought elementals were like fruit flies, not anything with an actual awareness. Bringing up evidence based on them… And we needed evidence. PUPI was based entirely on facts and evidence. We might know the killers had been there, but we couldn't prove it before the *Cosa Nostradamus.*

"These guys aren't classic serial killers or maniacs who will make a sloppy mistake," Pietr went on. "They're careful and clean and they don't leave anything behind to glean. How do we get proof?"

Venec lifted his head and stared at the wall, then said, "We go in and take it."

"Oh, man. This place gives me serious jeebies."

Nifty shuddered, and it wasn't playacting, either; his entire body was reacting to the atmosphere of the neighborhood, and we hadn't even gotten to the cement bunker yet. I had to admit, I was glad to see the big guy, and not just because of the physical protection he added. While we all worked different cases these days, it was unusual to go this long out of the office, and I'd missed him. I missed Nicky, too, but he'd gotten drained out working his hacker mojo, and Venec had benched him. He and Lou were now riding herd on the new kids, keeping them calm and busy in the office.

I didn't envy them that job, even knowing what we were about to face.

The bunker was actually an old warehouse of some sort, just beyond the outskirts of the city, beyond the shiny office buildings and the gentrified row houses. It was not the sort of area the tourists got to see, although there were plenty of indications that the locals didn't avoid it: the trash can on the corner had fast-food wrappers and newspapers in it, sodden from the previous night's storm but not decomposing, so they hadn't been there long, and the graffiti on the walls was more the "look at me" street-runner sort than "stay out" gang tags.

Rundown but not abandoned. Safe enough for strangers to come in and set up shop, but nobody would question the whys or wheres of what they were doing.

"Nift, you and Bonnie take lead. Sharon, up." Venec jerked his chin to indicate a rickety fire escape that had definitely not passed inspection on the closest building to our destination. It would have made more sense to send me up, since I was lighter, but I was also better at close-up fighting, if need be. Sharon still resisted hitting someone first.

There were two doors to the main floor, that we could see. According to the blueprint Andrulis had dropped off, with a "don't ask, don't tell" look on his face, there had been three doors, once. One was now bricked up. It might be a problem, but we weren't going to worry right now. Sharon got into position with a minimum of creaking metal and pinged us with a go-ahead: she could see the back door and was ready to incapacitate anyone who came out—or give us warning if anyone started in.

"Ready?"

"Do I look like a damned SWAT team?" I asked in return. I probably did, actually. Black jeans, black T-shirt, dark blue waterproof jacket, and high-top black sneakers—at least the socks were dark blue. And my bra and panties underneath were screaming yellow, even if only I knew that.

I wasn't used to having to think in terms of stealth: the point of PUPI was that we were aboveboard, totally in the *Cosa's* eye. Venec, though, seemed really comfortable in it, and Pietr…well, Pietr hadn't disappeared entirely the way he did when stressed, but his lean silhouette was almost impossible to see, his olive-hued skin blending into the night better than Nifty's black.

Me, I was like a damned flashlight, if anyone was looking, but Venec had vetoed Nifty's suggestion that they camo-paint Sharon and me to blend. I could only imagine the acne I'd have from that greasepaint…

ready steady came Nifty's touch inside my thoughts, and I nodded, moving forward as carefully as I could in his wake. Nifty outmassed me, and all of it was muscle. Let him be the target, if needed, while I was the unseen backup. That was the idea, anyway.

We got across the street without any obvious incident. In the distance a siren rose and fell, and there was a burst of men shouting, then some dogs barking, but nothing nearby and nothing coming closer.

The front door was a metal sheet set in a reinforced frame that had probably been seriously impressive once upon a time. Now, without any alarm system set up, it would be a simple matter of picking the locks and stepping in.

I put my hand on Nifty's forearm before he could do anything, and shook my head. This was why I was there.

My hand still on his thick forearm, trusting him to have my back, I slipped into a light fugue state, barely a breath between aware and gone, then opened my eyes again, waiting for them to refocus. I studied the door first, not wanting to go beyond just yet. It was metal, solid all the way through: ideal for spell-casting, as it would amplify the current and shove it right into anyone who touched it.

There was a faint tremor deep inside the door, and I nodded, satisfied. *doorbell* Basic spell, designed to inform the owner of who was knocking at his door; sort of a closed-circuit television for Talent. Nobody would think twice about this being here, especially sitting passively; at most they'd assume someone was squatting.

nothing else?

not outside

He bent down, his knees creaking a little, and pulled out his lock-pick kit. I had a matching one tucked into an inside pocket of my jacket, but Nifty had a better touch, for all that his hands were designed to catch a football, not do fine motor work. Pietr's trick with current wouldn't work here: that would set off the alarm the way Null tools wouldn't. That was why the Big Dogs didn't let us rely entirely on current.

The ease with which the lock opened was almost anticlimactic, except we hadn't even gotten to the really exciting stuff yet.

Seeing the space with physical eyes was strange—the angle was different, and things that had seemed large were smaller, the shadows less menacing somehow. It was just a warehouse, the smell of dry rot and mice shit stronger than any trace of blood or fear.

But the table was still there, in the middle of the open space. Where before it had seemed like some kind of mystical altar, draped in the residue of its victims, now the resemblance to a surgical table—the morgue table the bodies had been laid out on—was clearer. Change wood for steel, and they would have been identical.

"That can't be coincidence," I said, and Nifty shot me an odd look, having no idea what I was talking about. But Venec, brushing up against my thoughts, agreed.

doesn't matter right now. get on with it

I gave a mental salute that mainly involved my middle finger, and felt his reluctant chuckle.

"Torres, your attention, please?" Nifty didn't bother to whisper: if there was anyone else in the building, they knew we were here. The point of this exercise wasn't to hide.

"We really could have used a third person here," I muttered, moving to position at the head of the table. We needed Stosser.

We didn't have him.

I didn't want to touch the table: washed down or not, trace or no, there was going to be residue deep in the wood. But that was exactly why I needed to be the one to touch it.

Ellen was a seer: I was the one who could scry.

clear from Sharon, letting us know we had time. Pietr and Venec had us covered on the ground. The job was down to me and Nifty.

"I should have been a waitress."

"Yeah, and I should have been in the Hall of Fame. Maybe in another life. Stop stalling."

Nifty was going to be a fabulous mentor someday. He had the comforting, no-bullshit tone down perfect. I shifted my feet, let my shoulders relax, and placed my hands on the table as though I were going to give someone a massage—or was holding them down to be cut apart.

The wood was cold under my fingers, and inert. Something inside me let out a shivering sigh, but I didn't drop my guard. Not yet; not ever.

Nifty took up his place at the other end of the table, his face still and calm, like a mannequin's. He took a deep breath, preparing himself, and then nodded to me.

"In death, setting to life," I whispered, pulling current out of my core and sending it deep into the wood, even as I could feel Nifty doing the same thing to the air. "In death, setting to life."

You didn't need an actual spell to work current; that went out around the same time Founder Ben laid down the foundation of modern Talent. Venec, in fact, frowned on it, the same way he frowned on my scrying crystals and Lou's Magic 8 Ball. But he never refused a tool that worked, and right now, doing what we were doing...

Messing with the dead was Not Done. With properly directed current you could animate corpses, yeah, but that was someone's grandmother or brother you were messing with, and eventually, someone would find out. And souls... Wren had told me about her one and only encounter with a ghost. It was the only time I'd ever seen the Retriever cry. Spirits should not be held to the world, once they were gone. That was just selfishness and cruelty.

But there was a killer out there, even now looking for his next victim, and it had to stop now. We would not allow him to escape, kill seven more people, and then come back ten years from now to do it again. Because whatever he was looking for—he wasn't going to find it this way. And he wasn't going to stop.

"In death, setting to life."

And under my hands, a body formed. Not real—but real enough. The eyes of the victim stared up at me, green... no, brown...no, blue and then brown again, and my hands clenched around nonexistent flesh.

We'd done our job too well, or the victims had not gone far: we'd called them all.

No time to hesitate, to pause now would upset the balance of the spell, and as bad as it was to mess with the dead, I suspected it would be even worse to lose control of them.

"In death, setting to life," I finished, letting the current seethe through the table, holding the forms against the blood-soaked wood. The body/bodies struggled, but those shifting eyes kept staring up at me, unblinking, unwavering.

I expected to feel distaste, unease, a kind of regret. Instead, that gaze soothed me, urged me on.

The dead demanded satisfaction.

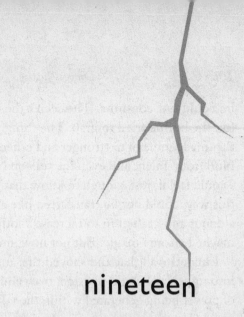

nineteen

"Hurry, hurry," I whispered, not meaning it: some things couldn't be rushed. But my arms ached from holding down a nonexistent body that pushed up against me, my core was draining too rapidly, feeding an endless strand of current into the table to maintain the body I was restraining, and my heart was breaking at the look in the ever-changing eyes that gazed back at me, stoic in death, giving me their agony without question or hesitation.

Around me, current snapped and cracked, making the air feel twice as thick with power. Nifty moved through it like a barge through fog, not letting it stop him as he mimed the cuts, over and over again, laying waste to bodies already gone, pausing to study, echoing the dance we had seen in the rolling display days before, when we didn't know what it meant.

Cut, and cut, and cut...

Now, the table under my fingers, the ghosts in my veins, I understood. It had lingered in the blade, their core sticking to it when the blood had not, tying them to it...driving the killer on, turn after turn, with the lingering taste of what

he could not consume. The secret the killer was searching
for, the key he tried to grab. The thing that made us Talent,
that made some of us stronger and others less so, that defined
Null from Talent and even the full-on Nulls from sensitives.
I could feel it, just enough to know that it could not be taken
this way, could not be transferred like an organ, taken from
a donor and grafted in to increase another. Maybe someday,
maybe by some magic. But not now, not this way.

I understood that and shoved that understanding as deep
into myself as I could manage, marveling instead at the flow
of power being generated within the table. Blood magic was
avoided not because it was inefficient or morally wrong but
because it was powerful—and addictive. Whatever reason our
killer had to begin his spree, I was amazed it allowed him to
take ten years off, and only ten victims at a time.

★!★

Venec's reminder put me back on track. I tore my gaze
away from those staring eyes and looked up at Nifty, who
was in a downward strike of his imagined scalpel, laying open
what would have been an arm. I could see the skin slice open
down to the bone, smell the blood, feel the body shudder
under my hands as pain ripped through them, their current
focused on trying to heal themselves…

A wash of nausea washed over me. Healing yourself was
almost as dangerous as leaving the wound open: without
training, you were as likely to fuse the wrong things or stop
your heart entirely. That was why the cause of death was so
screwed; the killer had taken too long, let them focus their
current on the wounds. They had killed themselves trying
to save themselves…and he felt cheated, because he had not
controlled the moment of death. The madness was driven by
frustration, the frustration fueled by madness. But…

Trying to understand a psychotic's mindset was not a good

place to go, particularly surrounded by the ghosts of his victims. I could feel them push against me, unsure now if I was savior or a torment of hell. My throat was dry and my skin slicked with sweat and I wanted to scream at Nifty to hurry up, to do something different, because, dammit, this wasn't going to work.

incoming!

Sharon's ping, hot and high-pitched, was all the warning we got before the swirl of current and a gust of cool, wet air told us someone had Translocated in.

Our proof had arrived.

holy shit, it worked came from someone, flush with surprise and shock. I would have laughed except the ping could have been mine, and then there was no time to think, only react, as a wash of current swept across the room like a tsunami. The ghosts surged and then disappeared, banished by the presence of their killer, and only the living were left.

Our theory had said that the killer, outraged by the invasion of his space, the use of his table, and surprised by our apparent—feigned—success where he had repeatedly failed, would be on the defensive, his opening blows distracted and—with four trained PUPS present—easily overwhelmed.

Theory didn't have a clue. The killer struck first, and hard. It caught me off balance and I fell forward, my knees buckling and my head slamming down against the cold surface of the table. Then there was another swirl of current, familiar as my own breath, and Venec and Pietr were there.

Four against one, except it was four against two, with another body appearing behind me just as I was getting up, grabbing my arm in an attempt to throw me back down again.

When I was twelve that might have worked. Might. After two years of sparring practice, it wasn't even a joke. I moved into his space, turning on my bent knee into his pace and coming back with my elbow into whatever I could reach. It felt like his rib cage—solid but bony—and I didn't have enough oomph to do any real damage. My next move, bringing my booted heel down on his instep, though; that worked.

Never bring dress shoes to a stomping fight.

I'd thought, when he attacked physically, that the assistant was a Null or low-res. The flow of current that hit me like a slap put paid to that idea. He wasn't as powerful as his partner, at quick estimate, but he was no Null, either. Young, untrained. A student; a new mentee. I pulled my current in from the table, taking the harsh recoil, and turned it back out again. Drained as Nifty and I were, the plan had been for the other three to do the heavy lifting on this part, but we'd underestimated.

need some backup

Sharon's assent came with a sense of a minute to hold on: with a current-fight going on, she wasn't going to risk Translocating in. Physics made that a bad idea, in terms of power and flesh occupying the same space.

"Yield." The shout, magnified by current, echoed against the concrete walls like the roll of thunder, ringing inside our ears. It was a magnificent gesture and had about as much effect as Nifty might have expected. My opponent took another current-slap at me, and I pulled back and wailed him one hard, sparks of green and black encasing my palm as I added the physical measure just for satisfaction.

He was just a kid. A mentee. But if we were right, he had held the bodies down. Had looked into those eyes and let them die in agony. Three deaths under his hands, maybe more, although the form that ducked and weaved around me didn't seem old enough to have been around for the past decade's murders.

I landed another blow, this one to the shoulder blades as I

ducked under and around, and my suspicion firmed. This was either the slightest-built adult I'd ever fought or a teenager.

The same age group as my fierce *chica* and her cohorts in Central Park.

The *Cosa Nostradamus* can be a rough place. You survive by your wits, your skill, and your connections, and all's fair, but there was no way I was going to hurt a kid. No way in hell.

My hesitation got me a spin-kick in the gut and a sharp spark of current that jammed from the bottom of his dress shoes into my flesh, stinging and spreading along my nerves. I howled and probably cursed, gathering all my current to-gether into a net of strands, planning to bring this son of a bitch down.

Then the shape of the fight changed, with a scuffle and a crack behind me, and instead of one-on-one I was sud-denly part of a larger whirl, as the first guy came around and slammed me one across the back of the neck, Pietr, Nifty, and Venec on his heels.

The sound of the door slamming against the wall was the only announcement, and then Sharon was there, too, five against two, and we were barely holding even.

One guy and a teenager should not be able to fight to-gether, physically and magically, well enough to hold off five pissed-off pups, even if two of us were drained down.

mentor

The ping came from Venec, to all of us, and a sense of comprehension that I didn't quite get. But it made sense: you were more tuned to your mentor than anyone else—the only thing that had ever trumped it for me was the Merge. If your mentor taught you how to fight, physically, then, yeah, it made sense....

And then it hit me. This kid had held the bodies down, had done so because his mentor told him to. A mentor who was supposed to train and protect him had instead turned him into an accessory to murder. Instead of protecting, this son of a bitch had destroyed.

I hadn't known I was capable of that kind of rage. It hurt, swamping me, searing the current in my skin with a shivering, crackling noise. I couldn't tell where it had come from: me, or the others, because without thought or intent, we slid into the fugue-blend Venec had spent years teaching us. An utter and instant awareness of each individual, calibrated to within a breadth of movement, aware of each other's core the way you knew how close you stood to a bonfire, close enough to warm but not get burned.

"Yield." This time Nifty's command was a whisper, but it carried equally well, the hiss of a cobra before it struck, giving you one last chance to get out of the way.

They didn't even bother to respond, just stood in the center and glared at us. I could see the kid more clearly now: he wore a baseball cap jammed over his head, shading his face, but there was a squared-off jaw with the suggestion of a shadow and scrawny, pale hands under a windbreaker that was just a smidge too short in the arms, like he'd grown out of it and his mentor hadn't noticed. Slacks, not jeans, and the dress shoes I'd noticed before. This wasn't some kid in the hood; I bet that if I knocked that cap off, the hair underneath would be neatly cut, too.

His current sizzled just underneath his skin: he wanted to use it, badly, but was holding back, waiting for a command.

The older man still hadn't said anything. Not tall, not short, not pale or dark, he was as close to a nonentity as I could imagine—enough that he reminded me a bit of Wren Valere, who took don't-see-me to a magical extreme, even more than Pietr because she did it intentionally. But this guy wasn't a Retriever—I'd been around Wren enough to know that. He was just...forgettable.

Until you looked with mage-sight and saw the current roiling under his skin, like living neon tattoos, forming and reforming shapes until it made you nauseous to watch. He hadn't found the secret to handling more current, he hadn't made himself more high-res...but he had figured out how to skim the edge of wizzing without falling over, inevitably, into madness.

that doesn't mean he's sane Ben, more worried than his face showed. And with reason: once someone wizzed, they didn't care about protecting themselves; all they wanted was more and more current-sensation. It wasn't so much a madness as an utter inability to give a damn about anyone else, a junkie in search of the fix they knew would destroy them. The fact that he had survived this long...

The kid. The pieces started to fit together, almost too late. Mentor and mentee, student and teacher. The bond was the most important thing among Talent, the way we counted lineage, the way we found our place in the world. And it was a two-way bond: I'd never once doubted J's love for me, ever. Making the boy part of this, he wasn't just a partner. He was an anchor. The more he probed for a way to steal current, the more he killed, the more the madness infected him. Having the boy there kept him grounded enough—prevented over-rush. Kept him intact just enough to keep killing.

over and over Sharon, adding her own piece. *neither of them's not old enough to be our first killer*

Ten years between each binge. Time enough for the student to become the mentor? The first death, the mentor... the start of a bloody cycle, how many years?

"What you're looking for. It doesn't exist." Venec stepped forward, breaking our circle, forcing the perps to watch him as well as us. The boy shifted, but his mentor didn't move. "You must know that by now. All the deaths, all the hiding and the running, the secrets…for nothing. Stand down. Let it go."

Ben didn't believe it would work. He was already steeling himself for what was to come. I exhaled and let what was left of my current slide back into my core, coiling it back into a ready position.

Cold, Bonnie. Cold like a winglet focused on repayment. Cold as a dragon forged in heat.

That slight movement was enough to distract the boy, who had started to think of me as "his" target, rather than keeping alert to the entire room. Bad move, not up to PUP standards, but then, he'd been trained on one target at a time.

"Say something, damn you," Venec said, stepping forward even closer, too close, inside the killer's arm-reach, a rookie mistake. Worse, a deadly mistake, and it could only have been intentional, with the boy distracted and the killer's attention on him.

A chance. A last chance, the last chance ever…

And then the killer struck, a howl of current rising out of the gut and blood and bone, his core emptying out into that one final strike, the knowledge of all lost and nothing left to gain, abandoning sense to sensation and the brain to current.

Overrush.

And as it hit, the boy struck in backup, as though following a long-held plan. He would not be left behind.

Even as the blast hit Venec, I was ready. My hands came up and found first Nifty's ham-size palm, then Pietr's more slender fingers curled around mine, and I felt Sharon connect, and we closed the circle, keeping the current contained.

I felt the power strike Venec, flinched and bore up under it. The urge to give him my strength, to let current flow into him, was squelched: I was too drained already, and my job, my responsibility, was here, to make sure that the killers did not escape. Venec would—

The circle faltered, the boy darting, trying to make a physical escape, crashing hard against Sharon, thinking she might be a weak link. Our combined power surged and struck, almost without intent.

The man screamed, the wind-torn shriek of a falcon, and then stopped, cut off like someone flicked a switch. He fell to his knees, and at first I thought he'd fallen out of grief or rage, until I saw the stream of blood coming from his nose, puddling on the washed-clean floor, red-black and sticky.

Venec exhaled, a harsh, ragged noise. And then there was silence.

Venec got a disposable cell phone out of the car we'd hired to get down here, and called Andrulis. Sharon and Pietr took the car and left, heading for Union Station and the haul back to NYC. None of us had the energy left to Translocate a sheet of paper, and I think they were just as happy to spend a few hours surrounded by the normalcy of the world, being lulled into a doze by the steady current-flow of the Amtrak rails.

Two cop cars pulled up about twenty minutes after, lights off and sirens quiet. There was no need for urgency now. Andrulis got out and met Venec at the door. They and the three cops with him went inside.

I waited for him, sitting outside on the cracked stoop of an abandoned warehouse down the street.

Half an hour later, Venec came out alone. I waited as he stared up into the sky. I thought maybe that he was counting the stars, even though they weren't really visible this close to the city. I could feel him breathing, as though he were standing right next to me, and knew that he was trying to decide what to do.

I took the decision out of his hands and went to meet him.

He didn't even look as I came up, but lifted his left arm and I slid underneath, like we'd been doing it all our lives instead of maybe three or four times.

"They'll take care of the cleanup. Call it, hell, I don't know, a fall-out among killers. Or maybe they won't call it anything at all."

"How long do you think it's been going on? Mentor to student, passing on the obsession, training them… Where did it begin?"

"I don't care. It ends here. Bonnie, that's enough."

He'd killed two men tonight. We all had. Never mind that they'd been mad dogs, a danger to the entire *Cosa Nostradamus*; never mind that they'd, in the end, given us little choice. We had not brought them to justice, only brought them down.

That wasn't what Stosser had created us for. I needed to understand the progression, the causes, so we could dissect it, lay out the facts and display them, to make sure that we'd recognize something like this if it happened again. If it had happened before. Find the pattern so we could prevent it.

Ben heard me without my saying a word. "You're a scientist at heart. You want things to make sense, to follow a logical progression. It doesn't. Not always. You have to just let it go. Otherwise, you won't be able to do the job."

I didn't agree, and he knew I didn't agree, but that was okay.

Three men had died in Philly. Five, if you counted the killers. But that meant seven men had not died, and ten more wouldn't die a decade from now.

I let Ben hold on to that thought and let him hold on to me.

Ian Stosser was cremated, as per his will, and we gathered—all the PUPs, and J, and a dozen other people I didn't recognize—on a narrow beach facing the Atlantic at dawn to say farewell.

The sky was still cloud-cast, but it did not rain. People spoke. I saw their mouths move and heard their voices, but I couldn't remember a single word that was said. My ears remembered the sound of the waves, and the hollow echo of the wind, and the calls of gulls and terns overhead, and how the sun warmed on our skin, even moments after it rose.

We wore black and walked barefoot on the golden sand.

Aden did not show up.

Two days later—nearly twenty hours of that sleeping in Ben's bed, his arms wrapped around me—I felt almost normal again. For some new definition of normal, anyway.

The doorman nodded to me as I came into the lobby, and the elevator door opened smoothly as I walked toward it, so I guessed Wren hadn't taken my name off her list, despite recent events. I shifted the foil-wrapped package in my hands and tried to focus on that, the good things.

I'd stopped by, on my way over, to check in with Danny. He'd looked like hell, but the grim, satisfied kind of hell. His girls had, in fact, been among those in the Park. The situation was, he said, "sorted."

He didn't want to talk about it. I didn't have the energy to push. Not now.

The apartment door opened, before I knocked. "Bonnie, hey—that's lasagna."

"Ever a master of the obvious. Do you ever go home now?"

"Not much," the demon admitted, taking the package from my hands, not even wincing at the remnant heat. The pads of his claw-tipped paws were probably a lot tougher than my skin. "I'll shove this in the fridge—they're in the living room. Go on."

A demon as housekeeper was probably one of the more amusing things I'd seen in months, but I wasn't able to muster more than the knowledge that it was amusing. I went into the main room, as directed.

Sergei was standing in front of the huge wall of windows, staring out, his hands clasped behind his back, and if I didn't know him I'd have sworn that he was posing that way. But I could see the tension in his back and knew that his hands were clasped to keep them steady.

"I brought a lasagna."

Wren appeared practically in front of me: my experience with both her and Pietr kept me from showing any surprise. "I think we're the ones supposed to bring you food, or something, aren't we? Bonnie." She paused. "I'm sorry."

For Ian's death, for not being able to find the file we'd needed, for something only she understood and I was too tired to chase down. And that was it. Sometimes you have to let it go for the world to move on.

"I came to—" I looked around, even though I knew already that Ellen wasn't in the room—or, in fact, in the apartment. "I came to see what you were going to do about Ellen."

"We were just discussing that."

Suddenly PB's desire to be elsewhere made more sense. Normally he'd be egging on the fight, but not this. This was too fragile a matter.

"She's with my mother."

Wren's mom was a Null. Nice woman, but couldn't see magic if you waved it in front of her face. I didn't know anything about Wren's dad and had never asked. She never asked about my folks, either.

"And…?"

Wren took a deep breath, let it out. "God, I really thought I was ready for this? She's almost an adult, Bonnie. Untrained but formed. I was young when I started, all my experience is there. We need somebody…" The Wren laughed, looking—for the first time since I'd known her—a little embarrassed. "She needs someone more flexible, strong enough to keep her safe, who can keep that already formed brain of hers occupied, while she's learning."

"So, back to the drawing board." The temptation to dump the problem on them was intense, but that wasn't how J had raised me. "She's okay with your mom, for now. Between the two of us, and my mentor, we should be able to find someone."

I knew, firsthand, what a bad mentor could do. We had to find the right person. Problem was, I'd thought I *had*.

"She seemed to enjoy working with you. Maybe…" Wren hesitated, aware that she was stepping into a mess. "I know things are going to be…complicated for a while, but…"

"We're none of us strong enough. Maybe Venec, but…"

But Benjamin Venec had his hands full already. This morning, he'd headed out to the office, going through Ian's paperwork. No more trying to go it alone.

That meant us, too. I still wasn't sure how I felt about that but…like Ian said, there's only so long you can be stubborn before it starts to spell stupid.

"Shame, really. She's got a useful skill set, for your line of work, once she figures out how to use it. It would certainly give her a reason to learn…."

Sergei, who had been staying out of the conversation until then, turned around. "Having had some dealings with young, undertrained Talent myself—" a snark at Wren, whom he'd met when she was still a teenager "—might I make a suggestion?"

I waited, and Wren gave him a look I couldn't decipher, part amusement and part…something else.

"Stay with her, Genevieve. If you give up on her now, she's going to take it to mean that she's not trainable, not worthwhile. From what you've told me, she's had a gullet of that already."

"But…" Something passed between them. Not the way Ben and I could ping; more like the way he and Stosser could—had.

The disbelief, the desire to not-accept, was still a physical pain, deep inside.

"He's right. I'm sorry. But he's right. Wren, if you give up on her…even if we find someone else…" I was a crap liar, as a rule; I could do it, but I hated it. Pietr had told me once that the secret was not to think about it like a lie, but a story. You were trying to get someone to react emotionally in the way you wanted—directing them, the way a writer or a musician or an actor did.

For Ellen, I could do that.

"Bastards." She flapped her hands, like she wanted to hit something, and then gave in. "Yeah, okay. I like her, I just… I don't want to screw this up."

"The fact that you don't is a pretty good indicator that you won't."

That wasn't entirely true. Zaki—my dad—hadn't ever wanted to screw things up, but he pretty much did all the time, right up to the time it got him killed. I didn't say that, though.

I left them contemplating the changes in their own lives, closing the door softly behind me. One last stop to make, and then I could go home.

Aden Stosser wasn't allowed within a set range of New York City, after her last attempt to "distract" us got a young boy killed. But I suspected she wasn't far away, and Aden

Stosser had never learned the meaning of "under the radar." A few phone calls to a few boutique hotels in Philadelphia and Boston with news of her brother's death, wasn't it terrible, but there were legal matters that had to be cleared up, and that easily, I had her location.

"I thought one of you would show up."

Aden Stosser was a feminine, stylish version of her brother, and it hurt to look at her. But her voice was nothing at all like his: cool and distanced, with none of the passion that had flared in his voice, filling him with heat and movement even when he stood still.

I was doing this on my own. I had to. I owed Ian that much, Council to Council.

"Guilty conscience?"

"What?"

"Did you kill him, Aden?"

She stared at me like I'd suddenly turned a shade of blue she wasn't sure was attractive or not. "He died of carbon-monoxide poisoning. Your idiot, cheap-end building had faulty wiring. The police report was utterly clear on that."

Of course she'd already gotten access to the reports.

"None of us had any signs of CO poisoning." We'd gotten checked out by a local doctor who handled a lot of Talent patients; the tests had taken longer, but they'd come out clean. "That means there was no leaking...until the last time, when it suddenly came out in lethal doses. At a time when the building was mostly empty—but Ian was still there. A leak that only seemed to hit our office."

She looked as though she were considering my words. "If someone wanted to kill him—why go through all the fuss with the false alarms?"

I didn't rise to her "you silly girl" voice. "That meant someone used the leak—studied our office, looked for a way in, and found it. A preexisting condition, to prevent it from being considered a homicide."

Her elegant eyebrows lifted at that. I guess I'd surprised her. "I still don't understand why you think it was a homicide."

"Because someone like Ian Stosser doesn't die of an accidental gas inhalation."

That got a laugh out of her, an elegant, pained sound. "I wish you were right."

Part of me wanted to believe her. Love should never turn to murder. But this was Aden Stosser, as poker-faced a player as her brother ever had been. And she had killed, indirectly, before.

"I can't prove anything. You know that. But if I even scent your signature anywhere near us…"

"What? You'll kill me?"

No, not that. Worse. "I'll use every contact I have in the Council—and out—to have you shunned forever, not just for a year."

I was the only pup who spoke fluent Council, the only one with contacts that could do what I was threatening. Like lying, threats weren't something that came easily to me. For Ian, who had given me my purpose in life, for the PUPI, who spoke for those who'd been silenced…I'd do it.

"You killed him, Aden. I know it." We had been warned. Seers don't see accidental deaths; that's too random for them to focus on. There was intent behind it, trying to shape the universe.

The dragons had indicated a debt that needed to be paid. Power, and payback, and balancing of the scales.

Aden stared at me, and something was going on in her head, but I had no access, I couldn't read her.

Then she blinked, and sorrow—and rage—were clear on her face.

"Go away," she said, her face shutting down again, even as she turned away to stare out the window at the Philadelphia cityscape.

I went, for once in my life managing a perfect exit, and landed on my knees in the middle of the living room of my apartment, wincing as the shock radiated through my bones.

"Should I give you the lecture about topping off your core before you start Transloc'ing anywhere, or should we just mark it as 'done'?"

"Not tonight, Ben."

I wasn't surprised he was there, even though I'd never given him a key or told him it was okay to just show up, unannounced, and make himself at home. I lifted my head, slowly getting to my feet in the proper fashion, making sure I didn't smack myself with vertigo or a headrush, and studied him. He was on the velvet sofa where he should have looked silly, his feet on the floor, a square-cut glass on the antique Chinese chest next to him, properly on a coaster. He'd helped himself to the booze, too.

If I'd a dog, it probably would have fetched him slippers.

"This building, it's…peaceful."

"Yeah." I sat down on the sofa next to him and reached for the glass. Not my usual; he'd brought his own whiskey. All right, I could deal with that.

"The building's on a good site," I said. "Everyone—every Talent who comes here notes the same thing. Wren used to live upstairs. That's how I found out about it."

"Something's upset you."

It was a stupid comment: had there been anything the past week that hadn't been upsetting? But he wasn't talking about any of that.

Dragons were about power and balancing the scales, about paying back every inch that was due. A dragon's sense of justice was cold, measured, and utterly merciless, to take the thing that mattered most to a person. Aden had already lost her brother: I had taken her chance for revenge.

Benjamin Venec, of all people, wouldn't judge what I'd done. Or if he did, it would probably be approvingly. Probably. But I wasn't ready to talk about it. Not now. Maybe not ever.

Dragons. I blinked, the memory creeping out of wherever it had been hiding. Fire in the sky, the deep, burning chasm of emotion, the hunger and anger…and the sense of something still waiting.

"It's been a miserable week," I said and handed him back his glass.

"Yeah." His right hand, the one not holding the glass, rested on his knee, palm up, and my left hand covered it, our fingers curling together, palm to palm. I'd lost my boss, my guidepost. Ben had lost his best friend. How the hell did you ease that pain? Even with the Merge, I felt helpless. So I did the only thing I could: I held his hand, rested my head against his shoulder, and matched my breathing to his, slow and steady, until I thought he might have fallen asleep.

Remember. Skimming, caught up tight against a dragon's chest, watching the threads of current bind us, earth and sky and water and even pain and joy…everything was connected. *Remember.*

Dragons. A dragon, holding and teaching. Why? The kenning still haunted me, so there was something left undone. What?

Into the silence, Ben said, "I brought files. Three new potential clients."

It used to be Ian's job, to vet the clients and decide which jobs we'd take on. Then he'd pass the details on to Lou, who'd sort out the details and work with Ben to decide who'd be assigned to what.

The pieces didn't so much shift in my mind as melt, flow, and re-form.

Once, not so long ago, Stosser had made a vague threat about making me his third in command, working the schmoozing side Ben was so terrible at. I thought I'd convinced him otherwise.

Bastard was getting the last laugh.

"There's someone we have to talk to, first," I said.

"I should have put on a tie."

"Do you even own a tie?"

"One. Ian bought it for me. Are you sure…"

"Relax. Honestly, you'd think you'd never—"

The elevator door opened before I could finish the sentence, and I could feel Venec tense up next to me.

"Bonnie." The maid was subdued, her face not wreathed in its usual greeting smile. "We heard. Are you all right?"

"Not really. But we need to speak with Madame, please? If she is available?"

"For you, she is always at home. You know that."

There was no sherry in cut-glass waiting on a silver tray, this time. We went directly into Madame's salon, a high-ceilinged greenhouse at the top of her Manhattan town house. She was curled, as usual, her long tail tucked alongside the hoard she had been collecting since well before Venec or I were born. Her elegant neck curved like a swan's, and her head lowered until she was, more or less, eye to eye with us.

holy mother of…

no, just Madame

There was no "just" about it. She was the Great Worm of New York, massive and powerful and not to be trifled

324   *Dragon Justice*

with, and only the fact that she was fond of J—and thereby, by extension, fond of me—gave me the right to impose on her like this.

"The Stosssser. Our regretssssss for your lossss."

"Thank you, Madame." I dug an elbow into Venec's side, and he recovered with a subdued "many thanks."

Madame's head turned and tilted, her great, faceted eyes studying him. Her red-rimmed nostrils flared, and I caught my breath. I should have expected that.

"Sssssssssso."

"Madame." I put as much gentle reproof into the word as I dared.

She huffed a little, delicate sulfur-scented flames escaping—a dragon's laughter—and pulled her head back, just enough for Venec's comfort.

"Madame, we…"

I hadn't thought this through. Or rather, I had thought it through endlessly, while getting dressed, while sitting in the cab heading uptown, to the one block of Harlem that had never needed gentrification, had never dared fall into disrepair, not in four decades, or more, and I still had no idea what I was going to say.

"Madame, if we don't raise two hundred thousand dollars immediately, our founder's debt will be taken out on us. On Venec."

She did not blink, did not react at all, despite my graceless haste and fluster. I reminded myself that she had known me when I was a teenager, that she was fond of me, that I had bargained with dragons before….

Lesser dragons, I had bargained with. Never a Great Worm.

"Gathering the money from other sources…would take too long, expose us to those who would take us down, shut us down." My hand slipped into Venec's, without intent. "Expose him to harm."

She had smelled the Merge, had scented out the connection. Would her fondness for J, that had extended to me, extend to him?

She contemplated us, letting the tension build. Never let it be said Madame did not enjoy her drama.

"For all thingssssss, there is a price, little Bonnnnita."

I swallowed and squeezed Ben's hand, warning him not to say anything. "I know." Dragons were Collectors. They were greedy. But they were also fair.

"I have watched you. I watch everything in thissss city."

Dragons, circling. Watching. Aware at all times of the ley lines that bind and shape this world. Not Old Ones, the Great Worms, but the oldest of us all. My kenning had told me it would come to this....

I had known. Before I came here, I had known. I just hadn't known that I knew.

She named her price.

twenty

To be a sorcerer, you needed to be high-res, highest of the high-res, even to be considered for their club. They forgot that high-res meant you were powerful, not invincible. Paranoia and suspicion only protected you against enemies you could see.

She and Ian used to play at this when they were children. Creeping up, current muted so low that they couldn't be sensed, bodies so controlled that they couldn't be heard. Then: a leap, a pounce, sometimes hands smeared with mud or aimed to tickle until their victim fell to the floor, giggling madly, calling for mercy, giving up.

Aden had no mud in her hands today, and they did not giggle. Their current surged up to protect them, but too late: she pulled her entire core, her hate and her fears, and struck not at them but against them, burning the air in their lungs the way they had done to her brother.

The mighty should be careful who they allowed into their homes.

"You shouldn't have done that," she said to the bodies at

her feet when she was done. Her breath was faster than she liked, but her voice was calm. "You were only supposed to box him in, not kill him. I would have been a useful ally, if you'd left what was mine alone."

Blood dripped from her mouth and nose, her knees holding her upright only so long as she locked them in place; the moment she released control, she knew she would fall.

She could feel the gathered current surging around her, looking for a place to ground. Temptation rose: she calculated the odds of wizzing, of losing herself in the maelstrom, if she took the current into herself, and found the results unacceptable.

The pup had thought she'd done it herself. She hadn't. Ian had been wrong, and dangerous, and if the only way to stop him had been to take him out of the picture entirely, she would have done it; but not that way. Not without honor, not without letting him know who was doing it. Not without giving him one last chance to back down with—there was honor in bowing to a stronger force. There was no honor in the way he had died.

She had only wanted them to cage him, to limit his influence. But they had seen her brother as a threat to themselves. She hadn't expected that. Hadn't assessed their paranoia—or his influence—properly. Her fault, for bringing them together.

And despite that, despite the fact that he had to know that, in his last breath, his last thought, Ian had called to her.

Honor required she answer. Honor had required that she write down what she planned to do and leave it where Benjamin Venec—and by extension, the rest of PUPI—would find it. There would be no question as to the rightness of her actions.

"You shouldn't have done that," she said again, although

there was no one left to hear. Her knees gave way suddenly, blood loss making her dizzy, and she folded gracefully to the floor of the town house, and waited.

Monday morning was tough. After our visit to Madame I'd spent nearly twenty-four hours curled in my loft bed, sometimes with Ben, sometimes alone. He'd done a lot of walking, standing up and leaving the apartment without a word, just... walking. Sometimes he came back with ice cream. Once, he brought back a single lily, the scent almost overpowering.

Funeral flowers.

On Monday morning, he threw the wilted flower out, we got showered and dressed, and went to the office.

The pack was waiting for us.

"Anyone who didn't sleep more than two hours last night, fess up and go home," Venec said, cutting off any questions, even as he hung up our coats in the closet, the simple familiarity of the act weirdly soothing.

Nobody fessed up.

I went over to the kitchenette and started prepping my coffee, almost out of instinct. I'd wondered how it would feel to be back here, after everything....

"I smudged the office last night," Nifty said, maybe picking up on my apprehension. "I don't know if it helped, but..."

"It did—" Sharon said, and Ben nodded. "Thank you. I should have thought of that."

Nobody gave that the scorn it deserved. He was Big Dog, but he didn't have to do everything. He'd remember that, soon enough.

Nifty said it first. "What are we going to do?"

"What we were trained to do," I said. "What did you think?"

They all wanted to protest, wanted to say they couldn't, we

couldn't, that we weren't able to move on without Stosser's hands on the reins. But nobody said a word.

Stosser would have kicked our asses if we'd curled up and died just because he was gone.

"What about the debt?" Nick asked.

I swallowed, hard. "It's taken care of."

"How? Bonnie, none of us have anything worth hocking, and anyone we borrowed the money from would have the same control over us, we'd never be seen as being impartial!"

Dragon Justice. It was cold, took in equal measure, and once the terms were set, there were no further strings.

"Madame has covered our debt."

"You bargained with a dragon?" Nicky's voice broke on the last word, like he was a scrawny preteen again. "A dragon?"

"She had been watching us," Venec said. "Judging." He still wasn't comfortable with that idea, but it wasn't as though he could do anything about it. Especially not now.

"We bring balance," I said. "She approves."

"So what, she just gave us the money as a gesture of good will?" Nifty was understandably dubious.

"No." I didn't want to share this part, but Venec and I had agreed: this affected them, too. "It's a birth-gift. *Cosa*-cousin to *Cosa*-daughter." Like a godmother, a cross-species mentor. The kenning of being held close and flying had not been for me, only for me to remember, when the time came.

My child. Our child, bound to the fatae, as well as Talent.

Intent shaped what a seer saw, what the kenning suggested, but the future wasn't set. Venec and I could have told the Merge to take a hike. Stosser could have left the building when Lou did. Aden could have accepted PUPI and saved us all some trouble. Wren could have gone to the office that night and choked on toxic fumes—like a dragon's breath—

with Stosser. Precognition wasn't Fate. All you ever got was a warning—and some advice.

There were blank stares from the rest of the pack while they digested what I'd said, and then the realization began to settle in.

Sharon's eyes went wide, and a look of unholy glee illuminated her, one step ahead of the others. "Bonita Torres, is there something you're not telling us?"

"What? Oh, *hell,* no," I spluttered, and I could feel Venec's shock turning to amusement and just a hint of wistfulness.

Eventually. Someday. When we were damn well and ready. Madame would just have to *wait.*

In the meanwhile, we were open for business, again.

★ ★ ★ ★ ★

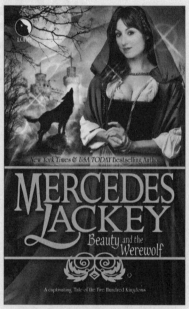

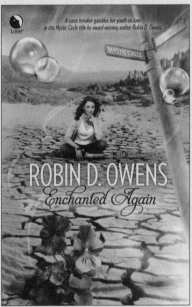

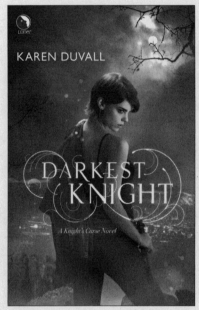